PAMELA K. FORREST
DESERT ANGEL

D0367540

ZEBRA BOOKS
KENSINGTON PUBLISHING CORP.

for my aunt, Virginia Mikesell, with love

ZEBRA BOOKS are published by

Kensington Publishing Corp.
850 Third Avenue
New York, NY 10022

First Printing: July, 1994

Printed in the United States of America

SPELLING LESSON

In the bedroom, Jim lowered her feet to the ground, but kept an arm around her slender waist. The room was bathed in the light of the moon, making a lamp unnecessary.

"Monday," he murmured as he lowered his lips to hers, gliding whisper-soft against them.

March stood quietly in his arms, slowly spelling the word to herself. It was one she had learned easily, and prided herself on remembering. The touch of his lips on hers was soothingly familiar.

"Tuesday." Jim traced the shape of her lips with the very tip of his tongue. His hands moved restlessly up and down the slope of her back.

Tuesday wasn't difficult either. There were only four letters with the word day at the end. His tongue was so warm and surprisingly soft.

"Wednesday." Jim lifted his lips from hers and pulled loose the ribbons at the bodice of her robe. The silky fabric slid freely down her arms to pool at her feet. With fingers eager to explore new territory, he traced the path of the thin straps over her shoulders.

March closed her eyes, hoping that she could better concentrate if she wasn't watching the fascination on Jim's face. Wednesday was a tough word, one she almost misspelled. How could he expect her to get it right when his touch was so tender, his fingertips so warm?

"Thursday."

Thursday was nearly impossible after he pressed his lips to her neck. . . .

TODAY'S HOTTEST READS
ARE TOMORROW'S SUPERSTARS

VICTORY'S WOMAN (4484, $4.50)
by Gretchen Genet
Andrew — the carefree soldier who sought glory on the battlefield, and returned a shattered man . . . Niall — the legendary frontiersman and a former Shawnee captive, tormented by his past . . . Roger — the troubled youth, who would rise up to claim a shocking legacy . . . and Clarice — the passionate beauty bound by one man, and hopelessly in love with another. Set against the backdrop of the American revolution, three men fight for their heritage — and one woman is destined to change all their lives forever!

FORBIDDEN (4488, $4.99)
by Jo Beverley
While fleeing from her brothers, who are attempting to sell her into a loveless marriage, Serena Riverton accepts a carriage ride from a stranger — who is the handsomest man she has ever seen. Lord Middlethorpe, himself, is actually contemplating marriage to a dull daughter of the aristocracy, when he encounters the breathtaking Serena. She arouses him as no woman ever has. And after a night of thrilling intimacy — a forbidden liaison — Serena must choose between a lady's place and a woman's passion!

WINDS OF DESTINY (4489, $4.99)
by Victoria Thompson
Becky Tate is a half-breed outcast — branded by her Comanche heritage. Then she meets a rugged stranger who awakens her heart to the magic and mystery of passion. Hiding a desperate past, Texas Ranger Clint Masterson has ridden into cattle country to bring peace to a divided land. But a greater battle rages inside him when he dares to desire the beautiful Becky!

WILDEST HEART (4456, $4.99)
by Virginia Brown
Maggie Malone had come to cattle country to forge her future as a healer. Now she was faced by Devon Conrad, an outlaw wounded body and soul by his shadowy past . . . whose eyes blazed with fury even as his burning caress sent her spiraling with desire. They came together in a Texas town about to explode in sin and scandal. Danger was their destiny — and there was nothing they wouldn't dare for love!

One

The sun had yet to clear the horizon, but the golden glow in the east proclaimed its coming as surely as heralds announcing a royal proclamation. In a few brief minutes it would peek from behind the mountaintops and then rise rapidly to dominate the sky. Effortlessly chasing away the coolness lingering from the night, its life-giving warmth would be welcomed by all the creatures beneath it. None who knew of its unforgiving nature, would argue that it was a mighty opponent only the foolish would challenge.

Melanie Travis stood on the veranda, her arms folded protectively around her protruding stomach, and watched as her husband mounted his horse. The cool morning breeze rippled the dark hair, as yet uncombed, that tumbled down her back. Her hastily donned dress, without benefit of proper petticoats, stretched snugly across her expanded middle and hung limply about her ankles.

Hours earlier the rattle of the chuck wagon as it moved out of the yard woke her from a restless sleep. Spring roundup was beginning, and would last for several weeks. It meant that she would be alone, except for a couple of cowboys who'd grown too old to follow the trail. Melanie didn't consider the two old men as companions. Their rough manners and blunt vocabulary offended her upbringing, back East men were unfailingly polite and indelicate language was not spoken in the presence of a lady.

"I'll circle around back home in a couple of days." Jim Travis sat on his horse, a worried frown creasing his forehead as he looked at his wife. "Woods and Hank will be around, if you need anything."

Melanie rubbed the mound of her belly and raised accusing eyes toward her husband. He had changed so drastically in the two years since she'd come from the rolling green hills of Vermont to the harsh land of Arizona. Gone forever was the gentle gallant who had wooed her with soft promises of a future that would be perfect, if only she'd consent to become his wife. In his place was a man hardened by his surroundings, who expected her to become as hard and brassy as the other frontier wives. Women who rode with their men at spring roundup, who roped and branded while sweat made trails down the dirt on their faces. Women who used the back of their sleeves to wipe away that sweat, and wore split skirts so that they could ride astride.

It seemed to her that Jim made no effort to understand that she couldn't change, couldn't become something that she was not. Five years ago, when he'd left her in Vermont to come ahead and build their homestead, he had seemed content with the woman that she was. But Melanie had seen the difference in her husband from the day of her arrival. The years of separation had changed him into a stranger . . . after two years he was still a stranger.

"Melanie?"

Jim noticed the distracted glaze in her eyes and guilt stabbed through him. This situation could not continue, but he didn't know what to do to change it. Far too late he had realized that the woman he'd admired and fallen in love with back East, was too gentle for the harshness of the west. The very things that had attracted his attention in Vermont, the exquisite femininity and retiring propriety that were eminently suitable for an Eastern drawing room, were a liability here.

He would send her back if he could, but both her parents had died in a flu epidemic last spring, and her only brother was in the cavalry stationed somewhere in eastern Texas.

Jim took off his hat and ran his fingers through his dark hair. Maybe when roundup was finished, he could spend more time with her. By then the baby would be here, and even though she showed less and less interest in its arrival, it would give her something to fill the long hours while he was gone.

The new house he had built for her was complete, with the ordered furnishings arriving almost daily. He looked at the white monstrosity so out of place in the foothills of the Santa Catalina mountains. Built with lumber brought down from the mountains at a tremendous expense, the two-story structure with its sweeping veranda and two-story ballroom was a recreation of the home she had left. He was well aware that its many glass windows and wood construction made it almost indefensible, but in his desperation to please her he had overlooked the many reasons that it shouldn't be built.

"Melanie?" he called again, biting back the need to defend himself for leaving her alone.

She looked at the man who had become a stranger, and let her thoughts drift to the man who had courted and won her. Of all her suitors James Travis had been by far the most handsome. With his coal-black hair and sky-blue eyes, he'd caught her attention at a party hosted by mutual friends. He'd been so incredibly gentle, holding her with infinite care as they swirled around the ballroom. She was half-a-head taller than most of her friends, but he made her feel tiny and feminine.

"Remember the dance, James?" Lost in memories, she missed the concerned look that crossed his face. "We danced and danced, until the matrons were whispering behind their fans in shocked dismay. Mama finally made me refuse to dance with you again." She raised sparkling eyes to him, swaying to the music playing through her mind. "Do you remember? I wore my new green velvet, and you said it paled when compared to my eyes."

"I remember . . ." Jim studied her, alarm squeezing his chest. "Melanie, are you all right?"

"Of course, James." Her laughter splintered the early morning silence. "Did I bring that dress with me? Mama said it would be too heavy to wear out here, but I couldn't leave it behind." Her brow wrinkled in concentration. "Now where did I pack it?"

Turning, Melanie walked back into the house. She didn't notice her husband's troubled gaze following her as she climbed the stairs toward the attic. Torn between the urge to reassure himself that she was all right, and the necessity to head out where the men waited to begin the roundup, Jim turned his horse away from the house. He'd see that everything was underway, he decided, and do his best to return home tonight. It would probably be after dark, but it was the best he could do.

Jim stopped at the front of the bunkhouse, where the two old men rested in the shade. Their only chores were menial ones, feed the horses that weren't taken out that day, repair an occasional broken strap, and keep an eye on the place.

"Sure don't miss roundup," Hank lied, as the yearning in his eyes screamed the truth.

"Man hankers for a little easy time when he

gets to be my age," Woods agreed, the longing in his voice belying his words.

"Sure ain't gonna miss all them days in the saddle, with blisters on my butt the size of a silver dollar." Hank turned his gaze to the open plains.

"Sleepin' on the hard ground and wonderin' if a sidewinder is gonna be sharin' your blanket come morning."

"Keepin' an eye out for the youn'ens 'til they get old enough to get smart."

"Coffee so thick you hafta cut it with your knife," Woods added.

"Yes, sir'ee, a man my age has earned a little relaxation."

"Man your age better watch that his relaxation ain't at the bottom of a six-foot hole with a marker on top," Woods snorted.

"Hell, you're older then me! You'll be a'smellin' the underside of a cowpie long afore I even give it a thought!"

Jim had inherited the old men when he had bought the ranch several years earlier. Their wisdom and experience more than repaid the cost of food and the small wages he paid them. Normally he would have smiled at the word play between them, but this morning too many problems rode his shoulders.

"Keep an eye on her for me," he stated bluntly. "Now's not the time to leave her alone, but I don't have any choice."

"Women get kinda funny when they's breed-in'." Woods spit a stream of tobacco juice into the dust at his feet.

"The West is hard on a woman," Hank agreed. " 'Specially someone as gentle-like as Miss Melanie."

"Don't be worrin' none about her, boy. We'll keep our eyes open."

Jim's gaze moved to the house in the distance, an eerie sensation of alarm creeping up his spine. Trying his best to ignore the warning that leaving her now was the last thing he should do, he nodded to the men and moved toward the open range.

By the time she had climbed the long flight of stairs to the attic, Melanie was breathless. Leaning against the door, she stopped to rest, rubbing the gnawing pain low in her belly.

If she had been another month along in her pregnancy, she would have been concerned that it was the first sign of labor. But she vividly remembered the night the child had been conceived, and knew that she still had three or four weeks of waiting before its birth.

A shiver of distaste at the memory of the last time Jim had used her body to satisfy his male needs made her move away from the wall. Not for the first time, she thanked God that Jim seldom demanded his husbandly rights. He had not bothered her once since the babe's conception and already she dreaded its birth, because it would free him from that restriction. Mama had warned her that it was a duty she must allow, but she hadn't been thorough enough in her explanation. Surely if a woman knew exactly what was expected of her, she'd never consent to marry!

With a shudder, Melanie opened the door. So newly constructed that it was nearly dustless, the huge attic was bare except for a few boxes and traveling cases. She searched for the trunk that was filled with the many ball gowns she had insisted on bringing to Arizona.

Kneeling in front of the heavy case, she unbuckled the straps, and threw open the lid that had remained closed since it had been packed two years earlier in Vermont. Tissue paper crackled as she freed one gown after the other from their confinement.

"Oh," she whispered, "I'd forgotten this one." She pulled out a ball dress of striped pink and white satin. The gauzy overskirt with its gathered flounce was made to drape over a tiny bustle. "I wore roses in my hair that night. Remember, Mama, how you fretted over those pink roses, because they wouldn't stay where you wanted them to?" Melanie smiled to herself. "You got so frustrated that you said a naughty word, and it startled us so much that we got the giggles and I was nearly late for the party."

The added weight of her pregnancy making her ungainly, Melanie grunted as she climbed to her feet. Holding the dress to her, she swirled around the empty room to the music only she could hear, smiling at the shadowy partner visible only in her mind. She batted her eyelashes coyly and lowered her head.

"My fan! Where's my fan, Mama?" Dropping the dress, Melanie dug through the trunk until she found the fan made to match the dress. Snapping it open, she held it in front of her face, just at chin level, and smiled sweetly.

"Why, Mr. Granger, whatever would people say if we were to dance together again . . . Mr. Holland, you turn a girl's head with your sweet words . . . oh, Mr. Walters, you flatter me . . ."

Lost in her fantasy world, hours drifted by and the attic grew warm as Melanie flirted with her imaginary lovers. Gowns of every imaginable color turned the floor into a rainbow of silk and satin.

Finally the heat and her own cumbersome body forced her to sit down on one of the boxes. She looked at the dresses scattered over the room and relived the memories from each.

"I'll miss the spring cotillion," she muttered, as her irrational thoughts carried her further into the past. "There's barely time to have a gown made! Why, I might have to accept a ready-made." A shudder of distaste shook her. "Mama, you can't let that happen . . . me, in a ready-made at the grandest event of the year! Never! Whatever will people think!"

Climbing to her feet, Melanie hurried out of the attic and down the stairs. "We'll go to town today, Mama. I saw the prettiest piece of yellow satin . . . well, of course, I can't wear yellow with my complexion . . . overskirt of green? No, I never thought of that . . ."

Melanie left the house, her slippers no protection against the rocks and thorns of the desert floor. Before she was out of sight of the house, her feet were bruised and several thorns were imbedded in the tender flesh.

". . . just the smallest train, such a problem when I'm dancing. Mama, do you remember last year when Alice Orson lost the entire back of her skirt, because Peter Simmons stepped on it?"

A ripple of inhuman laughter floated into the clear afternoon sky. The sun, a giant, blazing yellow ball, burned away the gentleness of the spring afternoon. Without the protection of a hat, the fair skin of her face soon showed signs of burning.

"I will not dance with him! Mama, how can you ask that of me!"

Melanie stopped and stamped her foot, unaware of the pain of multiple lacerations. Somewhere along her wandering path of hallucination, she had lost a shoe and was heedless of the bloody trail that marked her way.

". . . My hair! What will I do with my hair? Leave it down again . . . something like the style Mary Ann wore last Sunday, only with flowers . . . no, pearls!" She fluffed her mahogany hair. "Pearls will be so dramatic . . ."

Catching her breath, Melanie looked around the desert and saw the town of her youth. She

smiled graciously at the people who passed, the
men tipping their hats in respect. She listened
to the rumble of carriages and the voices raised
in argument or amusement. Breathing deeply,
she smelled the odors of food cooking and the
fragrances from the perfume shop they passed,
but above all was the scent of spring.

Spring in New England; trees and flowers and
grass, all with their own distinctive scent, a scent
that had been denied her for two endless years.

"Here it is, I was beginning to fear that someone else had bought it."

Melanie knelt down and plucked the tiny yellow flower from the cactus, heedless of the blood
dripping from her fingers, as a multitude of
thorns imbedded in her skin.

"What do you think? . . . no! I won't! . . .
You're so mean . . . I shall ask papa, he gives me
anything I want! . . . I will not wear a fichu like
some old woman or that flat-chested Letta! I am
a young lady, and it's time I allow the evidence
to be seen! . . . She'll be so jealous, my bosoms
are so much fuller than hers . . ."

An unearthly laugh filled the silence, floating
up and away as insanity grappled for supremacy
of a mind eager to relinquish the harsh realities
of life.

The sun began its descent, but was no less
fierce than before. Wherever it touched, it relentlessly burned skin unaccustomed to expo-
sure. Melanie's dress hung in tatters, shredded
by contact with the cruel thorns of the cacti. The

tender skin on her arms and face was slashed and badly burned, but her madness had driven her past that knowledge, far past the realization of the deadly game she played.

"It's so warm in here . . . Letta, dear, how lovely you look . . . my but that fichu is such a lovely addition, and so concealing . . . no, dear, I'm not chilled, in fact I was just commenting on the heat . . . a stroll in the garden, Mr. Walters? How lovely, yes, let's find a breath of coolness . . . I expect you to remember that you are a gentleman . . ."

There was no witness to her twirling dance of insanity. No one to stop her from falling into the arms of the giant saguaro or tripping over the smaller cholla, which left its silvery spines in her skin.

With the lowering of the sun, the life-threatening dehydration was lessened, only to be replaced with the very real possibility of hypothermia. The spring nights were still cold, making a coat a welcome addition. Without one, Melanie was in as grave a danger as she had been in during the burning sunlight.

"It's so cold, Mama," she muttered, her little-girl voice quivering. She folded into herself as much as her oversized stomach would allow. "Burr . . . it's dark! I'm scared . . . light a lamp, Daddy . . . please, don't leave me in the dark! . . . my belly hurts . . . I'm sorry I was bad . . . Mama, don't be mad . . ."

A barely visible sliver of moon drifted slowly

on its journey across the dark sky. Stars, like diamonds thrown from a giant's hand, twinkled merrily. The rustle of unseen night creatures and the lonely cry from a far off coyote were her only companions as the darkness, and madness, lingered.

"Damnit, you *couldn't* have watched the house all day, or you'd have seen her leave!" Jim rubbed at the muscles tightening the back of his neck with tension. He was exhausted and dirty, irritated by the necessity of the long ride back to the house.

After a day filled with one problem after another, it had been well past midnight before he had gotten back to the house. The front door had been slightly ajar, alerting him almost immediately that something wasn't right. Irritation had slowly turned to a gut-wrenching fear, when his initial search for Melanie had proved fruitless.

Now, more than three hours later, every room in the house, every closet, every cubbyhole, had been thoroughly investigated. The barns and all of the outbuildings had received the same vigorous inspections. A lantern had even been lowered to the bottom of the well. He didn't suspend the search for his wife, until he was finally forced to accept that she was gone.

"Been right over there by the bunkhouse all day," Hank defended himself. "Ain't moved 'cept to get a bite to eat now and again, and to make water."

"Been there beside him. Played a couple of games of checkers, took a little snooze midday, been sitting like a broody hen waitin' on her chicks to hatch," Woods added, pulling up his drooping galluses. He and Hank had been sleeping soundly, when Jim had come into the bunkhouse and roused them out of bed to help in the search.

"Didn't you think to check on her this evening, when there wasn't a light showing from the windows?" Jim asked in disgust. His answer came from the startled look that crossed the faces of the old men, confirming that neither of them had given it a thought.

"It weren't like Miss Melanie wanted company," Woods stated. "If 'en we'd a'comed up on the porch, she'd have chased us off with a broom."

"Miss Melanie is . . . ah . . ." Trying to be as diplomatic as possible, Hank searched for words that wouldn't offend his boss. It wasn't necessary to point out to the man that his wife was a pampered, spoiled missy, who needed her fanny warmed. "Miss Melanie, why, she appreciated us stayin' at the bunkhouse."

"Like I said, unfriendly as a bobcat with a thorn in his paw," Woods added bluntly. "She didn't like us none, and we did her the favor of stayin' out of her way."

Jim knew that criticizing the two men was unfair. Melanie had made it plain to anyone who would listen, that she didn't want any of the hired men around her. She also objected to the people on nearby ranches, and those she had met in town. In fact, in two years she hadn't met anyone she felt was suitable to be a companion.

A neighboring ranch had thrown a party when she had first arrived from the East. She had complained bitterly that their welcoming friendliness had been crude and unrefined, their speech uncouth, their manners vulgar. Melanie Travis had not endeared herself to any of them.

"Wanna go lookin' for her tonight? We'll saddle up." Hank's concern was genuine. He had lived in the desert long enough to be on first-name basis with its dangers.

"She can't be far," Woods offered. "Miss Melanie hates the desert almost as much as she hates us."

Jim looked out at the darkness as he pulled his watch from his pocket. Flipping open the plain gold top, he was surprised to see that it was nearly four o'clock. The search for Melanie around the immediate area had already consumed several hours, and dawn would begin lightening the sky in another hour.

He was a decent tracker in the light of day, but knew his own limitations at night. His greatest concern was that he'd inadvertently destroy her trail in his blind wanderings, then she would be lost . . . until the circling of buzzards marked her location.

She didn't deserve that, he thought, as anger from his own helplessness threatened to override his common sense. She didn't deserve any of this. He should have taken her back East long ago, but he'd kept hoping she'd adjust.

But she hadn't. Far from it, in fact. As time had gone on, she'd slipped further and further from his grasp, until he no longer even recognized the woman he had married back in Vermont.

Until he'd realized that he didn't love her, had never loved her. Until she became a burden he didn't have time to handle.

When he had realized how drastically his feelings for her had changed, Jim had been immersed in guilt. He knew he'd only been infatuated with the delicate girl, hardly more than a child, that he'd married and left behind.

During the years of their separation, he had worked hard to build a home for them and to get the ranch going, to make his dream into a reality. At night, when exhaustion forced him to his lonely bed, he'd dreamed of Melanie. Gradually, he had imagined her to be so much more than she really was, that by the time she'd arrived in Tucson, no woman could have matched his expectations. Gentle, refined Melanie had never stood a chance.

"Shame Breed ain't here," Hank said, interrupting Jim's useless recriminations.

"He'd find her, ain't no doubt. Yes, sir'ee, Breed can track a mouse after a stampede!"

The man known as Breed was the foreman on the Falling Creek Ranch. Jim had hired him in spite of the rumors that followed him wherever he went. With blond hair and blue eyes there was no doubt that the man was fully white, but it was widely known that he had been raised by the Comanche to be a Comanche. Even though he now lived as a white man, the past still clung, making him a formidable and intimidating presence.

If he had another name, Jim didn't know it and had never asked. In the West, a man offered information if he wanted it known. Breed did his job well, without complaints or demands. He had an astounding ability with horses that would make him an asset to any operation. As far as Jim was concerned, that was enough and would remain enough.

"It'll be daylight in another hour. We'll wait." They were the hardest words he had ever spoken, and he already knew that waiting the short time for the sun to rise would be the longest wait of his life.

"If I don't find her by mid-morning, then we'll send for him."

He did not need to add that by then they'd probably be looking for a body to bury.

The desert was unforgiving.

Two

Jim paced from room to empty room in the huge house, cursing the necessity of waiting until daylight before beginning the search for Melanie. Standing in the doorway of the dining room, he remembered that there was a load of furniture waiting in town for someone to pick up. He made a mental note to free up one of the men long enough to go get it.

Melanie had spent weeks poring over catalogs in search of just the right furnishings for each room. Jim had hoped that once they were settled in the new house she would be more content, but even before the furniture had started to arrive, he'd seen that the effort had been worthless.

Nothing and no one, even, he suspected, the baby she carried, could release her from the depression that overwhelmed her.

Slamming his fist against the door frame with helpless frustration, Jim turned and walked down the long hall to his office in the back of the house. This was the only room he had insisted on designing, everything else was to Melanie's specifications.

The dark-paneled room with a door leading outside had a huge, multipane window facing the mountains. One wall was entirely of stone, with a fireplace that was more than adequate to take the chill from the room. The other two walls had shelves with protective glass doors. Each shelf was filled with leather-bound books.

A rare and expensive pleasure in a time when few homes had more than a handful of books, Jim rarely indulged his passion for reading. He looked longingly at the books, knowing that it would be months before he could take more than a few stolen minutes to gratify his favorite pastime. Melanie had seen the books as a waste of money, but had only shrugged with indifference when he had insisted on the fully furnished library.

Just another of the many fundamental differences between them, Jim thought as he sat down in the leather chair behind his desk. He seriously doubted that she had read a book since leaving the expensive boarding school she had attended.

Leaning his elbows on the desk, Jim rubbed his forehead with the heel of his hands, hoping the pressure would eradicate the pain building behind his eyes. Every bone and muscle in his body ached in needless reminder of the physical labor involved in spring roundup. His tired body reminded him that he should have been asleep hours earlier. But concern for Melanie vied with regret and guilt to keep him wide-awake.

Where was she? Could someone, perhaps a passing renegade, have taken her? Most of the Apache had been settled on the reservation, but occasionally a young buck broke free of the constraints and went on his own private warpath. Geronimo left the reservation at whim, sometimes taking several dozen people with him, and rumors of the trouble he caused grew like wildfire. But in all the years Jim had been in Arizona, he'd never seen the famous war chief.

Thoughts of Melanie lost in the desert plagued him through the longest hour of his life. She was so meek, literally scared by her own shadow. She was terrified of snakes and spiders. What would a night spent alone in the desert do to her?

He refused to let his thoughts wander to the very real fact that she probably wouldn't survive the night. And never once did he acknowledge that if she died, so would their child.

Even before the first traces of daylight, when inactivity became impossible, Jim saddled his horse. Waiting impatiently for the final minutes of night to pass, he rolled a cigarette, struck a match against his denim-covered thigh, and inhaled the aromatic smoke.

"Want company?" Hank asked, his weathered features showing that he'd had little sleep.

"No." Jim dragged deeply on the cigarette. "I need someone to go to town for Doc. She's going to need medical attention."

"It'll be done," the older man replied, keeping his thoughts to himself, that Melanie would be more in need of the undertaker than the doctor.

Woods came out of the bunkhouse, a cup of steaming coffee in his hand. "Drink, boy. It's gonna be mighty dry out there."

Jim gratefully accepted the cup, hoping to derive some energy from the liquid. He was wide-awake, but his eyes felt as gritty as a dust storm, and his head ached with tension.

Slowly the landscape escaped the shadows of darkness. It was time.

Grinding the remainder of the cigarette into the sand and finishing the last of the coffee, Jim grabbed the reins of his horse and walked toward the house.

Hank found the first tracks a hundred feet from the front door; shallow prints, obviously made by a feminine foot. The trail was so easy to follow that even an inexperienced tracker would have had no trouble.

Jim walked his horse for a short while, mounting when the bloody track became painfully easily to see from the back of the animal. The steps went in no specific direction, twisting and turning, doubling back on itself.

An abandoned slipper, its satin shredded beyond repair, fluttered in the light morning breeze.

When the trail led to a large saguaro, he flinched at the bloody evidence of Melanie's passing. Numerous pieces of material matching the dress he'd last seen her wearing clung to smaller cacti.

Before the sun had warmed the morning air, less than a mile from the house, Jim found his wife. Dismounting, he grabbed the blanket from the back of the saddle, refusing to think whether it would provide her with much-needed warmth or become her shroud.

She lay on her side with her arms wrapped tightly around herself. As he knelt, his jaw tightly clenched at the sight of her burned and lacerated flesh. Carefully rolling her onto her back, Jim felt for a pulse in her neck, surprised to find a feeble quivering beneath his fingers.

"Melanie?" Jim put the blanket over her and opened the canteen of water. Dribbling a few drops on her parched lips, he watched as it ran down the side of her face.

"Come on, Melanie, try to drink some water." Again there was no response, and knowing it was useless, he closed the canteen.

Melanie moaned when he raised her to a sitting position and wrapped the blanket around her. There was no place on her battered body that wasn't sunburned or lacerated by the cactus thorns. As he remounted the horse with her draped over his thighs, Jim was glad that she was unconscious. The pain would have been unbearable for her had she been awake.

By the time he'd made the short trip back to

the house, Melanie was muttering hoarsely and trying to push away his restraining arms. Woods met him at the front door, grabbing the reins to the horse and holding the animal still, as Jim carefully climbed from the saddle.

"Hank took off for town right after you headed out." Woods looked at the battered bundle in Jim's arms and shook his head in regret. No one, even an uppity Easterner like Melanie, deserved the abuse she had taken. "I got some water on the fire. I'll bring it up and then take care of your horse."

"Thanks, Woods." Jim entered the house and carried Melanie up the stairs to her frilly pink and white bedroom.

Everywhere he looked his gaze clashed with pink or white ribbons and bows, lacy flounces and fancy embellishments. As he laid her on the bed, he wondered why he'd never noticed that the room was decorated more for a young girl than for a woman Melanie's age. If he had bothered to notice, he realized sadly, the bedroom would have given him clear evidence of her refusal to leave her childhood behind.

The clopping sound of Woods coming up the stairs broke through Jim's contemplation of the bedroom. He hurried out to the hallway and took the heavy buckets from the old man. Carrying them into the room, he mixed equal amounts of hot and cold water into a bowl, located tweezers, a soothing lotion, and a bar of scented soap.

A search through the bureau drawers produced a soft cotton nightdress, and clean sheets that Jim tore into more convenient size to use as washing cloths. When everything was assembled, he could no longer delay the formidable task that awaited him.

With the removal of each tattered garment, he grew more appalled. Her feet, legs, hands, and arms were slivered with embedded thorns. The tender skin of her arms, neck, and face was severely burned, and even though her dress had provided some protection, her back and abdomen hadn't completely escaped the penetrating rays of the sun. He found himself praying that she wouldn't return to consciousness before he was finished.

He averted his eyes from the mound of her belly as he covered her with a clean sheet, refusing to allow himself to think about the baby. As gently as possible, he dabbed at the flesh pulled tightly over her face, stopping frequently to dribble some water between her cracked, shriveled lips. In spite of the severe burn, there were no blisters, her body had too little fluid to make the welts. Dampening several rags, he layered them over her face and head, attempting to bring down her temperature.

Freeing one of her arms from beneath the sheet, Jim sponged away the dried blood, carefully removing as many thorns as possible. Most of them were deeply embedded and would require further attention later on, but for now his main concern was to examine the extent of her injuries and to make her as comfortable as possible.

Placing damp strips of cloth on her arm, he returned to her face, dribbling water into her mouth and reapplying the rags to her head. Time had no meaning as he worked unceasingly, cleaning one spot, then returning to previous areas to redampen the rags. Always, he took long minutes to dribble water between her parched lips.

Melanie mumbled incoherently, twisting restlessly on the bed and even reaching out to push Jim's hand away, but she didn't regain consciousness.

"Be still, Mel." Jim replaced the cloth she had dislodged from her face. "Where in the hell is that damn doctor?" he muttered. He had done as much as he could; he needed the experience of a man of medicine.

The knock on the bedroom door brought a sigh of relief, as Jim turned from the bed and threw open the door. Hank's worried features greeted him, and a scan of the hallway proved that the old man was alone.

"Where's the doctor?"

"Doc left early this morning for the Stand Down Y spread. One of their hands got gored yesterday." Hank's voice was filled with apology, as if it was his fault that the doctor wasn't available.

"Damn . . ." Jim turned from the old man,

his gaze resting on his wife. The Stand Down Y ranch was at least twenty miles west of town. A round trip from the Falling Creek Ranch to the Stand Down Y would take more than a day. Melanie didn't have the luxury of time.

Jim knew of only one person who could make the trip there and back in a matter of hours. The man rode a horse as if he and the animal were one, the horse responding to some unspoken command of his rider.

"Find Breed."

"He followed me into the yard," Hank informed his boss. "Guess he figured somethin' were wrong, when you didn't show up this mornin'."

Jim nodded, not surprised that the foreman suspected trouble when Jim didn't return to the roundup that morning. Breed seemed to know instinctively when something was brewing.

"Send him up to see me."

"He ain't gonna like that."

"Just pass the word." Jim closed the door and returned to the bed, automatically removing the hot rags from Melanie's head and replacing them with cool ones. Well aware of Breed's discomfort in a white man's house, Jim would have normally met him outside, but right now he didn't have the time or patience to pander to him.

An abrupt rap on the door announced the arrival of the foreman. Jim wasn't surprised that he'd hadn't heard Breed approach; the man moved with the silent grace of a mountain lion. Covering Melanie, he called for Breed to enter.

"I need you to go for the doctor." Not turning to look at him, Jim carefully moistened Melanie's lips.

Breed stood at the foot of the bed, his restlessly moving eyes the only indication of his discomfort. He looked, once, at the woman, and knew that no one of this earth could save her. If he had more time or if her wounds weren't so severe, he could prepare a poultice of jojoba or maybe yucca, but the healing properties of the desert plants couldn't help someone who had already chosen to depart this life.

"It will be after dark before I can get the man back here." Breed left unsaid the knowledge that the woman wouldn't last that long.

Dropping the rag back into the pan of water, Jim turned. He looked into the guarded pale blue eyes, reading their unspoken message.

"I have to try. Even if she were a complete stranger, I'd still have to try."

Breed nodded, his gaze drifting momentarily to the woman. "Your son is strong," he said quietly.

Jim's gaze flew to the mound of her stomach, and watched as the sheet fluttered with the child's movements. He closed his eyes with the pain of knowing that the baby might never see the light of day. She was so close to delivering, and yet the child would die, trapped inside his mother's body.

"Get the doctor, Breed." Rubbing his tired face with his hands, Jim threaded his fingers through his hair and listened as the door closed quietly. Melanie's best chance for survival depended on the skill of a man she had repeatedly called a savage. Perhaps his savage ability with a horse would be enough . . .

The hard physical labor of the roundup the previous day combined with the sleepless night, demanded a heavy toll as exhaustion weighed heavily on Jim's shoulders, and by noon he sat beside her bed capable only of changing the rags and dribbling water into her mouth.

When she continued to be unresponsive, he began to accept that everything he did for Melanie wouldn't be enough. She had opened her eyes several times and had stared at him, but there had been no sign of recognition in her unfocused gaze. The only hopeful sign had been the frequent movements of the baby, easily seen beneath the tightly stretched skin of her stomach. But in the last hour or so, even that had ceased.

On the lonely hillside the wind whistled mournfully through the spreading arms of a solitary pine. With his hat clutched in his hands and his head bowed as if in prayer, Jim stared at the newly turned earth at his feet. The hastily constructed white cross would later be replaced with a finely made marker of granite, and soon the elements would cover the harshness of the new earth. Only the stone would distinguish this as the final resting place of a woman far too young to have died.

After her ordeal in the desert, Melanie had never regained consciousness, slipping silently into the hands of death. Now it was too late for him to tell her of his regret that things hadn't been different. He knew he would live the rest of his life with a burden of guilt that he had caused her death.

He was wise enough to know that he hadn't chased her into the desert; he accepted that the sun and countless abrasions had taken their toll. But he would never be able to forget that she had given up, had refused to fight. It was easier for her to accept death, than to continue life in the hell he had forced on her.

And for that, for not seeing and understanding that his dream wasn't hers, he would never forgive himself.

He had made a mistake, thinking that she would fit into his life. It had been a fatal mistake. His dream had been to build a ranch in the growing West. He'd never given a thought to her dreams. Even now, staring down at her final resting place, he couldn't name one dream that had been hers. He'd told her of his plans, his dreams, but he realized now that he'd never once asked her what she wanted from life.

The untamed West was hard on even the toughest men. Why had he thought that Melanie could adapt? Before meeting him her greatest hardship had been keeping the hem of her gown clean on a rainy day. His selfishness and lack of foresight appalled him.

The decisions had all been his, without consultation with the woman whose life they would effect. He had taken one look at a sweet, gentle girl, and decided that she would make his life complete, without bothering to think whether he could make her happy or not. He had decided to move her to Arizona without considering that she would be a continent away from her family and friends in a land completely different from the gentle hills of Vermont.

"I'm sorry, Melanie," he whispered. "I know that doesn't make much difference, but I am truly sorry. I'll spend the rest of my life regretting what I've done to you."

"You did nothing to her."

Startled by the voice at his shoulder, Jim's head snapped up, and he turned burning eyes on the man who dared to overhear his confession. Breed's crystal blue gaze met his without flinching.

"Some people are not meant to live a long span on earth. Their beings are too fragile for this world. From the time of birth, they walk with one foot in this land and the other still in the spirit-land before birth. Their souls wander earth without first disconnecting from the other side, and they are too willing to return to the place of peace."

"A man of God, Breed?" Jim asked with a smirk in his voice.

Understanding the pain that Jim harbored, Breed took no offense. "The Comanche have many gods, many spirits that do good or bring harm. A man must learn to court the first and avoid the second. If he allows himself to live in regret for mistakes he has made, then his life will forever be plagued by sorrow, if he thinks constantly of those who have departed this world, then his spirit will be joined to them and he'll miss the joys of life."

"And if a man does something that causes another's death?"

Breed shrugged and looked toward the horizon. "If a man spends his time looking at the past, he can see all of the mistakes he has made. The future doesn't tell us which decisions are correct for ourselves and for others, only the past does that. But a man can't live in the past, he can only learn from it."

"I've learned that women don't belong in the West. It's too harsh, too ruthless for them."

"It is women that make the homes, bear the children, give a man the gentleness he needs to find peace. If the women don't come here, it will make the Indian happy, for without women the white men will return to their homes in the East."

"That's not going to happen. The white men are here to stay."

"And so are their women."

"I'll never ask another woman to endure this life." Jim turned and looked at the land spread around him—his land. "This is what I want for my life, but I'll never ask another woman to make my dreams hers."

"All women aren't the same. Some crumble at the slightest difficulty, while others grow stronger. Some scream at the sight of a snake, while others shoot its head off and cook it for supper."

"For a man who was raised by the Indians, you know an awful lot about white women," Jim commented.

"Was I speaking of white women?" A slight grin tilted one side of Breed's mouth. "I thought I was talking about all women, of which I know very little. Any man who claims to know a lot about women is a fool. They are creatures put on this earth to make a man's life both heaven and hell."

The sound of an infant's angry cry drifted on the breeze. Jim's gaze turned toward the mourners who were gathered at the house. They had moved far enough away to give him some time alone to mourn. Only Breed had dared to infringe upon that solitude.

"She was sent to you for a purpose. Be grateful for the blessing she gave before her death." In the Comanche way, Breed was careful not to say Melanie's name. "Right now that purpose sounds unhappy."

"A life replaced with a life," Jim said quietly.

"She walked with the spirits, but held onto this world long enough to give you the greatest gift a woman can give a man."

Again the infant's cry drifted to them. "Thank you, Melanie," Jim said quietly, this time not concerned that another heard his words. "Thank you for the gift of my son."

Three

"You gotta do somethin'," Hank stated firmly.

Jim climbed from his horse, tired, dirty, and hungry. The sound of crying filled the evening silence. Roundup was well underway, in spite of the fact that he was spending more time at home than on the range. He knew that he owed it to Breed that things were going so smoothly. If only the foreman was as handy with a newborn!

"Get a woman in here or somethin'. I ain't no mammy," the old man grumbled.

"See if you're still a wrangler," Jim replied with little sympathy. "Take care of my horse, and I'll see about the baby."

"Hell yes, I'm still a wrangler," Hank bristled. "I may be old, but I ain't dead yet. There ain't a horse around that I can't handle."

Jim climbed the steps to the house and found Woods walking around in big circles in the kitchen, the baby cradled awkwardly in his arms. If he hadn't been so tired, Jim would have smiled when he realized that the old man was humming a song that Jim recognized as one the cowhands sang at night to the cattle. It worked well to soothe the cattle, but didn't seem to be having any effect on his infant son.

" 'Bout time you got home, boy. Where the hell you been?" Woods sounded so much like a disgruntled wife, that this time Jim had to smile.

"Been looking for strays," Jim offered. "What have you been up to today?"

"This youn'en of yores will be makin' me deef, if'en I gotta listen to him much longer. You got to get someone to take care of him, boy. Me and Hank is too old for this none-such."

Jim threw his hat on the table and took the child into his arms. The pitifully crying baby blinked deep blue eyes up at his father, and Jim grimaced at the wetness dripping onto his hand.

"When's the last time you changed his towel?"

"I ain't changing no dirty towel, that's Hank's job. I feed him his slop and beat him 'til he spits, but Hank does the towels."

Shaking his head, hiding a grin, Jim carried the baby up to his room. He discovered that the baby's towel, gown, and blanket were wet, and it was necessary to change everything. The stack of clean towels was vanishing at an alarming rate, and he knew that neither Woods or Hank would volunteer for the job of washerwoman.

Picking up the now dry baby, Jim walked back down the stairs and headed toward the kitchen. A row of dirty baby bottles lined the dry sink, like bottles set up for target practice.

Balancing the baby on his shoulder, Jim opened a tin can of Murdock's Liquid Food, and poured it into one of the remaining clean bottles. Prying the rubber nipple onto the bottle was a two-handed job that he managed to do with one hand, an elbow, and the corner of the sink.

"We got problems coming, boy." Jim sat in the rocker in the corner of the kitchen and held the baby in the crook of his arm. The infant grasped greedily at the nipple placed in his mouth, sucking hungrily. "I got you to worry about and roundup going on. Pretty soon there's going to be branding, worming, culling. How am I supposed to do it all?"

Looking up with big, blue eyes, the baby blinked as if in response. "Breed says those nesters are still down in the south line shack, a whole family staking a claim to my land. I'm going to have to go tomorrow and convince them to move on."

The baby squeaked in protest when Jim pulled the nipple from his mouth and raised him to his shoulder. Patting him gently as the doctor had instructed, Jim waited until the child had burped. Jim had found out the hard way, with a night spent walking the floor while the baby screamed in his ear, what would happen if he failed to accomplish this task.

"You're not in danger of starving, youn'en," Jim muttered, returning the crying baby to the crook of his arm. "If I didn't know better, I'd say that this is as close to magic as it comes. All

I got to do to stop your noise is shove this nipple in your mouth."

The baby sucked noisily, smacking his lips as he gulped. "So, what am I going to do? Doc's had the announcement posted in town for a housekeeper since the day you were born, but nobody's interested in coming way out here. You're about out of clean drawers, roundup is going on, the nesters are nesting, and Hank and Woods are threatening to find another place to sit around all day. We got us a real problem, and all you can do is gulp your dinner."

The blue eyes batted with sleep. "That's right, boy, sleep on it. Maybe a solution will come about midnight, when you decide it's time to eat again. You've been here for ten days, and I haven't had a decent night's sleep since then. How one little bitty boy can cause such a ruckus is beyond me."

Jim set the bottle on the table and put his son against his shoulder. He lightly patted the tiny back as he made his way up the stairs. Satisfied that the child had expelled the built-up gas, Jim laid him on his stomach as the doctor had instructed. He watched indulgently as the baby squirmed until his knees were beneath him, his padded bottom in the air. Placing a light blanket over him, Jim left the room.

Exhaustion had become a part of his life since the night of Melanie's disappearance. It had him dragging his feet by bedtime each night, and still dragging them when he got up in the morning. He knew that things couldn't continue like this, but he wasn't sure what to do to solve the problem.

Everyone for miles around had attended Melanie's funeral. He was sure that most of them came out of respect for him rather than fondness for her, but he appreciated their concern. Some, he knew, had come out of curiosity, wanting to get a good look at the new house he had built for his Eastern bride. He had made it clear to everyone that he was in need of a housekeeper, but no one had applied for the job.

Last Sunday a childless couple who lived in town had made the long drive out to the ranch. They wanted to adopt the baby, promising to love him like one of their own. Jim had turned down their offer, but with every day that passed he began to seriously reconsider it. Unless something changed soon, he wouldn't be able to take care of the ranch and his infant son.

Forcing his feet down the steps, Jim walked back into the kitchen. There was a couple of hours of work facing him before he could consider going to bed. Baby bottles and nipples needed to be washed, and then cooked in boiling water to sterilize them. The doctor had been very specific in his instructions on the care of the newborn. He had given Jim enough examples of the horrible fate that awaited the child if the directions weren't followed, that Jim was careful to do every thing exactly as instructed.

His own belly growled with hunger as Jim

poured water into a bowl to wash the bottles. Grabbing the heel of the loaf of bread, the only remaining piece, he wondered why he had never before considered white bread as a luxurious thing. Only when faced with doing without any did he realize how much he depended on it. As he chewed the bread, he knew that it would be the last until one of his neighbors took pity on him and brought some over.

It was a sure bet that neither Hank nor Woods would volunteer to bake bread.

Jim didn't know what he would have done without the two old men, or without Breed. A routine, or the form of one, had developed the morning after the funeral. He would get up, take care of the baby, and then head out, leaving his son in the dubious care of the two men. Breed was handling the heaviest part of the roundup, making it possible for Jim to return to the ranch house before dark each evening.

It wasn't a perfect routine, not even a good one, but it was working for now. He just didn't know how much longer he could continue it. Breed did what was necessary without a word of complaint, and the two old men did what they could with ceaseless complaints.

He had to find a housekeeper soon, or face the real possibility of giving up his son. He wasn't sure exactly what he felt about the child. It was difficult to develop a relationship with someone who cried, ate, and slept, but he knew he didn't want to let the town people adopt him.

After scrubbing the bottles and nipples, he rinsed them and put them in a pot of boiling water. Either Hank or Woods had left a pot of beans and a pan of corn bread near the fire, and feeling as greedy as his son, Jim finished them.

Knowing it was necessary, but dreading it nonetheless, he made a quick trip back upstairs, grabbed the baby's dirty linens, and carried them to the kitchen. His nose wrinkled with disgust as he opened the bucket lid and poured water over the contents. Using the scrub board from the back porch, he scrubbed each towel ten times, ignored the stains, wrung it out, and threw it into the dry sink.

By the time he had finished the towels, he estimated that the bottles had boiled long enough. Carefully removing them with a knife stuck in the opening, he saved the water and added the clean towels. Returning it to the fire, Jim sat at the kitchen table and waited for them to boil.

His head nodded and he rested it against his hand, drifting into a much-needed sleep. The sound of the baby crying woke him abruptly, and as he climbed wearily to his feet, he shook his numb hand. Pouring the remainder of the can of Murdock's Liquid Food into a bottle and capping it with the rubber nipple, he cursed at the necessity of dirtying one of the clean bottles.

Before he left the kitchen, he remembered to remove the boiling diapers from the fire. The baby was squealing in rage by the time Jim entered the bedroom. His face was flushed and he had managed to wedge his head into the corner of the baby bed.

"Hold on a minute, fella," Jim mumbled, as he set the bottle down and reached for the infant. "If you aren't the hungriest boy ever born, I'd sure hate to meet the winner."

He rolled the baby over and changed his dirty towel for a dry one. The baby squirmed and cried pitifully, tugging at his father's heart.

"It's coming, boy." In spite of the fatigue dragging at him, Jim smiled at the tiny infant. "If you'd hold still 'til I get this on you, then you'd get your snack sooner."

As always, the crying ceased abruptly when Jim put the nipple into the child's mouth. Leaning against the windowsill with the baby cradled in his arm, he looked out at the darkness. A crescent moon gave little light, but the display of stars was magnificent. Millions of tiny specks of light glittered in the night sky.

It was at this time of night that he felt the guilt for Melanie crowd into his thoughts. Trying to take care of the ranch and his son at the same time, he had a better idea of what her life had been like.

She had never herded cattle or taken care of an infant, but she had cooked, cleaned, and washed. Sometimes she had been alone for several days while he'd been on the range, seeing no one. She'd had no close friends to confide in, or other women to share her fears with.

For a woman who had been raised in a city

with maids to do her bidding and someone always within the sound of her voice, Jim realized
that the ranch must have been hell on earth for
her.

Guilt ate at him relentlessly; it had taken her
death for him to see her desperation. He wondered if he had paid more attention to her, or
listened seriously to her complaints, if she might
be alive now.

With a sad shake of his head for all the things
he should have done differently, Jim placed the
baby against his shoulder and gently rubbed his
back.

He had to finish the feeding, wring out the
wet towels, hang them over the porch railing,
and wash some of the trail dirt from his body,
before he could seek out his own bed. Five o'clock
came early on any day, but lately it seemed to be
coming hours too early for him.

As Jim approached the line shack, he checked
the Winchester rifle in the saddle scabbard and
unclipped the Colt .45 on his thigh. He knew of
more than one man who had met his death trying to convince nesters that it was time to move
on.

Breed had found the family in the line shack
several months earlier in the dead of winter, but
when he told Jim of the number of children,
Jim hadn't had the heart to chase them off. First
one thing and then another had delayed his trip

out here, but spring was well underway, and it was time for the family to move on. He'd use force if necessary, but he hoped it wouldn't be.

When he arrived at the shack, it was obvious that the family had moved in with the intent to stay. A garden spot had been scraped out of the dry soil and someone had constructed a chaparral brush corral. As he rode closer he counted at least nine people, adults and several children, wandering around the cabin that had been built as overnight shelter for one or two cowhands riding the lower range. He couldn't imagine all of these people crammed into the tiny structure.

Jim stopped beside the cabin, but didn't dismount. He waited for someone to approach him and watched as a man turned in his direction, hitching up his pants as he crossed the sand.

" 'Mornin', what cain I do ya for?" the man asked, his eyes shaded by a straw hat.

"I'm Jim Travis, owner of the Falling Creek Ranch." Jim's alert gaze noticed the interest of the others, particularly the two boys who were nearly grown. "You're on my land."

"Well now, I don't be knowin' 'bout that. There waren't no signs up sayin' this land be yores. We found the cabin and figured someone had done decided to move on, so we claimed it for ours."

The man's family had gathered behind him, and a quick count showed two adults and eight children ranging in age from a toddler still in towels to the two boys who were in their late teens. The woman, aged beyond her years, balanced the baby on her hip.

"The line shack is mine. You'll have to move on."

The man scratched his head beneath his battered hat and stared off into the distance. "I'd be happy to oblige you, but there ain't nowhere for us to go, nor no money to go on."

Jim had expected this and had already decided to give the family a little money. It was much better than the alternative, which might result in the death of the father, then he'd feel responsible for the rest of the family. He had enough problems without adding these people to them.

"How much do you think it would take?" Jim asked.

"Oh, a hundret, maybe a little more." The man looked slyly beneath lowered lids.

An idea began to brew as Jim looked at the oldest girl. She wasn't more than thirteen, but with this family of children he had little doubt that she knew more about child care than he ever would. He reached into his shirt pocket, already aware of the amount it contained.

"I'll work a deal with you." He pulled out the bills and held them in sight of the man. "I'll give you enough to get started, if you'll agree to leave in the morning. I'd also be interested in talking to your oldest girl about a job at my ranch."

"Well now, there be possibilities in that, yes,

sir'ee, thar just might be possibilities. Name's George Evans, git down off 'en that horse and sit a spell, and let's do some talkin'."

The man motioned for the others to go away as Jim dismounted. In the sparse shade of a cottonwood tree, they soon struck a deal. For fifty dollars, the man would pack up his family and leave, and the oldest girl would go back to the ranch with Jim.

"Feb, go get yore sister. Tell her to pack her belongin's, she's goin' with Mr. Travis."

As the boy moved toward the cabin, George turned to Jim and smiled cordially. "She's a mite peeked right now, it bein' her woman's time and such, but she's a good hard worker. Ain't never had me much trouble outta her, and what I did was soon beat away."

Jim hadn't thought his impression of the man could have gotten much lower, but it sank further with George's lack of concern of his oldest daughter's welfare. What kind of a man would let his child go off with a stranger, not knowing or caring how she would be treated?

Her few possessions in a roll beneath her arm, the girl moved slowly out of the cabin, her hand on the wall as if in support. She wasn't the same girl Jim had seen when he rode up. This one had been in the cabin until now.

She was so tiny that at first Jim thought she was far too young for his purposes, but as she drew closer he realized that she was older than he thought. Her badly worn dress was too small, ending several inches above her bare feet and pulling snugly over breasts impossibly large for such a small frame. Still young, maybe fourteen or fifteen, but old enough to be responsible for his son.

Her bewildered gaze rested on her father. "Pa, you're sending me off with him?"

"Don't give me no sass, girl," George said harshly.

She looked with disbelief, first at Jim and then at her father. Pa had done many shady things, some of them despicable and a few she suspected were illegal, but she couldn't believe he was doing this to her.

"We'll be movin' on come mornin'. Say yore goodbyes to the youn'ens and head out. If'en Mr. Travis won't let you on the back of his horse, you'll hafta walk."

"You know I can't ride a horse, Pa."

"Don't make no never mind to me if'en you ride or walk." Without a further comment, George turned and walked away, stuffing the money into his pants pocket.

"Ma? He's sending me away?"

The woman looked sadly at her oldest daughter, then turned and followed her husband. One by one the children came and hugged her, but none shed a tear for this sister they would never see again.

Wanting to be away from this strange family and afraid he had been foolish to offer this girl a job, Jim mounted his horse. He was already wondering what he would do with her if she didn't work out. His desperation had caused him to overlook his better judgment, and he prayed he didn't live to regret it.

"Hand me your things, girl." Jim held his hand out, then stuck her small roll at the front of the saddle.

Her big gray eyes looked up—way up. And what she saw was far from reassuring. The man was big, easily twice her size. The sun was behind him, making it impossible for her to see him clearly, but he looked like many of the men who hung around the cabin with a layer of trail dust clinging to his clothes and the stubble of a beard darkening his face.

His hat was pulled low over his forehead, making it difficult for her to see much of his face. She wished she could push it back, so that she could study his eyes. Mama had always claimed you could tell a good man from a bad one by studying his eyes.

"I can't sit a horse, Mr. Travis."

"Your pa explained that you were poorly." Jim felt uncomfortable discussing such a personal matter with a stranger. "If you sit sideways and hold onto me, you should do all right."

With a lot of help, she was able to get onto the rump of the horse. It was a precarious position with her legs dangling freely and only her grasp on his waist to keep her on the horse, but the discomfort and weakness that plagued her far outweighed her concern about falling off.

She didn't dare turn to take a final look at her family, and tears clouded her eyes. What would Ma and the little ones do without her? Pa didn't care if they starved or went without clothing. He wasn't concerned if they were sick. During her mother's many confinements, she was the one who made sure there was food on the table and a warm fire burning.

"What's your name, girl?" Jim asked as he slowly walked the horse back toward the house.

"March," she answered softly.

"March? What kind of name is that?"

"Mine." Wiping the tears from her cheeks, she wondered what was in store for her now. She'd already suffered dearly, surely nothing could be worse than that.

"How'd you end up with March?" he asked.

"I'm the third."

"Like in a calendar; January, February, March, April?" He wondered why it surprised him that someone would name their children after the months of the year. After seeing the lack of concern George had shown this girl, nothing should have come as a surprise.

"January and February are my two older brothers," she clarified.

"How many months are there?"

Trying to ignore the gnawing pain low in her stomach, she decided that conversation was better than silence. "The baby is September, but I was starting to suspect that October is on the way." Her voice grew softer. "I wonder if they'll name the new baby March, now that I'm gone."

Jim didn't know how to respond to her so he remained quiet. From what he had seen of the family, he thought that it would be a blessing to be free from them. They were white trash, pure and simple, and would never be anything else. But they were the girl's family, and he guessed that she would have some kind of feelings for them.

March was in so much pain by the time they reached the house, that at first she didn't see it. Concentrating on staying on the back of the horse when Jim dismounted, she kept her eyes lowered until he reached up for her.

Raising her gaze, she emitted a startled gasp. "You live here?" She had never seen anything as beautiful as the pristine white building with its many sparkling windows.

Jim looked at the house, and realized for the first time how much he hated it. It was Melanie's house. It stood for all the things that she had given up to come West, and it was filled with the memories of her unhappiness. He much preferred the adobe house they had lived in before building this monstrosity.

"I live here." He motioned up the porch. "Wait here while I go get the baby."

"Baby?" March's heart began to pound, as if she had run for miles.

"My son." Jim looked at the girl and noticed

the strange look on her face. "Why did you think I brought you here?"

March shook her head. She hadn't given much thought as to what he wanted. She had been in too much pain, and was too worried about her younger brothers and sisters to consider what her own fate was to be.

"I need someone to take care of my son. He's ten days old."

"His ma?"

"She died."

Jim watched as the girl reached for the handrail and climbed laboriously up the steps. The back of her dress was spotted with blood, and he cursed beneath his breath. She didn't know how to decently attend to her own problems, and he was expecting her to know how to take care of his son.

"I think you'd better tend to your needs, while I get the baby."

March turned her head back toward him. A fiery blush replaced the pallor of her cheeks, when she realized where his gaze rested and what must be there. Feeling a wetness roll down her legs, she knew it was getting worse.

"I need to lay down a bit," she mumbled.

Jim had a sudden urge to throw her on his horse and get her back to her family, before he lived to regret this day.

"You can sleep in—" His words were harshly broken off, when he saw her eyes roll up in her head and her legs begin to collapse beneath her.

He grabbed her before she could fall and roll off of the steps.

"Damn, I think I just added another problem to the list."

Four

March opened her eyes and found herself in a room unlike any she'd ever seen before. It was like the fairy-tale story Ma told them sometimes, when she was in a good mood. The prince always saved the princess from some evil, and took her to his castle that was filled with wonderful and exciting things.

Everywhere she looked there was something different to admire. The long windows had real glass, and were framed with bright yellow-and-white-checked gingham curtains. The highly polished floor was covered with a circular rag rug with every color of the rainbow in it.

Sitting up to better view the room, she saw that the walls were a pale yellow, while the furniture was painted white. Colorful pictures, some of things she couldn't identify, decorated the walls.

Her eyes came to rest on the baby bed in the corner, and her heart skipped a beat. She rose, moving painfully to the bed, reverently touching the soft, fuzzy blankets.

Biting the inside of her cheek as tears blinded

her, she thought of the baby who would never know such riches, who would never see a cloud or hear the sweet songs of the birds. The baby girl, her baby girl, who had been born too early and had never drawn a breath.

"You're awake."

Turning too quickly, March grabbed onto the baby bed for support, as blackness wavered in front of her eyes.

"Hold on, girl, or you're going to pass out again." Jim closed the space between them and grabbed her arm. He'd never realized that a woman could be so weak during her monthly time. But then he'd never realized what was involved in taking care of a house either, until he'd had to do it. He wasn't about to have a monthly so that he could find out about it the hard way, too.

"I'm sorry," March apologized. "I've never passed out before. I'll be all right in a minute."

Not sure what to say, Jim looked around the baby's room. "This is my son's room. You can share it with him. When you feel up to it, I'll show you the kitchen and such, but for now maybe you should rest."

"Where's the baby?"

"When you passed out on me I carried you up here and decided to leave him be for a time. Whenever you're ready, I'll go get him."

March wondered if she'd ever be ready to hold someone else's child in her arms. Her heart ached for her own baby, and yet there was a relief that the child wouldn't have to suffer as she had suffered. She'd had nothing to offer her daughter except a heart full of love, but love wouldn't fill an empty stomach or warm a cold body. And love wouldn't protect her when someone called her white trash or whore.

"I'm ready," she stated softly.

"Maybe you should . . . ah, clean up a little." Her blond hair was hanging in snarls down her back, and she was still wearing the bloody dress. It embarrassed him that she would have let such a thing happen, or that he would have to draw her attention to it.

He nodded toward the pretty yellow and white pitcher and bowl sitting on the dresser. "There's warm water in the pitcher. I'll go get the boy, and you come on downstairs when you're ready."

March nodded, watching as he left the room. Unbuttoning her dress, she pulled it over her head, horrified at the large bloodstain on the skirt. A lady was never careless enough to let blood get on her skirts, even if it was three days after giving birth. She'd never be able to look him in the eyes again. Knowing that he must be thinking all kinds of terrible things about her, March moaned in despair.

A thick cotton drying towel and smaller washing cloth hung on the rail beside the sink. Dipping the washing cloth into the water, she scrubbed as much of herself as possible. It had been months since she'd had an all-over bath. It was too cold to wash in the river during the winter, and they didn't have a bucket large enough to sit down in. As soon as it was warm, she decided, she'd find a creek and take a nice, long bath.

Putting on her only other dress, she carefully wrapped her stained clothes in a bundle and put them on the floor, taking great care that they didn't touch the rug. She would have to wash them and hang them out to dry, since she had nothing else to wear.

As she came slowly down the stairs, Jim noticed that the clean dress was badly wrinkled, and if anything, smaller than the one before. Her legs were visible several inches above her ankles, but it was obvious that she'd made an attempt to wash her bare feet. He tried not to notice how shapely her legs were or how the dress clung lovingly to every curve. She was tiny, but well filled out, and he forcefully reminded himself that she was just a girl and here to take care of his son, not him.

Her gaze glued to the bundle in her employer's arms, March forgot her earlier embarrassment. Her heart beat painfully hard as she reached out to pull the blanket away from the baby's face.

"How old is he?" she whispered.

"Ten days." Jim looked down at his sleeping son. "His mother didn't survive his birth." He saw no reason to tell this child about the horror Melanie had gone through.

Longing with every fiber of her being to take the baby into her arms, March clasped her hands behind her back. "What's his name?"

Jim looked up at the girl and then back down at the baby. In all the confusion, the work and worry, he'd never given thought to giving him a name.

"He doesn't have one," he finally admitted.

"What?" Her stunned expression made him feel sadly lacking. "Everybody's got to have a name. What have you been calling him?"

"Mostly just boy."

"You've got to give him a name, Mr. Travis."

"Jim," he corrected. They didn't stand on formality at the ranch.

"Jim," she seemed to roll the name around on her tongue. "That's a good strong name for a man, but maybe you could call him Jamie 'til he grows a little."

"No, *my* name is Jim."

"All the more reason to call him Jamie; it'll avoid confusion."

He noticed that her eyes were the deepest gray he'd ever seen, nearly violet, with thick dark lashes that shadowed her cheeks. Her hair was blond, streaked nearly white in places by the sun. He wanted her to be about fourteen, maybe fifteen, but looking at her now as she gazed down at the baby, he was afraid that she was considerably older than that. He suspected that she was fully grown, and that he was courting trouble by having her in his house.

"No," he mumbled to himself, uncomfortable that he was noticing her as a woman rather than a child. He pushed the baby into her arms. "There's bottles and tinned milk in the kitchen, clean towels in his room. I'm heading out, but I'll try to be back tonight. If you need anything, give a holler, Hank and Woods stay around the bunkhouse most of the time. They'll give you a hand."

March didn't see him grab his hat from the hall tree or hear the door slam behind him. The pain between her thighs and the exhaustion brought on by the simplest movement faded away. All that she was aware of was the warm bundle in her arms.

"Hello, Jamie. Do you like that name? Your pa couldn't seem to decide if he wanted you named that or not." She carefully unwrapped the sleeping baby, studying his long, slender fingers, counting his stubby little toes. His rosebud mouth puckered when she caressed the deep dimple in his chin, and she smiled when he yawned and stretched out in her arms.

"You're a beauty, little boy," she whispered as tears suddenly filled her eyes. She had lost her own baby, but had been given another child who desperately needed a mother. "I'll be a good mama, sweetheart. You'll never be hungry or cold, and I won't let anyone ever hurt you."

Holding onto the handrail for support, March slowly climbed the stairs, returning to the baby's room. She needed to wash out her dress before the bloodstains set. She didn't even know where the kitchen was, and her stomach rumbled with hunger. But she laid down on the bed, the baby snuggled safely between her and the wall. Her eyes slowly closed, and for the first time since she'd lost her own baby, March slept without dreams.

Jim returned home long after sunset and wasn't surprised to find that the house was dark. He hadn't expected March to wait up for him. Grabbing the lamp hanging beside the front door, he struck a match and adjusted the wick.

He was surprised that there wasn't a fire in the kitchen fireplace, or a plate of food waiting for him. Alarm raced through him when he knelt at the fireplace and discovered that the ashes were cold.

With a pounding heart, he climbed the stairs and went directly to the baby's room. He muffled a sigh of relief to find March asleep on the narrow bed, the baby cradled in her arms. He turned and left the room quietly before the light could disturb either of them, but the picture of his son snuggled against her breasts followed him back to the kitchen.

Remembering her exhaustion and weakness, he allowed that she probably hadn't felt up to doing anything other than caring for his son. In a day or two she'd be over the worst of it, and he looked forward to coming home to a hot meal. He hadn't realized how bad his own cooking was until he'd been forced to eat it day after day. He'd gotten accustomed to Melanie's cooking, and while not the best in the world, it had been far superior to his own.

Opening a can of beans, he leaned against the table and ate them straight from the can. Women definitely had a place in the world, he decided, the kitchen being the number one spot. Now that there was someone to take care of the baby, do the washing and cooking, and generally keep the house running in smooth order, Jim expected his life to go back to the way it was.

With a tired sigh, he put the can on the sink and picked up the lamp to light his way upstairs. For the first time in days, he could count on a night of undisturbed sleep.

Unbuckling the holster belt, he laid his Colt on the dresser beside the lamp. Putting first one foot and then the other in the bootjack, he pulled the boots off and then his socks, rubbing his itchy feet on the rug. Slipping the suspenders down his arms, he rotated his tired shoulders, trying to work some of the kinks out as he unbuttoned his shirt. Lord, but he was tired. The bed would feel like heaven, he thought, as he threw the shirt in the general direction of the corner where he knew a pile of dirty clothes waited.

Reaching for the buttons on his canvas trousers, he stopped when a noise interrupted the silence. It was a furtive whisper of sound, like someone walking quietly, so that they wouldn't be heard.

Jim grabbed the Colt, blew out the lamp, and walked toward the door. He opened it slowly, grimacing when it squeaked. Staying near the wall, he stepped into the hallway and waited for his eyes to become accustomed to the darkness. Another sound drew his attention to the bottom of the stairs. There was someone in the house, someone who didn't want to be heard.

Finding the stair rail, he tried to move soundlessly down the stairs, muffling a curse when he stubbed a bare toe on a step. Hobbling, he followed the sound of the steps toward the back of the house, narrowly avoiding a chair, only to collide with the kitchen table.

"Who's there?" a feminine voice called.

"It's me, damn it." Recognizing March's voice, he lowered the Colt and rubbed his thigh where it had banged into the corner of the table. "What in hell are you doing down here at this time of night?"

March was glad for the darkness, as she felt her face flame. "I needed to find the . . . ah . . . necessary."

Not so shy, Jim shook his head. "There's a chamber pot under the bed."

"Yes, well, ah . . . yes . . ." March stood helplessly, embarrassed down to her toes. "It was dark and . . ."

"Why didn't you light a lamp?" Did she have no more sense than the old mule out back?

"It's dark—"

"We've already established that," he interrupted.

"I didn't know where the matches are."

"Oh . . . well, light a lamp now."

Jim waited for her to comply, beginning to wonder if she was a little dimwitted. "You do know how to light a lamp?"

"Yes, Mr. Travis," she stated, feeling the beginnings of anger. "I know how to strike a match and light a lamp."

"Then do it, girl."

"I assume that there is a lamp down here somewhere, and matches, but you'll have to tell me where, or we'll be here all night while I feel around for one!"

Feeling more than a little foolish, something he hoped wouldn't become a habit around his new housekeeper, Jim felt for a lamp on the sideboard, laid down the Colt, and found the matches in a small wooden box.

As he adjusted the flame, March saw that he was dressed only in his trousers and was unwillingly fascinated by the play of muscles over his strong back. She watched as the muscles bunched in his arms when he picked up the lamp and turned her way. There was so much latent strength in him that she backed away, realizing that he could overpower her without any effort.

"Here, girl," he stated gruffly, seeing her sudden fear and not understanding it. "Take the lamp and go do what you got to do. I'm going back to bed."

Setting the lamp on the table, Jim picked up the Colt, turned, and headed back to his room, muttering about his throbbing toe and women who wandered around in the dark.

March returned from the outhouse and carried the lamp up to the bedroom. She closed the door behind her and realized for the first time that it didn't have a lock. Surely he didn't intend to bother her, she thought, as she put the lamp on the dresser. He needed someone to tend to his infant son, but in the kitchen it had become glaringly clear to her that they were alone in the big house.

Her past experience with men had given her more than enough reason to be suspicious of his intentions. Now that she knew that pretty words and small gifts led to other things, she had no intention of getting involved with a man ever again.

Except maybe this one, she thought with a smile as the baby squirmed in his bed, bringing her attention to him. At his first mewing squeak, she turned him over and set about changing his wet towel.

"Hungry, little man?" she whispered. "Don't be so impatient, let me get you dry and you can eat." She smiled as his fist accidentally found his mouth and he sucked hungrily.

When he was changed, she wrapped him in a warm blanket and carried him to the rocking chair set in front of the window. Opening the front of her dress, she freed one of her breasts and his eager mouth latched onto her nipple with greedy ferocity. It was such a new experience for her, that it startled her as he pulled, his tiny hand batting against the swollen skin.

She blinked back tears, because she had never held her own baby against her breasts, giving her nourishment from her body. Swirling the long hair on the top of his head into a curl, she thought how strong he was, how eager to live.

"So, what do you think, Jamie? You need a mama and I need a baby. Do you think we'll do all right hitching up together?" She smiled as he grunted like a little piglet. "You sure aren't shy about where you sit down to dinner."

When one breast was drained, she patted his back to relieve the gas and then moved him to the other one. She had taken care of babies since she was little more than one herself. Her mother had a new one every year or so, and there was always a towel to be changed or a back to be patted. But she'd never before experienced the serenity of holding an infant to her breast and knowing that she was providing him sustenance.

In the quiet darkness, a bond was formed between the motherless child and the childless mother.

The sun was barely over the horizon when March woke to the sounds of the baby. Rubbing the sleep from her eyes, she climbed from the bed and mechanically changed his towel. Deciding that there was no reason for her to be up yet, she was still too weak to do anything, she carried him back to the bed. Holding him so that he could nurse, she closed her eyes and drifted back to sleep.

Other than the throbbing toe, Jim woke feeling more rested than he had in weeks. He climbed from bed and dressed. Strapping on the Colt as he walked down the hallway, he wondered what magic March had performed during the night. He hadn't heard a sound from his son's room.

Since the door to the nursery was still closed, he decided to let her sleep in. He'd make sure that he got home this evening with enough time to explain her duties to her. All he had done yesterday was to throw the baby into her arms and head out the door, hardly a friendly welcome.

Knowing that Hank would have the coffeepot on the fire and fatback frying, Jim headed for the bunkhouse. He'd breakfast with them and tell them about the new housekeeper. They had witnessed her arrival yesterday and would be concerned.

"How's the little missy this mornin'?" Hank asked as he handed Jim a steaming cup of coffee.

"Still sleeping, thought I'd let her get a little extra sleep today." The coffee was strong enough to dissolve a spoon, just the way he liked it. "She was doing all right last night though."

" 'Bout time you got somebody, I was gettin' mitey tired of playin' nursemaid." Hank grabbed a plate, scooped the eggs and fatback onto it, and handed it to his boss.

"Need you to keep an eye on her for me."

"Ain't she big 'nough to keep an eye on herself?" Woods asked between bites of food.

"Just make sure she doesn't get into any trouble while I'm gone."

"Leastways she's easier to watch than that youn'en, and don't have to worry 'bout her drippin' like that boy done. I swear, I ain't never seen no kid that leaks like that'en." Hank sighed with relief. It had been a strain on his tolerance to watch over the baby, and he was delighted that it was over.

"I'll try to get back a little earlier this evening." Jim stood and grabbed his hat. "We'll be in the south branch of Falling Creek."

"Water's still running pretty high," Woods offered.

"Gonna have a whole bunch of 'em bogged down." Hank referred to the calves who got stuck in the mud and were too weak to pull themselves free. If not found in time, they would starve to death.

Jim left the bunkhouse, a feeling of freedom carrying him toward the barn. It was good to have things back to normal.

* * *

With the baby in one arm and her dirty clothes in the other, March stood at the bottom of the stairs with her mouth hanging open. Last night in the dark she'd had an impression of the size of the house, but now the morning light showed her exactly what she hadn't been able to see.

"It's a castle, Jamie," she whispered to the baby. "I've never seen anything so beautiful in my life."

Stepping slowly off of the highly polished stair, she didn't know where to look first. Through the double doors to her right was a room twice the size of the shack she'd been living in with ten other people. The fireplace was large enough to roast a steer, and the green patterned rug stretched on forever. Large boxes and crates sat in the middle of the room, but she didn't dare enter to peek.

March looked into each room where a door stood open. She was disappointed that most of the rooms were empty of furniture, carpeting, and drapes, but just the size was staggering. She didn't open closed doors, afraid that somehow Jim would find out that she'd been nosing around and would get angry.

Wandering down a long hall, March found one room that was more magnificent to her than all the others combined. Spellbound, she stood in the doorway until the squirming baby attracted her attention.

"Look, Jamie," she whispered in awe. "Just

look at all the books. Aren't they beautiful?" She kissed the baby and readjusted him in her arms.

"I'm gonna read them, Jamie. Someday I'm going to know every word in those books. Someday all those funny lines and circles are going to make sense to me.

"Before I die, I'm going to learn to read." It was a promise and a prayer. "Even if the learning kills me."

Five

The kitchen was a big, square room with windows facing the east. A smooth oak table, flanked by eight chairs, occupied the middle of the room, while endless shelves, cabinets, and work space lined the walls. March marveled at the hand pump that drained into a tin-lined sink, making endless trips to the well a thing of the past. She pumped it several times and grinned as the cool, clear water splashed into the sink and then down the drain hole.

Out of necessity, she had discovered that the door at the back led outside, but in spite of curiosity that was nearly painful, refrained from opening the other two doors in the room. Her stomach rumbled noisily, reminding her that the only food she'd eaten yesterday had been at breakfast.

"What am I going to do with you, while I try to find something to eat?" she asked the sleeping baby in her arms. She couldn't bear the thought of leaving him alone upstairs.

Returning to his bedroom, stopping frequently to admire all the delightful things that surrounded her, March grabbed the soft blanket from his bed. She carried it to the kitchen, folded it into a thick pallet near the table, and carefully laid him in the center.

Feeling like a thief in search of hidden treasures, March opened one cabinet door after the other. They were filled with such marvelous treasures that her thoughts of food were forgotten in her desire to determine what was in each. She tried to convince herself that she wasn't being nosey. After all, she couldn't cook without knowing what the kitchen contained, could she?

One entire cabinet section was filled with dishes. March carefully picked up a plate and traced the delicate flowers and vines painted on the white surface. She discovered a small chip along the edge, but it in no way detracted from the beauty of the china.

The sunlight through the open window sparkled on the edges of cut-glass bowls, reflected onto the white walls, and turned them into a tapestry of rainbows. Struck by the incredible beauty, she put her hands behind her back so that she wouldn't be tempted to touch, afraid that she would accidentally drop something and break it.

She found more cooking utensils, wooden bowls, and stoneware jugs than she had ever seen in her life. The shelves closest to the fireplace held iron cooking pots and skillets, while still others held foodstuff in bags, boxes, and cans. Some of the labels had a picture of the product inside, but most were just written words, and she felt denied of some of the magic because she couldn't read the label. What wonderful treat was stored inside the tinned can? Some new and exotic treat? Something as common as beans? Short of opening the can, there was no way for her to know.

Shaking the cans did little to help determine their contents. The picture on one drew her like a magnet. Picking it up reverently, her mouth watered and she licked her lips, her finger lightly tracing the picture of a bright pink peach.

"Oh, Jamie, they're wonderful," she whispered to the sleeping baby. "I had one once, and it was better than a peppermint stick. It was so sweet, the juice ran down the side of my chin."

With a sigh, she reluctantly replaced the can on the shelf, but turned the picture so that she could see it whenever she looked up. "They're so expensive. I'm sure your pa wouldn't be pleased if I ate them."

Kindling had been laid in preparation for the morning fire in the fireplace, a marvel of modern convenience. The andirons held a generous amount of wood, and two hooks could be moved so that the cook wouldn't have to reach over the fire to stir a pot.

A removable iron rack sat a comfortable distance above the wood, the perfect place for keeping things warm or for something that needed to cook slowly. And wonder of wonders, in the stone wall was an oven for baking bread and cakes.

Excitement rippled through her. This was so much better than cooking out in the open in all kinds of weather. She wouldn't have to worry about lighting a fire with wet kindling or keeping it going when rain threatened to smother it. No more trying to keep warm when winter winds blew up her skirt, or worrying about a stray spark blowing away and starting a grass fire.

March struck a match and held it to the kindling. When it had caught the flame, she turned to look for the coffeepot. The only cabinet she hadn't explored yet was a strange-looking iron one that sat between the two doors on the side wall. Painted black with pretty red trim, it was a large, boxy chest on four legs with a small door in the front. She spied the coffeepot sitting in the middle of one of the iron rings on top.

Holding it under the faucet, she raised and lowered the pump handle with delight. When the fire was burning brightly, she threw some coffee beans into the pot and put it on one of the hooks, swinging it directly over the flame.

"It's just amazing, Jamie." She grabbed a bowl and the ingredients to assemble biscuits. "Imagine me, March Evans, cooking in a kitchen like this. Why, I'll bet those ladies in the city don't have it this good.

"And the food," her eyes turned longingly toward the can of peaches. "I've never seen so much food, except in the mercantile. It may be just a little short on meat, but maybe your pa goes hunting every couple of days."

The peaches beckoned enticingly. "And peaches, Jamie. Someday, when you're a lot older, we'll have some as a special treat. Maybe for your birthday or at Christmas."

Making biscuits was second nature, done for years and requiring no thought. By the time the fire had burned down to a nice layer of ashes, she had the dutch oven filled with fat balls of dough. She put it in the fire, placing a thick layer of hot ashes on the lid.

The coffee was bubbling merrily, filling the kitchen with its rich aroma and making her stomach rumble louder. When the scent of the biscuits drifted out from the fireplace, she knew she'd die before she could eat.

Wanting badly to use the flowered plates, but knowing that something that pretty was kept for special occasions, March found a wooden plate and a tin cup. By the time she'd poured her coffee and given it a few minutes to cool, she knew she could wait no longer for the biscuits, or she'd truly starve.

When they were golden brown and light as a feather, March placed two of them on her plate. She sat at the table where she could look out at the mountains, and still keep an eye on the baby.

Longing for some fatback or some of the jam her mother had once made from a cactus, she bit into the biscuit. Her gaze was captured again by the peaches, and she closed her eyes to avoid temptation. Peaches were just too expensive, costing nearly a dollar a can.

Jamie obligingly slept until she had finished her breakfast. She watched contentedly as he began to wake, stretching first his arms and then his legs. His head came up off of the blanket and bobbed uncontrollably. When he began to whimper, March bent over and picked him up.

"Good morning, again, little man." Opening her dress, she smiled as he nursed hungrily. "You sure are the eatin'est boy I ever saw. If you keep this up, you'll be full grown before you walk."

The baby blinked big blue eyes at her, trying to focus. "I think when you've finished your breakfast, we'll see about giving you a bath. I've got to wash my dress, and get it out so that it can dry. Then, if you're real good, maybe we'll go exploring."

By the time March had bathed the baby, washed her dress, and cleaned up the kitchen, she was exhausted. Carrying Jamie securely in her arm, she climbed the stairs.

"Maybe we better take just a little nap." She kissed his soft cheek and laid him in his bed. "We can take a walk after you wake up."

March laid down on the soft bed and thought of all the fabulous things she had discovered in the house. Why, the bed had two sheets and a nicely made patchwork quilt. It was a treat to sleep in a bed instead of on the floor, and nearly impossible to imagine sleeping between sheets!

It truly was a castle, she decided. A lingering sadness threatened to overwhelm her. Mama had told stories about her childhood home in Virginia, describing the house that she'd grown up in. It hadn't been nearly as glorious as this one, though. She wished that she could bring Mama and the little ones here to live. It would make their lives so much happier. With a sigh, she accepted the idea as impossible, knowing that by now Papa had pulled up stakes again and was headed far away.

Forcing her thoughts away from her vanishing family, March slipped into sleep with visions of canned peaches dancing behind her closed lids.

By early afternoon, March was ready to go exploring. She made a sling that held Jamie securely to her chest, and walked through the kitchen and out the back door.

The house sat away from the other ranch buildings and there were no plants or bushes to soften the stark lines of the structure. March studied it for a while. She delighted in the many things inside, but didn't find any pleasure at looking at the outside. Somehow, it seemed out of place, as if it didn't match its rugged surroundings.

"Well, Jamie boy, it surely is a castle, but I think it belongs in one of Ma's fairy stories." She hugged the baby that laid comfortably against her breasts. "Ma would say I'm probably jealous because it's not mine, but personally I think everyone can state their opinion. What do you think?''

When the sleeping baby declined to answer, March smiled and walked toward an adobe building where she could see two men sitting in chairs under a porch. It was time for her to meet the other employees of the ranch.

"Good afternoon," she called as she approached. One of the men stood up from his chair and removed his hat, while the other one spit a stream of tobacco juice onto the ground.

"Where's the youn'en?" the seated one asked gruffly. "Got me an interest in him, since I spent so much time changing his towels."

"I changed his towels," the other man stated. "You fed him his vittles."

"You was always busy when that youn'en sprung a leak."

"Seems to me I 'member you handin' him to me and telling me to fix him."

"You're gettin' old; havin' trouble rememberin' things is a sure sign."

"Ain't as old as you!"

"Hell you ain't! Why you was already brandin' cows while I was still learnin' to ride."

"That's cause you still don't know how to ride!"

"I can outride you any day of the week!"

March smiled at the two men, enjoying their bickering banter. Only old friends who had spent years cultivating their friendship would feel able to argue as these two were doing, without worry of hurting feelings. She had never been in one spot long enough to develop that kind of relationship with someone.

"Lookee here," the old man who was standing pointed out to the other one. "You got this here girl laughing at you. Ain't you ashamed?"

"She ain't laughin' at me, are you, girlie?"

"My name is March," she informed them. "And I'm not laughing at anyone."

"She polite, which is more than I can say 'bout you." The standing one ran his fingers through his thin gray hair. "I'm Hank and this here is Woods."

"Where's the youn'en?" Woods asked again.

March pulled the sling back enough for them to see the baby's head, then readjusted it to assure that the sun didn't touch his tender skin.

"Why if'en that don't beat all! Got him all snug and tight, and still got your hands free."

"Women just seem to know how to do those kinds of things with a youn'en. Guess it comes naturally."

Woods nodded in agreement. "Just like cookin', cleanin', and bickerin'. Ain't never known no woman that can go long without findin' somethin' to sink her teeth into."

"Or someone, more like." Hank deposited another stream of tobacco juice in the dirt. "Women was born just to make man miserable."

" 'Cept for mamas," Woods added. "My ma used to be the bestest cook this side of the Big

Muddy. Ever' year for my birthday, she used to make me a big pan of Spotted Dog, just for me, said I didn't have to share unlessin' I was a wantin' to. Oowhee, I can still remember bitin' into it. Seemed to just melt in my mouth!"

"Back when you had 'nough teeth to bite into somethin'. Now you'd just have to gum it to death."

"What'd your ma make you for your birthday?" Woods asked with a smirk.

"Didn't have no ma or birthdays, either. Man don't need to be reminded that he's gettin' older. I know that every mornin', when I wake up a half hour before my body's of a mind to move!"

"Only place it moves is from yore bed to that rockin' chair."

"Seems like I 'member you still snorin' loud enough to shake a cactus, when I already had breakfast cookin' this mornin'."

"I don't snore! Why a body cain't get no sleep around here for all the noise you make. If'en you ain't snorin', yore snorting or talkin'."

"I'll see ya'll later." Shaking her head with amusement, March started to move off. They were getting ready for another round, and as entertaining as it was, she was curious to do some more exploring before Jamie needed to be fed again.

"Quiet little thing," Hank commented as they watched her walk back toward the house.

"Hardly said two words," Woods agreed.

"Real polite-like, too."

"Cute as a long-legged filly takin' her first steps. This'en just mite do a bit better than the other one."

"Woman should be quiet and polite. Why, I knew a woman once . . ."

At the corral March talked quietly to a couple of horses, who greeted her with soft whinnies. The chicken house was abandoned but in good shape, and an old worn-out mule happily scratched his rump against the fence rail. Peeking into the dark, cool depths of several barns and outbuildings, she decided to save them for later exploration. She was getting tired, and Jamie would soon be demanding his supper.

Walking back to the house it struck her how peaceful it was with only the occasional stamping of the horses and the twittering of the birds. March had always dreamed of a home that was without the constant bickering that she had endured as a child. It seemed to her that nothing ever made her father happy. He always had a complaint, whether it was about the food or the noise of the children.

Whenever something went wrong, as it frequently did, he always found someone else to blame. She had learned how to dodge his blows as a young child, and how to protect the little ones from his temper when she was grown. It seemed to her that he always had a plan to get rich quick, one that avoided any work on his part. He didn't object to anyone else in the family working, just as long as he wasn't directly involved.

It had always amazed her that her pretty, educated mother had ever married such a brash, insensitive man. March had asked her once, but her mother had gotten so upset that March quickly changed the subject. It was only during March's long hours of labor to give birth to her stillborn daughter, that Virginia Evans had told her the story, perhaps hoping that March would continue to fight rather than to give in to the pain and sure death that crept ever closer.

More than twenty years earlier, at the start of the war between the states, Virginia and her family, staunch supporters of the Confederacy, had hidden a wounded Rebel soldier in their home. His injuries were not life-threatening, but took a considerable time to heal.

The only child of a shipping magnate, Virginia was fascinated by the heroic presence of the soldier. During his lengthy stay, he told wonderful stories of his home in Georgia, of the cotton plantation his family owned and the life that waited for him once the war was finished. He was charming and gallant, captivating sixteen-year-old Virginia with great ease.

Perhaps, in happier times, Virginia's father would have investigated the soldier more thoroughly. Perhaps if he hadn't been concerned with the survival of his business interests, he would have convinced Virginia to wait. But he, too, was taken in by the soft-spoken man, and gave his only, beloved daughter to George Evans.

When George rejoined his unit, Virginia was pregnant with her first son. George returned twice more in the next couple of years, each time leaving his wife pregnant with another child. When the war was finally finished, the North claiming victory, George was eager to step into the shipping business owned by his father-in-law.

Instead of returning to the wealth and prestige he craved, George discovered that his wife and three small children were living in former slave quarters. Both of her parents were dead, and the shipping business bankrupt. The burned-out shell of her former home seemed like a skeleton taunting George that he'd never be anything more than what he'd always been, except now he was saddled with a wife and children.

To his credit, he did not abandon his family, but that was his last and only noble gesture. Selling the land to the first carpetbagger to show interest, George moved his family west. The plantation in Georgia was purely fictional, as were all of his other claims to wealth.

March leaned against the porch railing and stared unseeing into the distance. She could barely remember ever loving her father. As a child she had felt guilty, because she disliked and feared him so much. A child should run to her father for protection, instead March had run from him, frequently spending the entire night hiding from his terrifying rages.

She remembered all of the things he had done, things even a child recognized were illegal or immoral. They never stayed in one place long enough for the law to catch him, often slipping away in the dead of the night. She had lived with equal parts of hope and dread that he would be found out. When it happened, and it would someday, how would Mama support herself and all of the little ones?

A shiver ran down March's spine, and an unknown snarl crossed her face when she remembered the night her dislike for her father had turned to unadulterated hatred. For the rest of her life, she'd never forget or forgive.

Jamie mewed softly, snapping her from her thoughts. The snarl on her face gentled as she looked down at her tiny charge. This time Papa had unknowingly done something *for* her instead of *to* her. He had sent her to live in a castle, caring for a little boy who needed her as badly as she needed him.

Jamie opened his eyes, squinting against the brightness. He nuzzled against her breast, his tiny mouth searching for the source of nourishment.

"Are you hungry, again?" March asked, the baby's whimpers his only response. Turning, she walked into the house and climbed the stairs to his room. By the time she had changed his towel for a dry one, he was crying pitifully.

Sitting in the rocker and opening her dress, March smiled when his cries ceased as his mouth latched onto her nipple. She smoothed down his rumpled gown and caressed his tiny head.

"Remind me to thank Papa, if I ever see him again. I want him to know how happy he made me when he sent me here," she said quietly to the nursing baby.

"Then I'll gut shoot him, and stand back and watch him slowly bleed to death."

Six

First one problem then another had risen to prevent Jim from returning to the house until after dark. His frustration grew as he left the barn after unsaddling his horse and saw that the house was dark, even the baby's room was without light.

"Damn," he mumbled. He had wanted to interview his new housekeeper. The baby had been in her sole care for two days, and he didn't know anything about her. Hiring her had been a spur-of-the-moment decision necessitated by desperation.

By now she could have dug through every crook and cranny in the house looking for valuables to steal. Hell, he thought, as dark as the house was, she could be long gone, leaving the baby to fend for himself.

At the thought of his infant son being alone, possibly for hours, Jim rushed his steps, entering the house through the front door. He took the stairs two at a time, his spurs clinking against the wood.

The door to the baby's room was cracked open

and he pushed it violently, making it bang noisily against the wall. Startled whimpering from the crib drew a sigh of relief from Jim, as he moved more quietly into the room. He gently patted his son's back until the baby slept once again.

There was no sign of March in the room, but the evidence of the child sleeping quietly told him that she hadn't left during the day, which meant that she could still be around somewhere.

When a quick search of the upper floor didn't produce the girl, Jim made his way downstairs. The light from the coals in the fireplace illuminated the kitchen enough to show her sitting at the table, her head resting on her folded arms.

March heard him behind her and dread filled her as she slowly raised her head. Wetting her suddenly dry lips, she gathered together her trembling courage. "I know you'll want me out of here. If you'll allow it, I'll wait until Jamie is settled in the morning, and then leave."

"Jamie? Leave?" Jim stopped at the end of the table and looked down at her.

"Jamie, your son." March had never felt as guilty as she did when her eyes came to rest on the empty can sitting accusingly in front of her.

"Who named him that?"

"You . . . me . . . us . . ." Shrugging, she pushed her hair from her face. Freed from its usual bun at the nape of her neck, it hung in a cascade of living gold around her shoulders and down her back. "Yesterday, when I asked his name and you said he didn't have one . . ."

Fascinated by the firelight playing through her hair, Jim forced his attention back to his housekeeper. "Why do you want to leave?"

"I don't want to leave! You don't understand. When I tell you what I did, you'll demand that I pack up and get out."

Eyes narrowed, Jim reassessed her. "What did you steal? Most of my money is in the bank in town, but there's always some around for emergencies. Did you find Melanie's jewelry? I suggest you admit to your crime and return everything to me. It'll save us both embarrassment, when the sheriff gets here."

"Steal? Steal! I wouldn't steal from you or anyone else. I may be a nobody who owns nothing, but I don't take things that aren't mine." She moaned as her gaze moved to the empty can. "Well, I mean . . . I don't take valuables . . . I mean I wouldn't take your money . . ."

Jim crossed his arms over his chest, his blue eyes icy as he stared down at her. "Don't think that because you're female that I'll let you just walk out of this house with my money. I'll strip you buck-naked and search every inch of you until I find it."

"I didn't steal your money!" March jumped to her feet and began to pace. "I wish I had, because then I could just lay it on the table and be done with it."

Her long hair moved like something with life

of its own, flowing with gossamer tendrils with each agitated step. Jim noticed that the dress she wore was the same one that had caught his attention yesterday. It was too short, too tight . . . too enticing.

"What did you take, girl?" His steely voice demanded an answer.

"Well . . . that is . . . ah, you see . . ."

"Spit it out!"

"Peaches!"

"Peaches?" Prepared for nearly anything, Jim was stunned by her revelation.

Her shoulders bowed with guilt, March nodded slowly. "I fed Jamie and put him to bed. And I went to bed myself, only I couldn't sleep. Every time I closed my eyes, I could see that can of peaches. I found them when I was exploring the kitchen." She raised her head and looked beseechingly at him. "I didn't nose through the rest of the house, just the kitchen, because I couldn't cook without knowing where things are, and I had to open the cabinets and drawers to see where everything was and . . ."

Jim nearly smiled at her hurried reassurance. Her honesty stood out as clearly as the gold hair webbing around her shoulders. He didn't know how she could be so ethical with her father as an example, but he didn't doubt that she had her own measure of morals.

"The peaches?" he encouraged her to continue her story.

March closed her eyes, but the picture of what

she had done was so clear that she decided it was better to see him than the peaches. "I came down to the kitchen, and they were sitting on the shelf where I'd found them earlier. At first I just sat at the table, holding them and looking at the picture.

"I don't even remember getting up or searching for the punch for the can. Suddenly it was in my hand, and I was poking it through the lid. When it was open, they smelled so good! And I thought since it was opened, it wouldn't hurt if I just tasted the juice . . . just a sip of the juice."

A smile lingering deep in his eyes, Jim picked up the empty can and turned it upside down. "Just a sip?"

"I ate them." March looked down at her hands. "I ate every bite. Once I got started, I couldn't seem to stop. And then I drank every bit of the juice."

Squaring her shoulders, she raised her gaze to him. "I know what I did was unforgivable, peaches are so valuable. If you'll give me a little time, I'll manage to earn the money somehow and repay you. I'll get a job in town cleaning houses or something."

Shaking his head, he set the can back on the table. If this little girl went to town looking for work, there was only one kind of job she'd be offered, flat on her back. He didn't think he could stand knowing that he'd been the one to send her there.

"It's just a can of peaches."

"Please, I'd feel better if you'd yell at me . . . or hit me."

"Hit you?" She couldn't be serious, he thought, but one look at her face convinced him that she was deadly serious. She was such a tiny little thing that one blow from his fist would probably kill her. "March, I would never, ever hit you or any other woman."

Remembering the rippling muscles that corded his back and shoulders, March released a silent sigh of relief. The blows from her father's fists had been staggering, and had left bruises that lasted for weeks. And Papa's strength was feeble in comparison to this man.

"Thank you for that. If you've no objection, I'd like to stay the night. When I have Jamie settled in the morning, I'll be on my way. If you'll trust me, and I realize that you have no reason to, but if you will, I'll send you the money for the peaches as soon as I have it."

"March, it was just a can of peaches. I can't expect you to work here without eating."

"But peaches!"

"Did you enjoy them?" he asked softly.

"Oh, they were wonderful! I felt so guilty every-time I took a bite, but they were wonderful!"

Jim couldn't help but wonder what her child-hood had been like, what deprivations she had suffered that a simple can of peaches became a priceless treasure.

"If it's in the house, and it's edible, and you want to eat it, then eat it. When something is gone, make a list, and when one of the men goes to town, he'll replace it."

March's eyes grew wide with amazement. "You're not mad?"

Jim slowly shook his head. Reaching for the matches, he lit the lamp and set it on the table. "No, honey, I'm not mad. Is there another can?"

At her nod, Jim instructed her to get it. "I think I'm in the mood for a peach."

March dug through the cabinet, searching for the other can she remembered seeing there this morning. When she found it, she handed it and the punch to him. Licking her lips, she swore that she could still taste a lingering sweetness from the juice. Her eyes remained glued to the can as he opened it, reached in, and pulled out a piece of the fruit. Plopping it into his mouth, he licked the juice from his fingers.

"You're right, wonderful." His eyes twinkled as he held the can out to her. "Here, have one."

"Oh, no . . . no, I couldn't." March put her hands behind her back to help avoid temptation.

Her eyes were huge, filled with more longing than he'd ever seen on a human face. "Sure you can," he said, holding up another piece of fruit and sucking it into his mouth. "Better hurry or I'll eat them all."

Jim held the can under her nose, teasing her with the delectable fragrance. March raised her eyes to him, and he chuckled at her expression.

"Go ahead, sweetheart," he encouraged softly.

Slowly, giving him plenty of time to change

his mind, she reached into the can and dug out a piece of fruit. Raising it to her mouth, she nibbled off the tiniest piece, savoring the flavor that burst onto her tongue.

Leaning his hip against the table, Jim watched her eat the peach, marveling at the look of delight on her face. She didn't gulp it down as he had done, rather she relished one tiny bite at a time, her eyes closed. He had never known that anyone could make the act of eating an experience in sensuality.

She did. She held it to her mouth and just the pink tip of her tongue came out to taste. Then her lips parted and her white teeth sank into the succulent flesh, biting a piece free. The muscles in her throat rippled as she swallowed, and her lips glistened from the juice. Jim found himself longing to lick the sweetness from her lips, to taste the flavor of the fruit from her mouth.

Swallowing back a need like none he'd ever experienced before, he held the can out, offering her the last peach.

"Are you sure?" she asked as her fingers dove into the can to snag the fruit. When she finally finished, she delicately licked each finger, her unknowingly erotic actions driving an arrow of desire through Jim's body.

For God's sake, she's here to take care of your kid, his guilt-riddled conscious reminded him, as he handed her the can and watched her drink the juice. She's only a kid herself. You should be shot for the things you're thinking. But God, in another couple of years she was going to a beauty. Hell, she was already a beauty, standing there in her too small dress with her hair trailing down her back.

"That was . . . was . . ."

"Wonderful?" he asked in a husky voice.

March nodded, breaking into a smile that lit the room. "Even better than the first can."

"Why?"

"Because I don't feel guilty."

"You ate the other can of peaches, but didn't enjoy them?"

"Oh, I enjoyed them, but I felt so guilty because I knew I shouldn't be eating them. I guess I can resist anything but temptation," she admitted.

Temptation, Jim thought. Girl, you don't know what temptation is . . . but I do. Temptation is being alone in the dark with a beautiful woman-child and knowing that if I decided to make her mine, she wouldn't have the strength to force me to stop. Temptation is watching her smile so sweetly, and knowing that the taste of her would be sweeter than any fruit. Temptation is wanting her as a man wants a woman, and knowing that she is far too young.

"We need to talk."

"About the peaches?" she asked hesitantly. Perhaps she had misunderstood him, maybe he was displeased that she'd eaten them.

"No, not about peaches." Running fingers

through his dark hair, Jim looked at her standing in front of him like a child prepared to accept whatever discipline he cared to administer.
"March, you are welcome to eat anything in this
house. You do not have to ask permission, and
you don't have to feel guilty. If there is something special you'd like to have and they stock
it in the mercantile, just add it to the list and
it'll be purchased. Do you understand?"

"Yes, sir," she replied meekly.

"Good, now that that's settled, let's go to my
office and get better acquainted." He turned
and headed down the hall, assuming that she
would follow.

March grabbed the lamp and slowly trailed
behind him. Hesitant to intrude even at his invitation, she stopped at the doorway to his book-
lined office. A lamp burned brightly on the
corner of his desk, and she watched as he struck
a match and lit the stack of kindling waiting in
the fireplace.

When it was burning merrily, he stood and
stretched, trying to work a few of the kinks out
of his tired back. His spurs jingled as he unbuckled them, throwing them carelessly onto the top
of his desk. With a sigh, he lowered himself into
the massive chair behind the desk.

"Come on in, girl. Don't just stand there like
you're afraid that something in the room will
bite."

Setting the lamp down on a table, March sat

on the edge of a wing-backed, leather chair, her hands folded primly in her lap.

"Had any problems with the boy?" Jim asked.

"None, he's such a good baby, complaining only when he's hungry or needs his towel changed."

"Good. I guess you've had some experience with babies, if that crowd of kids I saw were any indication."

"Quite a bit." March's voice trailed off as she waited for his next question.

Jim was reluctant to ask about her health, feeling that a woman's time was her personal business, but he needed to know that she was capable physically of taking care of the baby.

"You're . . . ah, recovered?"

Blushing at the memory of her bloody dress, March nodded. "I'm much improved. I still get tired easily, but it's only been a week. I should be nearly normal by this time next week."

A week! Good lord, he thought, how long does her time last each month? The only woman he'd ever been around on a regular basis had been Melanie, but she always recovered in less than a week. He had never thought that it might be different for each woman, and that for some the process was much longer.

"Well, just take it easy, no need to push." Jim noticed her reddened cheeks and felt his own face flush with warmth.

"I rode past the line shack this afternoon," he said quietly, anxious to change the subject, but wondering how she'd accept the news that her family was gone.

"They've packed up and left," March supplied before he could continue.

Jim nodded confirmation. Sighing, she pleated the fabric of her dress. "Papa had heard about gold being discovered in Brodie. He'd been talking about heading there for months."

"He won't find anything but trouble. Brodie was played out a couple of years ago. The big strike was in '78, and 'bout the only thing there now is a couple of hurdy-gurdy halls and some old-timers who are too tired to move on."

"It doesn't matter, gold mining is hard work, and Papa isn't going to stick with anything that involves work. He'll hang around awhile and then move on." March looked toward the lamp and watched the flickering flame. "I just wished he would realize how hard it is on Mama and the little ones, always having to pack up and move when he gets a spur under his blanket."

"I know you'll miss them."

"Not Pa." Realizing that she shouldn't degrade her father, March looked at her employer. "Pa was . . . well, he was ornery on his good days and just plain mean the rest of the time. And I can't say that I'll miss Jan and Feb, they're too much like him, even though they were never mean to me. I never saw them do anything illegal, but I have a feeling when they're away from home they don't remember some of the lessons

Ma tried to teach them. But I'll miss Ma and the little ones."

"I appreciate your honesty, and I hope it will continue," Jim said quietly, recognizing her discomfort.

"Mama always said it was better to tell the truth. When you lie, you have to remember who you told what, and it can get you in real trouble."

"Your mother sounds like a remarkable woman."

"She is." Her voice lowered and filled with pain. "No matter what Pa did to her, she never forgot that she was raised a lady. No matter where we lived, she expected certain standards of behavior. We lived in a cave one winter up in Colorado, and every time we'd come in from outside she'd make us wipe our feet, so that we didn't track in snow."

Even though March held the memory as a fond one, Jim shivered at the thought of living through a Colorado winter in a cave. March was well spoken, far above a lot of people who had never suffered as she had done. He knew that she owed that to her mother.

"Do you think you'll be happy working here for me, or would you rather search for a job in town?"

"Oh, no, I like it here. This house is like a castle, and Jamie is an angel."

Remembering the nights he had walked the floor carrying the crying child, Jim decided that her definition of an angel vastly differed from his.

"Your duties will be those pertaining to the house. I expect you to cook my meals when I'm here. When I'm on the range, I'll eat at the chuck wagon. There will be several nights when I won't get back, but Hank and Woods are always available, if you have a problem while I'm gone. They also take care of preparing meals for the wranglers. You're to keep the house clean, do the washing and ironing, and any other domestic chore that arises. But mostly you are to see to the care of the baby.

"In exchange you'll be provided with room and board and ten dollars a month, paid at the end of the month."

"Ten dollars?" March's eyes widened incredulously. She had never had more than a couple of pennies in her life, and those she had carefully hidden from her father.

"It's yours to spend or save; it doesn't make a difference to me. I can't offer you a day off as I do the wranglers, since there's no one to care for the boy, but I'll take you to town once a month and let you spend your money if you want."

March had only been to town a few times lately, but she remembered the reactions she had received. "That's not necessary. I'll be content to just stay here."

"No, I insist, it's only fair." Jim leaned back, propped his feet up on the edge of the desk, and crossed his hands over his stomach. "I spend most evenings here in my office reading or doing paper work. You're welcome to join me. After a day spent with the boy, you'll probably need to see and talk to another adult. Bring your sewing or make free with my books. They're here to be read.''

If only she could, March thought as she looked with longing at the many volumes. "Thank you,'' she murmured, as if he had given her a gift.

"Is that dress and the other one your only clothes?'' he asked bluntly.

March nodded. She didn't need to be told that they were both too small and badly frayed. She had one other dress in similar condition, but had left it with her sister May, who would need it worse than she did.

"There's all kinds of fabric in one of the spare rooms upstairs. Enough to make you a different dress for every day of the month. Feel free to use whatever you need for dresses, nightshifts, and other necessaries.''

"I can't do that!''

"Why not?''

"Well . . . well, it's just not right, that's why.''

"The fabric was purchased by my late wife, and I assume she intended it for dresses and such. There's no reason for it to just sit there and rot when you can use it. You do sew?''

"Of course, but . . .''

"March,'' he sighed and slowly shook his head. "Right now the men are out rounding up the cattle, but within a few days they'll be back here. I realize that you're young, but as attractive as your legs are, I don't believe that they should be placed on public display. Neither of your dresses is fit for rags, and I've got a room full of cloth. I can't think of one reason why you shouldn't use it, can you?"

"No, but—"

"Now about the boy," he continued, ignoring her objections.

"His name is Jamie," she said firmly.

"Ah, yes, his name." Jim leaned his head back and stared at the shadows dancing on the ceiling. "I'm not sure that's what he should be called. His mother favored Bartholomew." He stopped, grinning at her wrinkled nose. "I see that you feel the same way about that name as I do."

"That is not a name for a little boy."

"True, but he won't stay little for long."

"That's not a name for a man, either."

"Agreed." He chuckled at her adamant expression. "However, I'm not sure I want my son to be called Jamie. It sounds rather . . . prissy to me."

"Jamie now, Jimmy when he starts school, Jim when he's grown."

"Got it all figured out, do you?"

"He needed a name," she replied with a shrug. "You didn't seem overly concerned about it. Seems to me that a man's first son should be named after him."

"He'll be my only son," Jim stated firmly. "I

have no intention of remarrying. This land is too hard on a woman."

March thought about his wife and knew that the bitterness in his voice was from losing her. How he must have loved her! And how hard it must have been on him to watch her die, while she struggled to give life to his child. Many women died in childbirth, and his wife's fate could have been the same even if she had lived in a big city, but obviously he chose to place the blame on the West.

"All the more reason to name him after you," she said quietly.

"I believe that I like the name of John better. That's what we'll call him."

"John is a fine name, but Jamie is better."

"March, he is my son." Jim slid his feet off of the desk and leaned his arms on its smooth surface.

"I can't argue that." She stood, pushing back the hair from her face. It had been a long day, filled with new impressions and excitement. Exhaustion weighed heavily on her slender shoulders, and she longed to stretch out on the soft bed and sleep, but it would be a while yet. Jamie would soon be waking and demanding to be fed.

"Why do I have the feeling that you're agreeing with me now, but have no intention of calling him John?"

"I can't imagine why you'd think that," she replied, her face so filled with innocence that

Jim had to bite back a chuckle. "If you want him called John, then that's what he'll be called."

"I'll get breakfast over at the bunkhouse for the next couple of mornings so that you can sleep in, but next week I'll expect you to have it ready and on the table by five."

"That'll be fine." March stifled a yawn as she moved toward the door. "Will you be here for supper tomorrow night?"

"No, don't plan on seeing much of me until after roundup. Spend the time sewing and getting settled in."

She nodded and turned to leave. "Good night, John . . . ah, Jim."

"Good night, brat," he replied with a chuckle. "Sweet dreams."

Seven

As the mid-morning sun blazed down on her head, March regretted not taking the time to search out a hat. Wiping the beads of perspiration from her brow with the back of her hand, she checked to assure herself that Jamie was protected from the burning rays by the sling that held him against her chest. It had been her intention to climb a small hill a short distance from the house, but now she wondered if she wouldn't be smarter to save her exploration for another day.

Puffing slightly, March finally managed the last few steps up the incline. Looking back at the house, she realized that it was only a short distance away, but it felt like she had walked for miles. She couldn't believe how easily she tired, and wondered how much longer it would be before she regained her strength.

Gazing down at the infant snuggled against her, March was saddened to realize that she hadn't thought of her own baby in several days. She had never held her daughter, in fact had only caught the briefest of glimpses of her before she was whisked from sight. The memories of her own child were actually little more than the remembrance of the pain of childbirth and a lingering sadness.

Each time Jamie drew nourishment from her breasts, the bond between woman and child grew stronger. Her memories of him multiplied daily, while her daughter dimmed into a shadowy keepsake of a time better forgotten.

Gently stroking Jamie's cheek, March realized that the hardships of her past were slowly slipping away. After living at the Falling Creek Ranch for over a week, she was beginning to feel at home. She had discovered that the wooden crates stacked in the various rooms held furniture. Jim had promised her that as soon as roundup was done, he'd find the time to help her unpack them. Dying to know what wonderful things were hidden in the boxes, she had been tempted to do it by herself. Only the fear that she'd accidentally break something kept her curiosity under control. But, oh, it was so tempting!

That temptation had driven her out of the house and given her the impetus to explore her surroundings. Turning away from the homestead, March let her gaze roam over the cactus-covered hills. In the far distance, purple-tinted mountains rose majestically, while closer mountains beckoned with the promise of coolness on their tree-covered slopes.

March's startled gaze came to rest on an adobe

house set in the base of the hill. She knew immediately that it was uninhabited, its general appearance being one of neglect and disuse.

This house, with its flat roof and walls nearly the same color as the sand, seemed to be a part of the land, unlike the castle Jim now called home. Following the well-worn path down the hill, March eagerly explored the old building.

The roof extended out enough to create a wide porch on the two connecting sides of the L-shaped structure. Windows, with heavy wooden shutters, opened out onto what must have once been an inviting patio.

The ornately carved wooden door opened easily, and feeling only a little guilty, March entered its inviting tranquility. She shivered at the delicious chill of the room. After being in the heat of the morning sun, the temperature change was a welcome relief. The eighteen-inch adobe walls seemed to have captured the coolness of the night and held it for its own.

March had expected the room to be empty, and was surprised to discover that it was well furnished. Except for a heavy coating of dust lying undisturbed on tabletops and the cobwebs draped in lacy intricacy in the corners, it was easy to believe that the owner had just stepped out for the day.

Exploring curiously, March wandered from one room to the next. There was a contiguous sequence of rooms in single file, one room opening directly into another. The main room led into the kitchen, the kitchen into a bedroom where the connecting leg of the L-structure led into the other two bedrooms. Each was fully furnished, including the spreads on the beds and curtains at the windows.

The house felt welcoming, an old friend delighted by her return. It was as different from the other house as night was from day, and it suited March's tastes more comfortably than the house she still considered to be a castle. In this house she already felt at home, while she knew she'd always be only a visitor in the other one.

"What do you think, Jamie boy?" she asked the baby who had begun to squirm as hunger brought him awake. "All I'd need is a dust rag and a broom to knock down the spiderwebs, and it would make a great place for us to spend our time."

She stood in the open doorway and looked out at the patio. A rosebush climbed lazily up the far wall, its dark green leaves not yet burned by the sun as they would be by late summer. That it had survived without attention was a miracle, but March was too drawn to it to consider that blessing. Living too long without beauty in her life, she was struck by the enchantment of the single bloom that gleamed blood red against the adobe brick. Gently stroking its petals, she leaned over and inhaled its sweet fragrance.

"Ah, Jamie, this is home," she murmured softly.

When the baby wiggled and squirmed, mewing against her breast, March reluctantly turned and headed back toward the homestead. She patted the mound of his bottom, grimacing at the wetness that met her hand.

"Next time we come, we'll bring some of your towels and then we can stay awhile." The baby rooted against her breast, searching in vain for his source of nourishment.

Reluctant to climb the hill again, March chose to walk around it and considered opening her dress to let the baby nurse. She had done it before when they had been out of sight of the house, but as she began to open the top button she rounded the hill and discovered that the other ranch buildings were much closer to the old house than the new. In fact, they were barely hidden by the incline.

The two old men, Woods and Hank, sat in their usual place on the porch of the bunkhouse. They looked up and nodded as March walked past. With Jamie's frustrated complaints to be fed growing louder, she didn't stop to talk, simply nodding in greeting and hurrying toward the house.

As March nursed Jamie, she thought about the adobe house. She knew that it must belong to Jim, and wondered why he had ever built this place. Oh, it was grand, filled with lovely treasures, but it wasn't a home. It didn't invite you to kick off your shoes and relax.

Placing Jamie in his crib for a nap, March stretched out on her own bed, her tired sigh drifted through the silence. Tomorrow, she decided, she'd take a rag and a broom over to the adobe house, and chase away some of the cobwebs and dust. Her eyes closed as she thought of the many things she'd have to do to get the house livable; beat the dust out of the furniture and curtains, wash the bedding, mop the brick floors . . .

Jim totaled the figures one final time, then nodded with satisfaction. The head count on the cattle was better than he had hoped for, and he'd easily make his quota with the federal government. With this shipment the ranch would finally start paying its own way.

For the last three years he'd been supplying beef to the forts, now with most of the Indians settled on reservations, his contract had increased to include not only the forts but also the reservations. There were whispers at the monthly Ranchers' Association meetings that some of the forts were to be closed, now that the hostilities between red man and white had ceased to exist.

As far as Jim was concerned, until Geronimo was captured—and held so that he couldn't escape again—hostilities were far from over. He had a grudging respect for the wily Chiricahua Apache medicine man. It amazed him how one man could constantly evade an entire army. He had been apprehended several times, but Jim wondered if Geronimo had ever truly been cap-

DESERT ANGEL

111

tured or if he had willingly let himself be found. He always managed to escape, sometimes with no more effort than simply walking off of the reservation with his small band of followers.

Even if the forts did close, Jim didn't worry about finding buyers for his beef, there was a big market back East. The local ranchers had recently gotten together to form a consortium to find not only a demand for their cattle, but the most economic way to handle shipping.

Jim held a firm belief that the smaller ranchers needed to work together, if they were to survive. Already some of the larger spreads up north had been sold out to conglomerates, even some foreign investors, who never set foot on the ranch and yet ran it with iron-fisted control.

Money was one worry Jim didn't have, having inherited a healthy sum from both his parents and grandparents, but he knew that most ranches survived from one roundup to the next, scrabbling to hold their own at the best of times, suffering deeply at the worst.

"Coffee?"

Jim looked up with surprise to find March holding a cup of steaming coffee out to him.

"Thanks." He took the cup from her and sipped cautiously. It was still weak, but a considerable improvement over her previous efforts. He bit back a grin when he remembered taking a big swallow of the first pot of coffee she had made for him a couple of mornings earlier. Not only was it so weak that he could see the bottom of the cup, but he'd had the unpleasant experience of biting down on a coffee bean. After he'd rinsed the acid taste from his mouth, he'd shown her how to grind the beans and add them to the boiling water. He still got an occasional mouthful of grounds, but even that was improving.

"Stay around long enough, and you'll make a decent cup of coffee yet," he teased.

Shaking her head, March wrinkled her nose in distaste. "That stuff isn't coffee. I'm sure it has many uses that we should investigate, such as killing the smell in the necessary on a warm summer afternoon, but it isn't something a body would want to put in her mouth."

Jim smiled at her quick mind. He had discovered that she usually had a humorous response when he teased her, and had found it a pleasant change from the whining he had become accustomed to from Melanie.

"Everything done?" Jim watched as she wandered over to the bookshelves and opened a door. Her fingers lovingly caressed the bindings, tracing the impressed titles with a longing that was visible.

"You're welcome to read any of them," he offered. "Pick one and join me. I've still got some paperwork to do, but I'd welcome your company."

March carefully pulled a book from the shelf, holding it reverently and wondering what wonderful words the printed letters inside told. "Jamie will be awake soon wanting to be fed . . ."

"John," Jim corrected, knowing that it was a battle he had already lost. The boy's name would be Jamie, which he really didn't oppose . . . except that he enjoyed arguing with his housekeeper.

"Whoever he is," March continued, hiding a grin, "will be wanting to be fed, and I've got a dress started . . . there was so much fabric, I had trouble deciding which to use . . ."

"March, sit down, put your feet up, and rest a little. You're always working, the house is spotless, my shirts have never been so well ironed, and your coffee is improving. You've earned some time to rest."

"Well . . ." She carried the book over to the wingback chair and sat down in its comfortable depths. Curling her feet beneath her, she opened the first page of the book.

Jim watched her for several minutes, liking her presence in the room. She looked so young and innocent, so enticing and sensual, as she turned the pages. A frown of concentration creased her brow, and he wondered what was troubling her to cause it.

"What are you reading?"

Feeling like a fraud, March raised her eyes from the circles and lines on the pages. "I'm not . . . I think I'm discovering that I can't sit and relax, when I know I've got work to do," she improvised. She couldn't bring herself to admit that she couldn't read. She was pleased when she recognized an occasional letter her mother had taught her long ago, before so many responsibilities had taken away the time necessary for lessons.

Jamie's wail drifted down and March sighed with relief at the excuse to leave. Jim pulled out his pocket watch, noted the hour, and smiled broadly.

"Right on time," he chuckled as he put the watch away and climbed to his feet. "It's been a while since I've done it, now that you're here, but I think I can remember how to change his towel."

"I'll do it, that's what you pay me for." March stood up and hastily replaced the book on the shelf.

"You fix his bottle, while I take care of him," Jim stated as he left the room. "I haven't seen much of him in the last few days. Hard to believe, but I've missed the boy. Guess he kinda grows on you."

Fix his bottle, March thought, as she went into the kitchen and looked at the many cans on the shelves. She couldn't begin to guess which one held the milk, in fact, wasn't sure if there even was any. She'd nursed the baby since her arrival, and hadn't worried about any other kind of feeding. She dug out a bottle and nipple from the cabinet and set them on the counter. Walking back to the office, she knew that the time had come to confess that she couldn't read. Jim would have to find the milk, or she'd have to nurse the baby.

"You'd think this boy hadn't eaten in a week, from all the noise he's making," Jim said as he carried the crying baby into the room. "Where's his bottle?"

"I couldn't find the milk," she admitted reluctantly.

"Are we out? Why didn't you say something sooner?" His large hand swamped the baby's small back as he patted it soothingly. "We've got a starving youn'en here, and nothing to feed him. I know from experience that he can keep this up all night."

"I'll feed him." March reached over and took the infant from his arms. "I'll bring him back down when I'm finished, so you can hold him for a while."

"What are you going to feed him, if we don't have any milk?"

"I'll . . . I'll nurse him, like I've been doing."

"What?" Jim grabbed her arm as she attempted to leave the room. "What do you mean, you'll nurse him?"

March turned her perplexed gaze up to his. "I've been nursing him since the morning I first arrived here."

"How can you—I mean, why do you—" Jim shook his head. "I think you've got some talking to do, girl."

"I don't understand." March tried to calm the baby who grew more frustrated as he rooted at her fabric-covered breast. "I thought that's why you hired me, to take care of your son."

"I did, but I think there's something here I don't know anything about." He watched his son nuzzle against her breast and realized that the baby was familiar with it. "Sit down, you owe me an explanation." He all but pushed her into the chair she had abandoned when Jamie began to cry.

"I need to go upstairs . . ." March's cheeks flamed with color. "To feed him, that is . . ."

"You can do it here," he stated gruffly.

"Here?"

"Do it!" Realizing the implications of the situation, he ran a hand through his hair as he leaned against his desk. If she could nurse his son, that meant she'd had a baby. Where was it? Had she deserted it to the care of her parents, when she'd come here? How could any mother leave her own child to care for someone else's?

"How old are you?" He watched, unwittingly fascinated as she reluctantly opened her dress and freed her breast.

"I'll be nineteen this summer." March felt her face flame as she exposed enough of herself to let the baby nurse. She wished that she had a blanket to throw over her shoulder to hide her breast, but Jim had brought the baby down in only his gown.

Jim couldn't tear his eyes away from her display. He'd never seen anything so lovely. Melanie had never allowed him to see her body, insisting that the lights be out and letting him raise her gown only to her hips when he made love to her.

He'd seen a few nudie pictures one of the cowhands had one time, and he'd visited one of the
light women in town a few times, but he'd never
seen a woman nursing a child.

March's breast was firm and smooth, the skin
showing tracings of blue veins. He'd only caught
a momentary glimpse of her nipple, but he felt
a familiar tightness in his own body when he
thought of it. Walking around the desk before
she could see the evidence of his sudden lust,
Jim lowered himself into his chair.

"You've had a baby," he stated the obvious.
"When?"

"Three days before I came here," March
couldn't understand his sudden questions. He
had said that Pa had explained her condition,
why did he seem so surprised?

"Where is it?"

March briefly closed her eyes at the expected
flash of sorrow. "She died at birth."

"A girl?"

"Yes, but she came too early. She never had a
chance."

"I think you owe me an explanation," he
stated again.

Trying to shield as much of herself as possible
with the bodice of her dress, she raised questioning eyes to him. "What did Pa tell you?"

"That you were having your woman's time,
and were a little weak."

March shook her head. "How like him, he tells
a lie easier than other people tell the truth. If

he thinks it'll save his hide or earn him some money, he'll lie."

Jim saw the pain in her face, heard it in her voice. "Tell me about it," he encouraged, fighting to control his own feelings that he had been used by her and by her father.

March leaned over and softly kissed Jamie's head. She loved him so much, his innocence, his acceptance. Even though she'd only taken care of him for a week, she thought he already recognized her voice. When she spoke to him his tiny head would bob up and he'd search for her.

When he knew the truth, Jim might decide she wasn't fit to be the caretaker of his son. What would she do if she had to leave Jamie, once again losing her baby, only this time because of her past? She felt again the anguish of betrayal, the humiliation of deception.

Jim watched the play of emotions cross her face. He saw her love for his son and her grief at the mention of her own child. Without the necessity of words, he understood her fear that she would lose another child if he took Jamie from her. He also recognized her embarrassment, but deep in her eyes, turning their stormy gray to deep violet, he saw a burning hatred.

"You were raped," Jim stated quietly.

If ever there had been a time in her life when she wished she could lie as easily as her father, this was it. She knew a simple lie would save her job and Jim's respect. But there were too many people who knew the truth, and would be all too willing to tell their version of it to him, once it became common knowledge that she was employed here.

She wasn't a tramp or a whore. She had too much self-respect to lower herself to that level. She was innocent of crime, betrayed by softly spoken words and promises that were made with no intention of fulfilling; guilty for believing that she was valued for what she was, not who she was.

Raising her troubled, violet eyes to him, she shook her head. "No . . . I wasn't raped."

Eight

March watched his expression harden at her denial. If she hadn't been raped, there was only one conclusion that he could reach. And who could blame him for that, she thought sadly as she lovingly caressed Jamie's soft cheek. A decent woman never allowed a man, other than her husband, to touch her. Only a woman of ill repute, someone without morals, would give herself outside of marriage.

Should she admit the truth? Even at the risk of losing her job and ultimately having to give up the child she loved, could she find the strength to admit it?

The truth had been so inconceivable, so shattering to her, that it had overshadowed even the shame of her pregnancy.

"Since you've been given the job of caring for my infant son, I think I deserve to know the rest." His icy eyes showed no mercy; his square jaw was firm with determination. Only one kind of woman had a baby without first having a husband, and he didn't want that kind taking care of his child.

"I don't think his innocence has been tarnished by his short time in my care." March fought back the tears of humiliation. She had known that this past week had been too good to be true, and that it would never last. Good things didn't happen to people like her. Hadn't that already been proven to her, did she have to have the lesson repeated before she could learn it?

"Well? I'm waiting."

March dislodged Jamie from her breast and raised him to her shoulder to pat the air from his stomach. Discreetly rebuttoning her bodice, she decided that the baby could wait a short while before finishing his meal. When this interview was over, she'd carry him upstairs and nurse him in private. Providing that her employer would let her stay long enough.

"If you don't plan to finish it, I'll take the baby." Relieved that her enticing flesh was covered from his gaze, Jim stood up from the desk and approached her.

March couldn't believe how deeply it hurt to know that she had been judged and found guilty, and that Jim didn't want her to hold his son any longer than absolutely necessary. It made it easier for her to decide to tell the truth, all of it. At this point, she had nothing to lose and everything to gain. She kissed the fuzzy head and reluctantly handed the child to his father.

When Jim was once again behind the desk, the baby cradled securely in the crook of his arm, he turned questioning eyes toward her.

"I met him in town—"

"Oracle?" Jim interrupted, naming the small town that was much closer than Tucson.

"Yes, it was just before we moved into your line shack. We'd been sleeping out in the open with only a lean-to for protection. Pa moved us into the shack when it turned cold. He said there was no reason for us to freeze, when there was a perfectly good cabin just sitting empty."

Jim sneered at her father's description of the line shack. It was little more than some boards thrown together with a leaky roof overhead. The holes in the walls wouldn't keep the frigid winter wind from blowing through. It had never been intended for permanent habitation, in fact it was barely suitable for temporary shelter.

March looked down at her hands, wishing she still had the comfort and security of the baby in her arms. "I'd found a job at the cafe serving meals and washing dishes. The woman that normally did it had broken her leg, and needed time off until it healed. I knew the job would only last a few weeks, but with winter coming on, we desperately needed the money I could make. Besides, at the end of the day I was sometimes able to take home some of the food that was going to be thrown out.

"He came in most mornings for breakfast. One day he asked if he could come calling. I thought he was serious about being a suitor. It certainly didn't seem to bother him that we didn't have a home, and that Pa was drunk nearly all the time. He ignored the little ones and was polite to Ma.

"It got so that he'd be waiting for me every night when I got finished with work . . . said that he would walk me home, because a lady shouldn't be out at night without protection."

March leaned her head back and stared at the swirling design in the plaster ceiling. "He never mentioned that the person I most needed protection from was him."

Her voice was soft but firm, nearly emotionless as if she recited a litany. But Jim detected the deep pain she was fighting to hide. Whatever had happened, and he intended to know it all before the night was through, he'd bet his best bull that this woman-child was not promiscuous.

"I thought he loved me . . . he said he loved me . . . I should have known better. People like him don't fall in love with people like me."

"People like him? What do you mean?" Jim's voice held a wealth of gentleness at the question.

"Rich people, people who have everything." She waved her hand around the room, unknowingly putting Jim in the same classification. "People who take things like books and peaches for granted."

"He's wealthy?" He tried to ignore the sting of her insinuation that he was spoiled and unfeeling, simply because he had a comfortable lifestyle.

"Yeah . . . you could say that. Not him, really, but definitely his father."

"Who is he?" He felt anger tightening his gut. He didn't want to know, not really, but the question was asked before he could stop himself. If he knew, he might come to feel that it was necessary to protect her honor. He might do something stupid, like find the boy late one night and beat some much-needed sense into him. He might forget to stop while the kid was still breathing . . .

March ignored his question. She knew that Jim would hear the story in town and find his own answer, it wasn't necessary for her to name the man. "He'd talk about his plans for the future," she continued as if never interrupted, "someday he'd inherit his father's spread and what he wanted to do to improve it. He talked about a wife and children, implying that I'd be that wife and those children would be ours.

"He'd sometimes bring me gifts, little things that I'd never had before . . . a ribbon for my hair, a chocolate candy, a bouquet of flowers that he'd picked while waiting for me to get off of work."

March smiled, a self-disgusted smile at the innocent she had been. She looked at Jim, unaware that the tension had left his face, replaced by an understanding sympathy. "I believed him, Mr. Travis. Me, with a father who wouldn't know the truth if it hit him in the face, believed that lying, conniving bastard. I was so stupid I deserve everything that happened."

Jim looked down at his son, watching as the

baby attempted to get his thumb in his mouth. He knew what was coming, knew what March would say. He'd sat in enough bars overhearing loud-talking braggarts boasting of their conquests. Some boys seemed to think it made them more of a man to have taken the innocence of a young girl. Jim thought it was about the lowest thing a man could do.

"Sally finally came back to work and I didn't have a job any longer. He came by one day with a packed wicker basket . . . said he wanted to take me down to the river and have lunch.

"I was the dessert. He talked of setting a wedding date. He kissed me . . . and I didn't make him stop. I was so happy that I was to be his wife that it didn't seem wrong." Her voice trailed off to barely a whisper. "It seemed so very right."

She had thought she'd cried her last tear for her lost innocence, but March found herself blinking back the moisture filling her eyes. She raised her head and met Jim's compassionate gaze. "I did nothing to stop him. I willingly went into his arms and let him have his way with me.

"If that makes me a whore, then I'm a whore."

"Don't use that word, March. It's too harsh a word to ever cross your lips."

"I've been called that and much more. He wasn't quiet about what he did, and long before the baby started to show, the good people of Oracle made it clear what they thought of me."

"They judged without knowing all of the facts," he defended quietly.

"Oh, they knew everything. The good Christians of Oracle preach forgiveness, but practice the opposite. Their lives can't be happy unless they can pass on malicious gossip. If the truth isn't colorful enough they'll add their own versions, and if someone's life is destroyed because of it, they justify themselves by thinking that's what the person deserved.

"In fact the tale, embellished by wagging tongues, spread so quickly that for several weeks afterward there was a regular trail of men coming out our way. My father beat me until he left bloody welts all over my body, because I wouldn't go with them. You haven't heard the entire story, Mr. Travis.

"You see, that afternoon when we returned, I thought it was to tell my parents that we were getting married. But instead, when we got there, he pulled out his money clip and handed my father fifty dollars. Told Pa that I'd been a virgin after all, but next time he'd only pay ten, unless I learned the tricks, then he'd consider paying more. He didn't want to waste his money on a woman who just laid there without moving."

Jim could see the innocent girl she had been, standing proudly, probably a little bashfully, in front of her father, waiting for the man she loved to ask for her hand in marriage. He couldn't begin to imagine her hurt and bewilderment, when she realized that it had all been a prearranged plan from the very beginning.

He uttered a harsh expletive, but Marsh didn't

even flinch. "Yes," she said, "I believe that is exactly what he said he had done to me, and that's what all of the others wanted to do.

"My father was delirious with delight. He had found a new gold mine, and all he had to do was hold his hand out and wait for the money to drop into it. He was most unhappy when I wouldn't cooperate, so unhappy that he began to beat me quite regularly."

March shuddered at the remembered beatings, and knew she'd wear the scars, both physical and mental, the rest of her life. When she had continued to refuse the demand that she service the men, the whippings had gotten so severe that, at first, she was afraid she would die from blood loss or infection. They continued day after day, until pain became a way of life, and she began to pray that she would die. It seemed to be the only way she'd ever be free of his rage.

"Didn't your mother try to stop him?" Jim asked incredulously.

"She did what she could, but I don't think you realize how helpless a woman is in this world, Mr. Travis. We are dependent on the men in our lives to feed and protect us. Men are considerably stronger, and if one of them decides to start beating on a woman, there is little she can do but pray he'll get tired before he kills her.

"A woman has to think of her children—all of her children. She can't protect one if it means that she endangers the others. She can't do what she'd really like to do to the man—kill him while he sleeps—because then she would be found guilty of murder, and her children would be left with no one. No court in the land would accept her defense that she was protecting herself. A man is allowed to beat his wife, his children.

"Men are judges and juries; they couldn't let a woman get away with murdering her husband, even if the evidence showed that she was simply defending herself. After all, he hadn't killed her. They believe in—and probably practice—the theory that a woman needs to be kept in her place."

"Not all men are like that, March."

"I know." She studied his warm blue gaze, knowing instinctively that he would never raise a hand to a woman. "For several weeks after the incident, I couldn't leave the safety of being with Ma and the little ones." She shivered, remembering the men who had come to the line shack in search of her. They had been crude and abusive, usually drunk enough not to care if they had to fight their way to her. More than once the only thing that had stopped them was the Winchester Virginia Evans held in her hands, pointed at their chest.

"The one time I went into town, I was approached by several men, and if the sheriff hadn't given me his protection, I'd probably would've been dragged into an alley.

"When it was obvious that I was going to have a baby, Pa started beating me every night instead of every other night. Said he'd teach me some respect, and he'd get rid of the baby. He told me, in no uncertain terms, that once the baby was gone, I would have no choice but to service the men who came calling. He threatened to tie me down with my legs spread, so that I couldn't fight it."

Her harsh laugh turned to a sob, the sound of a broken-hearted child. "My loving father even said that it didn't matter if I ever started to like it or not. He'd spent enough money providing for me, it was time that I started earning some, and I'd earn more on my back than I'd ever make working a job in town."

"March, don't—"

"He'd spent enough money providing for me! I owned three dresses, all of them too small and donated by the good Christians of Oracle. My shoes have holes in the bottom and, until I came to work here, I can't remember ever not being hungry! The only money he ever spent was on himself and his own selfish needs—"

"March, enough—"

"You wanted the truth, now you have it." She was unaware that her bitterness was overshadowed by her pain. "My own father sold my virginity for fifty dollars! It could only be sold once, but he decided he could still make forty or fifty dollars a day off of me as a whore.

"The good people of Oracle have called me white trash and a whore. They have looked me in the face and deliberately stepped to the other side of the road, so that they wouldn't be tarnished by being in close contact with me. I'm not trash and I'm not a whore!" She stood up abruptly and paced to the window. Her own face was reflected back to her on the wavy glass, but she almost didn't recognize the twisted, hatefilled visage.

"If I ever again see the man who fathered me, I promise you I'll gut shoot him, then I'll stand back and laugh as he dies. I want to be the last person he sees before he goes to hell, and I intend to wish him well on his journey!"

Jim looked at her, unsure of what to say or how to offer comfort. It surprised him a little that he wanted to comfort her, to find the words to ease her pain.

The man who had so cruelly taken her innocence deserved to be gelded with a dull knife, but Jim couldn't think of a brutal enough punishment for a man who would treat his daughter in such a way.

Jim's relationship with his own parents had been filled with love and trust, and he hoped to establish the same relationship with his son as he grew to manhood. He missed the closeness he had shared with his parents and still mourned their deaths, knowing that he would always miss them.

March was a fiery, intelligent, beautiful woman. He was appalled that her father had attempted to use her beauty for his own profit by turning her into a prostitute.

"I worry so much about May," March said softly, almost as if she was thinking out loud. "She's nearly sixteen, and I can't help but wonder if Pa will try to use her, now that I'm gone. At least while I was there he didn't pay much attention to her, but now . . . She's such a sweet little thing, and she's so terrified of him. I don't know if she has the strength to withstand his abuse."

"She can come here," Jim offered.

"It's too late. She's so timid and easily frightened that she'd never think about trying to find me again; she'd never consider running away." Leaning her forehead against the cool glass, March tried to let go of the pain of her father's betrayal. She told herself that it had happened months ago, and that she should be over it by now, but somehow that didn't help make her acceptance of it any easier.

And now she waited for Jim to pass judgment. She tried to convince herself that she didn't care, that his opinion didn't matter, but she knew she was lying to herself. It did matter, it mattered desperately. That baby laying in his arms had become her child, and she knew it would break her heart to be separated from him.

Maybe if Jim forced her to leave, she could find someway to make enough money so that Ma and the little ones could leave Pa. She didn't know what job she could do that would support eight people . . .

She'd become a whore, she thought with a

smile filled with sorrow. She'd do exactly what Pa had wanted her to do, only she would keep the money and use it to support Ma and provide a happier life for the others. Of course, she wouldn't be able to live with them, she wouldn't let her reputation tarnish the chances of the younger children making something of their lives.

It was a twisted kind of justice, she thought sadly. She'd become the very thing that had made Pa nearly beat her to death for refusing, only he would never profit from it. And she'd be the best whore in the West. Men would come for hundreds of miles, just to spend their hard-earned money for the opportunity to climb between her legs.

And every morning she'd count her money, until she had enough to build a house like this one and could afford decent clothes and schooling for the little ones. And when she had enough money, she'd pay a bounty hunter to find Pa and kill him, slowly, painfully.

And maybe she could fly to the moon on gossamer wings and collect stars in a silken bag, March decided with a resigned sigh. Just the thought of a man touching her intimately made her stomach roll with nausea. If it actually happened, she'd probably vomit all over him, and no man was going to pay money for that!

Jim heard her smothered sob and saw her sad smile reflected in the window. He was in a quandary, unsure of what to do. Convention demanded that he not have a woman with a reputation of low morals in his house, but convention be damned. There was no doubt in his mind that March had told him the truth, and he had no reason to be concerned about her morals.

She might have used better judgment, but he found that he couldn't blame her in any way for what had happened. She saw an opportunity to improve her life and took a chance. Had she been older and wiser, she might have seen the motives involved, but she was young and innocent. It was a hard lesson, one that was a bitter blow, but she would survive.

He had no doubt that the good people of Oracle would rush to tell him their version of the whole incident, once it became common knowledge that she was living in his house and caring for his son. He could hear them now, clicking their tongues and shaking their heads at the shame. They'd advise him, oh so delicately, that she shouldn't be anywhere around an innocent baby, that she wasn't fit for decent company.

And the men would give him a conspiratorial wink and a sly grin. Their questions would be double-sided, when they'd ask if March was taking good care of everything. What they'd really want to know was if she was sharing his bed.

Even if he stood on the steps of the church with a Bible in each hand, Jim knew they'd never believe him when he told them that March's only job was the care of his son.

Jim felt his temper begin to simmer again,

when he realized that the man who had done this to her would be completely forgiven. After all, he was young, sowing his wild oats. He'd still be accepted in the best homes in town, and if he was from the wealthy family that March suggested, then mothers everywhere would be trying to interest him in their eligible daughters.

No one would turn their heads away when he walked past, or talk about him behind their hands. In Jim's opinion, the man was guilty of a crime worse than rape, and yet he would feel none of the social degradation that would be imposed on March whenever she set foot in town.

Jim just didn't know if he wanted to buck the people who were his friends and neighbors. He felt sorry for March and was angered at the thought of what had been done to her by both her father and this unnamed man, but he didn't know if he wanted to take on more responsibility. He'd been visited by the local dignitaries when he had hired Breed as his foreman. They had done their best to get Jim to fire him, simply because the man had been raised by the Comanche, but he'd refused to be swayed by their ridiculous accusations.

Did he really want to go through that again?

He looked over at the woman standing at the window. She looked even smaller than usual, as if she had pulled into herself for protection, preservation. Her proud shoulders were bent with humiliation, her sparkling eyes dulled with misery.

Damn, if he forced her to leave, he'd feel like he had kicked a puppy. She was as innocent and as easily pleased as a puppy. He thought of her honest delight in a can of peaches. If he made her leave, he knew that he'd never again be able to eat a peach without thinking of her and feeling guilty.

Hell, he liked peaches too much to give them up because of a little bitty girl who was too trusting for her own good.

He'd known her for a little over a week and had been gone most of that time, but he'd found her to be honest to a fault. And there was no doubt in his mind that she adored the baby. In fact, it was hard to separate her from the child. She was constantly carrying him around, talking to him, touching him with loving hands.

He could see all kinds of problems that could be avoided, if he sent her on her way. If she stayed, her life wouldn't be easy, and he'd probably bust a few knuckles protecting her. Already he was impatient to get his hands on the boy that had done this to her.

It would be smarter to give her some money and put her on a train to anywhere. It would be easier to look for someone else to care for the baby. Since when, he wondered, had he ever taken the easy way out? With a sigh, Jim made his decision. There wasn't much of a choice, and he'd known it from the beginning.

He looked down at his tiny son, who stared at him with unblinking, deep blue eyes so like his mother's. Jim thought of the many mistakes he had made with Melanie. From the very first, he'd been wrong time and again about her. Guilt weighed on his conscience; Melanie would probably still be alive if he had done things differently. He knew he couldn't handle more guilt, and if he fired March, more guilt was exactly what he'd have to live with.

"I'll be damned," he mumbled, stroking Jamie's cheek with a gentle finger.

Startled, March turned. "What?"

"He's got eyelashes." Jim's voice held such amazed awe, that March couldn't help the small smile that crossed her face.

"Well, of course, he does."

"And eyebrows. They're so light that you can barely see them, but he has eyebrows."

"And ten fingers and ten toes." March had done a thorough inventory on the baby and knew that he possessed the correct number of everything. "What did you expect?"

"He needs you." Jim looked at her, his gaze gentle with understanding. "He's already lost one mother, I don't want to be responsible again for him losing another."

March tried to find the answer in his face, but was afraid that she was seeing what she so desperately wanted to see. She folded her hands in front of her and waited for him to spell it out.

"It won't be easy, girl. You might be happier

far from here, where no one knows the truth. Every time you go into town, someone is going to take great delight in spreading the gossip."

"I want to stay, if you'll let me." Her voice lowered to a whisper. "I just won't go into town; I'll stay here on the ranch."

"No, you're not going to hide here like you've done something you're ashamed of. What was done to you was not your fault, and you won't hide here like you're guilty. It won't be easy, but in time they'll find something—or more likely someone—else to talk about."

"You believe me?" she murmured, as a glimmer of tears clouded her eyes. "You really believe me."

"Yes, March, I believe you, and I wish there was some way I could wipe it all from your mind, erase the memories and let you start over again, but I can't. You've been treated very unfairly, but there is nothing I can do to change that, except to let you know that the job of caring for my son is still yours if you want it."

"Oh, I want it, Jim. More than anything in the world."

He nodded briefly, then turned to the baby who was beginning to wiggle fretfully. "I think his good mood is running out. Maybe you'd better finish his supper so that he can go to bed."

Tears coursed down her cheeks as March took the baby from his arms. She held the small, warm body against her own, and wondered how to thank Jim for believing in her.

"I apologize for forcing you to feed the baby in front of me earlier." He watched her cuddle her precious burden and knew that he'd made the right decision. Let the people in town rant and rave, he'd protect her to the best of his ability. "I realize that it embarrassed you, but I want you to know that it was one of the most beautiful things I've ever seen."

"Thank you . . . for everything." Her voice was so filled with emotion that there could be no mistaking her gratitude.

"Go feed my son, March," Jim replied gruffly. "And come back down if you want to."

"I think, if you don't mind, that I'll just go on to bed."

"All right, it's been a long evening for you. I'll see you in the morning."

Jim watched her walk away, the baby clutched lovingly in her arms. Yep, he decided, he'd made the right decision, but damn, it sure was going to cause some excitement when word spread. He expected that a few of his own men would be the first to cause trouble.

A wicked grin crossed his face as he decided that he would tell the whole story to Breed. That was one man few would want to cross. One look at the ice in those silvery eyes, and anyone with the common sense of a cactus would turn around and head the other way.

Jim was unaware of the expression in his own blue eyes, but anyone seeing it at that moment would have thought more than once before saying anything about her in *his* hearing. He wasn't a man looking for trouble, but he was the one who would finish it.

Nine

"Woman, what in hell are you doing?" Jim dropped his hat and spurs on the kitchen table, and watched as March struggled to lift a heavy cast-iron pot from the hearth.

March jumped in surprise, the heavy lid of the dutch oven barely missing her bare foot as it clanged to the brick floor. Eyeing the layer of fine ashes that coated the tops of the golden biscuits, she turned to Jim with a look of disgust.

"I hope you don't mind ashes with your biscuits. I'm sure jam would be tastier, but you'll have to settle for what you get."

"You've got it hot enough in here to cook them on the tabletop." He looked meaningfully at the merrily burning fire, exaggerating slightly about the temperature of the room, since the spring mornings were still cool.

Picking up the pan, March carried it to the work counter and blew gently at the tops of the biscuits. Most of the ash drifted away, but some clung stubbornly to the warm dough.

"Do you know of another way to cook?" Pushing the hair from her flushed cheeks, she turned the hot bread onto a plate and carried it past him to the table.

It was bad enough that she had overslept, taking the time only to pull on the dress she had worn the day before, then rushing to get breakfast started. Now she felt foolish with her bare feet peeking out from beneath the hem of her skirt, and her hair hanging in a golden snarl down her back. She had intended to get a filling breakfast on the table and escape to her room before Jim got downstairs. So much for good intentions!

"Why don't you try the stove?"

"Stove?" March halted in mid-stride.

"Stove—that black thing over against the wall."

Looking at the large black cabinet on legs, she felt her cheeks tinge with embarrassment. Of course, it was a stove, she thought, mortified that she hadn't recognized it sooner.

"You have seen a stove before, haven't you?" Jim watched the expressions cross her face, and wondered why he hadn't realized that all of her cooking was done in the fireplace.

"They had one at the cafe," she admitted. "But it didn't look much like that one. It was red and a whole lot bigger."

"They cook for a whole lot more people." Jim moved to the stove and opened the fire door. The kindling he had put in several days earlier was still there. "Come here, and I'll show you how it works. It takes a little getting used to, but you'll like it once you get the hang of it."

March watched with fascination as he told her how to regulate the heat, how to adjust the damper, and when to add more wood. It seemed amazing to her that an entire meal could be cooked without bending over a fire. The heat was evenly distributed, so that nothing would be overcooked on one side, while still raw on the other.

"It's getting too hot to be cooking over an open fire." Jim reached up and playfully tugged at her tangled hair. "And it would be a sin if this got in the way and was singed."

"Too late." March held out a strand that was scorched and discolored by the heat.

Jim reached up and captured the shriveled tendril. Unconsciously rubbing her silky hair between his fingers, he stared down at her and suddenly wished that she was younger . . . or older . . . or as ugly as the old maid schoolteacher who had delighted in whacking the back of his hands with a ruler every time he had done something she didn't approve of, which was most of the time.

But she wasn't. She was beautiful with hair of gold and stormy gray eyes. Her skin was lightly tanned by the sun, giving her a healthy dose of freckles across her nose and cheeks. Her voice was as soft as a new morning, and her mouth was made for smiling . . . or kissing.

And she was nearly nineteen, old enough . . .

The harshness of her childhood hadn't removed the innocence from her expression, or dulled the sparkle of life from her eyes. Her too small dress emphasized the body it sought to hide, needlessly reminding him that she was a woman . . . and he was a man.

I should have sent her away while I had the chance, he thought, his grip unknowingly tightening on her hair. *I should have given her some money and put her on the train in Tucson. She's trouble just waiting to happen.*

March watched his eyes darken, as she tried to free her hair from his painful grasp. She couldn't help but wonder what he was thinking, and prayed that he hadn't changed his mind about letting her stay on at Falling Creek. In spite of her audacious decision to become a lady of the evening, she knew that she'd never have the determination to see it through. But without an education or any real work experience, there was nothing else she could do to support herself.

"Please let me go." Her quiet plea snapped Jim from his thoughts. He saw the fear in her eyes, and realized that he had wrapped her hair firmly around his hand. Carefully releasing it, he watched as she backed away from him.

"I'll . . . I'll have your breakfast ready in just a few minutes." March pushed her hair over her shoulders and bent to retrieve a skillet from a shelf.

"I'll eat at the bunkhouse." Knowing that he had frightened her, his voice was harsh with regret.

"But it will just take me a few more minutes."

Jim looked at the golden brown biscuits, smelled the inviting aroma of the bubbling coffee, and noticed that her dress pulled snugly against her milk-engorged breasts.

"I'll eat at the bunkhouse," he repeated, forcing himself to pick up his hat and spurs. Damn, she was going to be trouble.

"Is something wrong?" She thought that the expression on his face resembled someone in pain, and worried that he might be sickening with something. "Do you feel poorly? Does your stomach hurt? Are you suffering with a fever?"

"No, ma'am, I'm not sick." Jim plopped his hat on his head and grabbed his spurs. He didn't like the direction his thoughts had taken, and he had to get away from her before he said or did something that would offend them both. "I don't have a fever, my stomach is growling with hunger, and for a man near to starving to death, I feel just fine. I'm just not hungry for ash biscuits or that brown water you call coffee."

Turning, he grabbed his jacket from the hook by the back door and stamped out of the kitchen. The gentle morning breeze cooled his thoughts, and as he slipped on his jacket, he inhaled the sweet fragrance of the new day.

He scanned the horizon in each direction, alert for anything that looked out of place. For as far as he could see, the land was his, and there was no place on earth he'd rather be. He intended to spend the remainder of his life on the

Falling Creek Ranch, and now that he had a son, he knew that his labors wouldn't be in vain.

The few men who hadn't travelled north with the herd were beginning to rustle around, nodding quiet greetings as he passed. In the past Jim had always gone on the cattle drive, but the members of the new ranchers' consortium had voted to share the duties, and each year different owners would go on the drive. That way no one man would have to be gone for several weeks in the spring, and then again in the fall to see to the safety of his herd. Jim had sent the majority of his men to help out, but had kept enough on the ranch to continue its day-to-day operations.

He spied Breed and decided that now was the perfect time to tell his foreman about March. As word spread there would be more than one saddle tramp looking for a good time, and Jim had no intention of letting March be frightened by a woman-hungry drifter.

"We need to talk before you head out," he said as he watched Breed saddle his horse. "Let me grab a cup of coffee first."

Breed nodded, lightly tossing the heavy saddle onto the back of his Appaloosa stallion. "I'll wait."

Jim headed for the bunkhouse and the thick brew that waited, looking forward to the start of a new day.

* * *

March left the biscuits on the table, pulled the coffee from the fire before it could become as thick as mud, and climbed the stairs to the room she shared with Jamie. Moving quietly so that she didn't disturb the sleeping baby, she found her stockings and shoes and a comb for her hair. Since he would sleep for at least another hour, she had time to make herself a little more presentable and enjoy a quiet breakfast.

Back in the kitchen, March sipped at her coffee as she forced the snarls from her hair. Twisting it deftly into a knot at the back of her head, she secured it in place with two long sticks that her brother Jan had whittled for her and had given her as a present on her last birthday. She tried not to dwell on the fact that they were the last gift she would ever receive from her oldest brother; the final gift from her family.

After nursing Jamie, March washed some of his dirty towels and hung them out to dry. With the baby sleeping peacefully on a quilt in the shade, she took advantage of the quiet to work on the skirt she was making. Finished except for the hem, the polished cotton fabric was the same deep green as the forest that had sheltered her family for so many months in Colorado. Memories engulfed her and tears made her vision waver. The sound of the younger children's laughter seemed to fill her ears, then intermingle with the memories of their whimpers as the winter winds blew and hunger clawed at their empty bellies.

No longer delighted with the skirt that had brought such bitter images to mind, she put it aside as tears made her vision waver. Resting her head on the back of the chair, March looked up to the clear blue sky. Soon it would be summer and almost unbearably hot. Already the late afternoons were hinting at the heat that would become a daily reality.

She would spend the summer in the coolness of the house, with plenty of water when she was thirsty and shade from the sun when it was at its peak. She couldn't help but wonder if June had shoes to protect his feet, or if little September would spend the summer covered in a rash because of the heat. Were they hungry? Did they have a safe place to sleep? Did Mama still cry herself to sleep each night, trying desperately to hide the sound of her weeping from the others?

Standing abruptly, March carried the skirt inside and laid it across a chair. Grabbing the sling she used to hold Jamie, she picked up the sleeping baby and cradled him securely against her chest.

Anger grew as she thought of Jim's dissatisfaction with her coffee, and his look of disdain as he explained the workings of the stove. Sure, he liked his coffee thick, she thought, but he'd never had to go without because there was no money for luxuries like coffee or tea or sugar. Who could worry about trivialities, when faced with the very real concern of whether or not there would be enough food for even one meal each day?

Who would spend money on something like a stove, when there was a child who needed a pair of shoes so that he didn't have to worry about cactus thorns or poisonous spiders? Who could take pleasure in having rugs on the floor or pictures on the wall, when a child might die because there was no money to pay for a doctor when he got sick?

And why was she the one who would have a soft bed to sleep in and plenty of food to eat, while her little brothers and sisters suffered because of the selfishness of a father too lazy to provide for them?

She would have allowed her father to sell her body time and again, if it had meant that her family would have the bare necessities of life. But she knew from past experience that the money would have been spent on whiskey and gambling, rather than food and clothing.

Knowing that there were no answers to her questions, March stepped off of the porch and headed toward the noise at the corral. After a lifetime of always being surrounded by her family, she was suddenly desperately lonely. Kissing Jamie's soft cheek, guilt overwhelmed her as she wondered why she had been given heaven, while her family was still suffering hell.

March was unaware of the appreciative male glances that watched as she approached. Most were respectful, a few were openly admiring, and a couple leered blatantly. One pair of silver eyes filled with all of the warmth of a winter blizzard, watched not the woman, but rather for the reactions of the other men. The two whose gazes were so filled with lust that they were aware of nothing beyond the bulge beneath their own belt buckles, would be gone before the sun began lowering in the sky. The others would be given a warning; only one. Breed never gave anyone a second chance.

Feeling secure surrounded by so many, March never gave a thought to the fact that her presence might be unwelcomed. She smiled as the men tipped their hats and then turned their faces back toward the action in the corral. Instinctively aware that she must tread carefully until they became accustomed to her, she stopped beside Hank and smiled warmly at the old man.

"What's everybody looking at?"

Hank gave the onlookers a censorious look, as March's soft voice drifted through the sudden quiet. Turning toward her, he tipped his hat and motioned with his hand toward the corral.

"They're waitin' to see if'en the boss has learned his lessons or not."

March could see a pair of dusty boots from beneath the horse. "What lessons?"

"Breed's been a'teachin' Jim how to break a horse the Comanche way. Some of the boys figure that only an Indian can gentle-break a horse, and they've got bets goin' on how soon he'll be pickin' hisself up from the dust."

The massive horse glowed a fiery red in the sunlight, as the soothing sound of Jim's voice danced around the nervous animal. Tail and mane as black as a crow's wing flickered with restless anticipation. March watched as Jim rhythmically stroked the animal, his hands never completely leaving the muscular body.

"Do you think he'll do it?" she asked, mesmerized by the gentle sounds and touches.

"Hell, ah . . . durn, missy, that horse ain't never held a rider. Ain't no reason for him to start now, lessin' he's of a mind."

"But do you think he'll do it?" Her gaze remained glued to the man and horse, as she waited for Hank to answer.

The old man studied Jim's quiet actions. "Ain't but one other man who'd ever get more than a leg up on that critter, and he's the one who's been a'teachin' the boss." He rubbed his chin thoughtfully. "I'd say he's got as good a chance as a snake findin' water in the desert."

Jim carefully placed a saddle blanket over the horse's broad back. Its ears briefly lay back, then slowly resumed their normal position at Jim's continued soft words and gentle caresses.

"Bet he don't talk that sweet to a whore, when he's trying to get between her legs," one of the men said with a smirk.

Critical glances were sent first in the man's direction, and then became apologetic as they looked toward March. She carefully controlled the expression on her face, keeping her eyes on the excitement in the corral. She realized that this really wasn't the place for a woman, and that the men had become quiet since her arrival. If she hadn't wanted to see what was going to happen so badly, she would have turned around and gone back to the house, but her curiosity was greater than her embarrassment.

His voice never changing in pitch, Jim lowered a saddle onto the horse. As if familiar with its weight, the animal never changed his stance. Every muscle, every sinew, every tendon stood in stark relief beneath the sleek copper skin, as he seemed to wait for the next move from the man at his side.

March caught her breath as Jim reached underneath the animal and grabbed the cinch strap. She wondered if she was the only one aware of Jim's vulnerability in comparison to the powerful strength of the horse. Jamie squirmed and cooed softly, as if agreeing with her that his father was in grave danger.

"Open the gate." Jim's voice never rose in pitch, and yet several men hurried to comply to his soft request.

Biting her tongue to hold back a natural request that he be careful, March watched as he mounted the horse. In a fluid, graceful motion, he and the animal became one. For a heartbeat the horse stood still, then became a storm breaking around the cheering men. After several bone-shaking bucks that failed to dislodge his passenger, the horse did as Jim had hoped he would, he headed for the open gate and the promise of freedom.

"I'll be gol-durned! He did it!" Hank slapped his hand against a fence post and chuckled with glee.

"But I thought you said he would?" March watched until man and horse were little more than a cloud of dust on the horizon.

"I just said that sos you wouldn't worry none, but, missy, there ain't nobody that ever mounted that animal afore."

"No one?"

"Hell . . . ah, shoot . . . that is the meanest critter on four legs. The boss been workin' with him all winter, just to get the saddle on him. Never figured that one would let anybody on his back."

"When will he be back?" Concern clouded her eyes.

"When the horse and man are as one." March turned toward the deep voice behind her.

The sun shining behind his head turned his blond hair to a mystical aura of white light. She was aware of his size and strength, and a gentle presence that gave her a feeling of protection. It was a strange sensation, one she had never experienced before. She knew that she was as safe with this man as Jamie was in his sling against her breasts, and yet he gave an outward impression of such fierceness that common sense told her to take caution.

"You are Breed."

"They call me that."

"Do you have another name? I would rather call you something that you are comfortable with."

He hesitated briefly, as if fighting with himself before he answered. "I have been called many things by many men. One is as good as another."

"No," she argued gently. "A man should be called by his name, not by a word that is meant to lower him in the eyes of others."

"A wise woman for one so young." A smile broke his face, and March caught her breath at his masculine beauty. "Breed is an insult to them, but to me it is a reminder of all that I am. I am white by birth, Comanche by fortune. Truly a half-breed, since I am not accepted by the people of my birth, and denied the people of my life."

The excitement done, the men slowly moved away from the corral and back to their chores. "This is not the place for a lady," Breed stated quietly. "The little one grows restless. I will escort you back to the house."

March looked again toward the desert, but saw only the things that belonged there. "Will he be all right?"

"A man will do what he must, to hide behind a woman's skirts weakens him in his own eyes and the eyes of others."

"So I'm not supposed to worry?"

"Worry is a woman's job, but it should be done so that her man is not aware of it."

"He isn't my man." March raised her chin defensively.

"Then why do you worry?" Breed grinned and reached for her elbow.

"Because it's my job?" She looked at him and matched his grin. "He really isn't my man, but if something happens to him, then who will raise his son?"

"He will return." His deep voice, so confidently sure, denied any other possibility.

"Ah, but will he be in one piece or many?"

"That we will have to wait to discover."

At the front steps of the house, Breed released her arm. "If you are in need of anything, Hank or Woods will be near."

"You sound like it might be days before Jim returns," she stated with alarm.

"The horse is one of the most powerful I've ever seen. It may take that long before he accepts what he can not change." He nodded, turned, and walked away.

The day dragged by, March searched for ways to keep occupied. She had to force herself not to watch continuously for Jim's return. Deciding that he would be hungry after his adventures, she lit the stove and began preparations for the evening meal—a meal he might not return to eat.

Once the roast was in the oven and beans bubbling gently on the stove top, she carried Jamie

outside. She had never seen any of the men
around the back side of the house, so she felt
no concern about nursing him as she wandered
around in the shadows afforded by the structure.

She decided that the perfect place for a garden was just outside of the kitchen door, protected from the burning rays of the afternoon
sun. Plenty of morning light would reach the
plants, but the house would provide shade when
the sun was at its highest peak. It was only a
short walk from the well, making the necessary
job of watering much easier.

Visualizing neat rows of corn, beans, and peas,
March was startled at the long, slow whistle of
appreciation that interrupted her thoughts.

"I ain't never seen nothing so pretty as that
tit that young'en suckin' on." Lust-filled eyes
rested on March's bare breast. "Why don't you
just pull him off of it, so I can show you just
what it was made for?"

Ten

Without taking her eyes off of the intruder, March attempted to cover her breast from his leering gaze. Cursing her own foolishness for exposing herself to his threat, she looked briefly toward the house. She knew it was just a few short steps to the door and safety, but it looked as faraway as the moon. Even as she accepted the fact that he'd reach her before she reached it, fear made her wonder if she should give it a try.

The glow in his eyes warned her that he would relish the chase, and his swaggering arrogance proved that he had no doubt who would win. March's only choice was to hold her ground . . . and scream loudly enough to waken the dead if it became necessary. Surely someone would hear her and come to investigate.

Since escape to the house was impossible, and reluctantly deciding that it would be a poor choice even if she could get to it since it would give him the advantage of privacy, March changed directions and backed slowly toward the corner of the structure.

"That's far enough, missy." His smile was so

filled with his intent that she cringed. "I like it hot and hard and with just a little pain to make it more excitin', but I don't need no witnesses. The boss might think you're his special territory, and we don't want no one tellin' him that I mounted his favorite mare while he was gone, do we?"

As she listened to his boasting, March felt anger slowly replace her fear. She had heard all of the threats, all of the crudities, before. She had lived before in fear that every man who saw her would insist on using her. Not again, never again! No one could live in constant fear, no one deserved to.

As anger grew to rage, she knew that she'd never back down from this arrogant man who, like a spoiled child, believed anything he wanted was his for the taking.

Squaring her shoulders, knowing that half of her breast was still exposed to his gaze, she refused to cower. "Turn around and walk away, before you live to regret it," she advised firmly.

"Now, little lady, you don't want me to do that."

"Yes, I do."

"But then you'd be missin' out on the best lovin' in your life."

"What you have in mind is as far from loving as chocolate cake is from loco weed."

"Honey, I'm a'bettin' that tit of yours will taste better than any chocolate cake, and will drive me out of my mind surer than loco weed."

He advanced several steps closer, forcing March to back further away. "I done told you not to move. You'd best be careful that you don't make me mad. You wouldn't like what I'd do to you, if I get mad. That pretty face of yours wouldn't look so pretty, when it's been beat up a little."

She smiled bitterly at the memory of beatings so severe that she'd been unable to walk, of bruises so deep they had taken weeks to fade. Misinterpreting her smile for one of derision, the cowboy clenched his hands into fists as anger reddened his face. No one—especially a woman—laughed at him!

"Honey, I'm gonna wipe that smile right off your face." His voice lowered to a growl. "I could'a made it good for you, but now when I get through, you ain't gonna be smilin' for a long, long time."

A long, lean shadow was the first evidence that they were no longer alone. March bit back a sigh of relief as Breed moved around the corner of the house. His alert silver gaze looked first at her to see that she was unharmed, and then at the baby in her arms. When he was satisfied that neither of them was hurt, he turned his eyes toward her antagonist.

"This ain't none of your affair," the cowboy snarled.

"You're threatening the lady—"

"She ain't no lady," he smirked. "Ever'body knows that ain't her kid, but she's feedin' it like any mama."

". . . A lady I've promised to protect. That makes it my business," Breed continued, as if he hadn't heard the interruption. "I don't make promises lightly." He turned toward March and nodded slightly. "Go into the house and take the baby upstairs."

His intentions were so clear that March shivered at the softness of his voice. She took several steps toward the house before stopping and turning back to him.

"Be careful," she said quietly.

"You're worrying again," he replied, a smile lightening his eyes.

"Just trying to do my job." March looked toward the cowboy who waited, his cockiness wilting as he realized that maybe he hadn't made a wise move in confronting the woman.

He was really only a boy, she thought sadly, too sure of himself to think or care about anyone but himself. He was about to discover, the hard way, that he had crossed the boundaries of common decency. She had little doubt that when Breed was finished with him, the cowboy would have learned a lesson he'd do well to remember. And maybe if he was smart enough, he'd grow old. But she doubted it. Some people never learned until it was too late.

"He isn't worth a drop of your blood."

"Or a minute of your worry." Breed motioned toward the house. "Go inside."

"Just don't forget to quit while he's still alive," she replied gravely, turned so that only Breed could see the twinkle in her eyes. "A body is such a nuisance to get rid of. It's too hot to dig a grave, and you'd have to ride a long distance so that the smell didn't drift back here."

"I'll remember." His voice was equally solemn, but a hint of admiration lurked deeply in his sparkling gaze.

Stark pity crossed her face as she glanced again at her attacker. Clutching Jamie securely against her, March walked away. Behind the closed door, she waited for some sound, some indication of what was happening. It wasn't long before the impact of flesh against flesh drifted quietly into the room.

After placing more wood in the cook stove and adding water to the beans, she climbed the stairs. She couldn't help but wonder why men always seemed to feel the need to prove their strength. First Jim, on an animal so powerful it was frightening, and now Breed, with enough strength at his command to reduce her attacker to nothing in short order.

And why did some men think that anything they wanted was theirs for the taking? Why did some of them bully anyone smaller or weaker than themselves, while others thought it was necessary to protect those who didn't want or need protection?

She had found that there was no predicting what a man might do or not do. He could be kind and gentle or mean and rough. His voice could scare the leaves from a tree, or be soft enough to soothe a frightened child. With a formidable strength, he could deliver the harshest punishment or the gentlest caress. Laughing and teasing one minute, he could become a killer with the blink of an eye.

Men . . . a mystery she doubted she'd ever live long enough to solve.

At first March wasn't sure what woke her. Jamie still slept in his bed, and there were no unnatural sounds from the house.

She hadn't intended to take a nap, but as she fed Jamie his midday meal, her eyes had grown heavy with sleep. A gentle breeze had ruffled the curtains at the opened windows, soothing her with a serene whisper and an invitation to rest. Lying down, she promised herself that she'd only close her eyes for a few minutes, and then get up. Now she had no idea how much time had passed or what had caused her to wake, but she sensed that something wasn't right.

Standing up and stretching, her nose wrinkled as the smell of something burning drifted up the stairs.

"Dinner!" Skirts flying, March rushed down the stairs and into the kitchen. A layer of gray smoke floated lazily near the ceiling of the room, while a thin stream drifted out of the cracks around the oven. Opening the door, she stood back, eyes burning as smoke billowed out. Fanning the air in front of her nose, March rushed to the back door and opened it wide. After doing the same with the windows, she reached into the oven and pulled out the roast that was now little more than an unidentifiable, charred lump. She discovered that the water had cooked away, and the beans were a gooey, gray mass burnt permanently into the pot.

Coughing fiercely and eyes tearing so heavily that she could barely see, March grabbed a kitchen towel and carried first the meat and then the pot of beans outside. The air smelled delightfully fresh as she took advantage of the towel in her hand to wipe at her eyes.

When the coughing was under control, she peeked into the kitchen and saw that the layer of smoke had dissipated, but left a heavy, burnt smell. Reluctantly, she forced herself to return to the scene of her culinary disaster.

"Easy to use once you get the hang of it," she misquoted with a disgusted smirk, as she eyed the stove with great distaste. "I either better get the hang of it real quick, or go back to the fireplace. At this rate we'll be in real danger of starving to death."

The sun was lowering in the sky and it wouldn't be long before Jim returned to the house—if he returned. For all she knew, the horse could have thrown him somewhere in the desert, and he was making the long walk home.

But if he came home, and she suspected that he would, he would be hungry and wanting to eat. She doubted that he would care to listen to the reasons that there was no meal on the table. And if there was one thing she didn't care to see, it was his condescending expression when she explained about burning his dinner.

She needed to make something—quick! There was no time to soak beans and allow them to cook. The roast had been one that Woods had brought over from the bunkhouse, and she could hardly ask him to replace it. For all she knew, it was the final piece of meat available on the ranch.

Staring through the open window at the withering blooms of the cacti that grew in such profusion, March was grateful for the gentle breeze that would help clear out the lingering smell. Running her hand through her tangled hair, she asked herself the age-old question of what to fix for supper.

Stopping on the back porch, Jim unbuckled his spurs and beat his hat against his dusty pants. His mood was far from pleasant, after the discussion he'd just had with Breed. The foreman had stopped him on the way to the house and told him about the confrontation earlier in the day. He was glad that Breed had been there to prevent March from getting hurt and that he had fired the man, but Jim regretted that he hadn't been the one to take care of the problem.

March had thoughtfully set a pitcher of water and a bowl on a handy table. He poured water into the bowl, then sluiced it over his sweaty face and the back of his neck, appreciating the coolness on overheated skin. Drying his hands and face, he pulled open the door and instantly identified the odor of burnt food.

The door of the oven still stood open, and the fireplace burned brightly. Obviously, her first attempt at cooking on the stove wasn't a success.

Jim felt his belly gnaw at his backbone, and wondered if his supper would be a can of cold beans. When he had tried to run the ranch while taking care of his son, he'd eaten enough of them to know that he'd be happy to never eat another can. He'd grown accustomed to March's cooking, and her hearty, simple meals were filling and tasty.

But if she was anything like Melanie, she'd be upstairs pouting, and her burnt attempt would not be replaced by something else. From past experiences with his wife, he knew that if he wanted something to eat, he'd have to fix it himself.

He was hot, tired, and irritable. That damn horse had run until Jim had begun to fear that it would drop dead rather than accept a rider. When the animal had finally come to the end of his immense strength, they'd been miles from the ranch. The trip back had been considerably slower, and as the horse had regathered his strength, Jim had been forced to constantly stay on the alert for an unexpected move.

The horse was intelligent, fast, and one of the

most stubborn creatures he'd ever encountered. If he ever got the animal broke to the saddle, Jim knew he'd be a worthy, dependable mount. But he wondered if they would kill each other before that had a chance to happen.

With a tired sigh, Jim ventured further into the room. He discovered that the kitchen table was set for dinner, and heard March's soft voice as she descended the stairs. He wasn't surprised when she entered the room with Jamie propped up against her shoulder.

He stared at the lovely picture she made with the babe in her arms and a welcoming smile on her face. Her golden hair had been tamed into a sedate bun at the nape of her neck, and she wore clothing he'd never seen before. Since he was aware that her wardrobe consisted of the two well-worn dresses, he easily guessed that she had made the dark green skirt and white shirtwaist that she wore.

"You look lovely," he said quietly, wondering if the cowboy who'd accosted her had found her as attractive as he now found her.

Delighted that he'd noticed her new clothes, March smiled, unaware of the impact it had on the man watching her. His shoulders stiffened, and his eyes narrowed as she approached.

"Thank you." March twirled in a graceful pose. "I've never had anything this pretty."

Jim didn't like the effect her innocent smile or fluid whirl had on him. He wasn't happy about noticing her ankles as her skirt had drifted up, nor was he pleased that the only shoes she had to wear were the worn-out leather ones. In fact, he wasn't pleased at all that he noticed her as a woman.

"Very nice," he said more gruffly than he intended. "But I'd be a whole lot happier to see supper on the table."

"Oh, I'm sorry. Of course, you're tired and hungry, and here I am showing off my new clothes, while you wonder if you're going to starve to death." Her smile lost some of its gaiety, as she took Jamie from her shoulder and handed him to his father. "Hold your son for a few minutes, while I get everything on the table."

"I didn't mean to growl." Her sad smile had torn at his heart. Of course she was thrilled with new clothes. While every other woman he had known had expected clothing as their due, to March they were a wonderful treasure. He felt guilty that he had denied her the excitement. Damn, he was tired of feeling guilty.

"You didn't growl," she replied gently. "But be patient just a few more minutes, and you can eat."

Feeling even more guilty because of her compassionate response, Jim pulled out a chair and sat, his son in his arms. He watched as March leaned over the fire, pulling out first a skillet and then a dutch oven. The appetizing aromas drifted to him, and his mouth watered at a glimpse of golden brown biscuits . . . and her shapely backside.

As she had promised, within minutes the table was set with well-filled bowls and plates. She settled the baby on a pallet of blankets near her end of the table, and sat down.

Other than the biscuits, Jim wasn't able to readily identify the foods he put on his plate. There was a golden fried chunk that could have been meat, a mashed vegetable that could have been potatoes except for the color, and something green that resembled snap beans.

It appeared to him that, not only had she taken the time to dress nicely for him, but she'd worked hard on the meal. As he heaped his plate to overflowing, Jim knew a feeling of appreciation. It had been a long time since someone had been concerned about him.

"Would you mind if I planted a garden?" March asked as she filled her plate. "There's a good spot right behind the house where the plants would be protected from the sun the hottest part of the day, and it's not too far from the well, so I could water it easily."

Jim picked up the biscuit melting with butter and bit into it. "Are you sure you want to go to that much trouble? We've always gotten fresh vegetables in town, and the mercantile has a big stock of canned goods."

"It wouldn't be any trouble," she hastily reassured him. "I thought I'd find a place where the baby would be protected while I work, so that he'd get plenty of sunshine and fresh air. All I need are some seeds. I'll do all of the work of planting and harvesting."

"It's fine by me, but I'll have one of the men plow the ground up for you."

"That's not necessary. I can do it."

"I realize that, Miss I-Can-Do-It," he replied, irritated by both her independence and determination not to be a bother. "However, you won't. I'll put one of the men on it in the morning."

He scooped up some of the mashed vegetable and looked dubiously at it. "I thought at first that this might be potatoes, but now I'm sure it isn't."

"Give it a try, I think you'll like it."

"Care to tell me what it is first?" His eyebrow rose questioningly.

"Don't you trust me?" she teased, eating the vegetable in question.

He watched her mouth open and saw her small, very white teeth close on the prongs of the fork. Her eyes smiled merrily, and just the tip of her tongue came out to catch a dab of white on the corner of her mouth.

In spite of himself, Jim noticed that the ruffle at the top of her shirtwaist accentuated her slender neck, and the multitude of tiny tucks at the yoke pulled at the fullness of her breasts. She looked extremely feminine with wisps of hair escaping the bun at her nape, and a rosy glow about her cheeks.

He tasted the vegetable, surprised at its pleasantly sweet flavor. It reminded him of the pineapple he'd had once while he was still living back East.

And he wondered if she'd taste that sweet . . .

Squirming slightly as his breeches tightened uncomfortably, Jim forked some of the bean-looking things into his mouth. He was again surprised by an unexpectedly strange but pleasant taste.

Realizing that she had failed to serve the coffee, March rose hastily from the table. Jim couldn't fail to notice how well her skirt hugged her narrow waist and flowed around her shapely hips. He watched the gentle sway of the dark fabric, as she rushed back to the fire.

Hell and damnation, he thought with an irritated sigh. Hiring her hadn't been a good idea. No, sir, not a good idea at all. She sure wasn't the young girl he had thought he was getting. She was a woman . . . all woman. Her new clothes would have pointed that fact out to a blind man. And she was sweet. Lord, but she was sweet. She was so gentle with the baby, a man would pay anything just to have five minutes of that gentleness for himself.

A new hunger, a familiar masculine hunger, began to gnaw relentlessly at his gut. He wanted her, all of her, with an intensity that was alarming.

"I'm sorry I forgot all about the coffee." March's full breast inadvertently rubbed against his shoulder, as she leaned over him to pour his coffee.

As if burnt by the steaming liquid, Jim flinched as he felt the feminine firmness against him. He had thought himself too old, too jaded by the realities of life to ever be susceptible again to a female. Yet here he was, near to bursting, like a young boy just discovering another use for the appendage at his groin.

"Mind telling me what I'm eating?" Cutting into the only untasted thing on his plate, Jim regretted that his voice was a growl as he fought back his thoughts. It had been a hell of a day, first with the stubborn horse, then with Breed's problem with the young cowboy, now he had to put up with his own body betraying him.

March smiled hesitantly, wondering why he was suddenly so irritable. Granted, he was eating unfamiliar foods, but they were well prepared and tasty, although she wasn't too sure how he was going to react when she told him what he'd been eating.

"The . . . uh, mashed one is mescal . . ."

"Century Plant? The same one the Apache use to make their own kind of alcoholic drink?" he asked with disbelief. He had seen more than one reservation Apache drunk on the beverage fermented from the long leaf, spikelike plants that grew everywhere.

March nodded as his eyes narrowed. "The green one is tumbleweed. It's not tumbling, of course."

"Of course," he agreed sarcastically, still holding the final offering untasted on his fork.

"You have to pick the stems when they're only two or three inches long."

"And this?" He held up his fork.

"That's . . . ah, well . . ."

"Let me guess." Jim looked at the strange food with the crisp, golden crust. He felt like he wanted to tear something into tiny little pieces. "Cactus, right?"

"Right," she agreed quickly.

Watching her sit with her hands folded demurely in her lap and her breasts pushing against her blouse, Jim didn't hear her answer. He was too consumed with an appalling need to taste her rather than the food.

Biting back a curse, he put the food into his mouth and chewed. It was firm and yet mushy, crunchy but slimy, and bitter. Good lord, it was bitter. Jim spit it out, wiped his mouth, and tried to drown the taste with a mouthful of coffee.

"My God, what is that?" he asked, shuddering with distaste.

"I told you—cactus. Fried, prickly pear cactus."

Jim's eyes narrowed and his jaw clenched. Ranching in Arizona provided its own special problems; the lack of water, rattlers the size of a man's forearm, and thorny plants that were waiting for the unwary to pass too close.

Was it too much to expect, at the end of a long day, for a man to come home and find a good meal waiting for him?

This was it, the final thing that destroyed his tightly reined control. He pushed back his chair with a violent shove that frightened Jamie into a whimper, and rose to tower over March.

"Lady, since I moved to Arizona, I've chopped down cactus, kicked them out of my way, and even picked them out of my butt, but I don't—I repeat—*I don't* eat them!"

Eleven

With the utter stillness in his office broken only by the occasional ruffle of a piece of paper, Jim had no difficulty hearing the quiet closing of the back door. He knew it was his restless housekeeper. He'd heard her quiet steps as she'd come down the stairs.

Hours ago, she had brought him a cup of coffee, offered him something to eat—which he had gruffly refused—and then said a quiet good night.

As he had watched her walk out of his office, he'd felt the desire to call her back and apologize, explain to her that his outburst had nothing to do with her choice of meals. But watching the gentle sway of her skirts had forcibly reminded him exactly what had put him in a foul mood.

How could he explain to her that it wasn't eating cactus that had caused his explosion? Granted, the prickly pear cactus had been so sour he would have refused it at any time, but it wasn't what caused his explosion of temper. Hearing her soft voice, seeing her gentle smile, watching the femininity in every movement, had needlessly pointed out to him that she was a desirable woman.

And damn it, he was horny!

Jim smiled at his own description. Accurate, but crass, he thought. A gentleman did not apologize to a lady using *that* as an excuse for his bad manners. In fact, he doubted that March would even know the meaning of the word. And then he'd have to explain it to her. He chuckled as he pictured her face turning scarlet with embarrassment.

His chuckle turned to a frown, as he thought of the fear that would replace the embarrassment when she finally understood that he wanted the same thing from her that the young cowboy had wanted this afternoon. He wanted her, but not at the expense of her fear. She'd had enough of that in her young life.

A shadow crossed by his window, and Jim rose to his feet. There was no moon to light her path, yet her steps didn't falter. Using the door in his office, he walked outside to join her restless prowl.

"Can't sleep?" he asked quietly, taking care that he didn't startle her.

March looked up, watching warily as he approached. "Just planning my garden," she offered lamely.

"There have been many nights when I couldn't sleep. I always found it relaxing to walk in the dark. There's something peaceful about being alone, while others are asleep."

"My sister May is afraid of the dark." Crossing her arms over her waist, March shook her head sadly. "She could never understand how I could venture out alone at night. As soon as it began to get dark, she'd dart for the light of the fire, but not me. I liked the night, I could hide from other eyes and think my own thoughts."

"Privacy."

Surprised that he understood, March nodded. "With a family the size of mine, there was never the time or the place to be alone, except in the dark where no one could see me."

"What did you think about?" Coming to a stop beside her, he detected the floral scent of her skin. Even dressed in clothing suitable only for the rag bag, she always smelled clean and fresh.

"Oh, things of great importance." March smiled softly. "Depending on my age, of course."

"Things like the color of a hair ribbon or a dress for a new doll?" he teased.

"No." Her single word reminded him that she'd had very few hair ribbons, and he wondered if she'd ever had a doll. He wanted to give her the things that she'd never had. She was a little old now for a doll, but he could shower her with hair ribbons of every color of the rainbow, new dresses, and ruffled petticoats, shoes without holes, and frilly bonnets that served no purpose other than to make their wearer happy.

"Things like how many stars were in the sky, and why did I only see them in the dark. And what fish do at night, how do they sleep while they swim. And more important things, like do all daisies have the same number of petals, and what does an ocean look like."

Jim refrained from telling her the answers to all of her questions, deciding instead to encourage her to read the books that would give her the answers. He was aware that she'd had little formal schooling, but her vocabulary and manner of speaking belied that fact. With a little self-help, few people would ever question her lack of education.

But no book could describe an ocean; only a person who had seen one and traveled one could do that.

"An ocean is all colors of blue, from the palest blue green to nearly black. It goes on forever, until it seems to touch the sky with waves of water that swell until they burst into bubbles of white."

"You've seen an ocean?" Her voice was filled with curiosity.

"Seen it, and traveled to Europe and back on it."

"Weren't you scared?"

"Only once." He paused, remembering the very real fear he had felt as the ferocity of the wind clashed with the power of the water in a vigorous contest neither could win, while almost destroying the insignificant ship caught help-lessly in the battle.

"What happened?"

"We were in the middle of the Atlantic, and ran into a storm they call a hurricane."

"What's a hurricane?"

"That's a wind that blows so hard, it makes waves into mountains of water taller than the masts of the ship. You look up and up and up, and still can't see the top of the mountain, and then suddenly the ship rides the shoulders of the giant, and you're on top instead of the bot-tom. But when you get up there, all you can see is the next wave and the next.

"And the wind blows until you're sure that the poor, feeble ship won't survive. It blows so hard that the rain comes at you sideways."

"You're teasing me," she accused with a chuckle. "Everyone knows that rain falls straight down."

"Not during a hurricane. I swear to you that it comes sideways."

"You were scared?" March was amazed that he so freely admitted to feeling fear. It was her experience that few men would admit to fearing anything.

"That's putting it mildly. I swore that if I ever got back home, I'd never venture out on the sea again."

"Have you?"

"No. Maybe that's why I chose to settle in the desert. It's as faraway and as different from the ocean as anything in the world."

"Have you traveled much?"

"Enough." Jim shoved his fingers into his pockets to stop himself from reaching out to gather up the threads of March's hair that blew in the gentle breeze. "I took a grand tour of Europe after I finished my education. And I've seen a lot of this country, enough to know that this is where I want to live until I'm an old, old man."

"If I had my way, I'd never move again," March mumbled.

"You moved around a lot?" he asked quietly.

"We were always packing up to move on to someplace new. We'd no more than get settled, before we were on the go again. I never had many friends, because by the time I met girls my own age, Pa was thinking of moving on. After a while, I just quit trying. Why go to all the work of meeting people, when I knew we'd only be there until we got run out, or until Pa heard of a better place and wanted to go."

It was a statement of her childhood, spoken without rancor, while asking for neither pity nor sympathy. Yet Jim felt sorrow for the young girl who had never had a chance to be a child, to experience the carefree existence inherent to childhood. But he couldn't regret that that same little girl had grown to become an intelligent, generous, and sometimes exasperating young woman.

Stars hung overhead, looking close enough to touch. In the distance, a coyote howled and was

answered by others of its kind. A gentle breeze
danced over the sand, and a poor-will whispered
its mournful cry.

"I'm sorry about losing my temper earlier,"
Jim said quietly.

"It's my fault. I shouldn't have served you cactus, but when the roast burned, I knew I needed
to fix something else, and that seemed to me to
be the quickest thing."

"I thought I detected the distinct aroma of
burnt something," he teased gently.

"It wasn't just burnt," March chuckled, as she
thought of the roast. "It was charred beyond recognition. I think we'd all eat better, if I confine
my cooking to the fireplace rather than the stove.
Next time I might burn down the house."

"As I told you, it just takes some getting use
to."

"So does starving!"

Jim enjoyed her sense of humor, but never
more than when she laughed at herself. Melanie
had never even smiled at her own mistakes, and
had sometimes pouted for days because she had
done something humanly stupid.

Melanie had been blessed with every advantage in life; loving parents, financial security,
and an excellent education. While March had
been denied those same things. Yet it was this
tiny little bit of a woman-child who so readily
accepted the things she couldn't change, and
smiled even when life was at its worst.

He hated the constant comparison he seemed

to make between his dead wife and March. It wasn't fair to either of them, and yet he seemed incapable of stopping. He remembered times when Melanie had been happy and carefree, but even then she hadn't had the sparkle of life that so easily rode March's thin shoulders.

The differences between the two women, not only physically but in outlook, was night and day. Melanie had suffered through life, March embraced it.

"In spite of the disaster of your first experience with the cook stove and your choice of substitute menus," Jim continued gravely, "I deeply apologize for my behavior. I have never eaten cactus before, and really would rather not again." He shuddered dramatically at the thought of the bitter taste of the prickly pear.

"I thought you kinda liked the mescal and the tumbleweed," she commented innocently, too innocently.

"I still can't believe that I ate tumbleweed," he shook his head with amazement. "I guess they weren't bad, but the other one . . ."

"It just takes some getting use to."

"I'd rather starve!" His smile gleamed momentarily in the darkness, then became more serious. "That wasn't why I exploded."

"No?"

"No!" He reached over and tapped her button nose. "I wasn't in the best of moods, because that horse and I had trouble coming to an agreement. And then when I finally got back to the ranch, Breed had a story to tell."

"I wondered if he'd mentioned that little incident."

"Being accosted by a man in what should be the safety of your own backyard, is hardly a little incident."

"Nothing happened," she reassured him. "Breed rode . . . ah, walked, to the rescue."

"But what would you have done, if he hadn't gotten there in time?"

"Screamed so loud that the owls would have woke up, kicked like a mule, and if necessary, bite any place available."

"Your self-defense techniques are admirable, but the whole thing should never have taken place. You deserve to feel safe in your own home, and I won't have a man on this ranch I can't trust.

"Breed fired him and escorted him off of my property. The others have all been given warnings that they are to treat you with the respect you deserve, or they'll meet the same fate."

"I think Breed did a little more than just fire him," she supplied.

"According to Breed, the man was still breathing when he dumped him outside the gates."

"Thank God. I don't want anyone killed because of me."

"If anyone tries something like that again, that is exactly what might happen. I won't have you threatened in your own home."

"But it's not my home." She was unaware that her voice was filled with longing, but Jim heard every nuance of a craving so deep it was bottomless.

"As long as you're in my employ, this is your home," he said gently. "I want you to treat it as such, and feel safe here."

"I do feel safe here. Safe and protected. It's a wonderful thing not to have to worry about anything except burning your dinner."

"I want you to always feel that way. I, and the men who work for me, will see that your safety comes first . . . or they won't work here long."

"Thank you," she whispered softly. "I've never had anyone give me a gift half so great. I may just have to stay your housekeeper until Jamie is ninety-five years old."

"I believe that would probably make you the oldest housekeeper in the world."

March looked into the darkness, and her voice became dreamy. "What do you think it'll be like in a hundred years?" She spread her arms wide to encompass the area. "Do you think all of this will still be here?"

"Of course, but I imagine there'll be a few changes." It didn't surprise him when she abruptly changed the subject. She never seemed to dwell for long on something she couldn't change.

Jim rocked back on his heels and made a clicking sound with his tongue. "Why, I expect by then that the fishes will talk, snakes'll have legs, and man will fly to the moon."

"Fish will talk?"

"Yep . . . it'll take all the pleasure out of going fishing. When you pull one up on the bank, he'll lay there flopping and yelling at you to throw him back."

"Snakes'll have legs?" she asked with a skeptical giggle.

"Umm . . . at least ten of them. Five on each side. He'll have to take care that he doesn't trip over his own feet."

"And you really think that man will fly to the moon?" Her chuckle filled the night air with joy. "I think you were out in the sun too long today."

Jim delighted in the sound of her laugh as it swirled warmly around him. It was something that he knew he could grow to like . . . too much.

"And I think you'd better go back to bed, or you won't get any sleep tonight. My son is an early riser."

"I think you're right." She turned toward the door leading into his office. The mellow glow of golden light was inviting as she stepped into its glimmer. "Good night, Jim, and thank you."

"For what, angel?"

"For everything . . . for making this my home, for trying to eat my dinner, but most of all for not taking your rage out on me."

His stomach turned with disgust as he realized that others had abused her in their anger.

"You've nothing to fear, March. I'd never hit a woman."

"I know, and that's a wonderful bit of knowledge."

"Sleep tight, angel," he whispered as he watched her disappear. "No one will ever hurt you again. I promise."

"What do you have planned for today?" Jim leaned his elbows against the table, a cup of coffee cradled between his hands. It had taken her a month, but finally the brew was exactly as he liked it, strong enough to grow hair on a tortoise.

He watched appreciatively as March worked efficiently around the kitchen, her flower-printed skirt flowing gracefully around her ankles. Because of her diligent effort, her wardrobe now consisted of several simple skirts and shirtwaists.

It had become their habit in the evening after the daily chores were finished, to sit together in his office until Jamie's last feeding. Jim usually did paperwork, compiling records or replying to correspondence. Sometimes he indulged in his passion for reading, while March sat across the room quietly sewing or, on a rare occasion, reading. He had discovered that she was a delightful conversationalist; sometimes witty, sometimes thought-provoking, and oftentimes maddening, as she looked at the world from a feminine point of view.

He was pleased that she had begun to trust him enough to freely express her opinions without concern that she would anger him. In fact, some of their most enjoyable evenings had been when they'd argued a point nearly to death, each trying to get the other to see a different angle. Always, no matter how heated the discussion became, when it was time for bed, March would smile and wish him sweet dreams.

Jim had come to look forward to the evenings with her, but too frequently lately, his dreams had been far too sweet, and when he woke in the morning, he was aching with a fierce need.

As he sat at the table, the sky turned from black to misty gray. He could hear the sounds of activity outside, telling him that the men were already at work. Breakfast was over, it was time to get the day started, and yet he found himself reluctant to move.

"So, what are you doing today?" he asked again.

"Not much." March folded the kitchen towel and hung it over the back of a chair to dry. "I washed shirts and pants yesterday, and I plan to iron them this morning, before it gets too warm to be messing with the irons. And I need to wash Jamie's towels, but I do that every day. And I noticed last night that nearly all of the lamp chimneys need to be cleaned. I'll probably trim the wicks, too.

"As soon as Jamie wakes up and gets fed, I want to get some bread rising, and maybe I'll make a pie or two. And then this afternoon, after the sun goes down a little, I thought I'd go out and work in the garden for a while. The seeds Hank got for me in town are really starting to sprout, but then so are the weeds."

"That's not much?" he asked with raised eyebrows.

"I reckon it'll keep me busy," she replied with a grin.

"I reckon . . ." Jim stood up and carefully pushed his chair beneath the table. "Do you know what day this is?"

March's brow furrowed as she gave the question serious thought. She didn't keep track of the days, usually letting one flow into another and rarely wondering which day of the week the current one was. In one town they had lived in, she had gone to church every Sunday, so she had been very careful to mark off each day. But they hadn't stayed there long, and she hadn't bothered paying much attention to the days since.

"Tuesday?" she guessed.

"Wrong . . . not even close. It's Friday."

"And tomorrow's Saturday and the next is Sunday, and then the week starts all over again. Thank you, but now that we've established that fact, if you don't mind I've got things to do, and so do you." She pointed toward the door and smiled sweetly.

"Not quite yet, angel. Do you know what else it is, besides Friday?"

A squeaking sound drifted down the stairs. It

was less than a cry, but loud enough to let the adults on the floor below know that Jamie was awake, and ready to demand attention in any manner necessary to achieve his goal.

"I know that in a very few short minutes, your son is going to attempt to scream the house down around our ears."

Knowing that Jamie had never missed a meal, mostly because of the amount of noise he could make, Jim grinned as he reached into his pocket and pulled out a coin. "It's payday."

With a dexterity that would make many a small boy envious, he flipped it to her. With a quick snap of her wrist, March caught it. She stared in wonder at the shimmering coin, a ten-dollar gold piece with its aristocratic eagle on the back.

"Mine?" Her voice was filled with awe, as she savored the feel of the metal still warm from his touch.

"Every penny." Putting his hat on his head, he walked past her toward the door. "What are you going to do with it?"

Her expression turning serious, March leaned her head to the side. "Can I ask you a question?"

"Angel, you can ask me anything, anytime."

Clutching the small coin in her hand, she hesitated. "How much does a house like this cost?"

"Is that what you want to do with it, buy a house?" he asked softly. At her nod, Jim smiled gently. "Honey, if you worked for me for the next twenty years, and never spent a penny of the money you made, you still couldn't afford a house like this."

"Oh . . . I'd hoped, I mean . . ." Disillusionment bowed her shoulders.

Jim forced himself to turn his back to her, trying to ignore the urge to take her into his arms to soothe her disappointment. "Get the baby fed," he said more gruffly than he intended. "I'll be back in an hour or so, and we'll head into town."

"No!"

Stopping with his hand on the door latch, he looked over his shoulder at her. "You haven't been away from the ranch in all the weeks you've been here. It's time to stop hiding, March."

"Jamie's far too young, yet." March squeezed the coin, until she felt it bite into her palm. "I think it would be better if we wait until he's a couple of months older before he makes the trip."

"He's almost two months old now. He'll make the trip just fine."

"Thank you, but I don't want to go this time."

"Don't make me force you to go, angel."

"You wouldn't do that," she stated, but her voice shook with the barely hidden fear that it was exactly what he would do.

The squeak from upstairs became a full-blown wail of distress. "Feed my son, March, and then pack whatever's necessary for him to be away from home for a few hours."

"Please, Jim . . . . I don't think this is a good idea."

March found herself talking to the door as it closed behind him. Like an old woman who had long ago lost the vigor of youth, she slowly climbed the stairs, Jamie's cry increasing in volume with each step she took.

The baby waved his hands and kicked his feet, his face red with exertion. His thick eyelashes were matted into spiky points, and tears ran down his chubby cheeks.

"Oh, sweetheart, don't cry," March crooned as she picked him up. "I'm sorry I didn't come sooner, but your father is being every bit as stubborn as you can be."

March efficiently changed his wet towel as he continued to cry plaintively. Unbuttoning her dress, she sat down in the rocking chair by the window and freed her breast. As his lips closed on her nipple, his tears ceased, only an occasional hiccuping sob and his spiky lashes gave testimony to his displeasure.

"What am I going to do, Jamie?" March smoothed his hair, noticing absently that the ends were getting long enough to curl. "I can't go into town, I just can't. The people there all give me dirty looks, and they talk about me like I'm both deaf and dumb and can't hear them when they call me bad names."

March sighed and leaned her head against the back of the chair. "Your daddy is just beginning to accept me, and to forget all the bad things he's heard. If we go into town, everyone will break their legs rushing to him to tell him the worst about me.

"And then he might change his mind." A lone tear slid silently down her cheek. "What'll I do if he does? Oh, sweet baby, what'll I do if he sends me away?"

Twelve

March sat on the buckboard on the trip to town, concerned with her reception when they arrived and Jim's reaction to it. She didn't see the beauty of the towering ponderosa pines, or the colorful poppies and mariposa lilies that carpeted the ground. She was immune to the cheerful songs of the birds and the waving of lush grasses.

As they rode closer to the town, March was consumed with a fear so great that nothing else made an impression, even the baby cuddled in her arms barely registered.

She had done everything she could to convince Jim that she didn't want to go to town. Fighting tears, she had pleaded to remain at the ranch, and had even gone so far as to point-blank refuse to make the trip, but Jim would not be deterred. With the remnants of her shattered dignity drawn tightly around her, she climbed into the wagon and faced the dreaded trip.

With tight-lipped determination, Jim guided the horses toward Oracle. The two-hour trip had never before seemed so long. He usually enjoyed the solitude and the beauty of the road, but now all he could see was March's face when he had given her no choice but to accompany him. It had taken every ounce of willpower he possessed not to cave in to her pleading.

But her fight to hold back her tears was almost his undoing. Actual tears would not have affected him as much as her steely determination not to cry.

In spite of his best efforts to get a conversation started, she had remained stoically quiet. As the silence lengthened, his guilt at his own high-handed manner had turned to frustration, and then anger. If she wanted to sit and pout the entire way into town, so be it. He was finished with trying to make the trip pleasant. She'd soon discover that her fears were groundless, that few if anyone would remember an event that had happened a year earlier which hadn't directly involved themselves.

The storefronts of unweathered wood, freshly painted signs, and a variety of canvas tents, all proclaimed that the town of Oracle was still in its infancy. It was a rough-and-ready place, having sprung up to service the many men who worked in the area mines. It provided everything from a shave, haircut, and warm bath to store-bought clothes, a companion for the night, and everything in between.

The prospectors were determined and rugged, and the names of the mines they worked were as colorful as the ore they hoped to find:

the Apache Girl Mine, the Comanche Copper Mine, the Southern Belle, the Hijinks, the Oracle, which eventually gave its name to the town.

After months and years of back-breaking labor, some of the mines had proven nearly barren, while others were rich beyond the wildest dreams of the men working them. One of the biggest discoveries was made either by accident or incredible luck, and became known as the Southern Belle.

Capt. John T. Young had staked his claim and worked diligently to find the elusive ore. His wife daily brought him his lunch and, one day, sat down on a ledge to rest while he ate. A whitish vein meandered through the ledge; using a hairpin, Mrs. Young dug at it until she had loosened several specimens. The discovery was to yield one of the richest strikes in the area.

Depending on the weather, the main street of Oracle was either a dirt path, or a quagmire of mud waiting to catch the unwary. Since it had been several days without any measurable rainfall, it was now at its dusty best.

Several horses were tied at hitching rails, and a couple of buggies lined the street. It was deceptively quiet, the calm before the storm.

Once a month, on payday Saturday, the town would fill to overflowing as miners came down from the mountains to rejoin civilization for a day and the cowhands came in from the ranches to spend their newly earned riches. A few would make the long journey to Tucson, but most found that it wasn't necessary to ride all those miles, when Oracle offered them ample opportunity to be parted from their wages.

Jim pulled up to the mercantile and climbed from the buckboard. Taking the baby from March's arms, he held his free hand up to her. Although her eyes pleaded for a last-minute reprieve, he ignored her as he helped her from the wagon.

"You have a good look around, while I take the horses to the livery. I'll be back shortly."

"I'd rather stay with you," March stated quietly, forcing her voice not to quiver.

Jim climbed back on the buckboard and released the brake. "I'll just be a few minutes. Go see what you can find to spend your money on."

Watching the buggy disappear down the road, March felt deserted and vulnerable. She couldn't believe that after forcing her to come to town, he had then deserted her and left her to face her worst fears alone.

With chin up and the baby clutched against her chest, March opened the door. Even the knowledge that she had money in her pocket that she could spend in any manner she chose, did nothing to lighten her spirit.

The store was surprisingly well stocked. Knowing that his customers could make the journey to Tucson to purchase their needs, the store owner kept a good supply of nearly everything, thereby keeping the money in his hands rather than in the hands of the merchants of Tucson.

On the left a long counter stood in front of shelves filled with canned goods, flour, blocks of salt, and sugar. In the back was another counter for the sole purpose of providing room to view the many bolts of fabric, ribbons, and laces. In between were displays of shovels, buckets, seeds, saddles, and boots. The far side of the store was set aside for ready-made clothing, mostly for men, but with a few things for the ladies.

A few customers, mostly women, wandered through the aisles or gathered in small groups to talk. Hoping to hide behind the displays until Jim arrived, March was drawn to a dress displayed on a form. Her gaze riveted to the lovely creation, she missed the interest her arrival had produced. Curious eyes watched her as she marveled at the garment.

The dress was made of shot silk striped in colors of rose pink, green, and brown, and trimmed with black velvet bands on the hips and shoulders. White lace trimmed the bodice, the wrists, and the hem. The front of the skirt was elaborately draped to emphasize a tiny, corsetted waist, while the back jutted out with an enormous bustle.

"Isn't it lovely?" a feminine voice asked from behind her.

Blushing, March turned and met the gaze of Mazie Wright, whose husband owned the store. Tall and bone-thin with a tiny bosom, steel-gray hair, and posture so straight she looked like she'd break if she bent over, Mazie didn't appear to have a kind thought in her head. Hands shaking uncontrollably, March tightened her grasp on Jamie until she hesitantly met the warm brown eyes staring kindly into her own.

"It's beautiful," she replied quietly to the older woman.

"My husband said it was utterly ridiculous to order something like it for a store like ours, but I said that just because we lived out in the middle of nowhere, didn't mean that we had to forego fashion. One does get tired of simple, home-made clothing, and occasionally longs for French fashions."

Mazie's gaze traveled down March's simple blouse and skirt, then returned to the straw hat she wore for protection from the sun. "We have some wonderful bonnets in stock, if you're interested."

"I'd like to just look around a little first," she said hesitantly. "That is, if you don't mind?"

"Of course, I don't mind, dear. You wander around to your heart's content. But remind me to show you our newest line of ladies' stockings." Her voice lowered to a conspiratorial whisper. "You won't believe it . . . we've some in black and some with lace inserts and even stripes. They're sinfully naughty and delightfully wicked!"

"Thank you . . ."

Mazie patted March's hand. "You have a good look around, feel free to ask if you need help or want to try something on." She gazed at Jamie sleeping peacefully. "I'd be delighted to hold the baby for you while you shop."

"No!" March blushed at her reply, fearing she had insulted the lady. "I mean, thank you, but no. He's no bother."

"New mothers!" Mazie smiled warmly. "They just don't want to let the little darlings out of their sight . . . not that I blame them. If Mr. Wright and I had been blessed, I doubt that I'd ever have let someone else hold mine either. But if you change your mind, I'll be around."

March felt a little guilty as she watched the woman walk away. She'd seen the longing and quickly veiled disappointment when she'd refused Mazie's offer to watch the baby.

But she wasn't entirely sure what the woman thought of her. She'd been friendly enough, but Mrs. Wright was nearly a stranger. March knew that Mazie was aware of her past. They had never been introduced to one another, but she'd passed the woman on the street several times and had served her when working at the cafe.

But Jamie unknowingly gave March a feeling of security, and she wasn't ready to relinquish him to someone else.

It was a pleasant surprise to March when the people in the store ignored her. Several women nodded, but none made an effort to engage her in conversation. Mazie worked at the back measuring fabric for a customer, while her husband was filling an order for a miner.

Relaxing slightly, March spent long minutes pleasantly occupied by the multitude of buttons on display. There were so many different kinds and colors, some made of wood and others of bone. She delighted in the knowledge that, if she wanted to, she could even buy some that struck her fancy.

Suddenly the small ten-dollar gold piece weighed heavily in her pocket. She could buy nearly anything she wanted in the store; even something frivolous, something totally unnecessary, bought simply because she wanted it. She could pretend to be a lady of great wealth, in town for a day of leisurely shopping with nothing more important to do than to decide how to spend some money.

Torn between sparkling pink buttons made of bone and wooden ones painted to resemble a lily, March was startled by the voice she had dreaded to hear. Pretense crashed around her heels as reality took voice.

"Well . . . well . . . well, what have we here? I thought you'd skedaddled out of town with the rest of that white trash you lived with."

March turned and came face-to-face with the man who had, in more ways than one, so brutally taken her innocence. A shiver of fear raced down her spine, closely followed by one of outrage, hate, and disgust. This was the man who had betrayed her trust, who had destroyed her self-respect.

"Leave me alone," she said quietly. "I have nothing to say to you." She returned to the display of buttons until a hand fell on her shoulder, and she was rudely jerked around.

"Don't turn your back on me, bitch. I wasn't through talking to you," he snarled. "You've become pretty uppity for someone who ain't nothin' but a white-trash whore."

"I asked you to leave me alone. I have nothing to say to you, nor do I wish to hear anything you might say."

"Now ain't that too bad." The hand on her shoulder kept her from turning away, and she knew she had no choice but to hear him out.

"You always did talk pretty, and you sure did clean up good." His lecherous gaze moved lingeringly down her body. "You thought that I'd take one look at you and want to marry you?" His laugh filled the store, heightening her embarrassment. "Well, honey, you're thinkin' wrong. I done popped your cherry, and you ain't got nothin' that I want. My wife ain't going to be no white-trash whore. But I might consider tossing up your skirts, if you asked me real nice-like."

Knowing that everyone in the store could hear this loud-mouthed braggart, March's humiliation overpowered her common sense. "Your crude, boorish behavior attests to your limited intelligence, and leaves one wondering who helps you to put on your clothes each morning. I wouldn't stoop to asking you to spit on me if I was on fire."

March saw the callous anger darken his eyes,

and could have bitten off her foolish tongue. She had been determined not to cause further talk, but now he'd not settle for a quiet exit. Dread filled her that once again her involvement with him would become a topic for discussion.

"Just 'cause you got somebody else filling you, don't make you nothing more than a white-trash whore. Well, just remember, bitch, I already been where he's going, and I got there first."

His gaze lowered to the infant in her arms, and an evil grin crossed his handsome face. "I heard tell that you was goin' to have my bastard. Is that it? Let me get a look."

March turned as he reached for the baby, prepared to use any defense necessary to protect the child. She could tolerate him for herself, but he wasn't getting anywhere near Jamie.

"This is not your child," she stated in a level voice laced with the strength protecting Jamie had given her. "Your daughter died at birth. At least she was fortunate enough not to have to live with the knowledge of the man who fathered her."

She realized that she had finally pushed him too far when he doubled up his fist and drew back his arm. March braced for a blow that never landed. She sighed silently with relief as his arm was captured by a hand much stronger than his. Turned around so abruptly that he staggered to regain his balance, he came face-to-face with an opponent of superior size and strength.

"I don't hold with a man hitting a lady, boy,"

Jim stated quietly. "I think it's past time for someone to teach you some manners, Fred Hamner."

"And you think you're the one to do it?" he asked with a sneer.

"I'm the one."

Fred didn't know much about Jim Travis, other than that he was well-respected by the local ranchers. The man kept to himself, but from the look on his face he was a law unto himself. Fred knew that Jim wasn't the least bit impressed with his father's money or influence.

"She ain't no lady, Mr. Travis, and don't need your protection. Me and her got a little unfinished business to attend to. She ain't nothing but a flip-skirt filly who needs to be taught to respect her betters."

Fred didn't notice the narrowing of Jim's eyes or the tightening of his jaw. Maybe if he had, he would have turned and walked away. But the younger man could not accept that the girl who had once openly worshiped him now looked at him as if he were something lower than a snake's belly.

"Listen close, boy. I want to be sure you understand everything I say." Jim's voice lowered to an angry snarl. "The *lady* is my housekeeper, and the child in her arms is my son."

"Your housekeeper?" Fred asked with a nervous snicker. "You sure know how to pick 'em. Get a whore to clean your house while you clean hers!"

"Fred, I think we need to go out back and have a little talk." Jim shoved the younger man toward the doorway.

"Jim?" March hesitantly called.

Jim turned to her and grinned in spite of the rage that bubbled through him. This was going to feel good, he thought. At last he'd found some way to relieve some of his frustration.

"I won't leave a body, angel. Pick out your buttons and give your shopping list to Walt to fill. We'll go find us some dinner when I get back."

"Take care, Jim," she replied softly. "He isn't worth a drop of your blood."

"No, he isn't." His gaze warmed as he studied her to reassure himself that she had come to no physical harm. "But you are."

March watched him push Fred out the door and was torn between a desire to run and hide from the curious bystanders and an almost overpowering need to witness Jim's savage form of retribution.

"Men!" Mazie took March's hand in hers and gave a gentle squeeze. "I swear, they're all just overgrown boys! They think everything can be made right by fighting. Lord love 'em, they come in all battered and bruised and expect their women to think they're wonderful."

March's gaze moved wistfully toward the closed door. "Wouldn't it be nice, sometime when you're so mad you don't know what to do, to just start swinging?"

"I do," Mazie confessed in a whisper. "When

I'm so angry with Mr. Wright that I can't stand another minute of it, I start swinging cabinet doors. There is something so satisfying about the bang of a door!"

March smiled, grateful that the woman had stepped in when she so badly needed someone.

"Now, let's get back to important things like these buttons . . . and we can't forget that I promised to show you those stockings."

With her arm securely around March's shoulders, Mazie ushered her toward the back of the store. She hovered around March protectively, her look daring anyone to make a comment of which she didn't approve.

Finally relenting and letting the older woman hold Jamie, March was thoroughly intrigued by the stockings when Jim returned. She missed the exchange of looks between Mazie and Jim; his asking, hers reassuring.

"What did you find to spend your money on, angel?" Jim asked, startling March from her contemplation.

Scanning him from head to foot, she could find little evidence of his activities. His shirt had a streak of dirt that hadn't been there earlier and his newly polished boots were dusty, but she sighed with relief not to discover bruises and blood.

"What's this?" One eyebrow raised wickedly, Jim held up a gray stocking with lacy inserts at the ankle.

"That's, um . . . that's . . ." March turned a fiery red as she stuttered in reply.

"I believe you know exactly what they are, young man," Mazie scolded with a gleam twinkling in her faded brown eyes.

"I hate to correct a lady, but, Mazie, you're wrong. I've never seen anything like this." The intimate apparel was silky soft and the lacy inserts beckoned enticingly. It took little imagination to picture March's shapely legs encased in the stockings.

"Well, when you get married again, you can buy your wife a pair as a wedding present." She took the stockings from his hands and carefully replaced them.

"Would you like that for a wedding present, angel?" Jim asked softly.

Completely startled by the unexpected question, March could do little but shake her head. Since the fiasco with Fred Hamner, and with her parents as an example, marriage was not something she contemplated anytime in the near future . . . probably never.

Her amazement was overshadowed by his. Jim didn't know where that question had come from, suddenly it was spoken and now he wondered why. He had no plans to remarry, once had been enough. Melanie had proven that the West was too hard on women, the responsibilities too great.

But March deserved the chance to marry and have a family of her own. She was a great house-

keeper and a wonderful mother. He enjoyed her
sense of humor and respected her integrity. He
could relax with her and not be concerned about
saying or doing the wrong thing. She was a
friend.

Suddenly, Jim realized that he didn't like the
idea of her leaving him to marry some stranger.

"Quit embarrassing the girl, Jim Travis,"
Mazie scolded. "She's had enough turmoil this
morning without you agitating her more."

"You're right, Mazie. It's my fault, I should
never have left her alone." He took March's
hand gently in his. "I apologize, angel. I knew
how worried you were and I thought it was just
your imagination. I arrogantly assumed that
you'd come in here and nothing would happen,
that you'd be surrounded by other ladies. I
didn't figure on Fred Hamner approaching you
in public.

"I am deeply sorry that you had to face him
alone."

He was apologizing, openly, in view of several
interested spectators. March had never, ever,
heard of a man apologizing. It just didn't happen. Men made decisions, and if those decisions
were wrong, they never let anyone know they'd
made a mistake. Never.

"Did you give your list to Walt?" he asked,
before she could gather her scattered thoughts
enough to respond to his apology.

"No—" March bit her lip, after everything else
that had happened, now she had to confess her

greatest shame, that she could neither read nor write.

"Well dig it out and give it to him. We'll go over to the cafe while he fills it, then come back and pick up your order and head on home."

Taking a deep breath, she raised her head proudly. "I don't have a list."

Staring into his warm blue eyes, she couldn't do it. She just couldn't do it. "You didn't give me much time, rushing me out this morning."

It wasn't a lie, exactly, she tried to convince herself. He did announce the trip to town this morning, allowing her barely long enough to prepare herself and Jamie.

"And you didn't want to go," he said softly. Tapping the end of her nose, Jim shook his head with regret. "No problem, we'll still go eat and then come back, and you can just tell him what we need."

March turned to take Jamie from a reluctant Mazie. "Why don't you leave him here with me, while you eat?" Mazie asked hopefully. "I'd enjoy playing mama for an hour or so."

"Well . . ."

"Sounds good, Mazie," Jim interrupted before March could reply.

"He'll need to be fed soon." March wanted to grab the baby from the older woman's arms. It was silly, she knew Mazie would take excellent care of the child, but she didn't want to be parted from him even for a short time.

"That's no problem. We've got all the fixings here in the store."

March raised her gaze to Mazie's. Mazie was aware that Jamie was Jim's child, and that his mother had died giving him birth. March was about to confirm everything Fred had said, but Jamie was more important than any fear of gossip. "I nurse him."

"Well, I'd say he's a lucky baby to find a new mama so quickly after losing his own." Mazie lifted the baby to her shoulder and softly patted his back. "He's perfectly content now, and if he gets ornery before you get back, I'll just fix him a sugar-tit. Now you two go enjoy your dinner."

"Let's go, angel, before our Good Samaritan discovers exactly how noisy one little boy can be and changes her mind."

Jim placed her hand in the crook of his elbow. He was aware that she was completely off-balance. Too much had happened too quickly for her to absorb the repeated shocks. First she'd been forced to come into town, then he deserted her when she most needed his support; meeting the very man she wanted most to avoid and being accosted by him and then befriended by Mazie; admitting that she nursed Jamie and therefore confessing that she'd had a baby; being forced to leave Jamie in someone else's care for the first time . . . no wonder she followed him docilely out the door.

Her acquiescent mood lasted throughout the meal, picking at the food placed before her.

They sat so that she could look out the window toward the mercantile. After repeated attempts to start a conversation and having her reply in monosyllables, Jim gave up and quickly ate his food. The sooner he finished, the sooner they could collect Jamie and leave.

He hoped that when they were out of town, March would rediscover her fiery nature. It wasn't always comfortable to have to face her quick wit, but it was infinitely preferable to this lackluster woman sitting across from him.

He looked at her plate and saw that the food had been moved around from one place to another, but hardly eaten. "If you're finished, we can go."

"I'm finished." March neatly folded her napkin and rose.

"He's perfectly all right," Jim teased as he escorted her across the street to the store.

"I know. Mazie wouldn't let anything happen to him." Her voice lowered, and she looked beseechingly at him. "I just want to go home."

"You haven't spent your money." Jim opened the door and let her precede him inside.

March's gaze scanned the room, searching for the baby. She relaxed slightly when she saw him still cuddled contentedly in Mazie's arms, but nothing less than having him in her own embrace would satisfy her.

"I'll send a man in with our list early in the week, Walt," Jim stated as he watched March embrace the baby. "Just be sure to put in several cans of peaches. My housekeeper has a fondness for them."

"Will do, don't be so long in coming back to town. That little girl has had a raw deal. She needs to see that not everybody backs down to the Hamner's money." Walt's warm brown eyes looked with concern toward March. He lowered his voice, so that his words would go no further than Jim's ears. "Watch your back. Hamner ain't going to be happy that you went after his son. He's got a lot of people convinced that boy can't do no wrong. And now that she's embarrassed him, Fred's going to be after March."

"It's going to be a good little while before Fred is going to want to be seen in public." Rubbing his bruised knuckles, Jim's anger flared as he remembered the vicious threats the younger man had offered during their confrontation.

"I'll be careful, and I'll alert my men to keep their eyes open." His eyes darkened threateningly. "I protect my own. Anybody coming after that girl is going to have to go through me, and Breed'll be at my back."

"Good man to have guarding your back."

"The best."

Running his fingers through his thinning gray hair, Walt turned and scanned his shelves. "You say that little girl likes peaches?" He placed a can on the counter. "Take this home for her. Tell her it's a gift from me. She made my Mazie 'bout as happy as a June bug, letting her keep that boy for a spell."

Jim accepted the gift for what it was, Walt's own personal sign of approval. There would be others in town who would turn their noses up at March, but Walt and Mazie Wright wouldn't be among them.

Holding the peaches, Jim watched as March approached. With the baby nestled in her arms, she should have looked like any other young mother, radiant with the glow of motherhood. But she wore a mantle of worry on her thin shoulders that marred the gentle warmth of her face.

"Ready?" he asked quietly. At her nod, Jim wrapped his arm around her. "Let's go home, angel."

Thirteen

Too restless to sew, March sat in Jim's study flipping through a book. He worked on some papers, seeming content to ignore her for now. The circles and lines on the stiff paper seemed to tease her, taunting her with the hidden mystery that she couldn't decipher.

Frustration combined with her agitation until she felt ready to shatter into countless tiny pieces. She knew that sometime before they went to bed, Jim would expect an explanation for everything that had happened that day. That would be intolerable enough, but this waiting for him to ask was unbearable. On the trip home from town, while she waited in dreadful anticipation, he had been strangely quiet. He hadn't mentioned Fred Hamner or asked her to confirm or deny the many things Fred had said.

By the time they had reached the ranch, March's edginess had been conveyed to Jamie, and the baby had become cranky and irritable. He had cried for hours and, making matters even worse, her milk hadn't flowed easily, forcing the baby to nurse viciously and leaving her with sore nipples.

She had planned to stay in her room after feeding Jamie, but her restlessness had forced her to come downstairs or chance waking him. And as much as she loved him, right now a crying baby would be one straw too many in the haystack of misery surrounding her.

All told, it had been a miserable day, and now she sat with a book in her lap that she couldn't read, and waited for Jim to begin.

Jim watched her fidget in her chair and knew that she was unaware that her repeated sighing had attracted his attention. "March?"

Looking up from the senseless pages, she felt her breath catch. This was it, she thought with dread. Now he would learn the entire truth, and she would learn her fate. Suddenly unnaturally calm, she waited for him to continue.

"That book doesn't seem to be holding your attention tonight." Jim had watched for nearly an hour, and had seen her restlessly turning page after page.

Closing the book, March traced the lettering on the front, then held it against her chest for protection.

"Do you want to talk about today?" he asked gently.

"No, there's not much to talk about. You heard it all." She lifted her chin. "Most of it's true, but you knew that before we went to town. I can't really even blame Fred. I was stupid to think that someone like him would want to marry someone like me."

"The only stupid thing I can see about it is that someone like you would want to marry someone like him."

Her startled expression brought a gentle smile to his face. "You are a warm, intelligent, beautiful lady. He is a spoiled, loud-mouth little boy, who doesn't know the first thing about how to treat a woman."

March rose from her chair and paced the room, from door to window and then back again, the book clutched against her chest. "I am not intelligent," she muttered with disgust. "I'm about as dumb as a turkey."

"I can't argue that turkeys are dumb, but you, angel, are very intelligent."

With a snort, she turned and approached his desk. Carefully laying the book on the polished surface, her touch caressed the leather cover. Why try to hide it, she thought with resignation. Sooner or later he'd find out the truth.

The coward in her said to wait until later, but March knew that she couldn't stand the suspense of waiting. Now was the time to tell him, get everything out in the open . . . now, while she still had the courage.

"I'll tell you how intelligent I am. Not only am I dumb enough to think that a rich boy would marry me, but—"

Hesitating, she took a deep breath and forced herself to stick it out. "Do you know why I didn't have a list to give to Walt today? Well, I'll tell you," she continued before he could reply, before her confidence fled. "I didn't have a list, because I can't read or write! This book is filled with words, and I can't begin to read one of them."

Her voice was laced with the pain of her admission. "I'm stupid and ignorant, and if you want to fire me, I'll understand, I really will. I wouldn't want someone as stupid as me taking care of my child, that's for sure!"

Her anguish cut through him like a thousand cactus spines. He saw the fear in her eyes that this final confession added to everything else he had learned about her, would be the one that made him decide to release her from his employ.

Her statement had shocked him, but only because of the many hours she had spent sitting with a book on her lap. Had he given it any thought, he would have known that she had never lived in one place long enough to attend school. But she spoke so well, with a larger vocabulary than normally used by someone illiterate, that he never gave her lack of education a thought.

Unable to resist her need for reassurance, Jim rose slowly and moved toward her. Leaning against the edge of the desk, he picked up the book, flipped through it.

"There is nothing to be ashamed of because you can't read," he said softly. "I can read every word in this book, but that doesn't make me smarter than you or anyone else who can't read. The only difference between us is that I had the opportunity to go to school, while you were forced to stay at home and help with the other kids."

He grinned wickedly, "Of course, when I was a boy I thought the worst thing in life was having to go to school. I couldn't understand what was so important about learning to read or write or cipher. One year, when I was about nine, I played hooky more than I went to school." He leaned a little closer and lowered his voice, "I had the seat of my pants warmed more times that year than any other two years combined!"

He sighed silently when the beginnings of a smile tipped the corners of her mouth. "I have no intention of firing you, angel. I don't think there is anyone in the world who could love my son more or be a better mother to him, and right now he desperately needs that love."

"You mean that?" she asked earnestly.

"Every word."

Tears of relief filled her eyes, and March tried to turn her head so that he couldn't see, but his hand on her cheek stopped her. With a gentle thumb he wiped away the moisture, lightly caressing her soft skin.

"You really won't make me leave?"

"Not until you're ready to go." A smile brought a dimple to his cheek. "Besides, you're finally making decent coffee. If you go, I'll have to start over with somebody else. You wouldn't want me to go through that again, would you?"

"Jamie has a dimple just like yours," she muttered inanely, fascinated as it magically appeared and disappeared.

"Then he'll grow up to be as handsome as his father," Jim said smugly.

"Probably."

"Do you think I'm handsome, angel?" His voice was whisper-soft as he studied her slate-gray eyes.

"Yes." March was suddenly breathless again, but this time for an entirely different reason.

Jim felt a nearly overwhelming urge to kiss her, to sample her lips and discover for himself if they tasted as sweet as they looked. His hand rested on her shoulder, and he felt a shiver course through her.

It would be so easy to bend slightly, to meld his mouth to hers, to find the answer to his question. With sudden insight, Jim knew that she wouldn't fight him, that she would allow him to do as he wished . . . out of gratitude.

He didn't want her gratitude. If and when he ever kissed her, he wanted her reaction to be one of honest emotion. But lord, it wasn't easy to turn away when his entire body was aware of her.

"Would you like to learn to read?" His voice was husky as he fought, and won, the desire racing through him with the power of lightning.

"Really? Really read?" she whispered. "You'd be willing to teach me to read?"

"And write." Tapping her nose, Jim laid the book on the desk and forced himself to cross his arms over his chest. "It'll take a while, and you'll probably get pretty frustrated. You may even get mad at me a time or two, since I've been told that patience isn't my greatest virtue. But if you want it badly enough, I'll teach you."

"Read and write . . ." March wanted to dance around the room or throw her arms around him and hug him or both. "I already know some of my letters. Mama started teaching me, but then the babies came, and she was so tired by the end of the day. She wanted to, she really did, but there was so much work to do taking care of them, that there just wasn't time. I'll work really hard so that you won't be ashamed of me, I promise."

"I'm not ashamed of you, March," he said softly. "How could I ever be ashamed of someone who works as hard as you do?"

"I'll work even harder. And I won't get mad at you, I promise."

"Don't make promises that may be impossible to keep," he chuckled.

"I'll keep these. And I won't neglect Jamie. I'll only work on learning in the evenings when he's asleep, and after you've finished your paperwork. And I'll be sure all my other chores are finished. And I'll—"

"Whoa! Slow down or you'll be too tired to

get started." He pulled a piece of paper and a pencil out of his desk drawer, and ushered her toward the kitchen. "You ready for your first lesson?"

"Now? This minute? You aren't too tired? It isn't too late?"

"Now, this minute, I'm not tired, and it isn't too late. We'll start by opening that can of peaches Walt sent home for you."

"That's going to help?" Her forehead wrinkled in consternation.

"Well, it sure isn't going to hurt!"

Jim opened the can and sat it on the table. Pulling back a chair, he seated March and then himself. Slowly, with exaggerated care, he wrote a word on the blank piece of paper.

For once the peaches held little interest for March, though she did enjoy the sweet fragrance drifting from the can. She was going to learn to read, to write. Nothing in the world could compare with that. Nothing.

Jim slowly pronounced each letter as he spelled out the word. "P . . . E . . . A . . . C . . . H . . . peach." Reaching inside the can, he pulled out a piece of the fruit and held it to her mouth. "Peach," he repeated.

Her first word, what a pretty word with its swirling circles and lines. Accepting the fruit, March knew she'd never forget the wonder of the moment.

Or the man who watched her so intently, his

body tingling from the innocent touch of her lips against his fingers.

As the days became weeks, March's ability to read and write simple words grew at an amazing rate. Unaware of the new maturity and pride this accomplishment gave her, she glowed with satisfaction, catching the notice of anyone around her.

Always ready with a smile and a gentle word, she was nonetheless a fiery adversary when challenged. It sometimes seemed to her that the men on the ranch—practical jokers one and all—strove to find ways to antagonize her, just to see her temper ignite! They had come to like and respect the gentle woman who always asked about their families or girlfriends, who baked cakes for birthdays and bear-claw donuts for an unexpected treat.

Their teasing reflected their feelings for her, always good-natured, without any form of malice. March knew their goal and promised herself that next time she wouldn't be caught off guard, but always failed.

Aware of their teasing, she was unobservant of the constant protection they quietly provided.

Jim had spoken to Breed, Hank, and Woods, giving them details of her treatment at the hands of Fred Hamner. The look in Breed's silver eyes promised a swift and sure retribution, while Hank and Woods both swore that the varmint wouldn't get near their little missy again as long as they were alive to draw breath.

As word spread, in greatly abbreviated versions, the other men on the ranch became as protective. Women in the West were still in a minority, and ladies even scarcer. None doubted that March was a lady. The few who mentioned that she lived alone with Jim were politely escorted off the ranch and told not to return.

March wiped the sweat from her brow, as she stirred the pot of beans gently bubbling on the stove. She had mastered the iron monster and knew that it was cooler than cooking over an open fire, but summer had arrived, and with it came the heat of the desert.

Jim came in each evening so hungry that a stranger could be forgiven for thinking that he hadn't eaten in days. She was amazed at the massive quantities of food he consumed, while never adding an inch of fat to his lean frame.

Jamie slept contentedly in a baby bed by the open kitchen window. Nearly four months old and active enough to squirm around, March never left him without the protection of the slatted bed when he slept. Every day he seemed to do something new. Earlier that morning he had discovered his feet and had been fascinated with them, growing frustrated when first one and then the other would slip out of his grasp.

The kitchen door opened, and March turned with a ready smile to greet her unexpected guest. It wasn't unusual for her day to be interrupted by a hungry wrangler or cowhand who had come in too late to eat at the bunkhouse, or someone with a sweet tooth searching out a cookie or piece of cake. They had learned that her generosity was endless, and she was always willing to provide a meal for someone who was hungry.

There was an unnatural alertness to the man as he surveyed the room, carefully noting that it was empty of people except for the woman and infant. His rifle was held at his side, but anyone who doubted that he could shoulder it and fire in the blink of an eye was a fool.

March stared at her intruder and felt a momentary urge to panic. He was an Indian, probably a renegade, possibly escaped from the reservation and now on the run.

His slate black hair, silvered with dust, hung to his shoulders, a wide band of dirty fabric was tied at his forehead. Tan-colored pants and shirt, both as dusty as his hair, were thin from wear and covered a body that had gone without proper nourishment for a long time.

Panic fled when she noticed that his eyes strayed constantly to the pot bubbling on the stove. He was just another man, admittedly one who could be dangerous, but obviously one who had come to her in a desperate search for food.

March had been hungry enough times in her life that she couldn't turn someone away, simply because she was frightened by him.

"Come in," she said quietly, but firmly. "You're hungry?"

Moving slowly, careful to keep her hands in view at all times, she got a bowl from the cabinet. Filling it to the brim with the beans, she reached into the warming compartment of the stove for several biscuits.

"Come sit down and eat." She placed the bowl on the table, feeling ridiculous as she added a fork, spoon, and napkin. Did Indians use silverware? With a shrug, she decided that it didn't matter whether he used them or not.

The Indian glided silently to the table and slid the bowl to the side, so that he could keep careful watch on the door, the window, and the white woman.

Dipping the bread into the beans, he kept a constant watch as he rapidly consumed the meal. When the bowl was empty, March refilled it, adding several more biscuits and a large glass of cool water.

"Would you like to try some jelly on one of those biscuits?" March split one open and spooned a generous amount of jelly on it. She held it out to him, smiling when he hesitated.

"Go ahead, give it a try. I bet you'll like it."

The Indian took the biscuit and bit hesitantly into it. A look of surprised delight flickered across his face, before his countenance resumed its former suspicious expression. Smiling, March fixed him several more of the sweet treats and moved away from the table.

He was finishing his third bowl when the back door was jerked open, and March found herself facing a rifle aimed in the direction of her stomach.

"Step aside, angel," Jim ordered in a voice that brooked no argument.

She flinched as a chair crashed behind her, and she couldn't help but wonder if a rifle was also pointed at her back. If it hadn't been so frightening, the idea would be funny. March was sandwiched between the powerful weapons, making both useless as weapons against the real opponents.

"Put down your gun," March said quietly.

"Get out of the way, before you're in danger," Jim demanded again.

"*Before* I'm in danger! God have mercy, I have a rifle pointed at my belly and another one I suspect is pointed at my back, and you say *before* I'm in danger!"

"Angel—" The affectionate name was muttered through gritted teeth.

"Put down your gun, Jim Travis," she demanded before turning toward the Indian. As she had suspected, his rifle was pointed directly at her. "And you put yours down, too. No man sits at my table and then has to fight his way out of my kitchen."

Without thought to her own safety, or lack of, she approached him and pushed the barrel of the rifle toward the floor. "Sit down and finish your meal. Do you want more biscuits? I think there are a few left."

The Indian slowly lowered himself to the

chair, his glance bouncing continuously between the woman and the man. Jim lowered the point of his rifle to the floor, but his very stance stated louder than words that he was prepared to attack at the slightest provocation.

He watched with amazed irritation as March serenely served the Indian, adding jelly to the golden biscuits and offering another bowl of beans. She talked to him quietly, even though he didn't reply. But from the expressions that crossed the dark face, Jim was sure that the man understood everything she said.

Jamie squirmed in his bed, drawing everyone's attention to him. March casually walked to the baby and lifted him from the crib. He was wet and hungry, which created its own dilemma. If she left to go upstairs to change and feed him, she knew that the two men would no longer refrain from attacking each other.

The Indian was desperate and would have no concern for his own life. Therefore he would fight with every bit of knowledge and skill he possessed. Jim, on the other hand, would be fighting to protect her and the baby. He would feel no compunction about killing the intruder.

March didn't want Jim to be hurt or killed because of her. She also didn't see any reason to kill the other man, simply because hunger had driven him to her back door.

Jamie whimpered and nuzzled against her full breasts. She turned and looked at Jim, who stood on the alert just inside the back door.

4 FREE BOOKS

TO GET YOUR 4 FREE BOOKS WORTH $18.00 — MAIL IN THE FREE BOOK CERTIFICATE T O D A Y

Fill in the Free Book Certificate below, and we'll send your FREE BOOKS to you as soon as we receive it.

If the certificate is missing below, write to: Zebra Home Subscription Service, Inc., P.O. Box 5214, 120 Brighton Road, Clifton, New Jersey 07015-5214.

FREE BOOK CERTIFICATE

4 FREE BOOKS

ZEBRA HOME SUBSCRIPTION SERVICE, INC.

YES! Please start my subscription to Zebra Historical Romances and send me my first 4 books absolutely FREE. I understand that each month I may preview four new Zebra Historical Romances free for 10 days. If I'm not satisfied with them, I may return the four books within 10 days and owe nothing. Otherwise, I will pay the low preferred subscriber's price of just $3.75 each; a total of $15.00, *a savings off the publisher's price of $3.00.* I may return any shipment and I may cancel this subscription at any time. There is no obligation to buy any shipment and there are no shipping, handling or other hidden charges. Regardless of what I decide, the four free books are mine to keep.

NAME

ADDRESS _____ APT _____

CITY _____ STATE _____ ZIP _____

TELEPHONE
(   )

SIGNATURE _____
(if under 18, parent or guardian must sign)

Terms, offer and prices subject to change without notice. Subscription subject to acceptance by Zebra Books. Zebra Books reserves the right to reject any order or cancel any subscription.

ZB0794

GET
FOUR
FREE
BOOKS
(AN $18.00 VALUE)

ZEBRA HOME SUBSCRIPTION
SERVICE, INC.
120 BRIGHTON ROAD
P.O. Box 5214
CLIFTON, NEW JERSEY 07015-5214

She'd never seen such determination on his face, even during his confrontation with Fred Hamner.

Never patient in the face of hunger and uncomfortable with a wet bottom, Jamie's whimper became a cry as he arched against her.

"Take the baby upstairs," Jim instructed gruffly.

"No." She hugged the child tightly. "If I leave this room, I have no doubt that you two will try to kill each other."

"March, do as you were told!"

"No," she repeated defiantly. "I'll not have you two fighting in my kitchen, tearing everything apart and leaving the mess for me to clean up."

"A woman should do as her man tells her," the Indian said quietly.

"A great time for you to prove that you know English," March muttered as she patted the baby's back.

A twinkle entered the black eyes as the Indian crossed his arms over his chest, his rifle clutched in his hand. His gaze moved across the room to Jim. "She is a giving woman, sharing her food with others in need, and I think she is a good mother, but is she always so sure to have her own way?"

Jim nodded in response. "She is generous to a fault, and my son could not have a better mother. But I have an old mule out back who's only half as stubborn, and, until now, he's the most stubborn creature I've ever seen."

"If I were not running from your army, I would trade for her. She would be a wife to be proud of."

"If it weren't for my son's need of her, I just might consider your trade," Jim replied solemnly.

"Well, I never—I can't believe—" stammering with anger, March stamped her foot on the hard brick floor. "Trade for me? Trade for me! You arrogant . . . overbearing . . . *men!*" She said the word as if it were the greatest insult in the world.

"I refuse to stay here and listen to another minute of you talking like I'm some mare you want to possess. If you two want to kill each other, go ahead, you have my permission. I won't try to stop you. But before you die, you had better take the time to clean up the mess you've made in my kitchen, or so help me I'll . . . I'll . . . well, I'm not sure what I'll do, but you won't like it!"

Clutching the baby and her remaining dignity to her, March walked past the two men and rapidly ascended the stairs. She was so angry that she slammed the bedroom door, before she realized that she wouldn't be able to hear what was happening in the kitchen.

Well, let them kill each other, she fumed as she changed Jamie's wet towel. Let them beat on each other until their fists are bloody and their bones are broken. She had done nothing more than to offer food to a hungry man. If they couldn't live with that, that was their problem.

In the kitchen Jim casually leaned his rifle against the wall. It was a risk, but he didn't think that the other man would attack unless pushed into a corner.

"Do you need some supplies to take with you?" Jim asked quietly.

"My journey was unplanned. The chance to go was there, so I left. It was a foolish thing to do, but I could no longer live on the place the white man says I must live. There is no food, the water is bad, and the young children cry for their mothers who have died."

"It is wrong for your people to suffer," Jim agreed. "I would invite you to stay here, to make this your home. But the army would come and take you away, and then they would punish me. I can, however, give you a grubstake and a good horse." A smile creased his face. "If questioned, I can always claim that the horse got lost. Where will you go?"

"Some of my people still roam free in the mountains. I will try to find them."

"I wish you luck. If the army comes, I'll tell them you headed east."

"I think you are a good man. You protect your woman and child, and have the wisdom of a warrior. We could be friends."

"Another time, another place, I think we would be as brothers," Jim agreed somberly.

"But now you must hurry before the army picks up your trail."

Dark eyes traveled up the stairs. "She is a good woman, a gentle woman. Protect her from those who would use that against her."

"I will."

"Maybe I will return with many horses, and we will trade."

"No, my friend." His gaze also traveled to the stairs. He knew that March would be sitting in the rocking chair, lovingly nursing his son. Her voice would be gentle as she spoke to the baby, and the look on her face would be so filled with love that it was impossible to describe.

"You could come back with every horse ever to roam the desert, and you would still not have enough. She is my woman."

Fourteen

Jim waited patiently at the buckboard for March. They were heading into town for the day. Since the confrontation with Fred Hamner they had made the trip several times, but this one was special. In fact, this time she was so excited about going that she had been all thumbs as she tried to ready the baby.

He knew that some of her excitement stemmed from the fact that she had written the supply list last night, with only a little help from him. He was pleased, but not surprised, at her progress with reading and writing. Never before had he seen someone so determined to learn, and that determination was paying off. She could now read simple books and could write in a childish scrawl that was improving day by day.

The only problem he could see was her spelling. It was atrocious. She spelled words by sound, totally ignoring the fact that some words had silent letters, and that she sometimes mispronounced words due to her gentle southern accent. Some of her errors were so bad that he wasn't able to figure out what the word was supposed to be.

Jim grinned when he remembered their discussion the night before over a word. He still wasn't convinced that she believed him when he had told her that shoe was not spelled with a *u*.

He suspected that March and Mazie Wright, who had befriended the younger woman, had some plans up their sleeves for the Fourth of July celebration. Jim was so pleased that Mazie had taken March under her protective wing in such a motherly fashion, that he could overlook her occasionally autocratic demeanor. March missed her mother, though she rarely mentioned it, and she badly needed a woman friend. Mazie willingly filled both positions.

He hadn't apologized to March yet for his reaction the previous afternoon, when he'd walked into the kitchen and found the Indian eating at his table. Sometime during the long trip to town, he hoped to find the perfect opportunity to try to explain to her the danger she faced by so generously feeding total strangers. There were far too many drifters roaming around for her to continue opening her kitchen to them.

Not that it would do much good, he acknowledged wryly. March was too intimately aware of hunger to let anyone else do without, if she was in a position to prevent it. Maybe he'd be wiser to buy her a single-shot derringer that would fit into her apron pocket. She probably wouldn't be able to hit anything with it, but the noise alone would send someone to investigate.

He grinned when he thought of her actually shooting someone. She'd be on her knees trying to patch them up before help could arrive.

His expression sobered as he watched Breed approach. The grim look on the foreman's face warned Jim that he wasn't going to like what the man had to tell him.

"We've found three more." Breed stopped in front of Jim, his forbidding expression deepening.

"Like the others?" Jim questioned.

"Two cows and a calf, shot once through the head. Figure it happened sometime early yesterday or the afternoon before. Another calf was still beside its mama. We heard it crying, and that's how we found them. The calf was too far gone to save. I had to put it down."

"Damn!" Jim swore softly. Someone was almost systematically killing his herd. One of the cowhands had discovered the first carcass a couple of weeks earlier. Since that time, they had found eighteen more. Breed's latest find increased the count to twenty-one, plus the calf that had had to be destroyed.

Every rancher expected to lose a percentage of animals each season; the very young or the older ones who couldn't survive the stress of a hard winter or hot summer. A few were killed occasionally by an itinerant family, or by a roving band of Indians on the run from the army. Jim could accept and even tolerate those losses, because the animals provided sustenance. So far, except for two or three calves, all of the dead animals had been young cows in prime breeding condition. These weren't being killed for food; the carcasses were left where they fell.

"Did you find a trail?"

"Like all the others, nothing."

Jim knew that Breed was frustrated because he couldn't pick up a trail on the man or men doing the killing. They suspected that it was only one man, using a powerful rifle, perhaps a Sharps or a Winchester, that let him shoot at the animals from such a long range that no traces of his passing were left for evidence.

"Have any of the men heard anything in town?"

Breed shook his head. "Nobody's talking about killings going on at other ranches, and nobody's bragging about killing your stock. Whoever's doing it seems to have a grudge against you and means to make you suffer."

The only man Jim could think of who might have hard feelings against him was Fred Hamner, but Fred wasn't in the area. The elder Hamner had refused to join the rancher's consortium, claiming that he didn't want to lend his name to smaller outfits who were destined to go under. He had sent Fred East to locate outlets for his herd this fall.

"We're going to have to move them closer in," Jim stated quietly. He hated to move the herd, but he knew of no other way to protect them. "And we'll increase our night watch."

"I started the men on it before I came in."

"Good, that'll save some time." The horses hitched to the buckboard moved restlessly, reminding him of the planned trip to town.

He hated to disappoint March, but it would have to be postponed until another day. He couldn't very well go into town and leave his men to do the work of rounding up the livestock.

"I'll change clothes and meet you at the barn." Without waiting for a reply, Jim turned and headed for the house.

He heard March humming cheerfully when he entered the kitchen, and found her packing a basket with food for their noonday meal. She smiled merrily when she saw him.

" 'Bout ready. All I need to do is gather up your son and all his belongings, and we can leave."

"We're going to have to go another day, angel," he said softly, watching the smile leave her face. "There's been some trouble and I'm needed here."

"Trouble?" March stopped tucking the towel in around the edge of the basket. "What kind of trouble?"

"Nothing serious," he replied lightly. "There's always something coming up unexpectedly on any ranch operation and sometimes only the boss can make the necessary decisions."

He began unbuttoning his shirt as he walked

past her. "I'm sorry to disappoint you. I know how much you looked forward to the day in town. We'll go tomorrow or the next day."

"Don't worry about me. It's not your fault that you're needed here."

Jim had seen her quickly masked disappointment, and his respect for her increased when she didn't try to force him to change his mind. He'd make it up to her, he decided, as he climbed the stairs. Maybe he'd take her into Tucson. They could make it an overnight trip and he'd take her to supper at the nicest restaurant in town.

When he returned to the kitchen March was talking with Hank. Jim stopped long enough to ask the old man to unhitch the team from the buckboard, and to tell March not to wait supper for him. Locating several hundred head of cattle strung out over several hundred acres of land was going to take some time. And a lot of patience.

"Leave the wagon, Hank," March instructed as Jim walked out of sight. "I think I'll just go ahead into town on my own."

"I ain't thinking the boss is gonna be happy 'bout that, little missy," Hank replied.

"Hank, I've been to town many times by myself."

"Not since you've worked here," he reminded her.

"That's true, however, it doesn't change the fact that I *have* gone by myself and I've never had any problem. There's no reason for me not to go this time, too."

He removed his hat and scratched his head, carefully smoothing down the ruffled hair. "Walp, if'en you're set on goin', ain't no reason why I can't go with you. Ain't much goin' on here that I'll be missed for, and I ain't been to town since that youn'en were a few days old."

March liked the old man and found him pleasant company. It wouldn't be a hardship to make the trip with him. He always had stories to tell, many of which she decided he made up as he went.

"If you're sure, I'd welcome your company. But I don't want to pull you away from something you're supposed to be doing. I'd really looked forward to going today because Walt promised he'd have some dibs and hens waiting for me. He might sell them to someone else if I don't come claim them."

"What'ja gonna do with dibs and hens? This ain't no farm, it's a ranch."

"Eggs and fried chicken?" she asked with a smile. "You do like fried chicken, don't you?"

Eagerness lit his faded eyes as he placed his hat back on his head. "What'ja waitin' for, missy? If 'en you're willin' to make up some fried chicken, I'm willin' to eat it. It's been a long time since I've sunk these old teeth into fried chicken. Why I 'members when . . ."

March handed him the lunch basket and picked

up Jamie. It would be a pleasant trip into town, Hank's stories assured that.

"... You ain't never seen such nonesuch! And then that ole mule finally backs up right on Woods's foot!" Thoroughly enjoying his own story, Hank's throaty laugh ended with a cough as he tried to regain enough control to finish. "I'll tell you what, missy, I ain't heard such cater-waulin' since—"

Lulled by the rhythmic clopping of the horses' hooves as they struck the hardened ground and the jingle-jangle of the rigging on the buck-board, March was unprepared when the sound of a gunshot pierced the quiet, silencing Hank and spooking the horses into a run. Even as she realized that someone had shot at them, Hank began to slump to the side; the reins slipped from his grasp.

March grabbed for the reins as she tried to keep the old man from sliding from the bounc-ing seat. Glancing quickly at her feet to reassure herself that Jamie was secure in his box on the floor, she fought to slow the frightened horses.

Knowing that by stopping the team she was giving their attacker another clear shot, March momentarily debated letting them run. But Hank had been hit by the bullet and was dead-weight against her, giving her no real choice. She couldn't continue to support him and hope to hold the horses back, and she desperately needed to know how badly he was hurt. She wouldn't let herself even consider the possibility that he was dead.

Gritting her teeth, she used her meager strength against the power of the team, finally bringing them to a halt. Far from calmed, the horses stood restlessly, their sides heaving as they stomped their hooves in agitation.

Tying the reins around the brake handle, she glanced first at Jamie to find that he had slept through the wild ride, then turned her attention to Hank. Blood darkened the front of his shirt, and blared scarlet on the white of her blouse where he had leaned against her.

Sliding forward, she lowered him onto the seat. Reaching into the basket that contained Jamie's things, she found a towel and ripped open Hank's shirt. Folding the towel into a pad, March pressed it against his wound, appalled by the amount of blood he had lost.

"Hank, please don't be dead," she whispered in a prayer. "You don't deserve to die like this. Please, Hank."

"If he ain't dead yet, I got another bullet with his name on it."

Fighting to control the rage that flooded through her, March turned and met the grinning face she had once thought so handsome.

"Why?" she said through clenched teeth.

"Get down." If Fred heard her or understood the question, he gave no sign as he motioned for her to get off the buckboard.

"No." The refusal was a snarl of powerless fury.

Fred smiled and pushed his hat back from his eyes. "Get down, whore, or I'll shoot him again. And if you still refuse, that kid will be next."

"You bastard."

"Wrong, I got me a daddy; a rich, powerful daddy." His voice was almost pleasant as he motioned toward the ground. "Now get down. I'm getting tired of waiting."

Her hair had come loose from the bun at the nape of her neck, and blew freely in the gentle breeze. Pushing it from her face, March slowly climbed to her feet and stepped from the wagon.

"Get the brat," Fred instructed, waving his rifle in her face as a reminder of his threat.

"Why?"

" 'Cause you're going with me."

"But why take the baby?" The road to town was heavily traveled, and while there was danger in letting Jamie stay unattended in the buckboard, he'd probably be found in a short time. She wasn't so sure he'd be safe if she kept him with her.

"You're taking the baby because as long as you've got him to worry about I don't think you'll be giving me any trouble. You'll do everything I say—or he dies."

He was right, there was nothing she wouldn't do to prevent Jamie from being harmed. And her chances for escape, if escape ever became possible, were greatly reduced with the infant to worry about.

"Leave him here, I'll come quietly."

"Oh, you'll come quietly," he smirked, cocking the rifle and pointing it at Hank, "or the old man is dead."

"Why are you doing this?"

"You owe me, bitch. I spent nearly a month in bed, because of the beating your friend gave me. Now get the kid, you've wasted enough time."

March untied the thongs that laced the box where Jamie slept. Unfolding a small blanket, she placed several of his towels in the center, tied it closed, and slung it over her shoulder.

"Girl . . ." It was barely a whisper of sound, loud enough for only her to hear as she bent to free Jamie from his box. "Sorry, gal . . ."

Afraid that Fred would shoot Hank again, if he realized that the old man was conscious, March didn't reply. Her brief smile was meant to be reassuring, as she turned away with the baby in her arms and the make-do bag on her shoulder.

"I'm ready, Fred Hamner," she said clearly. "If you insist on doing this, then I'd say you're about to make a mistake that you'll regret the rest of your life, brief though it will be. There is a law against kidnapping, you know."

"Shut up!" He put the rifle in the saddle scabbard and reached for the baby. "Hand me the kid. I'll hold him, while you climb up behind me. We'll be miles away from here before they find the wagon."

March had no choice but to comply. Hank's and Jamie's lives depended on her doing as he said. But as she handed the infant to Fred, she made a silent promise to herself that he would deeply regret this someday.

With Jamie in his grasp and March behind him on the horse, Fred reached over and untied the reins on the buckboard. Slapping his hat against the rump of the nearest horse, he startled them enough to get them running.

"Oh, God, no," March murmured as she saw Hank slip to the floor. The horses were running wild, and she could only pray that they would come to a halt before further tragedy happened.

"He ain't gonna help none, so you can quit praying . . . if a whore knows how to pray." With a chuckle, he turned the horse toward the desert.

The sun blazed down on her uncovered head, but the sweat disappeared as quickly as it came. For nearly two hours Fred traveled at a killing pace, until the horse was lathered and it audibly gulped for each breath.

"If you don't slow down, we're going to be walking." As much as she hated sitting so closely behind him, she hated the thought of being on foot even more.

"We ain't going much farther. He'll just have to make it."

"What are you going to do if he doesn't? Shoot him, too?"

"Shut up! If I want your opinions, I'll ask for them. But don't hold your breath, any opinion from a whore ain't worth shit."

March obediently closed her mouth, but only because it suited her. She worried that if she further agitated Fred, he might do something that she'd regret. As long as he held Jamie in his arms, she would do nothing to instigate his anger.

She had tried several times to look around his shoulder to reassure herself that Jamie was covered from the sun, but her position on the back of the horse was too precarious to give her the necessary leverage. The baby had been quiet, almost too quiet, but she refused to let herself worry that something might be wrong with him.

Except for the mountains in the distance, the land looked deceptively flat. That they had been riding up a gentle incline was proven as the roof of a shack came into sight. March soon recognized the structure, and couldn't believe that this was Fred's intended destination. Surely he didn't think he'd get away with keeping her on Jim's own land!

"I thought it was fitting," Fred smirked, as he pulled up beside the dilapidated line shack that had been her home for several months. "No one will think of looking for you here. I really wanted to take you back to our picnic grounds," he grinned, referring to the spot beside the river where she had innocently promised love, but had learned betrayal. "But then I got to thinking that someone might come along and ruin my plans."

"You're a bigger fool than I thought," she muttered, regretting her quick tongue when his body stiffened.

"Get down!" he snarled.

March slid from the back of the horse, her legs buckling briefly.

"Catch." The single word was the only warning she had as Fred smiled evilly and literally dropped the baby into her arms. Catching him, she hugged him tightly, lifting the blanket from his face to discover alert blue eyes. Usually unhappy with his face covered, it was as if the baby understood the danger they faced and hadn't complained.

"Hello, sweetheart," March murmured, as she loosened the blanket around him. It was a wonder that he hadn't smothered in its folds.

Fred climbed from the horse as she walked toward the cabin. Trying to ignore memories of her family as she had last seen them, she pushed open the door. The inside was stifling hot, but at least it did provide some protection from the sun.

She wasn't surprised to discover that the room was totally bare, even the bed and bed frame were gone. Her father had been his usual thorough self, taking everything that wasn't nailed down.

In a corner away from the open door, March made a pad out of the blanket for Jamie and efficiently changed his wet towel. Leaving him on the floor wasn't the best solution, but at least he wasn't scooting around too much yet. If she kept an eye on him, he should be safe enough.

"Get out here, bitch," Fred ordered, his eyes gleaming savagely as he watched her. "Unsaddle my horse and rub him down." He threw the reins at her and lowered himself to the ground. Leaning against the side of the cabin with the rifle across his knees, he waited, as if anticipating her refusal.

Knowing that exercise would work the kinks out of her sore muscles, she approached the animal and patted his lathered neck. Woods had once told her that you could judge a man by the way he took care of his horse. From the look of the abused animal, anyone could guess that Fred wasn't worth the price of a bullet to kill him.

"What do you hope to accomplish with this . . . this stupidity?" March grunted as she caught the heavy, silver-inlaid saddle as it slid from the horse.

Enjoying his power over his helpless victim, Fred tilted his hat back and looked toward the sky. "When you're done with that, you can fix my dinner."

"He'll find you, you know." She rubbed the horse with the saddle blanket. "You took his son, and he'll come looking."

"Let him come." Fred stroked the butt of the rifle. "I owe him. Yes, siree, let him come."

"Is it worth getting hanged?"

"I ain't the one who's gonna die," Fred bragged confidently. "I'll be long gone before they find you, and they ain't never going to know that it was me. Everybody saw me leave a few weeks back on my way East. I even made it a point to talk to a few people in Tucson, before the train pulled out.

"What they don't know is that I got off in Phoenix, bought that nag out there, and came back here. I been having some fun thinning out your boss's herd a little. That Indian of his ain't too happy that he couldn't find me, but I can be real smart.

"I been getting them off guard, so I could get to you. It kinda surprised me when you headed into town today with just that old man. I thought I'd have a tolerable wait before I could get you, and here you just go and walk into my arms."

"Hank knows it was you."

"Hank? The old man I shot?" At her nod of confirmation, he snickered. "He's dead by now. But even if he ain't, who's going to believe him? It'll be my word against his, and nobody around here is going to cross me, or they'll have to answer to my daddy. When a man's got money, he can get away with most anything, if he's careful."

"There's not enough money in the world to buy your freedom when you commit murder."

"Gotta get caught first," he said conversationally. "Why, when I get home from back East, and hear tell how you and Jim Travis was found dead right here at his own line shack, I'll be really sad. Won't nobody know that I was involved."

Jamie began to whimper with hunger as March led the tired horse toward the small corral beside the shack. His whimper quickly became a full-blown bawl when his demands weren't instantly met. He was a good-natured baby, crying only when hungry or wet, but he expected immediate attention then.

"Shut that kid up, or I will." Fred raised the rifle threateningly.

"He's hungry. He'll quiet down and go back to sleep as soon as I feed him." March hurried into the shack and knelt beside Jamie. She turned her back to Fred as she opened her blouse.

"Turn around. I wanna watch him chew on you a little."

March recognized the lust in his voice, and knew that she was helpless to protect herself should he decide to attack her. Shielding her breast as best she could with the edge of her blouse, she reluctantly turned and leaned against the wall.

Jamie nursed happily, his tiny hand kneading the soft flesh. Rubbing the back of his hand over his mouth, Fred's eyes hungrily ate the sight of her. Framed in the doorway, with the sun at his back and the rifle hanging loosely from his hand, he appeared larger than normal, and suddenly March knew that he intended to hurt her as much as possible before he killed her. She had been instrumental in his humiliation, and he wouldn't let her live.

"Ain't that pretty," he drawled sarcastically. "Don't let the brat take it all. Ain't never had me a taste of tit-milk, but I'm thinking I'm gonna like it.

"Sure didn't get much from you the first time. Paid that old man fifty dollars just to bust your cherry, so I figure you owe me more. You're a whore born, and with just a little learnin', you'll take to it real good." Leaning the rifle against the wall outside of the door, Fred slowly approached her. "I was gonna wait until later for this, but shit, why not do it now, and then again later? Get that kid off of your tit, it's my turn."

March hesitated, wondering frantically how to prevent him from raping her. She had no doubt that he would be brutal in his possession, deriving pleasure from her pain. A knot of fear resting just beneath her heart started to grow, threatening to suffocate her.

The bright light from the doorway suddenly dimmed, leaving the room in deep shadows. Intent on his victim, Fred was slow to react. It was only when he saw the smile flit across March's face that he realized someone was at the door. Remembering that he had left his gun outside, he reached for the knife on his thigh.

At first March thought that Jim or possibly Breed had discovered her location, but a quick study of the new arrival showed that he was much smaller than either of the other two men.

March dislodged Jamie from her breast, and discreetly covered herself. Standing slowly, she slid along the wall so that she was no longer behind Fred. If the unknown man at the door decided to shoot, she didn't want to be in the line of fire.

There was something about the new arrival, something familiar. The brightness at his back prevented her from seeing his face, but his stillness and the long hair ruffling in the breeze brought back a memory.

"Well hello." March greeted the newcomer with a smile of relief when she recognized him.

A nod in her direction was his only response, as his alert gaze remained on Fred.

Fifteen

"You ain't got no business here, Injun, so just turn your butt around and head back to the reservation, or I'll have to report you to the sheriff."

Eyes narrowing as he judged the distance to the door, Fred bounced the knife in his hand a few times, testing its weight. He was pretty good with a knife, had even won more than his share of impromptu contests with some of the men on the ranch from time to time. Of course, he was better with a rifle, but he figured he was good enough with the knife that the Indian stood little chance. The more he thought about it, the more he began to relish seeing the handle of his knife protruding from the chest of the red man.

" 'Course, no one would blame me, if you was to die before that happened . . . just one more dead Injun for the buzzards to pick clean."

Fred wasn't afraid of this Indian or any other, never had been. All of his life he'd heard the horror stories about the atrocities credited to the Indian, but he figured they were works of imagination rather than real events. The few Indians he'd been around were too stupid and too scared to attack the son of such a wealthy rancher. They knew that if they harmed him, then they would be hunted down like dogs and hung from the nearest branch.

The Indian ignored the white man's blustering. He was like so many other white men who thought they owned the earth, who were too selfish in their demands to share with another. They were successfully destroying a way of life his people had known for centuries, were in fact killing his people in their greed.

He should have been miles away by now, but last night he'd been visited by a vision. His sleep had been restless, every night sound magnified in the silence. He couldn't even swear that he had slept, except that in his vision the sun was bright in the sky, and he was on the horse the white man had given to him.

A wolf, old and weary from many battles, but still magnificent in his pride, had stopped in front of him. His horse had stood quietly, as the old one had paced back and forth several times, and then had leisurely turned in the opposite direction and taken several steps. He turned occasionally, as if to assure himself that his human companion was following.

Upon waking the vision was still with him. He had seen too many visions to doubt the wisdom of following this one. For some reason the old wolf had called for him to return, so he had turned away from the mountains that had been his destination, and had headed back toward the ranch he had just left. He knew that only time would explain.

At mid-morning he had seen the man and woman racing across the desert on the back of a single horse, and had been intrigued when the sun had shone on the long golden hair of the woman. It had reminded him of the white woman who only the afternoon before had filled his hunger for food, and created a hunger of a different sort. So he had followed them at a distance, staying out of sight, but never losing their trail.

Now the Indian looked briefly at March, and recognized the woman he would always think of as Giving Woman. His dark eyes narrowed at the sight of the blood on her blouse.

"You are hurt?" he asked quietly.

"No," she replied, as she plucked at the stiff material. "It is the blood of the man who was with me and was shot by this one."

"Get out of here, Injun," Fred snarled. "I ain't gonna tell you again."

"The child is unharmed?"

"He's fine."

"You agreed to come with him?"

"No . . . he stopped my wagon, shot my friend, and forced the baby and me to come with him."

Satisfied that the woman and child were all right, he turned his attention to Fred. "I will take Giving Woman and her child back to her man."

"Giving Woman! That's a hoot! You sure did name her right. Promise her anything and she'll give everything," Fred smirked.

He turned the knife so that the tip was held between two fingers. "But you ain't taking them nowhere. Maybe you didn't hear me right, Injun, so I'll tell you one more time, real slow-like so that you can understand. Get . . . out . . . of . . . here! This ain't none of your business, and I don't want to see your ugly face again."

He was a warrior, with scars on both body and soul, who had followed his war chief into many battles. He was prepared when Fred threw the knife. It lodged with a sharp *twang* of sound in the doorframe beside the Indian's head.

But Fred never saw it sink into the wood. The sound of the rifle reverberated around the tiny cabin, startling Jamie and making him scream in fright. March watched Fred clutch his chest, as the blood poured between his fingers. His lips moved, but whatever he had been trying to say was lost forever, as he crumbled into a heap on the floor.

"Come." The Indian motioned to March.

Stepping carefully around Fred's body, she wondered briefly if she were becoming a bitter woman. She felt no regret that he was dead, only that he hadn't died a little slower.

"I can wait here," she said when she reached

the Indian. "Surely the sound of the rifle will draw someone's attention."

"No, there is danger here for you alone."

With an ease learned so long ago that it was a faded memory, the Indian swung onto the horse and held his hand out to her.

"Wait, I need to get the baby's things."

"Give me the little one, I will hold him.

Without concern for Jamie's safety, March handed him to the Indian and stepped around Fred's body to retrieve the bundle of towels. She returned outside and was pulled onto the back of the horse.

When Jamie was secured between their bodies, the Indian turned the horse. With a battle whoop that sent a chill of apprehension down March's back, he dug his heels into the animal's side.

In a matter of minutes, March realized that they weren't heading toward the ranch. In fact, she was appalled to discover that she no longer knew exactly in which direction the ranch was located.

"Aren't we going the wrong way?" she asked, pushing the hair out of her face.

When he didn't answer, she decided that he hadn't heard her, even though a little niggling of fear told her that he had. She could find no reason for the twisting, turning route. Several times he circled back on his own trail, and once she thought she saw the roof of the line shack.

Finally, when she began to think he had lost

all sense of direction, he turned toward the mountains in the distance. Several times March tried to talk to him but when he remained quiet, she finally grew silent.

She didn't know what he was planning, but as the afternoon waned she began to wonder if she had traded one kidnapper for another . . . had gone from the clinging coils of the rattlesnake to the clamping jaws of the wolf. For there was no doubt, of the two men, this one was by far the most dangerous.

But while she had constantly been aware of a gnawing sense of fear while with Fred, she felt security with the Indian. Something, perhaps his gentleness when handling Jamie, reassured her that he didn't intend to harm her.

Nor, she began to think, did he intend to return her to the ranch.

Just before sunset, when March knew she couldn't stay on the horse much longer, he stopped at a small creek. Swinging his leg over the horse's neck, he gracefully slid to the ground. Without a word, he held his hands up for the baby. March handed Jamie down to him and watched as he was cradled securely in confident arms. Gurgling in a language only he understood, Jamie reached for the bright-colored beads resting on the man's chest.

March looked down, way down, and knew her dismount from the horse would in no way resemble his graceful descent. She'd be lucky if she didn't land on her face. Her legs were numb from the knees down, and were riddled with pain from the knees up.

"Come." Shifting Jamie, he held up his free hand, waiting for her to dismount.

"I don't think I can. My feet are gone."

A smile broke his sober countenance. "They are still at the end of your legs," he replied with a chuckle. "Come, Giving Woman, I won't let you fall too far."

"How reassuring." March wrinkled her nose in distaste. "It would have been much more confidence-inspiring if you hadn't added the 'too far' part of that statement."

"The ground is soft."

"Easy for you to say," she muttered, swinging her leg painfully over the horse. "You aren't the one who's about to land on your bottom."

"Your son is waiting. Surely the mother of this fine warrior isn't afraid of falling."

"No, I'm not afraid of falling. It's the landing that has me bothered."

Leaning over slightly, March placed her hands on his shoulders. There was no other way to do it, she decided, but to slide off and hope for the best.

As she made the final move, a strong arm came around her back. When her feet touched the ground, March bit back a moan of agony as pain shot up to her hips. He held her until she was sure her legs would support her.

Walking like an old woman—or someone who had been on a horse for hours—March waddled toward the tiny stream. It was only a couple of inches deep; kneeling carefully, she scooped some onto her face. The water was tepid after the heat of the day, but felt wonderfully refreshing on the tender skin of her face and neck.

The Indian waited patiently with a fretting Jamie in his arms, until she climbed back to her feet.

"The little warrior is hungry," he commented as he handed the child to her.

"That is nothing unusual. This boy was born hungry and hasn't filled up yet."

He led the horse to the water as March looked around for someplace private to nurse Jamie. She just wasn't accustomed to baring her breast to someone else's gaze, but the only place that offered her any kind of shelter was a towering saguaro cactus.

As Jamie grew more strident in his demand and the Indian continued to ignore her, March realized that she had no choice. Turning her back, she reluctantly opened her bloodstained shirt. As she knew it would, the baby's cry ceased the minute his lips closed greedily around her nipple.

March found a fairly level bit of ground and slowly sank to the sand. She studied Jamie, relieved to find that he had suffered no ill effects from their eventful day. His face was red, but more from his display of temper than from the sun. Blue eyes gazed trustingly up at her as a small hand reached for her face. March nibbled lovingly on his tiny fingers and smoothed his ruffled hair.

"You are a loving mother," the Indian said quietly, coming to sit across from her. "That is good. A child should know that his mother loves him."

March's sunburned face heated with embarrassment as he watched her nurse the baby. He seemed unaffected by her display, as if it was something he had witnessed many times.

"I don't know your name," she muttered, hoping to distract him.

His dark eyes traveled up to hers. "Until I went to the reservation, I was called One Who Runs With the Light. But your people decided that all Indians should have a white man name and so I was called Charles Smith."

"Charles Smith?" March didn't attempt to hide her grin at the thought of this man being called Charles. It just didn't fit.

"It is a funny name?" he asked seriously. "I was told by many that it was a good name."

"Oh, Charles Smith is a perfectly fine name, a strong, proud name. But it just doesn't suit you."

"It was not my choice." His head rose proudly, and March knew she had offended him.

"I'm sorry, I wasn't making fun, but you have such a wonderful name, One Who Runs With the Light, even if it is a mouthful."

"Mouthful? Your mouth is full when you say

my name?" Perplexity crossed the dark face as he tried to understand her.

"What I mean is, most white people have two names like Charles Smith. Or like mine, March Evans, or the baby, who is Jamie Travis. One Who Runs With the Light isn't very easy to say quickly."

"What would you have me called, March Evans?"

March knew the question was one of seriousness for him, one that would perhaps stay with him as he learned to live in a white man's world. "I think I would call you Light," she finally replied quietly. "Light Smith."

He nodded, the name seeming to settle comfortably on his shoulders. "You have given me a white man's name, as I have given you an Indian name—Giving Woman."

"Giving Woman . . . that's lovely, thank you."

Again he nodded and then looked back at Jamie. "We will eat, and then we will ride more."

"More?" March bit back a moan. No way would she get back on that horse!

"Until the sun is gone from the sky. I have ridden slowly because of care for you and your son, so we still have many miles to go before we reach the safety of the mountains."

"Ah . . . Light, I think it's time for us to discuss our destination. I don't want to go to the mountains." She watched as a shutter dropped over his face, until his friendly expression might never have been.

"You will go."

"Even if I don't want to?"

He rose to his feet and went to the horse. Digging through the saddlebags, he pulled out a once-clean white cloth that was now browned with dust. March recognized one of the napkins from her kitchen, and was amazed when he opened it and saw that it held several of her biscuits.

Of course, she thought as she took one of the biscuits he offered, Jim had given him some provisions, as well as the horse and saddle.

"I have given it much thought," Light stated as he chewed. "You will be my woman, and your son will grow to be a fine warrior."

Now that her fear was put into words, March found that she felt honored by his choice, rather than terrified. However, that didn't change her desire to return to the ranch.

"Thank you, I'm sure it is an honor to be your woman, but I'd really rather go home."

"You can not become my wife until you are no longer feeding your son," he continued, completely ignoring her protest. "It will give you time to learn our ways."

This wasn't going to be easy, changing his mind. He appeared to be on the rather stubborn side. "Ah . . . you mustn't think I'm not appreciative of your generous offer, but I really must insist that you take me home."

"Finish your task so that we can leave." He

chewed his biscuit washing it down with water from the creek.

"You speak English very well so I know you haven't misunderstood me." March switched Jamie to her other breast and took another biscuit. They were dry and crumbly, and more than one grain of sand crunched between her teeth, but she was so hungry that even a feast couldn't have tasted better.

"I learned the white man's tongue when I was still a boy."

"You speak it very well. Who taught you?"

"We had several white captives. One, a boy about my age, taught me to understand his words, and I taught him to be a warrior."

"Well, you can be very proud of yourself, you speak better than some white men I've heard."

"Your son is done." He nodded toward the baby. "We can leave. I will get the horse."

March looked down and saw that Jamie had fallen asleep and her nipple had slid from his mouth. Cheeks flaming with embarrassment, she looked furtively at Light, only to discover to her amazement that he had gotten up and was heading toward the horse.

Fred had watched her nurse the baby, his eyes nearly glazed with lust. Light accepted it as a natural part of life and ignored it. Light, who was considered a savage, was much more of a gentleman than Fred, who had been raised as one.

"Come, Giving Woman." Startled from her thoughts, March looked up and found Light on his horse, his hand reaching down to her, the expression on his face tolerating no argument.

She wasn't going to argue, she decided as she shifted and her legs protested her slightest movement. She wasn't getting on that horse again tonight.

"No," she stated quietly.

"Hand me your son, and I will help you to mount."

"No. I'm not getting on that horse. I'm staying right here until morning, and then you can take me home."

His hand recoiled, and he slowly squared his shoulders. Slipping his right leg over the horse's head, he slid to the ground. Every vestige of friendliness was gone. Left in its place was the hardened warrior.

Panic nibbled at her as he approached. Perhaps she shouldn't have been so resolute in her refusal, March decided as Light stopped at her knees. She should have found another way to convince him that this was a good place to stop for the night.

"You will come."

Staring at his beaded moccasins, greatly impressed by the intricacy of the pattern and wishing she had more time to thoroughly examine them, March slowly shook her head. She had stated her position; she couldn't back down now.

"No, I'm tired. I'm scared and I want to go home."

Light reached down and grabbed a handful

of her silky golden hair. He pulled just hard enough to force her to rise to her feet, but not enough to cause real pain.

"Your home is now with me." His black eyes burned with intensity. "We will ride many more miles before we find sleep this night."

Tears burned the back of her eyes, but March refused to give in. She didn't think he'd really hurt her . . . at least she hoped not.

"No," she repeated.

With a snarl in a language she couldn't understand, Light released her hair and stalked away. His disgust was as much with himself as with her. He knew that he could force her to mount the horse and ride with him. He could take the child from her arms, and she would come. Or he could bind her hands and feet and throw her across the horse's rump as a captive.

But he found that he could not hurt her. Her strange eyes, the color of clouds before a storm, swimming with tears she wouldn't shed, spoke more loudly than words her determination to have her way.

Light wasn't sure what to do. An Indian woman would never disobey her man in such a way. If she did, then he would beat her until she followed wherever he led, whenever he said. But this white woman just raised her chin a little higher each time she refused.

March realized that he was fighting with himself about what to do next, and knew that it was a struggle with his male pride in jeopardy.

"Please, Light?" she asked softly. "I'm so tired. I don't think I can even get on your horse."

"A woman does what her man tells her to do. It is the way," he stated firmly.

"A man knows when she is too tired to go on, and allows for her weakness." Pushing her hair back from her face, March sighed tiredly. "I didn't mean to anger you. I really didn't, but I can't go on. Not tonight."

His gaze seemed to pierce through her. "We will stay—this time. But never again will you refuse me."

"I probably will," she warned. "I'm not good at quietly taking orders."

"Then I will beat you."

"My daddy beat me once until I nearly died, but I still refused to do what he demanded."

Light turned away, obviously disgusted with her and with himself for complying. As she watched him stalk away, March refrained from sighing in relief. He wasn't more than two or three inches taller than she, but his heavily muscled shoulders and arms divulged a far greater strength. And he was from a society that allowed, and applauded, male superiority and dominance. She wasn't sure why he had given in to her pleas for rest, but was grateful that he had.

March stared toward the lowering sun and wondered which way home was. Sinking back to the sand, she spread out Jamie's blanket and lay him in the center, using her own body to provide protective shade.

All day she had forced her thoughts away from Jim. Now, with the angry man behind her quietly tending his horse, she let her mind drift.

She knew the agony of fear he would feel when he found that his son was gone, and wished she could reassure him that nothing would happen to the child, as long as there was breath in her body to protect him.

Jim would be frantic when he found the buckboard with an injured Hank, but no sign of her or his son. She knew he would immediately begin a search, and doubted that it would take long for him to discover Fred's body.

From there the trail wouldn't be as easy to follow. Now she realized why Light had taken his twisting, turning path. It would confuse followers, taking them longer to pick up the actual trail and giving Light more time to disappear.

But Jim would come. He would follow to the ends of the earth, for his son.

March sighed and rested her head against her bent knees. She wondered what it would be like to be loved that intensely, to be the most important person in someone's life.

Jim's face in all its moods—laughing, sober, teasing, fierce—whirled through her thoughts. An uncharacteristic feeling of self-pity forced her to blink back tears.

Once, just once, she wanted to know a love that was stronger than the majestic mountains that surrounded her, a love without beginning or end.

Sixteen

Every tightly stretched nerve in his body urged Jim into action. Each superbly honed muscle and sinew demanded that he respond to the overwhelming need for physical activity. Staying seated on the horse was the hardest thing he had ever done in his life. The animal, unconcerned with the problems of his rider, munched contentedly on the silky grass at the side of the road, his tail flipping occasionally at an annoying insect.

Breed moved cautiously around the area, reading the signs as easily as another man might read a book, taking great care not to accidentally obliterate a clue because of carelessness, or overlook one because of haste. Several of the signs had been wiped away by the men who had rescued Hank, and it was taking Breed longer to separate one from another than it would have done had he been the first on the scene.

Which was the very reason Jim had to remain on his horse. Simply by stepping in the wrong spot he could accidentally wipe out a clue that could be valuable in locating March and his son.

Jim had always considered himself to be an even-tempered man, not one to head out on wild tangents fueled by excessive anger. But now he knew that he had simply never been given the necessary incentive. He had discovered that he was capable of experiencing towering rage that he could not harness.

And he relished it, savored each and every shred of anger striving for control. He stayed on his horse only because common sense told him that the sooner Breed could pick up the trail, the sooner he could release his fury. He sat with a steel-boned stillness, alertly watching each move his foreman made.

Later, when he had March and Jamie back, he could analyze the fear that had been his first emotion when one of his ranch hands had ridden out to find him and tell him the news of their abduction.

Later, he could remember the pain he had felt when the doctor had told him that Hank might not survive the bullet wound. The old man hadn't been found until several hours after the shooting, and had lost a considerable amount of blood.

Later, he would think of his overpowering need to hold March in his arms and know that she was safe.

She had been through so much, had suffered one humiliation after another, and had come through it all with her head held high. She had fought an inner battle as well, thinking that she was even less respectable because of her illiteracy. Her need to learn, to know, was awesome, and once begun, he knew that it would become a lifelong commitment.

She was everything feminine, everything desirable. She had an inner core of strength that was pure steel, and he found himself praying that she would call on that strength to survive this ordeal.

He had no fear for Jamie. Granted, he wanted his son back, but as long as he was with March, the baby could not be safer. She would fight the devil himself to protect his child . . . her child.

Hands tightening into fists, he savored the moment when he could use them on Fred Hamner. Hank had regained consciousness long enough to name his assailant, and to plead with Jim to find March before it was too late.

This time the younger man would not have a few bruises that kept him in bed for a couple of weeks. Jim smiled, a smile completely devoid of humor. This time Fred Hamner's rest would be permanent.

Lost in his thoughts of revenge, Jim was startled when Breed mounted his horse and moved slowly out from under the trees. Following his foreman, Jim tried to see whatever it was that was guiding the man. There were so many hoofprints, that one pretty well blended into another, making a trail impossible for Jim to see.

But Breed saw it. His pale blue eyes, trained by master trackers, knew where to look and what to look for. He stopped and motioned for Jim to join him.

"You've found it?"

"For now." Breed looked forward into the desert. "I started looking in the wrong direction," he admitted with no sign of embarrassment for his mistake. "I was wrong to think that he'd head on up the mountain. I hope he was prepared for the desert, because there is nothing between here and Tucson but miles of sand and a few hundred cactus."

"Damn," Jim swore under his breath. March and the baby couldn't survive for long under the blazing sun. And it had already been several hours since the abduction.

Without wasting time or exchanging further words, the two men began following the trail. Jim was relieved when they were able to pick up their pace; there was nothing to interfere with the trail left by the galloping horse.

Within a very short time, both men realized that the trail was heading toward the line shack. Breed was still cautious enough to watch for the track in case it unexpectedly veered off, but Jim's attention was captured by dark specks circling in the horizon.

He knew they had found their quarry, but the buzzards could only mean one thing. No longer able to hold back, Jim spurred his horse into a gallop.

As the shack came into sight, they saw that several of the massive birds were on the ground in front of it, while still more circled overhead. Their strident squawking ceased abruptly, followed by the sound of wings flapping furiously as they made their escape from the approaching humans.

"The smell of man has kept them outside." Breed slowed his horse and studied the deserted cabin. He was too well trained in warfare to approach a structure without being concerned for ambush.

Jim, more concerned with finding March and Jamie than with his own safety, was not nearly as cautious. He drew his .45 from its holster, but made no attempt to slow the horse until he was at the door.

The lowering sun shined brightly into the shack and onto the body in the doorway. Sighing with relief that it was a man rather than a slender-framed woman, Jim dismounted.

The bloated body already decomposing in the heat, Jim used his foot to turn it face up. He wasn't surprised to discover that it was Fred, but had to swallow back his bitter disappointment that someone else had had the pleasure of killing the man.

A quick search of the tiny room proved empty of March and Jamie. Where were they, he wondered, as a new fear crept up his spine. If she had ventured into the desert, she could be dead by now. Without water she would die of thirst. Without a gun to protect herself, she could be bitten by a snake and might die an agonizingly slow death from the poison.

Facing his own agonizing pain, Jim left the shack, slamming the door closed. As far as he was concerned, the buzzards could have Fred's body. But he knew Fred's father would want to bury his only son.

Breed had seen the single body in the shack, and hadn't bothered to dismount. He didn't waste valuable time examining a dead man. The sun was lowering rapidly, and with it came the darkness that made tracking impossible.

Again, Jim found himself waiting for his foreman to pick up the trail. The soft whinnying of a horse drew his attention to the corral. The animal's saddle had been removed, and the horse came willingly when Jim approached the fence.

Why hadn't March taken the horse? Why had she left the cabin on foot?

Reaching for the reins, Jim led the animal from the corral and mounted his own horse.

Breed was too far away to make conversation easy, but Jim didn't join him until Breed signaled that it was all right.

"What did you find?"

"She isn't alone." Breed's eyes narrowed against the glare of the sun. "I'd say your visitor from yesterday found her."

"The Indian?" Jim asked, perplexed.

"The trail circles back on itself several times. It's an old trick, used to slow down the tracker so that there is more time to escape. Not too many white men know how to do that."

"So where does it lead?"

"I don't know yet. We'll follow it for as long as necessary."

"I don't want to waste the time," Jim snarled as frustration built.

"If we pick up a false trail, we may lose even more time." He looked toward the sun to judge how long it would be before it set. "We still have a couple of hours. We might pick up the trail before then."

"If we don't?"

"Then we'll find it tomorrow."

"Damn!" Jim thought of the renegade who had taken a liking to March. If he had found her, then he wouldn't be overly willing to give her back.

Breed moved away from his boss, and began the time-consuming task of following a trail that was deliberately misleading. His respect for his adversary grew as the trail repeatedly returned to its original starting place, while giving no clue to its final destination.

A feeling of helplessness fed Jim's frustration as he faithfully followed along behind Breed. There was nothing he could do except stay out of the way, until the foreman found the real trail.

The old wolf found the female and moved to her side. Her thick, luxurious fur gleamed with a golden cast in the bright morning light. Her eyes, the color of gathering storm clouds, sparkled with an intelligence and wisdom far past her years.

Raising her head, she glanced curiously at him. Had she met him earlier, she might have shown an interest in becoming his mate. He was a strong, vibrant male, emitting that mysterious something that attracted the attention of any female. He carried his age as a mantle of knowledge and wisdom.

Yes, he was one whom she would have chosen, if she hadn't already given her trust to the other one, the one with whom she would spend the many years of her life.

Excited by her scent, he sniffed appreciatively, ignoring warning snarls. He was, after all, the male; she the female. It would take time, but she would learn.

He tried to mount her, but she daintily stepped away. Once more he assumed the position and tried again to mount. This time she turned, a swirling fury of golden fur and silver eyes.

Not ready to concede defeat, he forced her to change her direction to his own. Nipping at her heels and the scruff of her neck, the old one guided her for several miles.

At a water hole, she stopped and dropped to the ground. Night was coming on, it was the best time to hunt, but she made no effort to rise. He knew he couldn't leave her to hunt on his own, or she would be gone when he returned. Given no other choice, he lay beside her.

But he found that his rest wasn't as contented as it

should be. His belly rumbled with hunger, and his ears hurt from her sorrowful cry. He hoped that she would soon accept him and become the mate he so badly needed.

It became the pattern of the next few days. Each morning he would try to mount her, only to be fiercely rejected. She only moved when he forced her, never hunted for food, and cried long into the night.

Her fur soon lost the vibrant glow of good health. Her tail curled between her legs, and her ears lay flat against her head. She was going with him, but she was allowing herself to wither away.

Finally he accepted that he could keep her, but could never have her as the mate he desired. He would have to let her go or watch her slowly die.

He couldn't just walk away. He had to assure himself that she was safe. The morning light barely broke the darkness from the sky, when he began retracing the path they had already taken.

She followed slowly behind him, her look wary, as if she expected some trick. As the day drew on, she began to realize that he was returning her to her home. Yipping with a joy so absolute it hurt his heart, the old one watched as she hurried on ahead.

Traveling all that day and night, it was early the next morning when they were back at their meeting place. Feeling older than his years, he watched as she sniffed the ground, renewing her own scent in place of the faded odors.

He knew the moment she discovered a different scent than her own. Watching her, he saw her stiffen momentarily and then raise her head. With a howl more

*beautiful than any he had ever heard in his many
years, she jumped into a run.*

*Curious, and not quite ready to relinquish his hold,
he followed her. Within a short time his curiosity was
satisfied, in a way he wished he could deny.*

*On a hill waited a young male, not much older than
her, his black fur gleaming with youth and health. At
his feet were several pups, gamboling about in the morning dew, their fat little bodies a combination of her golden
fur and his ebony pelt.*

*The old one turned away from the happiness that
was nearly more than he could endure. A soft, sweet
call drifted down to him, and in spite of himself he
stopped and turned around.*

*She took several steps in his direction, puppies roll-
ing playfully at her feet. Once more she howled softly,
while at her side her mate stood proudly.*

*The old one turned back toward his own territory,
his steps self-confident; his pride was restored. It was
done, but her final cry had told him that he would
have been her choice, if he had found her sooner.*

The cry of the wolf still echoing in his ears,
Light knew that further sleep was impossible.
He rose, checked on his horse, and then lowered
himself to the ground beside March, and watched
her sleep. She was curled protectively around the
baby, her arm a barrier against harm. Her golden
hair was spread over her shoulder, and into the
sand at her back.

He struggled against the vision that had haunted

his sleep. He would have to take her back. There was no choice. The old one had sent him to protect her from the white man who had meant to harm her, but he hadn't intended for Light to take her as his own.

He knew that she would never adapt to the lifestyle of his people. Her spirit would forever mourn the mate she had been forced to leave. She would become a bitter, cruel woman; far from the gentle, giving woman she was now.

He had nothing to give her, not a home or family or even a people. He was running from the white man's law, his actions branding him as a renegade in the white man's eyes. Life on the run was not what he wanted for himself and this woman.

Briefly, Light let himself think of a time when life had been good, when food was plentiful and his people were content. It would never be again as it once was, and he would forever mourn the loss.

As he would forever sorrow for what might have been with this woman, if things had been different.

Taking the knife from its sheath on his thigh, Light separated a clump of her hair and easily sheared it off. Wrapping the golden strands around his hand, he waited for her to wake.

March shifted, the hard ground penetrating through layers of sleep, until she was forced to open her eyes. Light sat cross-legged beside her, his dark eyes unfathomable. She focused on the knife in one of his hands and the strand of her hair in the other. A shiver of apprehension rippled through her.

"Take me home, Light." Her voice was husky with sleep, her eyes deep pools of silver.

Without acknowledging that he had heard her, Light rose gracefully to his feet, returning the knife to its resting place on his hip. Watching him walk away, March sighed and sat up. Jamie squirmed and stretched and rolled to his back. Grabbing his feet, he looked up at March and smiled a toothless grin of pleasure at finding her so close.

Muttering meaningless nonsense to him, she changed him with his last clean towel. She had washed his dirty ones last night in the shallow creek, but hated the thought of putting them on him. The water was so low that there was no way she could get all of the sand out of them, and she knew that it would soon irritate his sensitive skin.

Light did not reappear until after she had nursed Jamie and had taken care of her own morning necessities. Hunger gnawed at her backbone, needlessly reminding her of her limited food the day before, and bringing back memories of a time when hunger had been a way of life.

It had been several months since she had felt real hunger, the kind that made all other problems trivial, when even inedible things were seriously considered as a possible source of nourishment. She remembered the time her mother had boiled the leather from a pair of boots, trying desperately to make a broth. Their meal that night had been little more than tasteless, funny-colored, hot water.

Since becoming Jim's housekeeper, she had not had one day of hunger. Food, even things that were considered luxuries, was in abundance. Nor had she spent a moment worrying about her safety, or fearing each time a voice was raised in anger that she would be the target.

She had so quickly come to expect three meals a day, a warm bed at night, and the absence of fear. Her thoughts turned to her mother and the little ones, and the sad knowledge that hunger was still very much a part of their lives.

March watched as a tiny bug climbed a mountain of sand only to reach the other side, and find another mountain waiting in its path. With a determination to conquer the sand, the bug began its laborious journey upward.

Raising her gaze toward the approaching man, March knew she would use the same kind of determination to return home.

"Take me home?" she asked again.

"Eat." Light held out another of the biscuits, now hardened with age.

"I won't be a good wife. I'll try to escape any time I can."

"You shouldn't give warning."

"I'll remember that." March nodded wisely as she chewed on the bread. Had she bothered to look, she would have seen a teasing gleam in Light's dark eyes.

"I can't cook over a fire," she lied.

"You can learn."

"I won't sleep on the hard ground night after night."

"You can stand up."

"I won't wear moccasins."

"When your shoes are worn through, you can go with your feet bare."

"I won't get on that horse."

"It is a long walk, but that is your choice."

Frustrated because he responded so mildly, March jumped to her feet and gathered the towels that had been spread out to dry. Folding one of the squares into a triangle, she wrapped it over her head for some protection from the sun. Using another, she made a sling for Jamie to rest against her chest.

"I'm leaving," she stated firmly.

"Which direction will you go, Giving Woman?"

"That way." March waved her hand in the general direction they had traveled the day before.

"Take care you do not find yourself in the land of the Mexicans. They are not friendly."

Pointing in a more northerly direction she stated, "That way!"

"Your hair will make a fine trophy for a young warrior to show, when he knows no one will tell of him owning it."

Turning, she took several steps away from him. The desert stretched endlessly in front of her. The giant saguaros and smaller cacti waited to catch her clothing and tear her skin.

She had sworn to get back home, but also to protect Jamie from harm. She knew that walking into the desert without food or water would not protect the child. It was sure death, waiting to strike in a variety of different ways.

Until he came to a halt beside her, she had been unaware that Light had mounted his horse. Reluctantly, she grasped the hand he held down to her, and was pulled onto the animal. He waited until she was securely seated with Jamie in his sling between them, then moved out at a slow walk.

March felt the tears slide down her cheeks with each step the horse took. Of course, Light hadn't argued with her earlier, he knew that she had no choice and just waited for her to arrive at the same conclusion. Why waste words arguing, when it wasn't necessary?

Light heard her soft sobs and knew he had made the right decision. Already her spirit was bleeding, if he had forced her to stay with him, it would have fled to a happier place, leaving only the shell of the woman behind.

But he wasn't ready to tell her of his decision. Like the old one, he would cherish this stolen time with her, knowing that it would end far too soon.

Jim and Breed had been on the trail at the first sign of light. At dark the evening before,

Breed had found the trail, and now they could travel at a much quicker pace. Knowing that they needed to get as many miles behind them as they could before the sun heated the day and made travel hard on both horses and men, they rode at a fast pace.

Jim hoped that having March and Jamie with him had slowed the Indian down. Breed knew that it wouldn't matter to the renegade. He would travel at his own pace, giving little concern for his captives.

At mid-morning Breed's attention was captured by movement in the distance. He watched as it slowly moved closer to them, before he pointed it out to Jim.

"Someone's coming." He pointed toward the horizon.

Jim stared at the tiny figure, but it was too faraway for him to be positive of an identification. At this distance it could be anything.

Light saw the two men approaching, and knew his time was up. He wanted to change his direction and make a run for it, but the memory of the old one surfaced, guiding him forward.

After several long, agonizing minutes, Jim realized that it was a mounted man approaching. He reached for his rifle when he was finally able to identify the Indian they had been searching for.

Breed reached over and stayed Jim's hand. "She is behind him," he said quietly, pointing out the long tendrils of golden hair blowing from behind the Indian. "If you shoot, you take a chance on hitting her."

"Will he give her up?"

"He is bringing her back," Breed stated.

Breed slowed his horse, forcing Jim to do the same thing. Frustration ate at Jim's self-control but he allowed Breed to set the pace. His foreman had been raised among Indians and was a better judge of how to handle the situation.

Light stopped his horse long before reaching the two men. He turned to the woman behind him and longed to stroke her golden hair and caress her silky skin.

"Get down," he said firmly.

March looked around, but saw nothing but the desert. "Why?"

"You ask too many questions, Giving Woman. I think I should have called you Nosey Woman."

About to question his decision, March heard the sound of approaching horses. Leaning around Light, her eyes widened when she identified Jim and Breed.

"Jim?" she whispered, suddenly impatient to get off of the horse. "Oh, God, Jim!"

She didn't remember grabbing Light's arm or sliding from the horse, but when her feet touched the ground, March flew toward Jim. Her cry of delight echoed back to the man who had followed his vision.

Jim threw his leg over the horse, slid from the saddle, and gathered her into his arms. Taking care not to crush the baby, he held her to him and felt his heart beat raggedly in his chest.

"Are you all right?" he asked quietly, not quite ready to release her.

"I am now." March buried her face against his shirt and relished the security of his arms. "I was so afraid, but I knew you'd come. I knew you wouldn't let anyone take your son."

Jim rubbed his cheek against her silky hair. With her safe in his arms, he could admit it to himself, if not to anyone else. He hadn't come for his son. He had known that the baby was safe with her.

With her head against his heart, her arms around his waist, Jim knew she was exactly where he wanted her to be.

He had gone to hell and back, and he had found heaven in the arms of an angel.

He had come for her.

Seventeen

"Go home, little missy," Woods commanded. "You've been here all evenin', and that youn'en is needin' his mama."

March looked across the room where Jamie was being entertained, while entertaining a bunch of cow punchers who were more accustomed to handling newborn cattle than newborn humans. Being passed from hand to hand didn't seem to bother the child. He tried his new powers of conversation, cooing repeatedly and capturing the hearts of his father's employees.

Tough men who daily met the dangerous challenges of handling wild horses and cattle melted at the toothless smile and wide blue eyes of the boy. Only once had a raucous commotion drifted over to March and Hank. That had happened when Jamie had firmly wrapped his tiny fingers around a well-maintained, handlebar mustache. The owner of the mustache, being duly proud of the whiskers that had taken him years to grow and to train into the long swirl of hair, was torn between saving his pride and joy and possibly hurting the child by pulling his hand free.

March had saved the day by gently unwinding Jamie's grasping fingers without the loss of a single hair. As soon as the cowhand was free, she expected him to hand Jamie over to the next man waiting his turn to hold the baby. But she discovered that it was such a rare treat for the men to hold an infant, that none was willing to forgo the pleasure. She hid a grin as she watched the man continue to hold Jamie, while keeping a careful grasp on the tiny exploring hands.

March knew that she was out of place in the bunkhouse. When the men returned from the range, it was their place to relax and unwind. They had been extremely polite when they had arrived and had discovered a woman invading their domain, but no one had complained. They understood that she was there because of her concern for Hank, and each of them harbored the hope that if they were ever in the same position as the old man, that someone would care for them that way.

"Go on to the house, missy," Woods repeated. "This ain't no place for a lady."

Hank moaned softly, wrenching at her heart. It was because of her that the old man lay here fighting death.

"He'll be all right," Woods reassured her when he saw her distress. "He's too mean to die. God don't want him messin' up heaven, and the devil is scared of him."

"Don't even joke about something like that." She wrung out a rag and placed it over Hank's hot brow. Beneath the flush caused by the fever, his skin was pasty white.

"We'll watch over him, little lady." Woods lightly touched her hand. "He's one of us, we won't let him go without puttin' up a good fight."

The tone of Jamie's gurgles changed abruptly, and March knew he would soon demand a feeding; his good mood was rapidly running out.

"Promise you'll come for me, if he needs me?"

Her pleading eyes were so filled with pain, that the old man would have promised her anything to wipe away some of her worry.

"He ain't gonna need you. All he needs is a good night's sleep." He patted her hand awkwardly. "And so do you. You're plumb tuckered. You take that boy home and put him to bed. And if you sleep good, you can come back tomorrow and check on ole Hank. You'll see I'm right. He'll be as prickly as a cactus come tomorrow."

Reluctantly, March stood from the chair Woods had placed beside the bed for her, and went to claim Jamie. The men were as reluctant to give up the baby as she was to leave, and her promises to bring him back the next evening were met with delight.

"Promise you'll come get me, if he gets worse?"

Breed waited at the door to escort her the short distance from the bunkhouse to the main house. With her back toward him, she missed the silent exchange between him and Woods.

Breed's icy blue eyes warned the older man that he would regret making such a promise.

"It ain't gonna happen, so we'll see you in the morning . . . but not too early. Don't want you bargin' in when one of the hands is still in his longhandles."

At least ten pairs of eyes shifted toward her, and March turned a fiery red with embarrassment. Mumbling a hasty good night, she walked into the darkness with her silent companion.

Jim had not yet returned from town, where he had gone to report the incidents of the day before to the sheriff. The house was eerily quiet in the consuming darkness. It had never before bothered March to be alone at night, and she didn't like the gooseflesh that dotted her skin as she rushed to the nearest lamp. Breed followed her inside, and waited while she lit several lamps.

"Do you think he'll survive?" she quietly asked the foreman.

"I've seen men die with lesser wounds, and live with greater ones. He is an old man, but his spirit is strong."

"Which doesn't exactly answer my question." March smiled tiredly. "Thank you for seeing me home. I'll be all right now, if you want to leave."

Uncomfortable in the big house, Breed nodded. "I won't be far away. Scream."

March couldn't hold back a chuckle at his single-word command. "Hopefully I won't have to, but it is reassuring to know you'll be there. Thank you."

Watching him leave, March looked around the roomy kitchen. Suddenly, the eerie feelings she had felt were gone. Taking a lamp from the table, she blew out the others and climbed the stairs. The shadows cast on the walls as she passed were as comforting as old friends. Nothing could harm her here. This was peace. This was sanctuary.

This was home.

Jim went in search of March. Since the house was dark, he checked first at the bunkhouse. Woods had told him how he had finally chased her home by promising that he would come for her if there was the slightest change in Hank's condition.

On the long ride home the day before, Jim hadn't had the heart to tell her that the old man was probably dead. He had been relieved to find Hank holding his own, still weak and fighting the beginnings of what would soon become a raging fever. March had immediately wanted to move him into the house, but Jim and Woods had finally convinced her that the old man would be more comfortable in his own bed. The grandeur of the big house would intimidate a man who had spent all of his life in simple surroundings.

He had learned from Woods how she had

spent the afternoon and evening, lovingly sponging Hank with cool rags and offering sips of water when he was lucid enough to respond. She had left his side only when it was necessary to tend Jamie.

Finding himself envying the old man, Jim wondered what kind of a fool would want to be gunshot, so that he could be the center of her attention.

After searching through the lower floor of the house, he headed upstairs. He finally found March in Jamie's room. Standing quietly at the doorway, he watched as she nursed his son, softly murmuring to the child who looked up at her with worshiping eyes.

He had seen that same tenderness time and again. The Indian had been right, he acknowledged. She was a giving woman; giving to others without taking for herself.

Not once in all the months she had lived with him had she asked for anything for herself. She was delighted by anything given to her, whether it was a can of peaches or seeds for her garden. Each gift was so graciously and sincerely received, that the giver was made to feel that he had given her the greatest treasure in the world.

There wasn't a grasping, greedy bone in her body . . . except maybe when it came to peaches, Jim thought with a grin. But even then she was careful to share equally.

March had been aware of Jim from the moment he had stopped in the doorway. She still felt a little embarrassed about the way she had thrown herself into his arms yesterday morning, clinging to him as if he'd disappear if she let go. When long minutes had crawled past and he still hadn't said anything, she raised her head and smiled tentatively.

"Hi."

Her smile cut into him, and he felt his breath catch. He wished he could take this moment from time and wrap it in cotton batting to protect it forever. He'd treasure it until his dying day, taking it out whenever he needed the loveliness of her smile.

She was a picture created to warm any man's heart . . . not to mention the rest of his anatomy. The glow from the lamp on the dresser turned her hair to strands of molten gold. Her dress was open to allow Jamie to nurse, and his small hand pushed against the slope of her breast where her skin had the appearance of rich velvet.

Jim wanted to put his lips to the spot where her exquisite neck met her shoulder. He wanted to taste her skin, to discover if it were indeed as soft as it looked. He found himself envying his infant son's innocent touch, as much as he had earlier envied Hank.

He had to get away from this picture of innocent seduction, before he did or said something that he would regret. Having been through enough terror in the last twenty-four hours to last her a lifetime, she didn't need him adding to her unease.

"When you've finished, come downstairs for a while."

March lowered her gaze to the baby in her arms. How much she loved him! She couldn't love him more if she had given birth to him. He was her child, her son.

"If you don't mind, I think I'll just put Jamie to bed and go to bed myself. It's been a long day."

"March . . . I think we need to talk."

"Please? Not tonight?" The talk would come, as she knew it must, but she needed some time to compose herself, some time to make plans.

Jim studied her sunburned face and saw the signs of exhaustion. "All right, angel. Tomorrow will be fine."

A tear slid silently down her cheek. Caught in the light of the lamp, it rested briefly on her cheek like a sparkling jewel, before she reached up and wiped it away.

"Oh, angel, don't cry." Jim slowly approached her, her tears driving a wedge of need in him to hold her, just hold her and wipe away her newest pain.

"I'm sorry." Her voice was thick with emotion that she tried desperately to hide. "I guess I'm just more tired than I thought."

Wiping at her wet face, March smiled feebly. "Don't mind me. I'll be fine in the morning, after a good night's sleep."

"Will you?" he asked softly. "Or will you spend the night remembering?"

Bending, Jim scooped her into his arms, her slight weight nothing to a man who was accustomed to throwing calves who were easily twice her weight. Getting the three of them positioned comfortably in the rocking chair took some doing however, but eventually he was able to set the chair into motion.

At first, startled by his abrupt action, March had to force herself to relax in Jim's embrace. Leaning her head against his shoulder, she felt the tension slip away with each creaking rock of the chair.

"I never used to cry." The tears seemed endless as she tried unsuccessfully to stem their flow. "I learned early on that tears were useless." Her lower lip protruded in an unintentional pout. "It seems like I'm always crying anymore. I hate to cry!"

"I sometimes wish I could," Jim said quietly.

"Men don't cry!" So startled by the thought of this big, tough man crying, March leaned forward.

"Exactly. Men don't cry. But sometimes things get so bottled up inside a body, that I can't help but wonder if a good crying spell would help."

Smiling at her amazed expression, Jim pulled her head back against his shoulder. "I can remember one time when I was about six or seven years old and I was crying—can't remember why—and Mama held me on her lap." His voice

softened as he leaned his head against the back
of the chair, his eyes closed. March could tell
that it was a good memory for him, the kind all
children should have of their parents.

"She smelled of rosewater and bread dough.
Her hands were so incredibly soft, except for a
scar she had at the base of her little finger. She
whispered soft words and hugged me. It was
such a reassuring feeling to know that she was
there and that she cared.

"I don't think there is a kid ever born who
can't wait to grow up. They hurry through childhood and then suddenly, for the rest of their
life, they're adults, and they discover that it sure
would be nice to go back to those days when
nothing was more important than winning the
spelling bee or deciding whether to go swimming or fishing or both."

Jim gently stroked the line of her jaw with the
backs of his fingers. "Mamas are special people,
there's no one else in the world quite like them.
They spend the best part of their lives raising
their children, knowing that the end result will
come the day that child leaves them. They scold
and soothe, defend and cherish, all the while
knowing that someday that child is going to become an adult, and when that happens, they
have to let go.

"I miss Mama," March said so quietly he
nearly didn't hear her. "I wonder if she's all
right, if she's hungry or cold or sick." Her voice
caught with a smothered sob. "I realized the

other day that I could write to her. I was so excited that I looked for a clean piece of paper and an envelope. But then it dawned on me that I couldn't write to her, because I didn't know where to send it.

"My mother and brothers and sisters are somewhere in this big country, and I have no idea where."

"You can still write to her, angel." Jim smoothed her hair back from her face, enjoying the silky texture of it against his rough fingers. "You can write a little each day, telling her what you're doing, and then put it away in a safe place until the next time you see her."

"Do you really think I'll see her again?" she asked hopefully.

Jim thought of her money-hungry father with distaste, and knew they hadn't seen the last of the man. "I'll bet you will. In fact, I'll bet you a can of peaches that you'll see her again before Jamie's first birthday."

March almost smiled at the mention of peaches. Since the day she had guiltily opened the first can and then admitted to her crime, they had shared many cans of the fruit. It had been the first word she had learned to write, laboriously practicing each letter until she had it perfect.

For the rest of her life, each time she saw a can of peaches, March knew she would always think of Jim and these halcyon days on the Falling Creek Ranch. Even when things were at their worst, she would remember that for a short time she had been a princess in a fairy tale castle with a knight of her very own.

"I won't be here then," she stated softly, firmly.

Jim heard the resolution in her voice, and knew that he had to tread carefully. "Why? Where will you be?"

"I'm not sure yet, but it won't be here." March looked at Jamie as he nursed contentedly. "You were right about mothers. There is nothing they won't do for their children. This baby is as much mine as the little girl I gave birth to. I won't do anything that might harm him in any way."

"I know that, angel. When I came looking for you, I never once feared for his safety. I knew you wouldn't let any harm come to him."

"And that's exactly why I have to leave."

"You think that leaving him now, when he needs you more than anyone else in the world, is the best for him?"

March hugged Jamie tightly. "I have to go."

"Why, angel? Make me understand what is chasing you away."

"I think there's something about me that men recognize." She hesitated, searching for the words that would explain. "Both Fred and that cowhand thought that I was an easy woman. They took one look at me and decided I was the kind of woman who should be working at the Golden Nugget.

"Maybe I am a whore, and just don't know it yet. I don't guess any woman just wakes up one morning and realizes that she's a bad woman. I figure that's something that takes some time to accept. I'm not sure what I am, but whatever it is, I know that I'm not fit to be this child's mother.

"He can't grow up hearing stories about me. It would be better for him, if I'm not a part of his life."

"I've never heard anything so ridiculous in my life," Jim replied with derision. "I don't know of anyone more fit to be this boy's mother. You're everything a mother should be. You're kind and gentle and loving. What more could a child want?"

"A mother who isn't a whore."

Fighting his own temper, Jim looked down at his son. He realized that Jamie had fallen asleep, and March's nipple had fallen from his mouth. It was cherry red and swollen, and Jim wanted to take it into his own mouth with a need that was overwhelming.

He couldn't let March know of his desire, for fear that she would equate him with Fred. Which would, of course, confirm her own low opinion of herself. She would think that he wanted the same thing from her that Fred had wanted.

And he did, Jim acknowledged as he tore his hungry gaze away from her breast. But he wanted more, so much more, than just the pleasure of her body.

Oh, he badly wanted her in his bed and the freedom to touch her in all the private places reserved for lovers. But he also wanted her gentleness, her caring. He wanted to know that she waited at home for him, when he came in from the range or just from the barn.

Having her body wasn't enough for him. He also had to have everything else that made March the kind of woman she was.

He figured he was stuck between a bull and a cactus; either way he turned he was destined to get jabbed. If he convinced March that she wasn't a loose woman and then approached her as a lover, she'd think he lied. If he tried to convince her that love shared freely was a gift of God, she'd think of the only examples she had seen, her parents, and again accuse him of lying.

The cactus or the bull? Which pain was less, which more quickly healed?

March nestled in Jim's arms, secure in his embrace. With his fingers tangled in her hair, she could have purred at his gentle touch. She unknowingly twisted her head so that he could reach the back of her neck and sighed at his exploration, her eyes closing in momentary contentment.

It felt so good, so right, to have him touch her, to learn that his hands could be so gentle and tender. That those same hands were capable of an equally terrifying strength gave her a feeling of security rather than fear.

It was a good feeling, a wonderful feeling, to know that he would protect her. It would be as hard to walk away from that security, as it would be to leave Jamie.

She felt greedy admitting that even to herself. There could be no comparison between her need for security and Jamie's need for a respectable mother. She was an adult, fully capable of taking care of herself. He was just a tiny baby, about as helpless as anything on earth.

She wasn't really his mother, she reminded herself. He'd had a mother, one who had died giving him life. She had been hired to take care of him, and was paid a good wage for her services. But in her mind, she had become his mother the first time he drew nourishment from her body.

Stroking Jamie's soft cheek, March thought of Melanie. "How sad that she never held her own child," March murmured, not really meaning to speak her thoughts aloud.

"Who?"

"Melanie."

"She didn't want him," Jim said harshly. "She didn't want him or me."

"What? You must be mistaken." She clutched Jamie more tightly to her, unknowingly relieving Jim of the sight of her swollen nipple.

"No, there's no mistake. She spent several months telling me often enough, so that I would have no doubt about her feelings. My highly respectable wife didn't want a child, and she definitely didn't want me. She wanted my name and money. She was very good at playing pretend, but she wasn't capable of handling reality.

"Melanie never grew up. She was spoiled and

pampered by her parents, and expected me to continue it after our wedding. I didn't have the time or the inclination, but, unfortunately, I wasn't aware of her misery with our marriage, until it was too late to do anything about it.

"I was so busy getting the ranch on its feet, that I spent too little time with her. I was gone for days sometimes, and when I got back, I figured she was just pouting because I'd left her alone.

"Melanie was . . . too . . . delicate for the West," he continued, choosing his words carefully. "And until I met you, I thought that this was the kind of life that was destined to destroy a woman.

"You came along and proved that a woman could be tough enough to take everything that is handed out to her, but gentle enough to be all woman. You've been kidnapped, molested, and beaten, but instead of fading away into a shell, you show nothing but kindness and gentleness."

"You make me sound like something special, instead of what I really am," she replied, blushing at his description.

"You are something special, angel." Jim gently tugged her hair until she lifted her gaze to him. Unable to resist, he lowered his head until his lips softly met hers.

Jim bit back a groan at the taste of her. She was honey sweet and just as tempting. Before the startled expression at the surprise of his kiss cleared from her face, he pulled away.

"You are not a whore nor a clinging vine. You are wonderfully generous, dangerously so sometimes. Men see you and they want some of that sweetness for themselves. Some men don't ask, because they know instinctively that you'll refuse, so they try to take.

"This is a lonely land . . . why do you think prostitutes make so much money? Men go for weeks and months sometimes without seeing a woman. They forget their manners, or maybe never had any in the first place. They grab for what they want, before someone else can come along and take it away from them.

"There isn't a man on this ranch who wouldn't die trying to protect you. But those very same men would grab at the opportunity to make you their exclusive property. And in the grabbing, they might forget that first and foremost, you are a lady."

As abruptly as he had lifted her onto his lap, he now set her on her feet. Steadying her until she regained her balance, Jim rose from the rocking chair.

"I'm going to give you a few things to think about tonight, other than Fred Hamner. In the first place, did you know that every summer schoolteachers from back East flock to places like Denver and Phoenix. And do you know what they do all summer?"

Not giving her time to reply, Jim continued. "They spend the summer making extra money, because teaching school doesn't pay very well, and I imagine they get pretty bored being so moral and upstanding all the time. And, angel, they make that money by prostitution."

He didn't try to hide a grin at her startled look. "You're kidding me, right?"

"No, baby, I'm not kidding. I've met a few of them in the past. Furthermore, and don't take off at a run when I tell you this . . . I want you every bit as badly as any other man." His eyes became a blue fire as he admitted it to her. "I want to make love to you until you don't know, or care, if it's daylight or dark outside. I want to learn every inch of your delectable body from head to toe, and when I'm done, I want to go back to the beginning and start all over again."

He walked to the door, stopping just over the threshold. "And one final thing . . . I think we should get married. Real soon."

Smiling at her open-mouthed expression of utter disbelief and confusion, Jim turned away. " 'Night, angel. Sleep tight."

Eighteen

"Catch, Miss March, catch!"

Forced into the game of ragtag catch, March smiled at the excited voice, adroitly caught the ball tossed to her by the child, then threw it to someone else before she could be tagged. She chuckled at the squeals of a little girl who caught the ball, then was thrown into the air by her father to protect her from being tagged.

Children were everywhere. Their smiling faces and happy laughter floated into the summer air in a litany of praise to the perfect afternoon. Beneath a cloudless sky they played games like bobtail run and catch the spider, inventing their own rules as it pleased them, delighted when an adult forgot his dignity enough to join in.

The sun was a bright yellow ball in the sky, but no one seemed affected by the heat. The day was one of celebration, Independence Day, and everyone was intent on having a good time.

March leaned against a tree, grateful for the shade it provided. She scanned the clearing, searching first for Jamie and then for Jim. Jamie was being passed from person to person, and was completely at ease with the situation. Jim stood with several other ranchers, and from the frequent gesturing and occasional raised voice, she imagined they were embroiled in a good-natured argument about stock prices, or some other matter important to ranching.

Allowing herself a brief moment of admiration, she admitted to herself that Jim was a fine-looking man . . . very fine. His thick brown hair, so dark it was nearly black, hung in gentle waves nearly to his white shirt collar. His tan hat sported a band of woven horsehair with a silver ornament that glistened in the sun. It was pulled low over blue eyes she knew from experience could burn with rage or desire.

March forced her gaze away from him before anyone could notice that she was staring, but not before she saw the way his tan shirt lovingly hugged his wide shoulders. He had removed his coat earlier in the day, and had rolled his sleeves up over his forearms. Black leather suspenders crisscrossed over his broad back, and seemed to guide her eyes down to his narrow hips and long legs. She blushed as she remembered the muscled virility she had felt in his thighs when she sat on his lap. He was whipcord lean and all muscle, with a strength that could be incredibly gentle.

Trying to ignore the shiver of awareness as he threw his head back and laughed with genuine amusement at something that had been said, March looked around the clearing and decided that nearly everyone from town, as well as the neighboring ranches and mines, was in attendance.

Earlier, the tables made from slabs of wood and sawhorses had been piled mountain-high with foods of all kinds. It had rapidly disappeared to the accompaniment of the expected groans of gluttony, and now everyone waited in eager anticipation for the ice cream that Mazie and Walt Wright had promised. March had learned that it was their special contribution to the gathering each year, enthusiastically greeted by children both young and old.

There were plenty of willing helpers to turn the handles of the churns, and an equal number to offer advice and encouragement. March eagerly awaited the treat. She had never had ice cream before, but had been told numerous times that it was something she would like. Jim had added that Walt was making one batch with peaches, and had teased her that she'd probably like it so much she wouldn't want to share it with anyone else.

Since that night earlier in the week when Jim had told her of his startling decision that they should get married, March had been leery of him. He treated her as he always had, but there was a gleam in his eyes that hadn't been there before.

She had attempted to bring the issue up on several occasions but he always managed to change the subject by telling her that they would discuss it again when Hank was better and she wasn't so tired.

Yesterday morning she had arrived at the bunkhouse to find that Hank's fever had broken. Today he was so much improved that she had reluctantly agreed to leave him in the care of Woods and join the party on the riverbank just outside of town.

She had dressed carefully in a newly made blue serge skirt and a stiffly starched white shirt-waist with a high neck and numerous tiny tucks across the bodice. She had added a wide red sash around her narrow waist, tied in a big floppy bow at the back, and a white straw hat.

Her appearance was perfectly proper, exactly what a lady should wear to a summer picnic, but March was well aware that clothes did not make a lady, and she had worried about her reception. By now everyone would have heard of Fred Hamner's attempt to kidnap her and the story of his death at the hands of the renegade.

She had been surprised when she had been greeted with open friendliness and genuine pleasure, but suspected that Mazie was respon-sible. She had such a formidable personality that few people could withstand her dictates. Jim had stayed by her side, introducing her to everyone, until he felt her relax.

Watching the fun and excitement, March was glad she had come. She had never attended a party before, and was amazed that everyone was so willing to do their part to make it a success.

"Whew," Mazie fanned herself with a wilted handkerchief as she approached. "Whoever it was that decided Independence Day should be in July, never spent a summer in Arizona."

"Who did decide it?" March asked with curiosity.

"Honey, the history books try to tell us that it was the day we became a country independent of English rule, but I really think that the men back East decided that a summer holiday was necessary, since all the other holidays come in the winter."

Mazie smiled at her own nonsense, then leaned closer to March. "Wanna do something a little bit naughty while we wait for the ice cream to finish?" she asked in a conspiratorial whisper.

"What if we get caught?"

"Why, honey, that's half the fun! Who wants to do something naughty if no one finds out about it?" The wicked gleam in the woman's faded brown eyes proved that she wasn't as old as she ought to be, nor as mature as she should be.

Unable to resist Mazie's sparkling mood, March nodded and then followed the older woman as she led toward the river.

"I've looked forward to this all day." Obviously prepared for the event, Mazie plopped down on a log, pulled a buttonhook out of her pocket, and started unhooking her shoes. "Only time of year I can do this and get away with it."

"What are you doing?" March watched with amazement as first one shoe and then the other was kicked free.

Mazie looked over her shoulder to be sure they were still alone, then reached beneath her skirt and rolled down her stocking. "Why, sweetie pie, as soon as you get your shoes and stockings off, we're going wading."

"Wading?"

"Come on, it's fun. And it sure will feel good."

"But, Mazie, I can't swim."

"Ah pooh, that don't matter none. The water here is only a few inches deep, not even up to your knees." Mazie reached over and began unhooking March's shoe. "No one will see us."

March didn't want to argue anymore. It sounded like fun, and there was no denying that the cool water would be refreshing. But more than that, for the first time in her life, someone was inviting her to share in the fun of friendship.

Shoes and stockings were soon neatly set aside. March followed Mazie into the water, holding her skirt up to her knees and safely out of harm's way.

"Careful you don't step on a slippery rock or you might find yourself a mite bit damp."

"This is fun!" March smiled happily, her eyes glowing with pleasure. "I've had more baths in a river than in a tub, but they were a necessity."

Mazie looked at the younger woman, a smile

of pleased fondness crossing her face. "Ain't you never done this before?"

"Not in a long, long time." March wiggled her toes and watched the sand float up from the bottom. "When I was a kid, there just wasn't time. I always needed to help Mama with the little ones. And when I got older, somehow it just didn't seem to be something I wanted to do."

Enthralled with the tiny fish that darted between her legs, March missed the look of pity that crossed Mazie's face. "Walp, I'd say it's about time somebody taught you how to play."

"I know how to play," March replied in surprise.

Mazie raised her leg and kicked at the water, laughing at March's amazed expression when it sprinkled in her face. Responding in kind, March splashed water back at the other woman. Soon they were both laughing, and very wet.

Looking down at the once carefully starched and ironed shirtwaist that now hung limply against her breasts, March shook her head. "I think everyone is going to know what we've been doing."

"They'll just be envious that they didn't think of it first." Mazie bent and splashed water on her face, pushing hair from her eyes that had come loose from the bun at the nape of her neck. "Besides, we'll be dry in just a few minutes, and then they can only try to guess what we've been up to."

"Having fun, children?" Jim called from the riverbank. He had been searching for March for several minutes, and had been drawn to the river by the feminine laughter. He'd watched the graceful and enticing display of legs as the two women had played, and had felt his own body heating up beyond the natural warmth of the day.

Mazie turned with a grin, while March tried to decide whether to lower her skirt and protect her modesty, or leave it raised and protect the skirt.

Leaning against a tree with his arms crossed over his chest, he watched with appreciation as March battled with her decision. He wasn't at all adverse to her leaving the skirt exactly where it was. It gave him a very nice view of her shapely legs.

"You're wicked, Jim Travis," Mazie said, trying, but failing to sound stern.

"Yep," he replied without moving his gaze from March.

"Ain't you ashamed of yourself, staring like that?"

"Nope."

"How long you gonna stay there?"

"As long as the view stays this fine." Pushing his hat to the back of his head, he grinned. "And it sure is a mighty fine view . . . mighty fine."

"Purely wicked!" Mazie's chuckle was equally as wicked as she walked out of the water, allowing her skirt to fall when she reached shore. She wasn't concerned with Jim seeing her legs, he had yet to take his eyes off of March.

March turned crimson at his continued stare. Naturally it had to be him, who had discovered her cavorting in the water like a child. Nearly a hundred other people of various ages were just out of sight, but, of course, it was Jim who found her with her skirt hiked up to her knees and her blouse soaking wet. So much for proper, she decided with a silent sigh.

"You're gonna miss the ice cream, if you stay in there much longer," Jim told her. "And the last time I saw him, Jamie was starting to get riled up. He's probably wanting his mama."

"Go away."

"I will."

"When?" she asked suspiciously.

"Just as soon as you come out. I have to stay and make sure you're safe."

Neither one of them noticed when Mazie grabbed her shoes and stockings and walked away. Neither one of them heard the laughter up on the hill, or the sweet song of the bird in the tree above Jim's head. Neither of them saw the beauty in the sparkling creek, or felt the sun on their heads.

Both were too aware of the other.

"Come here, angel," Jim called softly.

With a will of their own, her feet carried her to shore and into his open arms.

Her hair had slipped loose from the knot she had so carefully fashioned it into, and hung in golden strands around her face and down her back. Her blouse was wet, the fabric clinging faithfully to the cotton chemise beneath it. A large water drop clung to an eyelash, and Jim couldn't resist reaching up to catch it on the tip of his finger.

"Lord, but you're beautiful, angel." His voice was a husky whisper, filled with a longing that both scared and thrilled her.

"I'm a mess," she replied, finally remembering to release her skirt.

"A beautiful mess." Unable to resist, he leaned forward, his lips gently settling on hers. His tongue flicked out, never staying for long in any one spot as he learned her taste.

March discovered that his lips were surprisingly soft and shockingly warm. He teased her as he repeatedly rubbed his mouth lightly over hers. She wasn't aware when she leaned against him and wrapped her arms around his neck.

But Jim was.

He felt the heat from her breasts, so soft against the hardness of his chest, and savored the touch of her hands on his skin. With one arm around her narrow waist and the other buried beneath her hair at her neck, he pulled her tightly against him.

The world and everyone in it disappeared as he slowly deepened the kiss, until a fire sparked and threatened to become a flame. Careful not to frighten her with a need that was rapidly growing out of control, Jim slowly raised his lips from her, pressing his forehead against hers.

Breathing deeply, he closed his eyes and tried

to regain some kind of control. All he wanted to do was lay her on the ground and merge his body with hers. This was neither the time nor the place, and she had already had that kind of experience. He wanted her first time with him to be as perfect as possible, but lord, it sure wasn't easy pulling away.

Whoever said life was easy, Jim thought to himself with a grim smile, as he raised his head and reluctantly stepped back.

"When we make love, we're going to light the world on fire." His voice was husky with suppressed desire.

"Make love?" She blinked with surprise, her face so filled with innocence that he smiled.

"Yes, sweetheart, we're going to make love, and I promise you that you'll never regret a minute of it. Behind a closed door, a lady can do anything she wants with her husband."

"Jim, I think—"

"Don't think, March." He tapped her nose and turned away. "Get yourself back together and I'll go fetch Jamie. This will be a nice private place to feed him, and then we can go eat some of Walt's ice cream."

Flustered, March nodded in agreement and watched as he walked out of sight. Sitting on the log, she grabbed a stocking, but left it dangling between her hands instead of putting it on.

So that was a kiss, she thought, a real kiss. It was wonderful. It was exciting. It was thrilling.

It was as scary as hell!

She had been so involved in feeling, that Jim could have done anything to her and she wouldn't have resisted. All of her resolve to be a moral, proper lady had shattered at the sound of his voice. With the simple touch of his lips against hers, she had flung respectable out the window and grabbed for more of his forbidden pleasure.

When he returned, March had one stocking in place, but was just staring at her shoe, as if she didn't know what to do with it. He smiled to himself, pleased with her befuddlement. If he could keep her that way long enough, he'd have her married before she realized what was going on.

A decision had been made, one he hadn't even been aware of considering, as he placed the baby in her arms.

"Feed this monster, while I put your shoes and stocking on."

"He isn't a monster!" she defended the fussy baby. "He's hungry. And you can't put my stocking on."

"Why not?" He held up the white cotton garment.

"Because you don't know how."

"Sure I do . . . feed that kid before someone comes to see if we're hurting him!" Jamie's full-volume scream left no doubt that he was tired of waiting for supper.

Keeping a leery eye on Jim, March unbuttoned her blouse and lowered her chemise. He dutifully kept his eyes away as he rolled the stocking and slipped it on her foot.

Sweat beaded on his forehead, as he rolled the stocking up her leg. It was the hardest thing he had ever done. So many places to look and touch. So much soft white skin within reach, and he had to act like this was the most natural thing in the world. It was a tortuous agony no man deserved.

March blushed as his fingers came to rest briefly just above her knee, but he was so matter-of-fact about it that she relaxed as he pulled her skirt down in place.

Slipping her feet into her shoes, Jim found that it was a difficult job hooking the leather thongs over the buttons without a buttonhook, but it kept him occupied while she nursed Jamie. He was very much aware of the sounds his son made, of the flesh barely hidden from view, but he forced himself to concentrate on his chore.

When he finished his chore, March was still feeding Jamie. He had seen her embarrassed flush when she had freed her breast, and knew that she wasn't comfortable with him being there. But he wasn't about to walk away and leave her there alone. Earlier, someone had broken out a few bottles of whiskey, and the miners and ranch hands were starting to get a little rowdy. Normally, they were extremely respectful to a woman, but with a few rounds of rotgut under their belts, they'd been known to act first and apologize later.

He couldn't endanger March by leaving her alone, neither could he continue to sit at her feet like a worshiping slave. A few more minutes of seeing her exposed flesh, and he'd be more of a danger to her than any of the miners.

Jim rose and walked over toward the river. He was oblivious to its serenity, wondering with something akin to disgust, when he had started to think like a sixteen-year-old after his first time with a whore.

His physical relationship with Melanie had been far from satisfying, in fact she usually made him feel like he had defiled her body with his infrequent attentions. He couldn't remember ever wanting her the way he wanted March. And lord, but he wanted her!

Marriage was the only answer. He wouldn't treat her as she had been treated by Fred, using her body for immediate satisfaction. But if she was his wife, then he could provide protection for her, while enjoying the privileges of marriage.

He hadn't planned to remarry, some might even consider it far too soon, but the longer he thought about it, the more he liked the idea. Jamie needed a mother who would always be around to provide maternal guidance. March needed the security of a home, the kind of protection that a wedding ring would provide. And he'd have a woman around to tend to the needs of the house, to wash his clothes and cook his meals.

She had already proven that she was intelligent and clever. Now that she had mastered the cookstove, she was turning into a good little cook. There was always a ready supply of clean clothes in his dresser, his shirts had never been so neatly ironed, and all of the buttons were good and snug. His boots were frequently polished, and his hats brushed free of dust.

She was a fine seamstress; the skirt and blouse she was wearing were perfect examples of her abilities. She was friendly, generous to a fault, and honest beyond most men.

And she even managed to make a nearly decent pot of coffee.

With his hands buried in his pockets, Jim rocked back on his heels. It would be a perfect arrangement for all of them. And if he got the added benefit of a bedmate, well, that's as it should be. A woman needed a man, that's all there was to it. And if the man happened to desire the woman he wed, then all the better for him.

Yep, he decided smugly, marriage it would be. And the sooner the better.

Unaware of the decision that would radically change her life, March buttoned her blouse and rose from the ground. With the sleepy baby balanced against her shoulder, she waited for Jim to realize that she was finished. Finally, when long minutes had passed and he hadn't turned away from the river, she walked up to him, stopping at his side.

"All done?" he asked, surprised that she had finished so quickly.

"Do you think we've missed the ice cream?" Her voice had a little-girl quality to it that made him smile.

"I don't think so." He took Jamie from her and balanced him in the crook of his arm. "Let's go see if we can find some of that peach ice cream that Walt's been bragging about all day long."

As they climbed the hill, they discovered that the volume of noise at the clearing had lowered considerably, and they soon found it was because everyone was too busy eating ice cream to do much of anything else.

Jim found a shady spot for her with some of their neighbors, handed the baby to her, and went to get some of the ice cream. March wiggled with anticipation, silently urging him to hurry. Smiles and sighs of pleasure were so prevalent, that she knew the treat must be wonderful.

And it was . . . the most wonderful thing she had ever tasted. Jim had returned with a bowl so heaping that she was nearly embarrassed. He announced loudly that Walt had scooped that up himself just for her, and that she was to eat every bite.

March put a spoonful into her mouth, surprised at the coldness of the creamy confection. That surprise lasted only briefly, soon obliterated by the rich flavor of peaches. She closed her eyes to better savor the texture and flavor, missing the smile on Jim's face.

It surprised Jim to discover that he felt such pleasure, knowing he had introduced her to the treat. Ice cream wasn't new to him, he couldn't even remember the first time he had tasted it, but surely his face hadn't reflected the near-ecstasy that was currently on hers.

"Like it?" he asked needlessly.

"Surely it must be a sin for anything to taste so good." March licked her lips as she scooped up another spoonful.

"If it is, then Preacher Davies is in danger of going to hell along with everyone else." He pointed to the preacher, who was obviously enjoying his ice cream as much as everyone else.

"You shouldn't say things like that about a man of God," March scolded.

Chuckling, Jim rose. "I need to talk with Walt for a few minutes, enjoy your ice cream."

March licked her spoon and made a face at his retreating back. He could go talk to each and every person at the gathering. He could talk about the weather, the price of beef, or black versus brown suspenders. She didn't care.

She was going to sit here in the shade with Jamie sleeping contentedly at her knees, and indulge herself in something that just might be a little bit better than peaches.

Closing her eyes, March let the flavor melt on her tongue. She wasn't about to miss one bite of her ice cream for any reason short of . . . Grinning to herself, she acknowledged that she couldn't think of *anything* that would make her give up this special treat.

Nineteen

Jim disappeared for longer than a few minutes. March finished her ice cream, sighing regretfully when it was gone. Leaving Jamie asleep on the quilt in the care of a neighbor, she carried her bowl back to Walt and volunteered to help with the clean up.

"Thanks for offerin', but that's all taken care of." Walt took the bowl from her and dropped it in a bucket of water. "What did you think of your first taste of ice cream?"

Licking her lips, March smiled. "It's better than anything I've ever tasted. There can't be anything in the world that's even half that good!"

"Walp, there might be a body or two who'd disagree with you on that." Walt's eyes twinkled with merriment. " 'Course, ever'body's entitled to his own opinion."

"Do we have to wait until next summer to have more?"

"Nope, we make it twice a year; Fourth of July and Christmas Eve."

"Hurry, hurry Christmas!" When other people appeared with their bowls, March wandered away, searching for Jim as she greeted the neighbors she knew and nodded to others who were still strangers.

With something closer to contentment than she had ever felt in her life, March stood beneath the shade of a ponderosa pine and scanned the area, looking for Jim. It had been a perfect day, quite possibly the best in her life.

Instead of standing on the sidelines and longing to be a part of the group, for the first time ever, she felt as if she belonged. It was a heady feeling to know that these people accepted her, even if somewhat begrudgingly.

How she wished that Mama and the younger children could have been here. The little ones would have loved the games and the ice cream. She could almost see their eyes opened wide with wonder at the cold confection.

Regretting that the day was almost over, March knew she was old enough to accept that nothing lasts forever, but still young enough to hope it would go on and on. Everything, good or bad, had to come to an end, but why did it always seem that the good ended a whole lot faster than the bad?

"You filthy, white-trash whore!"

March heard the harsh words as a hand on her shoulder jerked her around. Torn so abruptly from her mood of contentment, she was unprepared to face the snarling, hate-filled visage of the man who held her with a hand on each of her shoulders, his strong fingers digging into her flesh.

She had never seen him before, but she knew immediately that he was the one person she had most dreaded seeing at the picnic. His features were so distorted with his vindictiveness, that she realized he was dangerously beyond reasoning.

"You killed my boy!"

"Mr. Hamner, I—"

"You wiggled your tight little ass at him, and when he did what any boy would do, you cried rape!"

"Mr. Hamner, I never—"

"You bitch!" His voice vibrating through the sudden silence as everyone's attention was caught, he began to shake her with such violence that March feared her neck would snap. "You lying slut! I'll teach you a lesson you'll never forget! I'll make you regret the day you were ever born! When I'm through with you, there won't be anyone around who won't know exactly what you are! You'll be sorry—"

"Let her go, Bud."

If she could have, March would have sighed with relief at the command in Jim's voice. Later, she promised herself, she'd remember to thank him for his intervention. For now, she was more concerned with freeing herself from this madman, before he could do irreparable harm. She saw that Walt and a couple of other men had gathered beside Jim, silently offering their help to defuse the situation.

"Stay out of this, Travis, this is none of your damn business!"

"You made it my business when you attacked my housekeeper. Now back off."

His fingers tightened until March was sure they were drawing blood. "This tramp needs to learn a lesson or two, and I'm just the man to do it."

"Let me handle this, Travis." Another voice, deeper, older, broke into the tense silence. "Bud, let the girl go."

"Leave me alone, Sheriff. I own you, now get outa here."

"You're wrong, Bud. You may be the wealthiest rancher around, but you don't own me, the town council pays my wage." The click of a hammer being pulled back on a gun echoed through the clearing. "I don't want to use this on you, Bud. We've been friends for a good many years, long before this pig path became a town, but I won't hesitate, if it means saving that girl's life."

"You're gonna choose a white-trash slut over me?" Hamner released one shoulder, moved his hand to around March's neck, and turned to look at the sheriff. "You call yourself my friend?" he asked with a sneer.

"I'm the best friend you've got, Bud, 'cause I'm not going to let you do something you'll regret for the rest of your life. Now, let her go."

"I could break her neck before you can pull that trigger."

"But you'd still be dead a few seconds later. At this range, I can't miss."

"Ain't got nothin' to live for no how, now that my boy's dead."

Jim stood with his hands clutched into fists, cursing his inability to save March. He had no doubt that one wrong move, and Bud Hamner would snap her slender neck as easily as snapping a twig.

"Mr. Hamner, I didn't kill your son," March said quietly, her voice filled with more composure than she actually felt. "I fell in love with Fred, and thought he wanted me to be his wife."

"Wife, hah! Why would you think my boy would look twice at the likes of you?" He turned away from the sheriff and looked at his victim.

"I wondered the same thing, but every evening he came by the cafe and walked me home. He talked about you and the ranch and his plans for the future.

"I felt like the luckiest girl in the world, when he started talking about marriage."

"Marriage? To you? Not likely!"

"I thought so, too, but he did, Mr. Hamner. He offered me all of the things that I'd only dreamed about for most of my life." March felt his hold on her neck loosen slightly, and took a deep breath. "I found out too late that he had paid my father for the use of my body."

"You're lying. My boy was a lot of things, but he didn't abuse women. I taught him better than that."

"He didn't abuse me, Mr. Hamner. He used me, paid my father, and then walked away. He took with him my self-respect and all my dreams for the future."

"White-trash sluts don't deserve no future."

"Even white trash, as you've labeled me, is human." March squared her slender shoulders, pride in every line of her small body. "I hurt, I get scared. And I bleed, Mr. Hamner. If you push a knife in, you'll discover my blood is as red as yours.

"And always, even when I didn't have a pair of shoes for my feet or my belly growled with hunger, I still had my dreams. The cruelest thing you can do to someone is rob them of their dreams."

Her voice softened, so that the interested audience had to strain to hear her every word. Her eyes had deepened to a liquid lavender, filled with understanding and pity for the older man.

"But you know that, don't you, Mr. Hamner? You had dreams . . . so many, many dreams, for your ranch and for your son. But someone robbed you of those dreams, someone took the very soul from your body and shredded it into tiny little pieces. Now you need to make me suffer, as you are suffering.

"As God is my witness, I didn't kill Fred." She watched as the expressions chased across his face, from blinding fury to heartrending sorrow.

"If my death at your hands will help you to accept that he is gone, then go ahead, do it. I can't stop you." She motioned to the men behind him. "They can't stop you, the deed will be done before either one of them can react."

Tears clouded the old man's eyes, and his shoulders slumped. "Damn you, God damn you," he whispered in a choked voice. "You took away everything I had to live for."

She felt his hand slide from her neck and briefly closed her eyes in a silent prayer. "I'm truly sorry for your loss, Mr. Hamner," she said softly.

Slowly, tentatively, she reached out and placed her hand against his cheek. "I know that no words can ease the pain of losing your child."

"You can't know that! You can't know what it's like to wake up every morning and know that you'll never hear his voice, that it's just one more day to get through without him."

"I lost my baby, she came too early. I never saw her face or heard her voice, but my grief is no less than yours," March replied gently.

He raised his head, his cheeks wet with tears. The single word, a question, was forced through a throat choked with pain. "Fred's?"

"Yes . . . his daughter."

"Oh God." Bud Hamner forgot that the entire town looked on with avid interest. He forgot that he had come to make this girl suffer. He forgot that just moments ago he had threatened to kill her, had fully intended to kill her.

Suddenly, his loss was doubled. He was torn

by a pain so great, he felt as if his heart would break.

Jim stiffened when Bud reached out again to March, then relaxed slightly as he pulled her into his arms. Need met need, and March did what she had always done . . . she gave of herself. Putting aside her own agony, she gave to a man who was suffering beyond what he was capable of handling.

March wrapped her arms around his shoulders, and held him as he cried. Tears clouded her own eyes, as she shared his suffering, his loss. She had lost her baby, but he had the double loss of his child and his grandchild.

She knew she would someday have more children to love, would perhaps suffer greater losses and learn to accept the things she couldn't change. But never again would anything affect her quite as deeply as being a part of Bud Hamner's pain.

"I loved him," Bud muttered, clutching to March with painful intensity. "He was all I had, and I gave him everything. He was a bit spoiled, but he wasn't a bad boy."

He pulled away from March, staring into her eyes. "He wasn't a bad boy. He had some wild oats to sow, that's all."

March nodded, keeping to herself the memory of Fred's final actions that caused his death. There was no reason to share that with Bud; no reason to inflict further pain.

"I'd like to have seen her," he said quietly. "My granddaughter."

"Me, too." March smiled gently. "My Mama said she had a head full of dark hair, and was as tiny and dainty as a little doll. She said she was a real beauty."

His tear-rimmed eyes studied the delicacy of her face, the golden hair that curled riotously every which way, the wisdom and understanding in her gray eyes. He tried to clear his throat, but his voice was little more than a harsh whisper. "She'd a'had to have been, if she looked anything like her mother."

Bud released her abruptly, dropping his hands to his sides. "I ain't apologizing for none of this, and I hope we never cross paths again. I won't be able to look at you without thinking of my boy . . . but I'ma thinking we both missed out on something special, because we didn't meet a whole lot sooner.

"Your daddy might be nothing but white trash, but you . . . you're a lady who deserves better than you got."

With a nod at her, ignoring everyone else at the clearing, Bud turned and walked away. March folded her hands together and watched until he was out of sight, tears for his loneliness and sorrow dampening her face.

"Come here, sweetheart."

Never had an invitation been so welcomed or more readily accepted. Jim took her into his arms and held her tightly against him. He felt her slowly relax, her arms coming to rest around his waist.

"I was so scared," she whispered.

"I've never been prouder of anyone in my life." Jim rubbed his cheek against the top of her head. "You are the most giving person I've ever known. Bud was intent on causing you pain, and you turn around and offer him understanding and sympathy!"

"He's so desperately hurt."

The observers moved away, most discussing March's gentle strength and understanding, some clearly disappointed that the ending had been so sedate. Several of them looked at her with new respect, and more than a few decided that maybe they had been too harsh in their original judgment of the girl.

A wagon pulled up beside them and March looked up, surprised to see Mazie holding the reins. "Come on with me, sweetie pie," the older woman called. "Let's make a quick trip into town, and get you spruced up just a little."

"Mazie, I'm fine." March pulled away from Jim, but still kept one arm around his waist. "A little worse for wear, but so is everyone else by this time of day."

"Go with her, angel," Jim coaxed. "By the time you get back, everybody will have forgotten most of it, and will be anticipating the finale of the day."

"Jamie?" March looked toward the quilt, relieved to see the baby snuggled contentedly in experienced arms.

"He's fine. Go on now, get away from here for a few minutes."

"This is ridiculous, you're both acting like I'm some delicate maiden, who's going to swoon any minute." Letting Jim lift her into the wagon, March settled beside Mazie.

Sitting with her hands in her lap, she was surprised to discover that they were shaking. Maybe it was a good idea for her to leave the picnic for a few minutes. The trip into town and back wouldn't take more than a half hour. By the time she returned, she was sure that she would be in better control of herself.

Reluctant to let her out of his sight, Jim watched as the wagon pulled away. He and Mazie had made some hasty plans, one of which was to get March into town for a while. Now it was his turn to handle his assigned tasks. His eyes narrowed as he searched the clearing until he located the man he needed.

With a satisfied nod, Jim headed in his direction.

Mazie tied the team to the hitching rail in front of the store, and pulled the keys from her pocket. Unlocking the door, she opened it wide and ushered March inside.

"Whew, it sure is good to be out of that sun for a few minutes." Her smile was reminiscent of the one she had worn when she invited March to do something naughty. "I have a surprise for you . . . a present, if you will."

"A present? For me?" March's eyes widened with astonishment.

With a chuckle, Mazie pulled her toward the back of the store. A large, white pasteboard box with a big pink ribbon sat on the counter used for cutting fabric. March's fingers shook as she untied the ribbon, carefully wrapping it around her hand, so it could be saved to use later.

Lifting the lid from the box, March was speechless as she looked at the contents. "Oh, Mazie, you can't mean this for me?"

"And why not, young lady? It's mine to sell or give away as I see fit, and I can't think of anyone else in this town or even Tucson who will do this dress half the justice you will."

Reverently, March lifted out the striped silk dress that had caught her attention the first time she had come to the store. She hadn't dared to touch it then, and now she marveled at the luxurious fabric, the softness of the velvet trim.

"Let's get you upstairs, and see if we can't find some water to wash with, then we'll see how it fits."

"Mazie, I can't wear this."

"Why ever not?"

"I don't know how."

"Then it's time you learned. I won't take no for an answer. If you keep arguing, you're going to make me mad and hurt my feelings." Mazie grabbed her arm. "Now, no more of your non-sense. When we go back to the picnic, they're going to think that a princess has decided to honor them with her presence."

March learned a new lesson . . . it was difficult, if not downright impossible, to argue with someone, when you didn't want to win the argument in the first place!

Jim waited as patiently as possible for March to return. He had changed Jamie's towel, and dressed the baby in a clean gown he had found in the bottom of the bag.

He had combed his own hair, rolled down his sleeves, and put his coat on. He was as nervous as a stallion in rut, he thought. Smiling at his own analogy, he realized it was far too true, though he'd never admit it to anyone other than himself.

The sound of a wagon approaching snapped him from his lusty thoughts. Mazie pulled up beneath one of the trees, and Walt helped the ladies descend.

Jim's breath caught and held in his chest at his first sight of March. She was beautiful beyond his imaginings. The pink, green, and brown striped dress fit her perfectly, hugging her narrow waist and accentuating her golden coloring. Rather than hiding her full bosom, the high-necked gown seemed to emphasize her feminine roundness.

Her hair had been pulled up to the back of her head, and left to hang in ringlets around her slender shoulders. A perky pink and black hat tilted enticingly over her brow, while a saucy green feather teased her eyebrow.

Mazie had insisted that they leave the bustle off of the dress, stating that, fashion or not, it made March look like she had a deformed backside. The extra fabric flowed in a graceful train behind her.

March felt a combination of embarrassment and pride in herself. No one else at the gathering was dressed even half as nicely, and everyone stared wide-eyed, the men appreciative, the women envious.

She looked nervously around the clearing for the one pair of eyes that mattered the most, and couldn't have been more pleased at his expression. He held Jamie against his shoulder as his gaze moved slowly from the top of her head to the tips of her new shoes, barely visible at the hem of the gown.

Feeling like a pretender, March slowly walked toward him, her chin held regally high, as she waited for his response. It wasn't long in coming.

"You are incredibly beautiful, Miss Evans." Jim took her hand in his and carried it to his mouth. He placed a chaste, social kiss on the work-roughened back, then turned it over and bent again.

This time his actions were those of a lover, as his tongue darted out, circling the center of her palm several times. Gently, so that he caused no real pain, he nipped at the base of her thumb, then laved it to remove the sting.

Startled, March pulled her hand free as her face flamed with pleasure. Curling her fingers into a fist, she savored the impression of his lips against her skin.

"The celebration is nearly finished." Jim smiled as he noticed her clenched fist. Acting as if the taste of her hadn't nearly driven him to his knees, he put a hand beneath her elbow and turned her, so that they faced the far end of the clearing. He was relieved that they didn't have to move from beneath the trees, since he wasn't sure that his legs would support him if he tried to walk.

March looked, but didn't see the excitement taking place at the other end of the clearing. Her mind was a swirling eddy of confusion, incapable of registering anything beyond the burning in the center of her palm. She could still feel his tongue pressed hotly against her hand, and had to force herself not to look down to see if there was a permanent imprint.

Good heavens, he had kissed her twice today! But never, ever, in any romantic imaginings she'd ever had as a young girl, had she guessed that something so simple as his lips against her skin would feel so . . . so . . . wonderful!

March blushed to the roots of her hair at her thoughts. Even his hand so casually holding her elbow sent a flash of heat up her shoulder. She felt hot, yet shivery, and her breathing was labored, as if she had run to town and back without stopping.

Wondering if she was sickening with something, she swallowed hard. Sure enough, her throat was tight and her head felt light. Maybe it was too much sun or too much excitement. The day had been one emotional peak after another. Perhaps she wasn't as strong as she liked to think she was. Maybe the meeting with Bud Hamner had been more trying than she had thought.

She blamed her feelings on anything but the real cause. March wouldn't let herself admit that Jim's kiss was the culprit. If she did, then she'd have to wonder why it affected her so deeply, and she wasn't ready to face that answer.

"You're going to miss it, angel." Jim leaned over and whispered into her ear, his breath warm against her skin.

"Miss what?" March forced herself not to lean into him, to be closer than was considered proper. In fact, she was having a difficult time remembering what was proper.

"The cannon." Jim smiled to himself, more than satisfied with her reaction to him. She was finally aware of him in a way she had never been before.

"Cannon? What cannon?"

He fought the chuckle that was trying to force its way free. Knowing he should feel just a little guilty for causing her inattention, he was too pleased with himself to give it much thought.

"Russ Willis always brings his cannon every year, and fires off several rounds at the end of the Independence Day celebration."

The cannon was Russ Willis's pride and joy. He had salvaged it from one of the forts that had been abandoned at the end of the war between the states. Several times a year he pulled it out of the shed he had built specially to protect it, and fired several rounds into the air.

The children loved it, but the adults greeted it with mixed emotions. Several of the men had served in units during the war. The sound of the cannon brought back bittersweet and painful memories of the battles they had fought, the loved ones they had lost.

Seeing someone light a torch, Jim leaned over to her. "Here, hold the baby and cover his ears. It gets pretty loud."

He handed the infant to her, watched as she pulled his head snugly against her breast and covered his free ear with her hand. Knowing what was coming, Jim reached up and covered her ears with his hands.

At the ground-shaking *boom* and puff of smoke, a cheer went up from the crowd. Even with her ears protected, the sound was so loud that March wondered if the men closest to the cannon would become deaf.

Jamie turned toward the sound, his eyes widening with surprise. March worried that he would be frightened, but instead he seemed pleased with the muffled noise.

Again and again the cannon rang through the clearing. Each time, even though she watched them load it, March jumped with startled surprise. A thick layer of gray smoke drifted on the breeze just above everyone's head, the smell of sulfur was almost overpowering.

When the final round was fired, the men who had done the work turned and bowed dramatically to the crowd. They were greeted with a rousing round of applause and cheers.

Jim removed his hands from March's ears and slipped his arm around her shoulders.

"That was different, but slightly noisy," she said with a smile.

"I always imagine what the noise of a battle must have been like." His voice reflected the lingering regret that he had been born too late to go to war. "Imagine several cannons firing, the sound of rifles, and the screams of the men."

"And the dying, the suffering, the agony," she replied quietly. "Why must young men die in battle? Why must mothers mourn the loss of their sons when old men decide to go to war? Is anything so precious that it's worth dying for?"

"Freedom, March, the right to govern without someone else making the decisions."

"Seems to me that someone is always making my decisions for me. I don't think any war ever fought has ever brought freedom for any woman. It's men who fight the wars and make the decisions. All a woman can do is make the best of what she has to work with."

"A woman doesn't need to go to war. She has a man to protect her and provide for her."

"And beat her, starve her, abuse her," March mumbled.

"Never, angel." Jim placed his hand beneath her chin and raised her head. "Never again will anyone abuse you. I promise you, I will spend the rest of my life protecting you from harm."

His fingers were so warm against her chin, his eyes burning with a blue fire of promise. If she let it happen, she knew she could be mesmerized by his voice.

"Don't make promises you might not be able to keep." She intentionally repeated the words he had used weeks earlier, when she had promised to be a perfect student, if only he'd teach her to read.

"I intend to keep these."

"Only as long as I'm on your ranch."

"Planning on leaving?" he asked with a smile.

"It might happen someday." Her eyes turned smoky with sadness at the thought. "You might remarry, and your wife may decide she doesn't want me around."

"Oh, I definitely plan to remarry." His eyes sparkled with amusement.

March's head snapped up with shock. "Soon?" she whispered.

"Very soon."

Clutching Jamie so tightly that he protested,

March fought to maintain her composure. She hadn't expected this, nor had she been prepared for the shaft of pain that shot through her.

"I'm . . . I'm very happy for you," she whispered. "She'll be a good mother for Jamie? I guess . . . I guess I should be looking for another job, another home."

Jim felt a rush of guilt as he saw the sparkling happiness in her eyes turn to dull pain. "I'm sorry, angel."

Regretting that he had chosen to tease her in such an inappropriate way, Jim sighed with relief when he saw Mazie approaching. The time had come, and never before had he been so sure that he had made the right decision.

"Can we go home now?" The day had been so perfect that she hadn't wanted it to end. Suddenly, she couldn't wait to get away, to hide in the room she shared with Jamie, to shed the tears that were threatening to overflow.

"The day isn't quite over, March. There's one more event planned before everyone goes home."

He took Jamie from her arms and handed him to Mazie. At a nod from Jim, the older woman smiled and walked away. Turning to March, Jim smiled softly and gently stroked her cheek, reaching up to give the saucy green feather a flick.

"Preacher Daves has a final chore to perform, sweet angel," he stated quietly. "Will you marry me, March Evans?"

Twenty

Delaying the inevitable for as long as possible, March checked one final time on Jamie, adjusting the light blanket over the sleeping baby. She patted his rounded bottom, marveling at how much he had grown in such a short time. He was developing a personality, talking in a language uniquely his own, and grinning freely with an endearingly toothless smile.

After his final feeding each night, he usually slept until after sunrise. But March had started the habit of leaving a lamp lit, turned down low, in case she had to get up with him in the dark.

Reluctantly, she turned away, her gaze coming to rest on the neatly made bed that had been hers.

Months earlier she had thought she was the luckiest girl in the world to have that bed all to herself. A bed with real sheets and blankets, in a warm room with pictures on the walls and curtains at the windows.

Months earlier, filled with a sorrow that knew no beginning and had no end, she had been forced to leave her family, the only security she had ever known, and come to this castle of a house to care for another woman's child.

Months earlier she had been a little girl masquerading as a woman, but experience had forced her to mature almost overnight. As a brief flash of panic flared through her, she wished that she was once again a little girl, who could run to Mama and find the gentle love and understanding she so desperately needed.

March walked out of Jamie's room, knowing that she would never again share it with the child. From this night on she would sleep in the big bed in Jim's room, sharing it through the many years of their lives together as man and wife.

Wife! She pulled the door closed with hands that had started to shake. With a few words spoken in the meadow just a short time earlier, she had become a wife. She had vowed to love, honor, and obey, to spend the remainder of her life as the mate of a man she barely knew.

True, she had lived with him for the past few months, but as his employee, not his wife. A man could easily treat an employee in a manner completely different from that in which he treated a wife. If he abused an employee, the person could simply quit the job and leave. But a wife had no such choice, she was stuck, and if children were involved, she had the added responsibility of protecting them.

"God, let him be gentle," March prayed silently as she stood at the top of the steps, looking down at the darkened room below. At least he waited

for her in his study, rather than in the bedroom. It didn't help that she knew firsthand the degradation and humiliation that awaited in the marriage bed, and added to her prayer that Jim would be a considerate lover, unselfish in his demands and compassionate of her fears.

Clenching her sweaty hands into fists, she readily admitted that she was terrified. Her one experience had left an indelible scar that hadn't begun to fade even a year later.

Her knees seemed ready to collapse beneath her with each step, as she reluctantly descended the stairs. Trying to convince herself that Jim had always treated her kindly didn't alleviate her fears. She kept remembering that always before she'd had the choice of staying or leaving. Now the choice had been taken from her.

With an undignified plop, March sat down on one of the steps. This was getting to be ridiculous. For the last two hours, she had been dreading the moment Jim would claim her as his wife. Clutching her head between her hands, she wondered what had happened to her common sense. Had it flown out the window as she repeated her wedding vows? She had come to this house with a less than decent reputation and with two dresses in her possession. Jim had offered her a job, a home, and a security she had never known before.

He trusted her to care for his infant son. He had seen her desire to learn to read, and had taken time from his busy schedule to become her teacher. And in the weeks that had passed, he had become her first real friend.

So, she asked herself, what's all this nonsense about being afraid? He wasn't going to suddenly turn into a monster, because she was now his wife rather than his housekeeper. There was no unpleasant surprise waiting for her once they were in bed. She knew exactly what he would do, and while she didn't look forward to it, she knew she could always close her eyes and practice her spelling words, until he was finished. It would be over in quick order, and then they'd sleep.

Sighing at her own stupidity, March rose to her feet. Being a wife brought a good many changes, most of them pleasant. Jamie was now her son, no one could ever take him away from her. She had a beautiful, if somewhat large, home, plenty of food to eat, and a wonderful feeling of security.

If Jim wanted to claim his husbandly right once or twice a month, why, she could tolerate that. It wouldn't take all that long, and her spelling could always use all the practice it could get.

Straightening the skirt of the nightdress that had been a present from Mazie, March continued down the stairs. It was just a little awkward, this coming together the first time. After tonight, they'd find a routine, and within a week or two, it would be like they had always been married.

Jim had taken off his coat and rolled up his

sleeves. For nearly an hour he'd tried to occupy his time, and his thoughts, with something other than the woman who was now his wife. He'd had little success, and his nerves were stretched so tightly, that he felt like he'd break if he had to wait another minute. He knew she was scared, but putting it off was only going to make her anxiety worse. Time would prove that she had nothing to fear of him, or of their marriage.

Deciding that she'd had long enough to get Jamie to bed—hell, she'd had long enough to run halfway to town!—he knew he had to take matters into his own hands.

Reminding himself that he needed to practice extreme gentleness, Jim blew out the lamp on his desk and turned to the one across the room, beside the chair March usually occupied.

A flash of movement at the doorway attracted his attention. Suddenly, Jim forgot to breathe, as he stared at the vision that was his alone. The cream-colored nightdress and matching robe teased and enticed, emphasizing the very curves it sought to cover.

The entire bodice of the robe was made of lace that hid nothing of the plunging neckline of the dress beneath it. Long bell-shaped sleeves, also made of lace, gave alluring glimpses of the bare shoulders and arms. Feminine shadows beckoned with an irresistible temptation to touch, to explore, to taste. Silky hair nearly to her hips hung in an inviting cascade of golden tresses.

Jim remembered to breathe, when the room started to swirl around him. He couldn't tear his gaze from her, as he slowly approached, trying to force himself to act as normal as possible.

"New dress?" His voice was deceptively casual, while his eyes burned with a hunger bordering on starvation.

"Yes, do you like it?" March twirled in a circle, unknowingly making the hem of the gown float just above her slender ankles.

"Oh, I like it, angel." Jim's voice was a husky rasp. "I like it entirely too much."

"Mazie gave it to me as a wedding present. She said she knew that you'd like it," March smiled innocently. "I can't understand why she thought it was necessary for you to like it, when it's a gift for me?"

"Can't you, sweetheart? I think it is a wedding present for both of us; for you to wear and for me to admire."

"Something this pretty shouldn't be kept hidden in a bedroom. It should be worn for everyone to admire."

Putting his fingertips beneath her chin, Jim raised her head. "It is indeed pretty and you are beautiful, but I don't want anyone else seeing what's for my eyes only. They'll just have to wonder what's put a smile on my face."

March looked at his grim mouth. "Do you plan to do a lot of smiling?"

"Constantly.

"When are you going to start? You certainly
don't look too happy right now."

"Later, angel, I'll smile all the time. For now
I've got better things to do."

Jim traced the outline of her lips with his
thumb, pulling back the fuller lower lip to find
the delicate skin inside. He felt her tremble
slightly, and smiled with satisfaction.

"You're smiling," she mumbled.

"It's just the beginning, Mrs. Travis."

March's eyes widened at the title. "I am Mrs.
Travis, aren't I? I hadn't given that much thought
. . . March Travis . . ."

Without warning, Jim bent and swung her
into his arms. He turned and carried her from
the room.

Wrapping her arms around his neck, March
leaned confidently against him. Whatever was
about to happen, she could endure. It was such
a simple thing to do for him. He had given her
so much, surely she could give him this, she decided with a sigh. So far it had been . . . pleasant. His admiring gaze had been unexpected,
his gentle touch pleasurable.

Stifling a yawn with the back of her hand,
March closed her eyes as her head rested against
his shoulder. Soon it would be over, and she
could sleep. It had been a long day, filled with
excitement and new experiences.

Expecting his destination to be the bedroom,
March was startled when she heard a wooden
chair sliding across the floor. She opened her

to eyes to find that he had carried her into the kitchen. He smiled mysteriously as he lowered her to the waiting chair.

"I have a special surprise for you, Mrs. Travis."

After lighting a lamp, he walked across the room, stopping in front of a wooden barrel that hadn't been there earlier. March's curiosity grew as she watched him pry off the lid, and then scoop out handfuls of straw. By the time he freed the clay crock embedded beneath the straw, she was leaning so far out of her chair, that she was in danger of falling.

"Mazie wasn't the only one to give us a wedding present." Jim carried the bowl over to the table. "Walt made this specially for you, and said I was to give it to you when the time was right. I think about now would be the best time for you to have it."

Anticipation brought a glow to her stormy gray eyes, as she reached for the lid. The coldness that met her fingers confirmed her hopes.

"Ice cream!" March removed the lid, delighted by the creamy confection in the bowl.

"It's not going to last much longer." Jim dipped a finger into the melting cream. "The ice in the barrel is nearly melted, and this is a little milkier than usual. Walt knew it wouldn't last, but he wanted to give you something special to remember the day by."

"I don't think I will ever forget this day." Unable to resist for another minute, March stuck a finger into the ice cream. "But it sure was sweet of him to do this." She licked her finger clean, closing her eyes with delight.

"If you'll wait just a few more seconds, I'll get a spoon." Jim grinned at her. "I wouldn't want you to miss any of this."

He returned with two spoons and sat down beside her, pulling the bowl between them. Like greedy children, they consumed the ice cream, sharing the pieces of peaches Walt had mixed in. The heat worked quickly, turning it into liquid, but neither of them minded.

In the kitchen of the big house, with only the light from a single lamp, they began their lives together as husband and wife, by sharing the simple delicacy.

Jim entertained her with stories of his childhood, while growing more and more intrigued with her smile, her soft laugh, her sparkling eyes. By the time the bowl was empty, March was completely relaxed, and Jim was aroused to a fevered pitch.

"All gone." She sighed with contentment as she scraped the spoon over the bottom of the bowl.

Taking the spoon from her hand, he placed it on the table and put his fingers beneath her chin. Leaning over slightly, he softly kissed her lips, tasting the peach ice cream lingering there.

"I want to make love to you," he whispered.

"I know," March replied quietly.

"I don't want you to be afraid."

"I'm not." She smiled confidently. "I was, at

first, when I realized what you'd want to do to me, but then I got to thinking about it, and, after all, it only takes a few minutes, and I can practice my spelling while you're doing it."

"What?" Jim leaned back, letting his hand drop from her chin. "You plan to practice your spelling while I make love to you?"

"Sure . . . I mean, I won't take my list with me, but I can practice my days and months. And if I'm not sure about one of them, then I'll wait until you're done, and I can ask you. I won't interrupt you or anything."

Shaking his head, Jim didn't know whether to laugh in amusement or howl in outrage; somehow he was torn between both emotions.

"Sweetheart, making love isn't something to do alone."

"Well, of course not. I don't know much, but I do know that."

She was so innocent, he thought with an indulgent smile. For all her experience at the vile hands of Fred Hamner, she still didn't know the first thing about making love.

"You won't . . . ah, mind?" he asked, trying to hide a grin. "I mean, I don't want to interfere with your spelling."

"You won't." March patted his hand lightly, unaware of the open challenge she had just offered.

"Well, as long as you're sure . . ."

Jim blew out the lamp and again swung March into his arms. Guided by the light of the full moon, he effortlessly maneuvered through the room. Her long gown wrapped sinuously around his legs as he slowly climbed the stairs, her bare feet peeking from beneath the hem.

"I'm perfectly capable of walking." March snuggled contentedly into his arms. She knew he wouldn't drop her, and she found that it was nice to have someone to depend on. Granted, this carrying her from room to room was only for this one special night. But from now until the end of her life, she would have him to count on when she needed him.

Until she was relieved of it, March hadn't realized how much responsibility she had carried on her shoulders for so many years. Her mother had had so many children so close together, that she was usually either expecting or healing. As she had grown older, March had gradually taken over the burden of taking care of the little ones.

Her life now seemed almost leisurely. With only one child to care for, she had more free time than ever before. The anxiety over food, shelter, and clothing was one of the past. As Jim's wife, she could expect him to worry over such things, while she tended to Jamie and the house.

It was a heady feeling, to know that she suddenly had more freedom and security than she had ever dared to dream about.

In the bedroom, Jim lowered her feet to the ground, but kept an arm around her slender waist. The room was bathed in the light of the moon, making a lamp unnecessary.

"Monday," he murmured as he lowered his lips to hers, gliding whisper-soft against them.

March stood quietly in his arms, slowly spelling the word to herself. It was one she had learned easily, and prided herself on remembering. The touch of his lips against hers was soothingly familiar.

"Tuesday." Jim traced the shape of her lips with the very tip of his tongue, lingering slightly at the corners. His hands moved restlessly up and down the slope of her back, from her shoulders to her rounded bottom.

Tuesday wasn't difficult either. There were only four letters with the word day at the end. His tongue was so warm and surprisingly soft. She wondered if he would object, if she tasted him as he was tasting her. Of course, he would, she decided with a sigh. He was the one making love; she was practicing her spelling.

"Wednesday." Jim lifted his lips from hers and pulled loose the ribbons at the bodice of her robe. The silky fabric slid freely down her arms to pool at her feet. With fingers eager to explore new territory, he traced the path of the thin straps over her shoulders.

March closed her eyes, hoping that she could better concentrate if she wasn't watching the fascination on Jim's face. Wednesday was a tough word, one she almost always misspelled. How could he expect her to get it right, when his touch was so tender, his fingertips so warm?

"Thursday."

"Wait! I haven't gotten Wednesday right yet."

"That's all right, you can go back to it later." He bent and kissed the soft skin where her shoulder met her neck. Suckling lightly, he left a lover's brand on her creamy flesh.

"Thursday," he repeated, kissing his way up the side of her neck, as his fingers journeyed down the sides of her body from the fullness of her breasts, lingering at her tiny waist and over well-rounded hips.

Thursday was nearly impossible with his lips against her neck. The pressure of his suckling against her skin sent shivers of delight down her back. His hands were incredibly warm, burning through the light layer of her gown and into her flesh. No, Thursday wasn't easy.

"Friday." Jim teased himself as much as he teased her, letting his lips and fingertips learn her in ways he'd often imagined. The silky fabric of her gown and the silky texture of her skin were driving him to a burning need, one that he intended to satisfy very thoroughly, very soon.

March bent her head to the side, giving him freer access to her neck. His inquisitive fingers traced the plunging neckline of the gown where it dipped between her breasts, delving just beneath the fabric to the skin below. She wasn't sure she had spelled Friday correctly, which surprised her, since it was usually as easy as Monday . . . but then, she'd never been this distracted before, either.

She was surprised to realize that her breasts felt heavy and incredibly sensitive, her nipples were like hardened pebbles. That was a reaction she was familiar with when it was time to nurse the baby, but she had never imagined that she'd experience it at any other time.

"Sunday."

"Wait . . ." March moaned as the backs of his fingers trailed over the tips of her breasts. "I . . . I'm still working on Thursday."

"Sunday, sweetheart. Thursday was way back here." He suckled on her neck again, leaving another brand of possession.

"How am I supposed to remember how to spell Thursday when you do *that?*" she asked, moaning at the sensuous feel of his mouth on her skin.

"I'm sure you can figure something out." Smiling at the obvious distraction on her face, Jim stepped back and pulled the suspenders from his shoulders. He watched her watching him, as he freed the buttons of his shirt. "Did you ever figure out Wednesday?"

"Wednesday?" As the shirt came open, she discovered that his chest was lightly covered with dark hair. Wanting suddenly to reach out and touch him, March closed her hands into fists at her sides.

"Try something easier, like Friday or Sunday." Pulling his shirt free from his pants, he slid it from his shoulders and let it drop to the floor. Moving away from her, he locked the heel of his boot in the bootjack, and pulled his foot free. Soon his socks joined his shirt and her robe on the floor.

"Friday? That's . . . that's usually an easy one." March watched with utter fascination as he unbuttoned his pants and let them slide down his long legs. Covered only by his knee-length drawers, she swallowed hard at the obvious bulge. She knew exactly what was there, having cared for Jamie and her little brothers, but somehow it was so innocent when the male was a baby, and so . . . so exciting when it was Jim.

Satisfied that he had caught her attention, Jim lifted her into his arms and carried her to the bed. Lowering her slowly onto the crisp white sheets, he leaned over her and let his mouth make a trail from her shoulder to the beginning slope of her breast.

This wasn't at all like she expected, March decided as she looked at his dark head against her breast. Not at all!

"January." Jim pulled free the ribbons that tied on her shoulders and one beneath her breast, leaving the gown in place.

"I haven't finished the days yet," March muttered as his warm breath fanned across her. He slid his drawers from his body, giving her only a brief view of his masculinity before he joined her on the bed.

"February," he whispered, as he made a trail

down the center of her body, stopping just short of his ultimate goal. When he could stand it no longer, he slipped the bodice of the gown down to the tip of her breast.

"April."

"You forgot March," she reminded him with a moan, as his hand rubbed gently against her stomach, making wider and wider circles with each rotation.

"Never, ever, sweet March. How could I forget a taste as heady as wine? Skin softer than the softest velvet? The little moans of pleasure, when I touch or taste? No, angel, I could never forget March."

Jim kissed the slope of her breast, pushing the gown out of his way until the cherry pink tip was exposed. A fever of need soared through him, as he lowered his mouth and gently suckled. Taking care not to hurt her, he tasted his fill, then traveled to the other breast.

She had forgotten how to spell April! God above, what was he doing? This was something entirely new and unexpected. She wanted to clutch him tighter to her. She wanted to push him away, as she felt a frightening new sensation course through her. She wanted . . . she wanted to spell April.

"May." Jim raised her enough to free her from the gown. The moonlight fell softly on her skin, and he caught his breath at the beauty of her body. Her full breasts gave way to a waist he could span with his hands, and led to rounded hips and a flat stomach. The curls at the crown of her femininity were the same golden blond as the hair on her head, and he was eager to discover the treasure they protected.

"June." Kissing, tasting, teasing, Jim forgot why he was naming the months of the year. He forgot everything but the lovely woman who was his wife.

"July." With incredibly gentle fingers, he parted her thighs and found the warmth of her. Her moans of surprised pleasure were adding to his heightened enchantment, as he teased them both.

"August."

March thought she knew what to expect, but whatever that was, it wasn't this. Her body felt on fire, and yet shivers kept dancing across her skin. Her breasts ached, and there was an unfamiliar throbbing deep inside her.

"September."

She couldn't stop her hands from moving to Jim's back, tracing the heavy muscles, delighting in the warmth and smoothness of his skin. The hair on his chest tickled against her in a way that added to her awareness of him. When he parted her thighs and gently stroked her, she felt a tightening anticipation deep within her.

"October."

Jim lifted himself over her, resting comfortably between her silky legs. He felt the heat and the need, and knew he was as close to losing control as ever in his life.

"November."

March waited with her breath caught in her chest, for him to become a part of her, but he didn't seem to be in any hurry. With his hands buried in her hair, he kissed her neck, working his way toward her mouth. His lips were hot as they settled onto hers, his tongue invading in a dance of passion. His hips rocked slowly back and forth, while the hair on his chest rubbed deliciously against her sensitive breasts.

"Please?" she asked, pleading for release from the sensuous torment.

It was all the invitation he needed. One word that told him he wasn't alone in this ritual of mating. In her innocence she had thought she wouldn't be involved, and he had gently taken her on a journey of discovery of her own body.

Jim slipped into her eager warmth, sighing as she sheathed him protectively in her body.

"December."

Twenty-one

"Want another spelling lesson?" Jim felt her moan more than he heard it. She lay snuggled tightly against his side, her surprisingly long legs tangled with his.

"Did you ever figure out how to spell Wednesday?" he asked far too innocently. "I think that was the first day that gave you trouble."

When a muffled mumble was her only response, he smiled with male satisfaction. "I think I could get rather fond of April . . . and July is definitely tops in my spelling book."

"What did you do to me?" March felt as weak as a newborn kitten, yet her skin was so sensitive that the slightest touch filled her with awareness.

"You mean you don't remember? I thought I was just helping you practice your spelling."

"I think I got a little sidetracked." She wanted to roll over and stretch, but without something to cover herself, March felt much too bashful, even after the incredibly intimate act they had just shared.

"Well then, maybe we should work on it." Not

nearly as inhibited, Jim rolled her to her back and leaned over her. "Do you remember April?"

"April?" March felt her face flame as his gaze came to rest on her breasts.

"Yes, angel. April." Jim lowered his lips to the tips of her breasts, gently suckling. "And July." His hands drifted slowly down her body, until he found the enticing entrance.

March arched her back, bringing her nipple more fully into his mouth, and opened her thighs to invite his touch.

"I think I'll need to practice my spelling more than once or twice a month," she moaned, soaring with newfound desire.

"Once or twice a month? Sweetheart, I don't know where you got the idea that we'd only make love once or twice a month, but I assure you, it will be much more often than that . . . more like once or twice a day."

"I will be an excellent speller by our first anniversary." March reached for him, her eyes inviting his possession.

"Oh, I can guarantee that." Jim slid between her legs and slowly entered her. "And we'll always end the lesson with December."

"Didn't you forget Saturday?" March asked later, much later, with a sigh of utter completion.

"Umm . . ." Jim couldn't remember ever feeling as satisfied in his life. Rather than fearing him, March matched him touch for touch, kiss for kiss, following his lead when she wasn't sure what to do next.

"You remember Saturday? Follows Friday, before Sunday?"

"Oh, baby, I remember Saturday." He turned to her and pulled her into his arms. "When we finally get to Saturday, I promise you that you'll never forget it either."

From habit, Jim woke just as the sun began to chase away the darkness. Knowing that he needed to get up, but reluctant to leave the bed, he spent long, leisurely minutes studying his new wife.

In the morning light she looked far too young to be a wife and mother, too young to handle the tremendous responsibility. Yet she did handle it, and did an excellent job. Her features were delicately feminine, from her rounded chin to her upturned nose. Long, thick lashes of dark gold rested against her cheeks, and her slightly parted lips innocently invited him to sneak a taste.

He felt a stirring of desire and shook his head in rueful disbelief. It didn't seem possible that he could want her again. But there was no denying the awareness that was burning through him.

Wondering if he was dreaming, praying that he'd never wake up, he smiled ruefully when reality called.

The squeaking protest from the room down

the hall was a vivid reminder that he wasn't dreaming, and that a new day had dawned. Climbing out of bed before Jamie could waken March, Jim went to get the baby.

March heard Jamie, but before she could do more than battle to open her eyes, she felt Jim leave the bed. Rolling over and stretching, she smiled at the soothing sound of his voice and Jamie's gurgling response. The baby was always happy to see someone first thing in the morning, but his good mood would last only a very few minutes, before hunger took control.

March swung her legs over the side of the bed, startled to discover that she was slightly sore . . . in a very pleasant way. Pulling the sheet up over her breasts and holding it into place beneath her arms, she looked for something to cover her more modestly. The only thing available was her gown lying in a puddle of silk on the floor, with Jim's shirt a complementary embellishment on top and his pants staking a place of prominence to the side of it.

Her face flamed at the memory of him removing her robe and gown, of his kisses and intimate caresses. Heat grew as she recalled his whispered words tantalizing her, his own clothing, so casually discarded, joining hers on the floor.

Had she really allowed him to do all of those incredibly intimate things to her? Had it really felt so good, or was her memory playing tricks? What had happened to her determination to be a lady?

"Good morning, angel." Jim walked into the bedroom—serenely, nonchalantly, gloriously—naked! Jamie, held high against his shoulder, was his only covering.

March turned a bright red as she admired his long, lean body, hardened by years of work on the ranch. There wasn't a spare ounce of flesh on his frame, from the top of his head to the tips of his feet . . . just several feet, six to be exact, of wonderfully masculine body.

"Like what you see?" he asked with a leering smile.

"Very much," March replied in spite of her embarrassment.

"Glad to hear it, since it's all I have to offer."

"I wouldn't say that."

"No? Name something else." He patted Jamie's back, trying to quiet the squirming baby.

"You've given me a beautiful home to live in, lovely clothes to wear, plenty of food to eat . . ."

"Those are material things, angel. I have enough money to provide you with nearly anything you want, but I'm not so sure I can give you the things you need." Jim's light mood evaporated as he realized that she deserved more from him than a house or clothes or food.

March pulled the sheet more snugly over her breasts, and pushed her tangled hair from her eyes. "You have given me more than I've ever had in my life. For the first time I have security; I won't be moving in the morning or run out of town tomorrow night. No one is going to attack me or threaten me. I don't have to worry about hunger or being cold or trying to cook in a drizzling rain.

"I'm free." She waved her hand around the room. "Even if all of this was suddenly taken away, I wouldn't worry, because I know that you would be there. I've never had someone to take care of me, for as long as I can remember, I've always been the one to take care of others."

Jim was humbled by her honest gratitude. "March, I promise that you'll never again have any worry about security, but there are things a woman needs to make her life complete."

"I can't imagine anything I don't have now that I'll need in the future. I have a beautiful home, food, clothes, and a son. If there's something missing, I sure don't know what it is."

"Love, March," he said quietly. "Every woman needs love, but I'm not sure I can ever give you the love you need and deserve. I may have been wrong to rush you into marriage. Someday you might meet someone who can give you love."

He was being so considerate, his gentle voice filled with regret. "Jim, love is for young girls whose heads are filled with romance stories of princesses and knights on white horses. I'm not a young girl; I've never been a young girl. I know what's important in life, and a useless emotion won't feed you when you're hungry, or comfort you when you're cold.

"I'd say that love has caused more problems for people than any other single thing they face in their lives. And, to tell you the truth, I'm not even sure the emotion exists, except for the love a parent has for a child."

"So cynical for one so young."

"I'm far older than the number of years I claim." She smiled gently, her eyes drifting to Jamie, who was becoming very vocal. "I like you and respect you. I'll always be grateful for the things you've given me, and I'll try to be a good wife to you and a good mother to Jamie and any other children you give me."

Turning her head slightly, she grinned. "You do realize that we'll probably have a number of children. Mama never had any trouble getting caught, and I have a feeling I'm just like her. You won't mind, will you?"

He hadn't thought about children, her children, but a shiver of fear drifted down his spine when he remembered Melanie and the pain she had suffered. He didn't want to see this tiny woman swollen with his child, twisting and turning in agony to give it birth.

"We don't need to rush it any. We can wait awhile, before we add to the family," he replied firmly.

"I don't think we'll have much choice, unless you want to refrain from further spelling lessons?" she teased impishly.

Jim's throat tightened and a heaviness filled his body. Now that he had tasted her, loved her, he knew it would be impossible to sleep next to her night after night without making love.

"No," he said huskily.

"Good, me either. I think I'll soon become an excellent speller, but I do think we can do without this love nonsense, don't you?"

Jim wasn't sure how to respond. His intention in starting this conversation had been to reassure her, yet somehow he was the one being reassured. Jamie's howl vibrated through the room, threatening his hearing.

"Feed your son, madame, we'll continue this discussion at another time." He handed the baby to her and then climbed back into bed.

"Aren't you going to go to work?" March patted Jamie's rounded bottom, trying to soothe the hungry baby who was becoming very vociferous in his protest over the delay in his meal.

"Later." Remembering his one opportunity to view March nursing Jamie, Jim leaned back against the headboard and folded his arms over his chest, deciding that wedding vows gave him some unexpected pleasures. "I think the men can manage a few hours without me."

"Oh . . ." March wanted to ask him to leave, but didn't know how. There was no doubt that he was comfortable with his nudity. She, however, wasn't quite as relaxed with the new intimacy.

"Angel, if you don't soon feed that boy, he's going to bring the roof down around our ears." He smiled understandingly at her shyness, but didn't budge from his place on the bed.

Trying to keep her back turned as much as

possible, March reluctantly lowered one side of the sheet.

Denied the sight he most wanted to see, Jim studied her slender back. Held rigidly straight, he could count nearly every rib. She was delicately made, from her narrow shoulders to her tiny waist to her nicely rounded hips. He felt an overwhelming urge to press a lingering kiss on the dimples, where her back rounded into her buttocks.

Climbing to his knees, Jim moved up behind her. Gathering up her sleep-rumpled hair, he placed a light kiss on her shoulder. The action provided him with the opportunity to look down at his son.

"The most beautiful thing I have ever seen in my life, was the night I forced you to feed Jamie in my office."

His whispered words moved warmly over her skin, making her shiver in reaction.

"I knew how embarrassed you were," he continued softly. "I wanted to apologize, but I couldn't take my eyes off of you, and I was afraid if I said anything, you'd run from the room."

Jim wrapped his arms around her, pulling her gently back against his chest. Putting one arm under hers to help support the baby, he let his free hand rest against her stomach.

March was vibrantly aware of the warmth of his body and the solidness of his chest against her back, his thighs surrounded her hips, until she was enveloped by his masculine bulk.

Hazy sunlight filtered past the sheer curtains at the windows, as the quiet sounds of morning drifted into the room, adding their own sense of peace. Leaning her head against his shoulder, she felt embarrassment slowly slip away, replaced with a contentment of a different kind, one she had never experienced before.

The strength of his arms provided a comfort and tranquility that seeped into her soul.

It was security, an oasis from reality.

In the early morning quiet that surrounded them, it was sanctuary.

The morning of her third day as Jim's wife, with Jamie fed and in bed for his morning nap, wash hanging on the clothes line and beans soaking for supper, March decided to explore the house. Respecting Jim's privacy, she had never ventured into rooms with closed doors, even though her curiosity had been nearly overwhelming at times.

Starting in the kitchen, she opened one of the two doors that had remained closed in that room, discovering that it led into the dining room. The other door revealed a set of stairs leading down. Since the room below was shrouded in darkness, March lit a lamp and descended the steps. At the bottom she found a small pantry, lined with row after row of nearly empty shelves. It would be the perfect place to store the produce from her garden, she decided as she climbed the stairs.

On the lower floor, the only room that hadn't been explored contained a delicate desk with frilly curtains at the window. Several satin-covered chairs and gilded tables, set in groups of two and three, filled the room to overflowing. Obviously a lady's sitting room, she wrinkled her nose in distaste at the fussy room and quickly closed the door.

Upstairs there were three bedrooms other than Jamie's and the one she shared with Jim. Two of the rooms had only a bed and dresser, with plain curtains of a nondescript shade of tan at the windows. The third room was such a surprise, that March could only stand in the doorway and stare in amazement as foreboding spread through her.

It wasn't the pink frilly bows that covered every inch of the room that caused her feeling of un-ease. Nor was she bothered by the thick white carpet and lacy white curtains that draped grace-fully over the windows. Her gaze came to rest on the wide bed with its white canopy held back with pink bows. A mountain of satin pillows in every imaginable shade of pink were piled hap-hazardly on the far side of the bed. She shivered and crossed her arms over her chest, when she realized that the bed covers were thrown back as if someone had just left the room. The blanket and silky white sheets trailed onto the floor, where a slipper lay tipped on its side.

The vanity, with a lacy pink skirt and white bows, held a jumbled collection of bottles and jars, some with their lids open, while others were still wrapped in their original paper. A thin layer of dust coated the once-sparkling cut glass.

March backed out of the eerie room, softly closing the door behind her. There was no doubt that the room belonged to a lady, nor was her identity a mystery. What did remain in question for March, was why Melanie had a separate room from her husband.

The final door on that floor revealed a set of stairs leading up. The sight of Melanie's room hadn't prepared March for the chaotic disarray of the attic. The smooth wooden floor was covered by dresses, petticoats, and untold numbers of accessories; bonnets of every description, lacy colorful parasols, gloves, handbags covered with shiny beads.

March was appalled that such beautiful garments were strewn so carelessly around the room, as if by the hand of a maddened giant intent on destruction. She was even more horrified as she tried to imagine what would cause someone to so ruthlessly destroy things of such beauty and value.

Had Jim, in a fit of anger at his young wife's death, been compelled to obliterate anything of beauty that had been hers? Or had Melanie, for some reason March couldn't begin to imagine, done this to her own things?

"I think, at the end, she went a little mad."

Jim's voice from the doorway so startled March that she had to stifle a scream.

"I shouldn't have left her alone that morning." He continued into the room, surveying the scattered array with a deepening sorrow. "Her death was so useless, maybe if I had stayed with her, she would still be alive."

"A lot of women die in childbirth, Jim," March consoled quietly. "It's not something you could have prevented."

"She didn't die because of childbirth." His voice deepened with guilt. "If anything, Melanie died of neglect."

"Neglect?" March leaned over and picked up a bright yellow gown. Carefully, she began to fold it, so that she could put it in one of the open cases.

"I spent more time worrying about the ranch than I did about her." Jim leaned against a support beam and watched her work. It was time she knew the truth about Melanie, and perhaps learned a few things about him at the same time. "A ranch can't run itself, it takes a lot of time and energy. Melanie wasn't happy with her life. I knew it, but didn't do anything about it."

March heard his pain and wanted to take him into her arms to help chase it away, but she knew that sympathy wouldn't help him to find his way through his feelings of guilt.

"Pooh!" Dropping the yellow gown into the case, she reached for another one. At a different time, she would have enjoyed just touching the rich fabrics, but now her concerns were centered on her husband, and the pain he still carried.

"Pooh?" One eyebrow rose in surprise as he looked at March.

"Yes, pooh. No one is responsible for someone else's happiness. If she wasn't happy, then *she* should have done something about it, not sit back and wait for you to change her life for her."

"I'm not sure she knew how to be happy."

"Then that was her fault, not yours. It's not polite to speak ill of the dead, but she sounds rather spoiled to me. She had a beautiful home, lovely clothes, a son on the way, and a husband who loved her. If that wasn't enough to make her happy, then she wouldn't have been happy if you'd stood on your head and talked with your feet."

"I still feel that there was something I could have done, if I'd only paid more attention to her."

"Perhaps so, perhaps not." March folded a blue gown of such gloriously soft fabric that she couldn't resist stroking it. "I've seen her bedroom, and now this. I never met her, but from what you've said, I don't think she ever grew up. I think she wanted to stay a little girl forever."

"You're probably right, but that doesn't make it any easier for me to accept my cruelty to her."

"Cruelty is seeing a hungry child and not feeding it. Cruelty is watching a horse with a broken leg suffer rather than shooting it. Cruelty is telling yourself that it's your fault that Melanie wasn't happy." Suddenly the lovely gowns and trinkets weren't nearly as attractive to March.

They were reminders of a life wasted. "It's sad that she's gone, that Jamie will never know his mother. But life continues, day after day. Keep her as a gentle memory in your heart, and let the rest go."

"It's not that easy," Jim said quietly.

"Nobody ever said it would be, but you don't deserve to spend the rest of your life regretting hers. With time and a little practice, your memories will be pleasant ones. The sorrow and guilt will fade."

All ready Jim was beginning to find that the guilt of Melanie's death was lighter. Somehow this woman, with a few words, had helped him to see and accept that it hadn't been his fault.

"How'd you get so wise?"

"Nothing wise about it. Common sense tells me that she had everything to live for, and yet she chose to give it up. That wasn't your fault. Why should you be the one to suffer?"

It was the same things he had told himself since Melanie's death, but for some reason, it sounded more convincing coming from March. He could almost believe that he hadn't been at fault, that Melanie had been a spoiled, pampered little girl who wasn't ready to be a wife; who would have never been ready to grow up.

Maybe, someday, he would believe it.

Twenty-two

In the main room of the old adobe house, March sat on the multicolored rag rug that graced the floor, and smiled at Jamie's antics. The baby gurgled happily at her, his grin displaying four pearly white teeth; two on the top and two on the bottom.

Rolling over to his plump belly, he struggled to get his hands and knees beneath him. Successful, he turned to look at March, batting his thick eyelashes. With a shriek of carefree glee, he used his newly learned technique to crawl over to her.

"You're so silly." March picked him up high over her head and kissed his tummy, smiling at his pleased giggle. He was a beautiful baby with dark brown hair, and deep blue eyes surrounded by the thickest eyelashes she had ever seen. No longer content to stay where he was put now that he had discovered mobility, he was becoming a little person with a definite personality and a growing list of likes and dislikes.

Putting him back onto the rug and handing him a wooden toy Hank had carefully carved to fit a tiny grasp, March picked up her sewing. Adding the few final stitches to the shirt that was to be a Christmas present for Jim, she sighed with contentment.

She couldn't quite believe how happy and satisfied she was in her role of wife and mother. Jamie was a pure delight, the light of her life. With Jim, she found a contentment she hadn't known existed.

The old adobe house had become her own private domain, to her knowledge no one else ever entered the structure. Jim was aware that she spent time there several days each week, but never intruded on her privacy. With a few touches strictly her own, a colorful pillow here, a coverlet there, she had turned the abandoned house into a home.

She often wished that she had the nerve to suggest to him that they move into the adobe, but she was afraid that he would be offended. The big house was beautiful, the furnishings luxurious, but coldly impersonal. It would never have the appeal of the adobe nor the warmth of a real home.

Of course, they would soon need the extra bedrooms of the big house, March thought with a satisfied sigh. Since she'd had her monthly time only once shortly after their marriage four months earlier, she had every reason to believe that she was in the family way. It gave her a deeper feeling of contentment to know that she was carrying Jim's child.

Along with the shirt she planned to give him next month for Christmas, March decided to give him the news about the baby. By then it would be definite, not just a suspicion.

"What do you say about heading home, young man?" Folding the finished shirt, March gathered her sewing supplies together and placed them in the quilted bag she had made.

"It's getting late, and I need to get your daddy's supper cooking and give you another bath." She gathered the gurgling baby into her arms and bounced him on her lap. "How one little baby can get so dirty is a mystery to me. You seem to find dirt even when there isn't any. You've got enough under your chin to plant some corn."

March tickled his neck, delighting in his giggle. "We'll plant corn here." She tickled him just beneath his right ear, "And some beans along about here." Kissing the flesh along his jawline, she wiggled her fingers under his other ear. "And maybe some squash here, and a few potatoes beside them."

Suddenly the door to the house was thrown open with such violence that it bounced against the wall. Clasping Jamie against her chest, March looked up with alarm as she reached for the single-shot derringer in her apron pocket.

"Come quick, missy," Woods gasped between strangled breaths.

"What's wrong?" she asked, climbing hastily to her feet.

"Give me that youn'en and hustle over to the big house."

"Woods, what's wrong?" Alarm raced down March's spine as she clutched the baby tighter.

"The boss's been shot. It's bad, missy, real bad," he replied gruffly.

"Shot . . . oh, my God, no . . ."

"There ain't no time to waste. Breed said to get you there quick-like."

Knowing that Jamie would be perfectly safe in Woods's care, she placed the baby in his arms. Pulling her skirt up nearly to her knees, she raced from the house.

Jim had been shot! She couldn't believe that Jim, so strong, so vitally alive, could now be in danger of dying. Only last night he had picked her up in his brawny arms and carried her up to the bedroom. His lovemaking had been wickedly teasing, bringing her to the point of madness, before he had taken them both over the edge of fulfillment.

Was he still alive, or had he already been taken from her?

Never before had the distance to the big house seemed so long, or her feet so heavy. *Too late, too late,* her running footsteps seemed to mock. By the time the big house came into sight, March was breathing heavily and a stitch pulled in her side, but she didn't slow her pace. Her thoughts were centered on Jim and the very real possibility that she would, indeed, be too late.

The house was alive with activity, men seemed

to be milling around everywhere. Each one of them looked at her gravely, a few nodded, a few turned their faces away.

March flew up the steps, her gaze riveted on the open door of the bedroom she shared with Jim. Her attention was drawn immediately to the still figure on the bed, and the spreading red stain on his dusty shirt.

At her moan of anguish, snarling silver eyes lifted to her. Breed said something quietly to the man beside him, before he rose gracefully to his feet. His tall, powerful body loomed over March, as he reached for her shoulder and forced her from the room.

"He needs you," Breed said quietly when they were alone. "But he doesn't need someone to hang over him wailing with grief."

"How bad is it?"

"Bad."

"Will he live?" Though her words were whispered, her fear was a viable thing.

"I don't know." It never entered his mind to lie or to soften the blow with a half-truth. "He needs someone who is willing to fight for him. If you can't do that, then go back to your house over the hill."

March felt anger creep in around the edges of her fear. "I will not moan and groan, nor will I run away and hide. I've seen blood before and managed not to swoon. He is my husband; my place is at his side."

"Good." Breed nodded once, turned, and

headed back to the bedroom. He was aware of March at his side and the fact that the next few hours would take all of the strength of will she possessed, and then some.

The man at the bedside nodded when they approached, then left the room after a few words with Breed. A bucket of warm water and some clean sheets waited on the table nearest the bed.

March was proud of the fact that she didn't blink an eye when Breed pulled the big knife from its sheath on his thigh. Her teeth bit into her bottom lip, as she fought to remain quiet when he slipped it under Jim's bloody shirt, splitting the fabric from hem to neckline. Only the barest hint of a sound passed her lips, at the tiny hole low in his shoulder that oozed dark-red blood.

Breed was too busy to pay attention to March. If he had, he would have seen the tears that she made no attempt to wipe away. He only knew that when he started to remove Jim's shirt, she was there to help pull away the fabric. Her hands were steady as she sponged away the blood, giving them a better view.

"I need to roll him over," Breed stated, gently moving the injured man.

"Why?" She knew how badly he was hurt, and couldn't stand the thought of moving Jim unnecessarily.

He didn't reply as he carefully turned Jim to expose his heavily muscled back. Seeing what he'd expected to find, disappointed that there was no exit hole, Breed slowly lowered him back to the bed. He carefully palpitated the bruised flesh, feeling the grate of bone against bone in at least two spots.

"The bullet's still in there, and he's got at least two broken ribs we've got to worry about. There's no air bubbles around the hole, so I'd say it missed a lung, but one of the bones could still do the damage."

"He'll make it," March stated firmly. "Tell me what to do."

"You ever remove a bullet before?"

"No, but I will if I have to." She raised her chin, unaware that the tears on her face gave her a vulnerability even the hardened warrior admired. "I take it we don't have time to send for the doctor?"

"It'd be better, if we don't wait." Breed stood and looked down at her. "Besides, I don't want word getting out yet that he's been shot."

"Why?"

"Don't know who did it, or why. If they know he's alive, they might try again."

"You mean this was deliberate? Someone pointed their rifle at Jim, and intentionally pulled the trigger?"

He didn't answer, choosing instead to remove the remainder of Jim's clothing. "We'll need more rags, a bucket of hot water, some sewing thread, a needle, and whiskey."

"I asked you a question," March stated firmly. "Did someone intentionally shoot my husband?"

Breed dropped the dusty pants. "He came riding in alone, barely hanging onto his horse. His gun hadn't been fired, so he didn't do it to himself. Been more than one man who's found himself dead when his gun went off at the wrong time."

He removed the cloth thong that held the long blond hair at the nape of his neck and tied it around his forehead just above his eyebrows.

Annoyed that he hadn't answered her, March reached out and grabbed his arm. "I asked you a question; did someone intentionally shoot him?"

Breed looked down at her hand on his arm, but didn't shrug it away. "My guess is that he was ambushed. I'll look for signs later, but if you intend to see him live past tonight, we've got to get that slug out now.

"Go get the things we need while I get him ready."

As he moved away, March reluctantly left the room. Her thoughts were frenzied as she wondered why someone would deliberately shoot Jim. He knew most of the people in the area as friends, except maybe for Bud Hamner. The old man was grieving, but after their confrontation at the Fourth of July celebration, she didn't think he would harm Jim.

She thought briefly of Light, but discarded the idea almost immediately. The Indian had brought her back of his own free will, she couldn't believe that he would now go after the white man who had claimed her.

So the question remained unanswered for now. Whoever had shot Jim was still roaming free, while he was fighting for his very life.

With the help of two ranch hands, March gathered up the things Breed needed and carried them back upstairs. She had to bite back a protest, when she saw that he had tied Jim spread-eagle on the bed. His ankles and wrists had been wrapped in several layers of fabric, so that the ropes didn't cut into them, but she still objected to the cruelty of tying him.

"Is that really necessary?" She nodded toward the ropes.

"If you have the strength to hold him still, I will release him."

Unable to fight the wisdom of his decision, March made no further protest as she began to cut a sheet into usable sizes for bandages. The next hour and a half was torture, plain and simple torture, for both the injured man and the woman who helped to cause him further pain. From the moment when Breed had enlarged the bullet opening, until she carefully sewed the last of the fourteen stitches needed to close the wound, March fought back a constant need to cry against the agony they were causing.

After a thick pad had been placed on the incision and several layers of fabric had been wrapped around him to try to hold the broken ribs in place, March pushed her hair out of her eyes and stood in a daze as Breed untied the ropes.

She tried not to think of how difficult it had been to stick the needle into his flesh, nor how easily the steel shank had sunk into the damaged skin. She knew that for the rest of her life she would be haunted by the tugging and pulling sensation of the needle weaving in and out of him.

"You did good." Breed's compliment was all the more effective because of its simplicity.

"Now what?" she asked, as reaction began to set in and her hands started to shake.

"Now we wait."

"Wait . . ." March knew that the waiting would be the hardest part.

"When the fever comes we may have to tie him down again if he starts to thrash around. We should know one way or the other in three or four days."

"Three or four days . . . my God, I don't know if I can wait that long to know if he'll live."

"The wait will be far shorter if he dies."

"He won't die!" Looking around the room, March finally saw the soiled linens and buckets of bloody water. "I think I'll get this mess cleaned up, check on Jamie, and then sit down and have a good cry."

With Breed's help, the room was set to rights in a very short time. He left to find the baby for her, giving her much-needed time to be alone with Jim.

He was so pale beneath his tan. His eyes were closed, but she wondered if it was in sleep. He had opened his eyes only once during the time they had dug for the slug. His gaze had connected briefly with hers, before pain had driven him back to the realm of unconsciousness.

March gently stroked the hair back from his eyes. "Fight, Jim Travis," she whispered. "Your son needs you . . . I need you."

Her words surprised her. They had been unplanned, coming almost of their own. Not until she had uttered them had she known the extent of her need for him. They hadn't discussed love since the night of their wedding, but standing there watching him struggle for each breath, March began to wonder. Could this be love? Was love this overpowering need to protect him from further harm? Was the fear growing in her, because the man she loved was injured?

"I wish I knew what love is," she whispered more to herself than to the sleeping man. "I'm so confused. Am I so scared because I love you? Or is it a selfish desire to have you live so that my life doesn't go back to what it was before?

"How do I know love from self-preservation? Do I love you, Jim Travis? Or do I simply want to keep the many wonderful things you've given me?"

Kneeling beside the bed, March rested her head against the soft surface as exhaustion bowed her shoulders.

"I'm so confused," she whispered. "And so very, very scared."

March stilled, barely breathing, when she felt his hand come to rest on her hair. Only the stillness in the room let her hear his murmured word. Whether conscious thought or a mind so riddled with pain that it reached out to another time, it brought her a measure of comfort she so desperately needed.

"Angel . . ."

On the morning of the third day, with dark circles beneath her eyes and only bits of sleep snatched during the endless nights, March knew Jim needed more help than either she or Breed could provide.

Leaving him at the tender mercy of Hank, she went in search of the foreman. She was unaware of the crystal-clear morning air with just a hint of winter chill, or the softening of the desert as it awaited for respite from the summer heat.

Carrying Jamie balanced on her hip required almost more strength than she had left. By the time she reached the barn, she knew that the baby had gained at least twenty pounds in the last two days.

Breed was speaking in his quiet manner to one of the hands. She waited patiently for him to finish and send the man on his way. To her knowledge, the men were aware that Jim had been injured, but the details had deliberately been left sketchy.

"He needs the doctor. Go get him," she stated bluntly, too tired and too worried to take the time for diplomacy.

Breed saw the exhaustion pulling at her, and knew that only her determination and willpower were keeping her on her feet. During the past two days, he had spent many hours with her and deeply respected her loyalty to her husband. If anything, she was stubborn to a fault, insisting on being with Jim every minute of the day and night.

He almost smiled when he remembered checking on her late last night and finding her sitting on the floor beside the bed, sound asleep. He had picked her up and put her on the bed beside Jim, and now he wondered what she had thought this morning when she had awakened to find herself there.

"I said he needs a doctor," she repeated when Breed hadn't responded.

"It may be dangerous for him, if word gets out," he warned quietly.

"It will be *deadly* for him, if we don't do something. His fever is out of control."

"That is usual in such an injury."

"I don't want to hear usual!" she shouted. "He's dying. Do you understand me? While we stand here arguing, he's upstairs dying! Post a guard around the house, stand a man outside the bedroom door, find some killers for hire. I don't give a damn what you do, but I want that doctor here, and I want him here *now!*

"My husband's life is threatened and I expect you to do as you're told. Do I make myself clear? Get the doctor!"

Breed smiled. He knew it was the wrong thing to do, that it would just further ignite her rage, but he couldn't help it. She was a mother mountain lion fighting for her cubs, and, as are all mothers, she was magnificent.

When the grin slashed across his handsome face, March saw red. She had heard the expression used, but had thought it sounded kind of silly. Now she understood it . . . Lord, how she understood it!

Seeing his smile and misinterpreting it for derision, she wanted to attack him. She even went so far as to look around the barn for a safe place to put Jamie so that he wouldn't be in danger. Never, ever, had she been so violently angry or so powerless to retaliate.

"Sheathe your claws, little cat," Breed said quietly. "My humor is not at your expense. Since I left my people, I've never seen a woman so determined to protect her mate. Most white women I've seen are weak and helpless. They demand to be treated as fragile flowers.

"You are like the women of my tribe. You will bring about your own death to protect those you love. It has made my heart lighter to know that my friend has such a wife."

"Go for the doctor . . . please?" Tears clouded

her eyes, belying the strength she had shown earlier. His words had been so gentle and sincere, that she felt like the biggest fraud in the world. She wasn't strong . . . she just wanted, needed Jim to live, to be well, to return her world to the safe, dependable thing it had been before he'd been hurt.

"I will go. We will take the risk, if only because you need the reassurance the man of medicine can give you."

"You'll go now?"

"As soon as I saddle my horse." Breed reached up and stroked Jamie's soft cheek. "Take the little warrior into the house to be near his father. He will feel your presence, and know that he is surrounded by your strength and your love."

"I'm not strong," she sighed wearily. "I wish I were, but I'm not . . . I've tried so hard . . ."

"You are one of the strongest women I've ever known, either Indian or white. You are like the plants of the desert, you will struggle against any hardship, and then will blossom to show that you have won."

He reached for his saddle and carried it past her toward the corral. A shrill whistle pierced the air, and a magnificent Appaloosa stallion responded by raising his head. Another whistle, and the animal raced toward the man who beckoned.

In a matter of minutes the horse was saddled and restlessly pawing the ground in anticipation. When Breed mounted, it was difficult for March to decide which was the more impressive animal;

both were flawless examples of perfection, neither of them quite tamed.

"Go do your job, Angel of the Desert," he commanded, giving her a name that seemed appropriate for this tough but gentle woman. He found himself almost regretting that she was the wife of another. He had never considered taking a wife before now . . . now that it was too late.

"My job is to worry," she replied, a slight smile creasing her lips when she remembered their conversation so many months earlier.

"No, your job is to be a woman. You do it well."

Twenty-three

March stood at the kitchen window, a cup of coffee slowly cooling in her hands. As she stared out at the mountains on the horizon, she let her thoughts drift in a hazy web of exhaustion. It had been five days since Jim had been shot. Five days of hell, relieved only by occasional moments of intense relief when his fever would break and he would be lucid for a few hours.

At first she had been fooled into thinking that the worst was over, that he would survive. Now she knew better, for all too soon the fever returned. It would climb until he felt on fire, until his skin was too hot to touch.

The doctor had come, complimented March on the fine row of stitches, and commented on Breed's excellent care. Stating that there was nothing more that could be done other than to keep Jim as comfortable as possible while he fought the raging fever, he had gone.

March's own rage had known no bounds, as she had ranted against the seemingly indifferent doctor. It wasn't until she had seen Breed's smile that she had finally stopped raving. It was downright aggravating the way that man seemed to enjoy her anger!

She finally agreed with him that there was nothing the doctor could do that they couldn't. She knew that the doctor had other patients he needed to tend to, making it necessary for him to leave. But that didn't matter. Those people were strangers to her; Jim was her husband. The doctor could have, should have stayed just in case . . . just in case.

March shivered at the thought of what "just in case" meant. They had fought so long and hard to save him, surely they would be rewarded. He had to live . . . he had to! She couldn't let him go. She hadn't told him about the baby they had made together, or that Jamie could crawl across a room now . . . or that she loved him.

Sometime, during one of the endless nights, while the world slept and she kept a lonely vigil, March had accepted that she was in love with her husband.

The realization had come quietly, settling comfortably around her like a soft mantle. She had watched his fever-ridden body toss and turn, listened to his constant mumbling, and knew that her life would never be the same if she had to live it without him. She knew beyond a shadow of a doubt, that she didn't want to live it without him.

Leaning against the window frame, the coffee cup forgotten in her hands, March felt a restless yearning to find solace in Jim's arms, to turn back the clock to a time before he had been shot, so that she could tell him of her love.

She knew that he didn't love her, might never love her. She thought she could accept that, even understood why he might never be able to love again.

During some of his fever-induced ramblings, she had learned how his love for Melanie had slowly eroded to pity and dislike. Tears had filled her eyes, while she listened to him beg Melanie to forgive him, and she longed to offer comfort, to give him the kind of love he deserved, to wipe away his feelings of guilt because of her death.

But all she could do now, all she had done for days, was wait, wait for either the fever to break a final time, or for death to release him from his pain.

It was there again, that soft misty cloud with its pristine facade of newly fallen snow and its promise of tranquility. He didn't know his own name, or why he was being punished in such a tortuous way. He wasn't sure if he still lived. Maybe he had died, and this was hell with its unrelenting fires of eternal damnation.

He did know, almost instinctively, that if he just reached out, he would be enveloped in a mantle of coolness, the savage heat would be tamed. That it was a false promise was of little concern to him; after days of being burned alive, he cherished even the thought of reprieve.

He was tempted. It was an offer so filled with temptation, that he began to wonder why he hesitated. The desire, the need, the demand of his own body, commanded that he accept.

But each time he nearly gave in to the entice- ment, a voice called softly to him, staying his hand. A sweet voice, so filled with love and long- ing, begged him not to go.

He found that he could resist the lure of the cloud, but not that of the voice. Somewhere in his fever-induced delirium, he fought to identify the voice, to put a name to the person calling to him. It became a challenge to search through his jumbled memories to discover her name.

Finally the cloud drifted away, changing shapes as clouds are wont to do. First a beckoning hand, then a velvet field thick with soft spring grass, and finally a concealing curtain, each inviting him to come and explore. He was tempted . . . but then the voice . . .

Always the voice, calling sweetly through the pain, promising a world of paradise in words he couldn't quite understand.

A soft tapping on the back door released March from her thoughts. Expecting to find one of the ranch hands inquiring about Jim, she was startled speechless to see her father, hat in hand, a lop- sided grin on his face.

"It's me, girl. Ain't been that long since ya seen your pa that you done forgot my face," George Evans said jovially.

March had thought that if she ever saw him again, she would feel an overwhelming desire to cause him the kind of pain he had caused her. She was startled to discover that she felt nothing for the man standing on the back stoop; not love nor hate nor even revulsion. She tried to ignore the need to ask about her mother and the children. She wouldn't give him the satisfaction of letting him know that she cared.

"What do you want?"

"What do I want? Why, I come to see my baby girl."

George pushed his way into the kitchen, his wary gaze rapidly searching the room. Finding it empty except for them, he turned to his daughter. His manner was exceptionally meek, uncharacteristically humble.

"I heard 'bout you marryin' up with this rancher. Seems I done you a good turn, fixin' you up with him and all. Now it's yore turn to help out your old pa a little." He shuffled his feet and twisted his hat in his hands. "Jan and Feb runned off a while back. You know I ain't never been much with a rifle. I could use some vittles, it's been a bit since I ate."

"No." Hating for anyone to be hungry if she could do something about it, March frequently offered food to strangers. He was certainly no stranger, but she didn't care if he starved to death. She wanted him away from the house, before his taint of corruption could somehow infiltrate the room.

"How can you be sayin' no to me, girl?" he whined. "I'm your pa."

"No," she repeated, feeling a new strength begin to spread its wings. "You have never been a father to me. You don't even know the meaning of the word."

"I done the best I could!"

"How? Tell me one time that you considered anyone except yourself first."

"Why, there was many a time when I knew my babies was hungry, and I found money to feed them."

"Stole it, you mean. And then you spent it on whiskey. The only time we had money is when you came home drunk and passed out. Then I'd dig through your pockets and take what was left." March looked at the man who had fathered her, and felt a growing disgust that she was related to him.

George Evans felt a growing frustration. This wasn't going at all the way he'd planned. March was supposed to be scared, more than ready to accept his guidance. The woman facing him was a stranger, with a strength he wasn't accustomed to encountering in a woman. Of course, March always had been a stubborn one.

"You'd lie, cheat, and steal to get what you wanted. But you finally reached the bottom, when you sold me to a man who only wanted my innocence. You tried to make a whore out of me, and when that didn't work, you sold me again. A father doesn't abandon his child to a total stranger."

"I done you good!" he argued, his face turning red with anger. "Lookee here at this fine house! Why that dress yore wearin' is better than anything yore ma has! Now get me some food, afore I have to take my belt to you. I have a lot of decisions to make, and I ain't makin' 'em on an empty stomach."

Expecting instant compliance, George turned away. His greedy gaze noted the well-made furnishings and the trappings of a comfortable life. There was money to be had here, probably more money than he'd seen in his entire life.

"Get out of my house," March said quietly, a thread of steel lacing the words with conviction. "You aren't welcome here now or ever."

"Yore house? Well, ain't you the high-and-mighty one. You ain't been a widow a week yet, and you're already givin' orders! Well, you better be thinkin' about who yore tryin' to order around. I ain't some hired hand."

March didn't hear his entire tirade. She hadn't heard a word after his comment that she was a widow. How could he know that Jim had been shot? It wasn't common knowledge, since Breed had made every effort to keep it quiet.

Suddenly she had an idea how he knew, an idea so vile, it made her blanch. Breed hadn't found any traces of the shooting, since he had been unable to determine exactly where it had happened. It was a big desert, and the trail had grown cold long before he had been able to back-track it.

"Have you gone stupid on me, girl? Get me some vittles."

"You shot him," she stated quietly. "You shot my husband."

"Ain't no way you cain prove it." George puffed up, as pride filled him at his achievement. He hadn't lied when he had stated that he wasn't too good with a rifle. He figured that luck was on his side that day. "No siree, you cain't prove nothing."

"I don't need to prove anything to anyone. I know the truth, that's all that matters."

"I'll tell you what matters, girlie," he snarled, tired of her disrespect. "I'm yore pa, and yore a widow-woman who needs a man to take care of her. Me and yore Ma is moving into this fine house, and you'll do everything I say. Do I make myself clear?"

"Go to hell," she replied softly.

"I've had enough of yore backtalk." George crossed the room until he stood within reach of her. "I done what I had to do, just like I've always done what I had to do. There ain't gonna be no more talkin' about it. And from here on out, yore gonna do exactly like I tell you to do, or you'll be sorry."

March smiled as his threats drifted past her like snowflakes on the wind. He couldn't hurt her again. Finally, after all the years of painful beatings and harsh humiliation, George Evans couldn't touch her.

"Go to hell."

With a speed common to small men, George reached out and backhanded March. He watched with satisfaction, as her head snapped back and blood welled up from her lips.

"That's just a taste of it, little girl. Anymore of yore backtalk and you'll get a whole lot more. There ain't nobody to tell me what I cain or cain't do."

March wiped the blood from her mouth and looked at the bright red stain on her hand. One time, a long time ago, she had run from him when he had started to hit anyone near at hand. But that was a long time ago, a lifetime ago. She had been a child; now she was a woman.

March felt free, incredibly free. The pain of her split lip was negligible in comparison to the years of agony she had suffered at his hands. But now it was at an end. There was nothing he could do to her. He had tried his worst and failed.

Just a few months as Jim's wife and a lifetime of self-recrimination was put into its proper perspective. She had nothing to be ashamed of, nothing to regret.

She was free of her father's corruption. Free to be a wife to Jim, a mother to Jamie. Her hand came to rest on her still-flat stomach. She could hold her head up with pride, meet the gazes of friends and strangers, and know that she was as good as any of them, maybe even better than some.

"Go to hell," she said slowly, distinctly.

George's fist swung again, connecting solidly with her jaw. March didn't try to dodge that blow, but from the corner of her eye she saw his other fist aimed for her stomach. She twisted away; it landed on her hip with enough strength to knock her from her feet.

Fury unlike any she had ever known ran like fire through her veins. She could take the punishment for herself, but he was threatening the child that nestled within her body.

Rising from the floor, her hand sought the derringer in her pocket. She turned to face George, a magnificent mother protecting her offspring.

Holding the small gun in both hands with it pointed at his belly, her face was a twisted snarl of hate. Even at this range there was a slight chance that the bullet would miss him, since the gun was known to be inaccurate. It was a chance she would gladly take to protect her baby.

"Get out of my house, now!"

"Put that toy gun down!" George demanded. "I ain't gonna be threatened by my own daughter, and I ain't gonna forget it neither. You'll do as I say, or you may just find yourself havin' an accident someday."

March cocked the weapon. "This is your last warning. Get out!"

He raised his fist and swung, but it never connected with its target. Two shots rang out, one seeming to be the echo of the other. George grabbed at the burning hole in his stomach, and watched the crimson blood flow between his clutching fingers.

"Ya shot me . . . I'll be damned, ya really shot me."

Slowly, like a wind-up toy that has run down, he crumbled to his knees. March watched as his eyes turned glassy, and his body relaxed in death.

"Oh, my God . . ." she muttered, letting the gun slip through her fingers.

"It is done, a coyote has been destroyed," a deep voice said from behind her.

In shock, March turned in time to see Breed holster his Colt. "He was your father, for that I ask that you forgive me. A child shouldn't witness the savage death of a parent, whether he deserved to die or not."

"You shot him?" she asked in confusion. "Are you sure? I thought *I* had done it."

"It is my bullet buried deep in his belly. Your shot went wild, and is in the wall by the fireplace."

"I couldn't have missed." March shook her head with disbelief. "At this distance I couldn't have missed."

Breed's silver eyes softened with compassion. "It is not an easy thing to kill a man. It is harder still to kill your parent. At the last you turned your gun away enough that it missed.

"I wasn't so generous. My bullet raced true.

Had there been more time, I would have used other means to stop him, but I came into the kitchen when it was too late to do more than to protect you with my gun."

March believed him, maybe because, in the end, she wanted to. She stared down at her father, and remembered her promise so long ago to someday gut-shoot him and laugh as he died. She hadn't been the one to shoot him, and she wasn't laughing.

"He was going to hurt my baby," she mumbled quietly.

Breed looked at her hands protectively cradling her stomach, and understood her fear for her unborn child. "Your last memory of him shouldn't be that you were the one to cause his death. He wasn't a good father, but he was your father. Search your mind until you find a happy memory of him, and keep that with you. Let the pain of the truth drift away until it is gone."

"I know I should be sad that he is dead, but I can't find any sorrow in my soul."

"It is hard to mourn the loss of someone who brought you only pain." Breed reached out and gently touched the bruise on her chin. She had been so fierce, this tiny woman, taking the blows for herself, but protecting her child in the only way she could. He wouldn't let her carry the burden that she had killed her own father. Right now she was in shock, but soon the pain of guilt would raise its head, and she would agonize over it for the rest of her life.

It was only a small lie, one that wouldn't have been necessary had he arrived in the kitchen only seconds earlier. George would never have touched her had Breed been around.

Breed looked into her troubled gaze and knew that he would always regret arriving too late, but he would never regret the lie.

He also knew, as surely as he knew that the sun would rise in the east, that it was time for him to leave. A friend had written recently, requesting a favor of him. He would use that as his excuse, for how could he stay? If he stayed, eventually the truth would be known by all . . . he had fallen in love with the woman another man had already claimed as his own, a woman who carried the growing seed of life within her body.

"I ask your forgiveness, Angel of the Desert," he repeated softly, his hand unknowingly caressing her cheek.

"There is nothing to forgive." March found peace in his touch, the touch of a friend. "Thank you for being here when I needed you."

Breed reluctantly withdrew his hand and nodded. "Go upstairs to your son and husband. I will take care of things down here.

"My mother . . . how will I tell her what happened?"

"I will find her and bring her to you. She will know the truth before she arrives."

"I can't ask that of you."

"You didn't. Now go." The friendliness was

gone, replaced with his usual mask of indifference.

After March had left the room, Breed moved to the fireplace. With the point of his knife, he dug at the wood beside the structure, until the slug he had fired there fell into his hands. Dropping it into his pocket, he began the grisly task of removing all signs of the violent death.

March slowly climbed the stairs, a heavy weight of exhaustion riding her slender shoulders. Checking on Jamie first, she was amazed to discover that he had slept through the noise.

Moving into her own bedroom, her eyes widened when she realized that Jim was staring at her, his gaze clear and questioning.

"What's happening? Did I hear a gunshot?"

"Jim . . . you're awake . . ."

"And tired." He studied her and saw the weariness in her face and the darkening bruise on her chin.

He cursed silently at the weakness that prevented him from providing her even the most basic protection. He had no idea what had happened, but suddenly, the most important thing was that he touch her, hold her in his arms.

"Come here, angel." He patted the side of the bed, a slight smile crossing his face. "Come lie with me, and tell me what's going on. You can start with telling me the reason I feel like my horse threw me, trampled me, and ate me for dinner. After that, I'd really appreciate an explanation for your colorful face."

March laid a gentle hand on his brow and sighed with relief to find it was cool. The temptation to accept his offer was too great, the need too demanding, to refuse. She climbed into the bed beside him, snuggling up to his uninjured shoulder.

"Is Jamie all right?"

March had to smile. He had regained consciousness several times, and each time had asked the same questions. "Yes, Jamie is fine. I'm fine. Your cows are fine."

"They aren't cows, they're cattle," he corrected.

"Whatever . . ."

Jim tried to move to a more comfortable position, and bit back a moan as pain slashed through his shoulder. There wasn't a comfortable position. Every muscle and bone in his body ached. He remembered being told that he had been shot, but knew little else of the past several days.

"How long—" he began, only to be interrupted by his smiling wife.

"This is the fifth day. You've asked that same question nearly every day since it happened."

"How?"

The smile left March's face, as a shudder raced through her. "Pa," she stated bluntly. "He must have heard about our marriage and decided that living here was preferable to digging for gold."

Jim's only reply was to pull her more tightly against his side.

"He's dead," she said quietly.

Jim nodded, but again he didn't comment. "Your mother and the children?"

"Breed's gone to get them."

"Good, they can stay here."

"I thought, maybe, if you were willing, they could stay at the adobe."

"I thought, maybe, if you were willing," he said gently, "they could stay here." He knew of her fondness for the smaller house, and heard the hesitation in her voice when she mentioned them living there. "I've never been too fond of this house. It's out of place. It should be in some small town back East, not here in the middle of the desert.

"If you're willing, we could move into the adobe, and give this place over to your mother and the kids. I have a feeling those kids will give this monstrosity a life of its own."

March sat up and looked down into her husband's smiling blue eyes. "Are you sure? You wouldn't mind leaving here?"

"Are you sure you want to live in a smaller house?"

"Oh, Jim, I love the adobe. It's a home. It's warm and friendly and inviting . . ." Her voice drifted away, and she looked at him beseechingly. "Could I take the stove?"

Jim closed his eyes as exhaustion forced him to rest. There was so much he needed to know, so much had happened, but it was beyond his ability to stay awake for long. The answers would come later, much later.

"What will your mother cook on?" he asked sleepily.

"Oh . . ." The single word was filled with disappointment.

"Come here, angel, just let me hold you for a while," Jim urged her back to his side, sighing with contentment when he felt her settle against him. "We'll just have to go see if Walt has another stove in stock."

"Are you sure you don't mind?"

It was beyond his ability to answer, as sleep drifted quietly over him. But he heard her voice, if not her question, and knew that she had been the one responsible for pulling him back to life all those times, when it would have been easier to give up.

His unconscious mind had known what he hadn't been able to see. March was the other half of his soul; his reason.

Maybe, if he lived another fifty years, he could even find a way to tell her of his love.

Twenty-four

March stood with her hands clasped firmly at her waist, watching Jim and four of the hired hands manhandle the heavy cast-iron stove into the kitchen of the adobe house. Walt didn't keep cooking stoves in stock, so it had been special ordered and shipped out of Kansas City. Slightly smaller than the one in the big house, it was painted dark gray with bright yellow trim.

The flue had been installed weeks earlier and as soon as the stove was in place and attached she could begin cooking . . . that is, if they ever got it into the house. If muttered four-letter words and snarled hisses had been of any help, it would have been inside over an hour ago!

Once again, the men set the monster stove down, wiping the sweat from their eyes. The doorway, already expanded once, still remained too narrow.

"Angel, go over and check on Jamie," Jim ordered in an uncharacteristic demand.

"The older girls have him," she reassured. "He's just fine."

Jim walked around the stove to approach his

wife. Taking her by the arm, he led her away from the men.

"You don't understand, sweetheart," he said quietly. "The men are uncomfortable with you here. They're getting frustrated with this durn contrary contraption, and would really like to say a few things to it, but they feel it would be improper to use such language in front of a lady."

"Oh . . ."

"Yes, oh!" Jim smiled and tapped the end of her nose. "Go check on our son, talk with your mother, plan wonderful menus; just get away from here. I'll let you know when it's in place."

"Just promise me you won't do too much. You're still weak, and I don't want you to over-exert."

"Yes, ma'am." He smiled indulgently. During the last couple of weeks he'd become accustomed to her concern, and had grown to like it. It gave him a warm feeling to know that someone cared . . . that March cared. "If you'll go away, I promise I'll be a good boy. I won't do anything, but stand back and add to the colorful language."

"Don't make a promise you can't keep. You haven't been a good boy in your entire life."

"Well . . . I'm really good at being bad." His wicked grin was the perfect foil for his less than innocent comment.

With a knowing smile, March squeezed his hand and headed toward the big house. She had no doubt that as soon as her back was turned he would be in the thick of things. She just hoped that he used some common sense as well as brawn. It had been only four weeks since he'd left his sickbed. His strength increased with each passing day, but since Breed had left two weeks ago, Jim had been pushing himself to the maximum to complete the tasks around the ranch.

Breed's leaving had been bittersweet for March. She had grown fond of the taciturn man, the hours spent together caring for Jim had forged a strong bond of friendship. He had left after receiving a letter from Tim Hansen, the man who had helped him make the adjustment from the Comanche lifestyle to the white world. March wasn't sure what problems had arisen, since as usual he hadn't seen a need to confide in anyone, but she understood Breed's desire to help out his friend.

She would miss him, that quiet man whose mere presence could intimidate lesser men. Her lips twitched with a smile when she remembered learning his white name. She had asked the same question months before and he had refused to tell her, but for whatever reason, this time he chose to answer; Gideon Hansen. Gideon had been given to him by Tim, and he had adopted Hansen in honor of his friend. The name seemed to fit the tall, Norwegian-looking man who would probably always walk a narrow line between two worlds.

The sound of laughter floated to her, as she

climbed the hill. At the crest, she stopped and watched as her brothers and sisters played in the backyard near the well. Since moving into the big house the children had opened like flowers after a rain, their natural vitality no longer hidden behind a veil of fear. Their childish laughter had become a common and much-welcomed addition.

The house, once so quiet and empty, had become crowded and lively with the addition of seven children. March had longed for the day when Jim was well enough to move, delighting when less than a week had passed before he insisted he could travel the short distance to the adobe. It was heaven to be alone with him and Jamie in the smaller house.

Watching the girls jump rope while the boys played with a hoop, she thought of their arrival a month earlier. Breed had gone after Virginia Evans, but she had refused to come with him.

And he had refused to accept her answer. Instructing May to watch the younger children, the man who had been raised to be a Comanche warrior bound the older woman with rope, threatening to place a gag in her mouth to still her protests, and gently placed her on his horse.

March grinned at the memory of her mother's face when Breed had carried her into the house and set her carefully onto a chair. Once untied and left alone, their reunion had been tearfully poignant.

The children had loved the house, soon making it into a real home. May had sighed with total enchantment at the frilly pink and white bedroom. The fussy room seemed to be made for the feminine girl, who was rapidly becoming a young woman. Seeing her sister's longing and understanding the desire to have something pretty, March had arranged for her to have the room to herself.

Several days after their arrival, May had taken March aside and filled her in on the things that had happened during their separation. Tears had filled March's eyes when she learned that her mother had turned her back on her the day she had left with Jim, because of the anguish she suffered through her inability to save her oldest daughter. After that day, Virginia Evans never again spoke directly to her husband.

Now Virginia's smile was a common thing, as was her beautiful voice raised in song, filling the air with heart-wrenching melody. Woods, whose fiddle playing had come as a surprise to March, had started joining in for impromptu sessions. The lovely music filled the desert with a different kind of peace.

Leaning against a tree, time slipped away unheeded, as March thought of the many changes in her life. Some things were still unsettled. Her mother refused to live at the ranch without finding a way to earn her keep, but so far a solution hadn't been found. The children needed to attend school, but the town school was too far away. George Evans's death had been reported to the sheriff and declared a justifiable homicide, but the years of his abuse had taken their toll on his children, who still weren't comfortable in the presence of the men of the ranch.

It would take time and patience to undo the damage, but time was now one thing they could plan on.

"Daydreaming?" Jim slipped his arms around her waist, pulling her against him.

Leaning her head back against his strong shoulder, March sighed with contentment. "Now my daydreams come true."

"I want all of your dreams, day or night, to be fulfilled." He bent slightly and kissed the soft skin just beneath her ear.

"Like the stove?" she asked, turning her head just enough to give him room to explore further.

"Like the stove . . . and the new, bigger window in the kitchen."

March turned in his arms, leaning back to look at him. "Bigger window?"

Jim shrugged and smiled a devilish little-boy grin. "It wouldn't go through the door. One of the men suggested we either leave it outside—which I knew you wouldn't like—or tear down a wall. That window will be real nice, once we get glass in it."

Shaking her head, she rolled her eyes heavenward. "Is brute force always your answer for everything?"

"Hum . . ." Taking advantage of the opportunity, he sampled the taste of her lips. "Right now I'd like to use some of that brute force to carry you off to the desert, and make passionate love to you until the sun forgets to rise."

"Too many cactus." March did some exploring and tasting of her own.

"Then we'll head to the woods." His hands slid down to the rounded curves of her bottom. As he pulled her firmly against him, she was left with no doubt about his building desire.

"Too many pine cones." Her own needs were growing apace with his, and she tried to tell herself that this was neither the time nor the place, but somehow that did nothing to stem the rising tide.

"Then we'll just have to steal these few minutes alone." The mood of his embrace changed, his kisses gentled, his caresses stilled. "Have I thanked you for calling me back when it would have been easier to let go?"

March's expression showed her perplexity. "When the fever raged in me, there was more than one time that I was tempted to let go, to see what death offered. But each time, you were there. Your voice called to me, begging me to fight to reach you."

His voice softened as he looked into her velvety gaze. "It was so filled with love and longing, that I knew I had to come back to find out the truth."

"The truth?"

He seemed to hold his breath for a moment, expelling it with his question. "I need to know if you could ever learn to love me, as much as I love you."

Tears filled her eyes and slid gently down her cheeks. The sun found the strands of gold in his hair, and made it gleam with warmth. The hollows beneath his cheeks had filled out, and the gray beneath his eyes had been replaced by his usual deep tan. He was once again the picture of health, a man in the prime of life.

"I was so scared. You were so sick, I didn't know if you would live or die. I sat beside you day after day, night after night, and watched you battle the fever. And everyday you seemed to get just a little weaker." She leaned her head against his chest and fought back a sob.

"I love you so much, and I didn't think I'd get the chance to tell you."

Jim's chest expanded as he gulped in badly needed air. He had waited forever to hear her words, and relief flooded through him. "Tell me again, angel. Don't make me wait."

"I love you, Jim Travis," she complied readily, raising her head proudly. "I didn't know what love was, until I nearly lost you."

Sighing, Jim briefly closed his eyes. When he opened them, March was amazed to see them rimmed with tears. "I love you, March. You're my love, my woman, my wife. I might never have known it, if it hadn't been for the fever. I heard your sweet voice calling to me, and I knew I had to fight, like I've never fought before, to get back to you. I wondered why, and suddenly I knew.

You are the missing half of my soul, the reason I was put on this earth."

March shivered and wrapped her arms around his waist. "I'm scared," she said quietly.

"Why, sweetheart?"

"Can it last? This love we feel is so strong, can it last a lifetime? Or will we wake up one morning to discover that it is gone?"

"I doubt that it will last for more than an eternity or two." With tender fingers beneath her chin, Jim raised her head and placed a soft kiss on her lips. "I don't think we'll have to start worrying about it for a couple of centuries."

"Promise?"

"Forever."

"Even when I'm old and gray and wrinkled?"

Jim grimaced as he looked at her smooth skin and golden hair. "You planning on doing that anytime soon?"

"No . . . but I've thought about getting fat."

His hands spanned her slender waist. "How fat? Fat like my horse? Or fat like the hog we're gonna slaughter next week? Or fat like Mrs. Quincey in town?"

"No, more like fat as in the family way."

She had planned to save her news until Christmas, but suddenly a week seemed far too long to wait. Watching comprehension dawn on his face was like watching the sun rise.

"You're going to have my baby?" he asked with a mixture of awe and dread. Melanie's agonizing death was still too new for him to easily forget it.

"I guess I take after my mother." March smiled, showing her delight at the situation. "I hope you like children, because we may well be starting a calendar of our own . . . you'll have to help me with my lessons, so that I don't forget how to spell them correctly."

"Twelve babies?" he asked in disbelief.

"I'm young . . . could be fifteen or sixteen before I get too old."

"My God . . . I don't think I've got that much life in me!"

"Don't worry, my sweet husband." March lowered her voice and her hand. "If all else fails, I'll remind you of Saturday."

Jim's lips met hers in a kiss of overwhelming tenderness, as memories of the lovemaking they had christened with the names of the days of the week drifted around them.

He wanted to name their new baby . . . she refused. She was stuck with March for the rest of her life, and it was a terrible name but not nearly as bad as his choice.

When she threatened to never spell another day or month in his presence, he grudgingly conceded; by now he knew that she always kept her promises. She named the baby Katherine Virginia, deciding that it was a beautifully feminine name.

He was soon calling her Katie. However, for the rest of his life, Jim always thought of his first born daughter as Saturday. He just hoped March never knew.

She did.